'Belton's account of one year of Schrödinger's life is bleak, judicious, thickly atmospheric . . . Belton never forces an analogy; throughout the novel, the images and metaphors are fastidiously chosen and beautifully sustained . . . the more you bring to this book, the more it gives back from its densely textured store of allusions, and the more pleasure you gain from its neat imaginative loops . . . This is a text you will remember for years, it is almost designed to be read, pondered, read around and then reread . . . The result is austere, authoritative fiction, a fine and melancholy novel, its poignant insights shimmering'

Hilary Mantel, *London Review of Books*

'Neil Belton's superb imagining of Schrödinger's life . . . Historical novel, tragic romance, war fiction, epic of ideas, *A Game with Sharpened Knives* is full of such menace . . . Belton, like John Banville, looks sideways straightfaced at a more comedic tradition of Joyce, Beckett and O'Brien, but this startling first novel bears such comparisons . . . With novels as good as this – worth reading and re-reading – it'll remain hard to displace'

Finn Fordham, *Guardian*

'Neil Belton's first novel is an improbable masterpiece. It is improbable because it requires the reader to imagine what it is like to be a scientific genius. It is a masterpiece because he pulls it off . . . this is a sophisticated novel and one thoroughly to be recommended'

Daniel Johnson, *Evening Standard*

'Truly brilliant. An intersection of science, politics, memory. We've been waiting for someone to write beautifully about science for a long time. I hope that it will win great praise. It really deserves it. The war scenes take the breath away'

Colum McCann

'Paranoia, betrayal, and the pursuit of scientific and emotional "truths" are themes at the heart of this densely woven debut novel by the award-winning biographer . . . Belton's novel is hauntingly powerful. As a good character study should, it takes its time to unravel the layers of experience that have made the protagonist what he is – a brilliant scientist whose intellect has flourished at the expense of emotional maturity'

Review

Neil Belton was born in Dublin and educated at University College Dublin. He works as an editor in publishing, and is the author of *The Good Listener, Helen Bamber: A Life Against Cruelty*, which won the *Irish Times* prize for non-fiction in 1999.

A Game with Sharpened Knives

NEIL BELTON

PHOENIX

A PHOENIX PAPERBACK

First published in Great Britain in 2005
by Weidenfeld & Nicolson
A Phoenix House Book
This paperback edition published in 2006
by Phoenix,
an imprint of Orion Books Ltd,
Orion House, 5 Upper St Martin's Lane,
London WC2H 9EA

1 3 5 7 9 10 8 6 4 2

A CIP catalogue record for this book
is available from the British Library.

ISBN-13 978-0-7538-1801-5
ISBN-10 0-7538-1801-9

Printed in Great Britain by
Clays Ltd, St Ives plc

The Orion Publishing Group's policy is to use papers that
are natural, renewable and recyclable products and made
from wood grown in sustainable forests. The logging and
manufacturing processes are expected to conform to the
environmental regulations of the country of origin.

www.orionbooks.co.uk

For Merel, Hendrick and Manus

And in memory of Sheila Lohan Belton, 1917–2004

Science is a game – but a game with reality,
a game with sharpened knives . . .

Erwin Schrödinger

Graz

1938

It was nine sharp. The secretary who had summoned him the day before had announced the hour of his appointment as though she were giving an order to open fire. After three weeks the most ordinary conversations had taken on a military snap, and manic urgency had become the new politeness. Her posture behind her desk was that of a ship's figurehead, and only her lips moved when she said that the Rector would see him now.

The big office on the first floor had grown larger: the soft chairs and most of the shelves had been removed; the room was stripped for action and redecorated in their favourite trauma colours. Only the busts of Goethe and of Fichte had survived. The man in uniform behind the desk pointed to a wooden chair. The peevish face on the giant portrait behind him, the leader in short leather trousers and flowery braces, only enhanced the Rector's vigour. He was young and fit, vibrating with optimism, gazing through shining, widened eyes. His voice was high and hoarse, the sound of a badly tuned radio.

'I'll come to the point, Professor. I admire your work. I see it as distinct from the degenerate cant that has taken over science. You believe in law and order in physics, or so I understand. Yet you have set yourself against the people, first in Berlin and now here. You have made speeches and comments notable for their cosmopolitan light-mindedness, their lack of German spirit. You bend to the false gods that ruined Austria. Your hostility is well known. It may be passive, but silent enemies are often the worst. You were a soldier and you know what happened in nineteen eighteen. I say to you frankly, we won't turn our back ever again on Alberich the dwarf and his sharp little knife.'

Schrödinger sat on the edge of his seat, trying to look earnest and manly. He remembered later the nervous discomfort he felt, and the hardness of the chair-edge under his thighs, and he had never been so aware of living in a naked body that could be tapped and broken like a fragile bulb. When he woke, as he often did, at four in the morning in his bedroom in Clontarf, this encounter was one of the memories that made him stare at the ceiling in an agony of revulsion, appalled at himself and the stupidity that comes with fear. He spoke haltingly, smiling, he hoped without irritating fulsomeness, saying that he was anxious not to go against the will of the people. He had no desire to do so. None. He had been mistaken in 1933 – 'And in 1938, it seems,' said the Rector, smiling in return – but he had been actuated not by hostility to the spirit of the new Germany so much as by a lingering distrust of *all* politics. The whole babble repelled him. He had not appreciated how the new movement had transcended the merely political. It was more like, he said, an outpouring of, as it were, brotherhood. 'But not fraternity,' the Rector permitted himself to chuckle. Not in the old sense, Schrödinger agreed. And he would not wish to stand aside from the people now. If there was any way that he could demonstrate his goodwill he would be profoundly happy to show that he was not hostile. Not one of the dwarves, he dared himself to say.

The Rector performed a little drum-roll with his fingers on the desk-top. 'Well, well, yes, the sincerity of your regret does you credit. There is after all a new spirit of brotherhood, of true liberty, true equality, and we must be generous. I will be completely frank and honest with you. We are speaking now as German men, we must see if we can find the German peace that our leader wants for all of us. It touches me to see how the renewal of our people can move even those we feared were lost to us. The sweet exchange of good cheer from heart to heart!' He looked archly at Schrödinger, who suspected he should recognise a quotation, and nodded sagely. 'Do you know what I think?' Solemn now, briskly businesslike, the Rector leaned forward. Schrödinger shook his head, and inclined his own body so that he was bending uncomfortably towards the desk, his forehead close to the

Rector's. 'You must write down what you have just said to me. Elaborate a little, but concisely. A single page. Send it to me in the form of an open letter. A letter to the German people, so to speak, a cry from the heart of one who is coming home. I feel sure that such a letter would have a tonic effect on other latecomers during the election, and that it would touch the hearts of higher authorities.'

Schrödinger nodded his head as emphatically as he dared. 'Good, it's settled then,' the Rector said, and leaped upright. Everyday life was now full of such ardent callisthenic gestures. Schrödinger had been in the room for less than ten minutes. As he marched his guest to the door the Rector spoke of his plans for the ancient foundation. 'Here in the marches where Germans held firm against Mongol and Muslim, we will create a world centre of racial science and medicine. We will perform wonders, and you will too. Good day, Professor, and Heil Hitler.' When Schrödinger bent his arm and said Heil Hitler, the Rector gave him a hard slap on the back. Later, in the mirror, he noticed a faint bruise between his shoulder blades.

His father would have said that a letter is a live thing: what is written down can never be retracted. As the proprietor of what he called a 'concern', his father knew about the consequences of letting go, about solicitude and worry. Stain a white shirt and it will never get clean. Schrödinger recalled these commandments of a life that had disintegrated as he walked home from his meeting with the Rector, dazed, but also springy with a demented sort of hope. We have a chance, he told Anny. They were standing in the kitchen, which was filled with the smell of rosemary and garlic and of potatoes roasting in the oven. A glass of red wine was dimming the freakish crackle of the Rector's voice. This is what lasts, he told himself. Food, drink, the feeling of being safe in a warm room. Anny was kneading a piece of thin veal with a rolling pin on a wooden board. They had been living on bread and cheese for days, eating at odd hours in different rooms of the house. This was their attempt to take hold, to eat a cooked dinner sitting down. Yet as she worked, the sight of the pink flesh whose fibres she was crushing disgusted him. He wanted her to look at him and listen, but she was distracted, as though she needed to show that this preparation of food was important: a protest against the dire fevers all around them. This stolidity of hers, her refusal to feel the urgency of the threat, shook his brittle good humour to pieces.

'Please listen to me. I have to write them a letter. He was sympathetic in a way. Crude, but not as vicious as I'd feared. He obviously sees some advantage in having me here. And there are decent people among them. They can't all be thugs. They must learn to deal with scientists in a human way. They can't uproot four hundred years of physical thought overnight.'

She straightened up, traces of pale meat adhering to her hands. 'Decent people who will do what they are told. Was there a station master in the old days before the war who didn't love the Emperor, who didn't feel a little importance by having his picture in his office? These people are ten times worse. He's doing exactly what is good for him. I think you should be careful.'

He clenched with irritation at her resistance to his need to find ordinary self-interest in that jumping jack in his stolen office. 'If I do nothing, we will lose all we have. They may demote me, sack me, or worse. If I refuse this, whatever it is, this olive branch, this journey to Canossa, we are through. They need their petty revenge, that's all. They don't care a damn about physics, but they may like the idea of having a few more of us around who've made a real contribution. They have driven away the Jews. Maybe what they've lost is starting to worry them. After I've done my penance we will be left alone.'

Anny faced him steadily, and her sanity, which had never been more obvious, enraged him. 'You know I'm not a clever person, but whatever we do now has to help us survive,' she said. 'None of them can be our friends. They're drunk when they're cold sober. Nothing you say can be enough for them. You can't turn yourself inside out. One minute you say they don't care about culture and science, and the next you think they worry about losing you. I think they're playing with mice. We could leave, just leave.'

'With what, the clothes on our backs? And go where, exactly? I turned my back on Oxford. Do you think they will welcome me back with open arms?'

'Don't shout. They don't beat people there because they are born with the wrong shape of nose.'

'There is *no way out*!' He squeezed his thumbs against his

forehead, burning the skin, then grabbed at the white ceramic roller and smashed it onto the piece of meat so that it tore like wet paper, threw the kitchen door against its hinges and ran upstairs.

He wrote draft after draft. By one in the morning the discarded sheets made the room look as it sometimes did when the child invaded it, trotting around examining and crushing things. The falsity of the thought was impossible to work. It twisted into vulgar shapes, so obviously ugly and mendacious, and he felt that the draft he gave her the following morning was no better than any of the others he had torn up. He had slept, at least, for the rest of that night. He called it his confection, something cunning, sweetened and empty, to diminish the nausea he felt at producing it. He imagined it being read in an office by some rigid senior official. It is no worse, he told himself, than the gross politesse of academic life, the well-turned vote of thanks for the dull visiting speaker, the oily praise for the book that no-one will read, the retirement eulogy for the man you despise. That afternoon he delivered it by hand to the Rector's office.

After two days he was feeling almost resentful that such an artful and hollow gesture had evoked no response. On the third morning he took the tram to the city, thinking that he might telephone the Rector's secretary. At the tram stop near the university a news kiosk displayed the front page of the *Tagespost*. At first he could not read it. Moving closer, he made out the block headline CONFESSION TO THE FÜHRER. He unfolded the paper along the crease that separated the massive letters from the smaller type beneath, and saw the full text of his letter over his name. He looked at the other sheets. The letter was in all that day's papers, the *Sturmer*, the *Volkischer Beobachter*, the placement varying, but always the text as he had written it, without a misprint or a word changed. He stood at the kiosk unable to move, holding the last paper he had unfolded. His mouth hung open; his eyes were staring. The newsboy said, 'This is not a café, Herr Doktor'. He put a note in the man's hand and walked off rolling the newspaper between his hands. The craven prisoner led around on a rope before the crowd, pleading for his hide. They had not needed to fake a word. He thought of Einstein in America reading this, of Born in Edinburgh reading a translation in *The Times*. Hansi reading it, perhaps at that very moment, in Vienna. And all they had

had to do was ask and there he was, grinning and talking unstoppably, spontaneous self-abasement.

Sitting in his office in Merrion Square, years and a continent away, he remembered Quinn telling him he knew that they had threatened him with Dachau. Why else would he have done it? He wanted one day to say to Quinn, the intelligent commit the worst crimes against self-respect because they think that what they say is just a form of words. We think we can keep our real meaning safe. But my father was right: the confection I baked was a mouthful of shit. Different drafts jumbled in his head, unforgettable phrases that he couldn't call back, never sure if the one he remembered was the one he'd sent.

Our country comes together in a joy that is not given twice in a thousand years, to affirm its destiny. At last we join in life and work our fellow Germans from whom we have been separated by an artificial frontier. As a natural scientist I may be permitted to observe that an energy barrier separates atoms; but our barriers were unnatural and painful. All at once our state of isolation has ended; our energies as united Germans flow as one. Of divided brethren a new and greater substance has been made.

Unfortunately there are some few of us who must in the midst of this great celebration hang our heads, avoiding the clear gaze of our compatriots. For they have understood simply and sincerely what we have failed to grasp until the very last moment, we whose cult of the abstract is our weakness. Yet we hope it is not too late for the deep heart of Germany to forgive the latecomer, to take the humbly offered hand of friendship. For nothing would give me greater happiness than to hope that I too can play a small part in bringing to fruition the hopes of all my German brothers.

In the election that will soon take place – more properly should it be called an acclamation that will record our freely given choice – the only permissible word that may be uttered is surely Yes. And until then let every affirmation that is not a yes to Germany and its leader be silent. With a glad heart I make this confession of faith public so that my repentance may be heard by those who still have doubts. To them I say: Come home, as I have done!

On a fine warm day, a few weeks after the letter was published, he sat on a train to Berlin. Everywhere, in the small halting places and the cities, the colour of the world was reduced to monotonous distributions of energy around the same predictable nodes. The relentless bombardment of his eyes' red receptors gave him a headache, and the black was everywhere absorbing the light, the white reflecting it like some dead spectral centre. Every train station looked ready to receive an important corpse.

At the house in the suburb of fine villas and old trees he handed his stiff invitation card to the young gatekeeper, whose precision was ostentatious. The lobby was newly painted in white, and tall vases full of white camellias and red roses stood on the floor. Planck stood in his well-cut evening dress, trim and upright, his shirt whiter than the flowers against the heavy new emblems in polished dark wood and iron. It was his eightieth birthday. The old world clung to him, even in the way he stood: he could never give himself that extra quotient of jut. Already in the vestibule the handshakes were a little too warm, and von Weizsacker with his smooth face, as bland as a cheese, clasped Schrödinger's arm as though he were a sinner coming home.

And there was Heisenberg, coiled and smiling, his wiry blond hair brushed back, radiating good cheer. Schrödinger could see him sitting in a circle around a camp fire, his bare legs outstretched, singing hearty songs, ballads about a Germany rising above rancour and strife. With his backpack and guitar, he marches up a valley followed by his faithful youths to a castle on a crag, in the flickering light of torches, under a Bavarian moon. He is the hiker into purity, finding runes under the moss on an old stone, as wholesome in his dinner jacket as he is in dungarees. He is animated by a country-boy energy, his soul shining and true. Believe in me, he seems to say, in my transparent honesty and rude drive.

He came up now and laughed, delightedly. 'You are back. It is wonderful, wonderful to see you. All of us, all of us here. Such a beautiful occasion for German physics. I could not be more pleased on today of all days, when our beloved Planck reaches the age of Abraham.'

'It is nice to see you too.' Abraham. And the rest of it. It struck him that this moment was so leaden with grudging not only because he felt nearly destroyed by him, intellectually disgraced, but because he found himself making notes, like a hostile editor, against every word that the younger man uttered. He had once been standing at a party with Reese, some gala occasion after he and Heisenberg had won their prizes. There had been speeches, one by Heisenberg, in honour of some other grand old man, and afterwards Reese had stood beside Schrödinger in that blissful saintly way of his, his near-autistic self-possession protecting his interminable silences. For long minutes that night he said nothing at all, while Schrödinger tried to find a crack in the glass that surrounded him, and of which Reese was entirely unaware. Eventually, he said:

'I say, you know when Heisenberg said just now we were all sitting on the floor of the Kapitza club in Cambridge the first time we met? That was not wholly right.'

'I beg your pardon?'

Reese looked at him with bright, childlike eyes: 'In his charming speech just now, when Werner said that we first met in those rooms at Trinity for the discussion club, he said we were delightfully informal, all sitting around on the floor.'

'Yes, I can imagine it. All of you stretched out on the boards talking physics. Cold, though, I should imagine, if it is anything like Oxford.'

'Well yes it was, but actually you see most of us had chairs around the wall. Some people had to sit on the floor. Not many though.' Reese made the seating arrangements sound like a matter of wonder and delight, but also strangely concerning at a deeper level than was yet fully visible.

'All our memories are not as clear as yours. It was a long time ago, after all.'

Reese would not be put off by soothing phrases. 'No, not really. Eight years is not that long.'

'A quarter of his life, but no, not that long. He shouldn't have to consult his diary. Why does it bother you?'

'Oh, I don't know.' Reese gazed at him, holding his glass limply against his thin shoulderless body. He stood motionless, like, Schrödinger thought guiltily, a psychiatric patient who has been let out for the day and told to be polite, with no idea what that really means. After at least another minute crawled by, Schrödinger growing tense with the effort of willing Reese to speak, he said, 'I think that sitting on the floor seemed to Werner more soulful. More like that youth movement of his. The little wandering birds or whatever they're called. He likes everything to be like a boy-scout camp.' Reese was smiling slightly now.

And that was it, Reese had caught it years ago, and tonight the patness was grating, that glib 'all of us' and the invocation of the Jewish prophet in a room where there wasn't a single Jew, the halving of Abraham's age. The pious stuff about German physics. These men had all made their German peace for the sake of German physics, but Werner had run at his with outstretched arms. The professors stood with their drinks in their hands with the trap closing around them like the teeth of the broken crosses on the walls. In the cheap sparkle of the thin champagne he could taste the revilement he had brought on himself. I've stood up and pissed myself in public for no other reason than to amuse them. That was my price. None of the others here, well-adjusted men who don't have tremors of remorse and ungovernable desires, will find themselves so botched. They go along; their distress won't get out of hand.

Planck himself came up to join them, genial and sweet. He laid a hand on his arm and said, 'I am truly glad to see you here.' For a heady moment Schrödinger relived the feeling that this old man's admiration had once given him, the feeling that all the striving had brought him to a state of intelligent grace. Planck's courtesy was unchanged. He asked after Anny; enquired how things were in Graz, as though it were an ordinary provincial town, as though this was not a wake. But after a little he leaned forward, subtly excluding Heisenberg, and almost whispered: 'It is important to save what we can, to uphold the morality of our calling. The pressures are immense, but we can keep our integrity, I know we can, no matter how stormy it becomes. I really hope you are well, my friend.' Schrödinger nodded his head and almost smiled. Oh God yes, we're having a spell of bad weather, you could almost make me think it's true. But all he said was, 'I am glad to be able to wish you a happy day, and many more to come.'

Planck took Schrödinger's arm and steered him, Heisenberg walking behind, into the long room next door. The silver, glass and linen on the tables were clean and heavy, catching and deepening the light. A man in a black dress uniform approached Planck, who turned from Schrödinger. The room filled up. Heisenberg was at his side again, gazing around like an impresario. 'Look at what we have managed to save. What great things we can do with our science! Yes, *our* science, not theirs.' He looked Schrödinger defiantly in the eye.

'It is not merely ours any longer, is it?' Schrödinger said. Planck's arm was now in the grip of the uniformed officer.

'But what you don't realise is that we defeated the fanatics. The ones who would have taken us back fifty years. No relativity theory, no uncertainty relations, no wave mechanics. Not even that. They'd have had us working only on better ceramics and artillery shells. It has not been easy.' He spoke as though he were a veteran of exhausting battles, privy to a world that Schrödinger was too naïve to understand.

Not even that. He felt the neat sting. 'And we won't help them get better at killing. It could indeed be worse.' He tried to smile, to make light of it, but the sharp *sekt* was making him more reckless than he ought to be, and he knew that anything he said was too much. Heisenberg shook his head pityingly and tapped his right forefinger on his glass in time to his words. It made a sound like a little dampened bell. 'We can *do – good – physics*. Our revered teacher is right. That is what is important. In those days of upheaval, you know, we had to make a choice: remain at our posts and preserve what we could, or leave our beloved country and our German science. It has been worth sticking it out for the sake of those who will protect what really matters to us.' Oh your bland elisions, Schrödinger wanted to say. You don't speak this cosy fraternity argot, it speaks you. *Our revered teacher.* Heisenberg pressed on, oblivious to his companion's dumb sulk. 'The good side, the harmony will emerge from the noise and we'll be a happy country again, I'm sure of it.'

'The music of pure thought. I'm glad to hear it. Perhaps we'll still have to sing for our supper, just a little.' He knew he should stop, fall into step, but his defiance was lifted by the sickly effervescent wine.

Heisenberg shook his head, good-humoured and confident. 'My friend, you're the same as ever. You want a world that died at the turn of the century, when our guest of honour found that energy comes in units we can't divide. You long for a world that's whole and continuous and obeys nice sensible laws. You do! You want to be able to say for sure what is and what happened, capture the nature of the world in a pretty picture. You've never accepted what the equations tell us. All this nonsense about connecting what we do to experience, I mean come on, Erwin, *really*. The world's just not like that. Any coincidence with the rules our fathers left us is accidental. Inside the atom you can't observe the position and momentum of electrons at the same time, that's it, their energy jumps instead of flowing, they do inexplicable things. There's no underlying reality, no warm current deep down that might explain why things are the way they are and ease our hurt. You should stop expecting more; it brings worse grief. If I may be frank, you should stop dragging around your suffering nostalgia for something that couldn't have survived anyway. In the time between observations there is unobservable darkness. Not even that. Nothing. Forget between. We create the real by looking for it. What will have happened in between will be determined later, when we next look.'

He laughed, as though a little embarrassed by his eloquence. Schrödinger was sweating. He felt dragged down by the heat, the drink, the deep fragrance of the roses, the white flowers like memorial offerings, and he was losing control. He looked around the room at the black suits and chalk-white shirts and had the sensation that he was in a gathering of the already dead. They were going through the motions of an academic jubilee, but only Heisenberg seemed untouched by the event's horrible sleepwalking quality; he was positively humming.

'You know,' he went on, 'I am sincerely glad you've made a choice at last. We have to work with what we've got, as I've always said. But since we're friends again I hope you won't mind me admitting that your waves harmonising the subatomic world – you know, I always found them a little, well, nauseating. Forgive me. I thought the whole thing was an Asian river of wishful thinking, the brown tide of the Ganges, those mystical conundrums, the lower-caste human mass moving over the dry plains. I couldn't help seeing in your waves the hordes rolling towards us across the steppe. The sea that would sweep us away if we didn't erect barriers against it.

Things don't flow as we'd like them to. You were lucky with your waves: the world sometimes behaves as if they were real. That is all. Truth is a decision, a leap to a point of view. That is what makes our world, our world here in the West. Cut and move on.'

Schrödinger was silent for a moment. He was thinking: You're working for them, but measured another way you're just minding your own physics. But to Heisenberg he said, 'You see the real in different lights. It's a great skill to have.' He was daring too much, and he felt his face darken. Waiters emerged from side doors carrying silver tureens as the guests took their seats. The brilliance of the polished glasses and the sheen of silver took him back to that other banquet before the Great War, when he had been waiting his turn and Planck was already old.

'These are unstable times. One must act for the best, and then understand what it is that one has done. We cannot wring our hands on the sidelines or walk away. As you have not. You won't regret it.'

As Heisenberg released this weightless little balloon of good cheer, he raised his eyebrows roguishly, and on the left shoulder of his defeated rival he laid a comforting hand.

Back in Graz the following night he found a letter on the hall table. The envelope was brown and flimsy. Inside there was a single typed sheet under the new swastika letterhead of the Dean of the Faculty in Vienna: '*Your authorisation to participate in instruction is withdrawn.*' Now that he could see it, he knew that it was the only possible reality, that this was the cold taste at the bottom of the cup. But did the right hand know what the left hand was doing? Who had known last night, when the letter was already in the mail, at the moment when he was shaking hands with Planck and thinking he was safe? Heisenberg, surely, would not have performed as he had if he'd known the knives were already out. That hand on his shoulder felt like an obscene caress, and years later it still made him shudder, more enraging with time than it had been then. The way he talked about the past – 'in those days' – he was talking about nineteen thirty-three, for Christ's sake, a bland amnesiac nostalgia making just five years ago a half-timbered folksy haze in which the details blurred. He's the experiment of himself, not knowing yet what his position will have been.

He still had his job in Graz then, half of what they paid to get him back, though his courses were barely attended. Bored young men slouched around the university, and from their clubs you could hear them roaring at enemies who had vanished. The faculty was purged. They had thrown the elderly professor of Hebrew into the river. But letters from colleagues arrived, and the usual journals, as though nothing had changed.

It was not until he was living in this state, through days in which he could not even breathe deeply lest it give him false confidence, that he understood what had happened to Boltzmann here, when the rabid German students stole a bust of the Emperor from a University hall and insulted His Majesty as a defender of Slavs and Jews. A mongreliser. Boltzmann had to discipline them. The police chief watched to see how he would handle himself, and behind him was the Governor, and observing them all the Emperor in Vienna. The students went on torchlit marches; they wrote him threatening letters, screamed abuse as he rose to speak amidst the fantastic energy of their derision. He had to channel all that rage, the Emperor's sewer. Once they start in this city, the revels never stop, Schrödinger knew that now. And what had there been to hate? A man who thought of founding a journal that would report only experiments ending in failure.

One afternoon a porter who had read some of Schrödinger's essays took him down to a dark corridor in the basement. They walked beside lagged heating pipes to the end, where the man unlocked the door to a storeroom whose shelves were full of dirty glass, stray wires and sheets of foil and lead. Something at the back had a dustsheet thrown over it. The porter lifted it out and removed the sheet.

'See,' he said, 'it even has differential gears. It's very clever.' The porter was a wiry, serious man who always carried a book in the pocket of his brown coat. He looked at Schrödinger intently. 'He was a great man, sir.'

Schrödinger nodded. There seemed no need to say anything more as they stood in the dusty basement, and he was just afraid enough not to dare confirm that he understood what the man was saying to him. He took the model bicycle from the porter's hands and turned one of the cranks so that the shaft connecting them moved, and the wheels turned, like the electric currents they symbolised, two masses whose motion and position are given by cyclic co-ordinates, their flows of interacting energy mimicked by the machine. Boltzmann's serious toy.

He stood with the bicycle in his hands and said, finally: 'Thank you for showing it to me. It's beautiful. A machine that is a picture of the world.'

'Not any more, sir', the porter said, as he took the bicycle from him and walked back into the storeroom.

One warm June afternoon his mother-in-law rang the doorbell. He was surprised to see her. Her disdain for him rang out clearly in the distance she kept between them. In her steady remorseless disapproval he could feel the cost of the compromises she made in order to pretend she liked him. They kissed lightly on each cheek, and stood, making an effort to talk, until Anny came down and the coffee was on the table.

She was pale and tense, he noticed, when she did consent to sit down. She drank coffee and ate a piece of cake, but clutched her handbag between her feet, pressing her legs almost indecently around the smooth leather. After covering the weather and the train and the inconvenient remoteness of Graz, she put down her cup and blurted out: 'I am a good Austrian. I cannot go against my country. This is for my daughter's sake. I should go to the police. But here it is.'

With a jerk of the straps the bag came up, snapped open and a piece of paper slipped underneath his cup. Anny took tight hold of Erwin's knee. He felt sudden, terrible fear, and his hands prickled with it. The thought of the police, what that now meant, entangled itself with the white paper. 'If I am asked I will say that I never had this. The Dutchman who came from Zurich said you would understand.'

On the sheet of notepaper, neat handwriting formed a fragment of English:

The right twigs for an eagle's nest. Institute of Advanced Studies, Dublin. Yes or no?

Part One

January 1941

In the hallway of the Institute, which was dark because they were so careful now with light and heat, he felt again how poor his eyes had become. It was not merely the onset of evening; the door was blurred as though the fog outside in the square had drifted into the passage with the brass rail along the wall, the dark mirror and oak bench. His eyes, still clear and blue behind the strong round lenses, apparently so undimmed, narrowed to a squint. I've reached the age when I'm lost without my glasses, he thought. For months he had been feeling that turbid water was falling between him and the world, and that it was slowly absorbing more and more light. He flinched as he pulled open the door, and then the fear of deterioration was swept aside in a spasm of hurry, one of many things he could not bear to think about, a premonition of something like shame. It was a bitterly cold evening. Last night they dropped bombs near the South Circular Road. It would already have become an accident, in the adjustment of reality by those whose job it was to shape it. The telegram of apology or denial would have reached the office of the Taoiseach around the corner. The German Minister would be on his way to explain, or bluff: the British trying to discredit us, again. Yet however it was, in the cloudless night the planes found themselves over the canal and the tiny Jewish quarter, and the synagogue in the terraced house was damaged and the street littered with broken glass, or so the porter said. How well they see in the dark.

Long cirrus clouds drifted slowly overhead. Hundreds of bicycles stood tilted sideways and chained to the railings around the garden at the centre of the square, black and heavy machines, immobile, he thought, like devices for the crippled thrown aside after a mass cure. He unlocked his bike from a cold iron rail and swung across it, athletically for his age, a little showily, though not as showy as his dismounting, when he would throw a leg forward over the handlebars so fast that his hands seemed incapable of making way for his leg. He pushed off from the kerb. He was a slim rangy man, younger than his years, and there were times when he wished he could play the sober professor, but the mask never stayed in place for long. With his rainproof cape and leggings, his rucksack and his hair brushed back from his high forehead, he made an impression of which he was aware: the vigorous savant on his two-wheeler.

The row of flat house-fronts behind him, built of good brick and stone, pleased the eye with their high windows and fanlights over the doors guarded by little Doric columns. But he rarely noticed their elegance now. He thought, how familiar everything is, I am seeing so little. Yet he liked the way the Irish had of living in a city they half despised, as though they were trying it on like a suit of clothes they had inherited: it made him feel a little less the stranger. I should be grateful, he thought, and the square is beautiful. They had considered, he was told, filling the garden in the square with all the old statues they could no longer stand to see: Queen Victoria laying a wreath on the head of a dying man, generals and dukes. There would have been a park full of upright human figures outside his office window, rows of them silent among the trees, Nelson's Pillar towering over them all. It would have been like working in a graveyard.

He cycled past the gates of the ducal palace where the parliament met. The policemen stood at ease in their peaked caps, the soldiers in their battledress had their rifles sloped, posted lest the enemy attack. Though which enemy? that was the question in a state of peace that was armed, a state of war very like peace. It was not done to call it war. He thought of a small head breaking the surface of the ocean, breathing carefully, feet slowly moving underwater. The sea was so close; ships came up the river and moored a few blocks from the General Post Office. He could smell the docks from his open window the previous summer, his first in Dublin, an odour of malt and petrol and dung. The burning and sinking went on not far out there beyond the bay, and he never heard a whisper. It was like that strange effect of large explosions: as you move away from the blast the sound attenuates, and then intensifies once more many miles away. In the war before this he had been told how his huge gun on the bare limestone hills above Trieste could be heard far down the coast, but sometimes hardly at all from a village nearby, and he wondered what happened to the sound waves when they rose to the thin air of high altitudes. At the time, he thought it must be the increased amplitude of the waves at such inhuman heights compensating for the diminishing effect of the less dense atmosphere on the sound's intensity. It was a conundrum, this zone of silence, and now he was living in it.

As he rode on, the cone of light from the lamp on his handlebars playing on the fog, he could feel the sheer weight of the saturated air. The fog shut him in with the feelings he wanted to escape. He was aware this winter of the city's watchfulness and foreboding; more oppressed than he had ever been at first by the mild meanness of the weather, the wind that chilled the summers and drove the endless winter rain along the promenade by the sea near his house at Clontarf.

And the memory of that encounter before Christmas in Grafton Street was disturbing the balance he thought he had established here. The restraint and cold sobriety of the people had unnerved him from the start, the way they left him alone. So when the man beside him at the window of the bookshop turned to him that evening and raised his hat, and smiled at him, he shrank back, fearing an intrusion, an enquiry about the meaning of relativity, or of life, on which he could not pronounce to save his own, still less on the meaning of quantum mechanics, except to say none of us knows what it means, or how it meshes with the forces that draw the stars together and keep the lights burning, and he thought of the crank letters, the rants in capital letters accusing him of heresy and atheism. Because he was feeling feverish, his head drowsy with a cold that would not go away, he had drunk a hot whiskey in a pub on his way to buy presents for Anny and Hilde. He found the bookshop window restful. Books stood upright, propped open by little wooden blocks. The space was lit by a soft illumination that conformed to the law and made the colours of the book jackets glow, made the books objects to be displayed on small polished tables in a light like this, not things to be handled and read.

The man loomed at him, his face bending towards his own with disconcerting familiarity. Schrödinger was confused by the shifting light on the street and the passing close by of so many bodies, quick and well-dressed women in headscarves on their way to the expensive stores. He had not been aware of the man standing there. He seemed to materialise noiselessly in the way that a servant might, or a policeman. Schrödinger took a step backward. His bicycle balanced on a pedal on the kerb. A horse harnessed to an open trap, driven by a figure wrapped in plaid rugs, lifted its tail and let out a chain of turds smelling of hay.

The fellow was looking eagerly at him in the dim light, and seemed to be nodding his head, his smile showing large tobacco-stained teeth. Schrödinger felt embarrassed at the way he had flinched. The man had wide, pale, unblinking eyes and a curved scar over his left eye, as though the scalp had once been peeled back. It was a raw outdoorsman's face, framed by big ears and centred by a craggy nose, and Schrödinger could see flickers of amusement playing over it. They were of an age, both past fifty, but the man was brutally vigorous, bursting out of his heavy coat. The insolent assumption he embodied was menacing, his bulk interfering with the space around him. His face had an odd hectic flush. It struck Schrödinger that it was not weather-beaten so much as engorged, the face of someone who had eaten and drunk too much for too long. There was a gigantic frustration about him, as though he spent his days tied down to a few acres of wet grass. Schrödinger could imagine him drinking whiskey in some country pub and the bully in him coming out. The locals would be too small for him; he would patronise and annoy them.

Suddenly the space between the two men shrank even further, so that Schrödinger could smell the other's cigarette breath, dark and tarry. 'I hope you will achieve great things here. The Irish are a lucky nation.' When Schrödinger merely nodded, the man's hat rose and tilted, concealing for a second the ruddy features with an oval of shaved wool, and he stepped back. Schrödinger turned to his bicycle.

He had been spoken to in German, German with a tone of sing-song complaint. Bavarian, perhaps. He thought he should say something to him, but when he looked up again the man had vanished and a well-dressed couple were examining the books in the window.

He should have forgotten the incident, but its unfinished aggression had lodged in him. It left him feeling exposed, no matter how he pushed it aside or told himself that the man had been some bore cut off by opportune silence. A whiff of some urgent unhappiness clung to his memory.

The noise of an engine startled him, and he swerved to the side of the road. This hour of the evening was silent because the office workers were still sitting at their desks, as she would be, typing memoranda on a black upright machine, and since Christmas motor cars were rare. They said that soon even priests would not be given petrol. The dark sedan pulled out to pass him. He saw the big moustached face smiling, flanked by a hand raised slightly in a busy important salute, then the car swerved right into the mist, heading south. So many of them lived on that side of the river. The minister in that car, an old comrade of the Taoiseach's, a hard jovial man with a thin stubborn mouth and a long nose, had killed policemen in his youth. Now they had firing squads for men like he had once been. Schrödinger had met him; he disliked the way his protected status made him so visible to all of them. He was de Valera's mascot, and so the inner circle tolerated him with their hearty courtesy. But it was said that only ten people in the world could understand the theory of relativity and that the Taoiseach was one of them, and Schrödinger sensed that having another of the elect around took some of the shine off the legend. Ten just men to save the world. Or ten clever men to ruin it, break it apart. He thought of a drop of water on the mouth of a tap, elongating slowly and dividing, the drop falling and a new one forming, the slow splitting of a liquid, then the drop splitting new drops violently fast, a drenching rain.

The same minister once said to him, lowering his voice and leaning in: 'I can't make my mind up about this war,' as though he were offering a confidential tip. Around them the guests at the reception held up their glasses and cigarettes to each other like trophies under the chandeliers. He could not tell what the minister was really telling him; could never read the minds of those who had been together for so long that they understood each others' intentions without the use of words. But Schrödinger was aware of them feeling their way with infinite care as the world outside was closed to them, as though a great ship had turned off its lights and was moving nearer and nearer to them in the darkness. And he knew that none of them would save him.

And now a power with whom they were not at war had bombed the city, just a little, and he wondered why. Perhaps to show that they can, that it's a helpless body they can cut as they wish. The surge of anxiety made his arms ache, and he was aware of a sluggishness in his heart, and of a slight breathlessness. He was cycling too fast, curving out and around the slow horse-drawn wagons, and despite the cold he was beginning to sweat. He slowed down as he cruised along the side wall of Trinity College and noticed a group of good-looking students sauntering by. They walked with their long scarves over their coats like believers in a cult of happiness into which they had been born. He envied them, as if he had been expelled from the marvellous thing they formed together. I was like that, he thought, in Vienna before the last war, when being half a century old was inconceivable. Had Hamilton, he wondered, been as handsome and naïve, before it all went wrong? He must have been happy when he found, almost casually, that light and matter can have the same expression, the movement of particles and rays of light reduced to the same action. He was so young. A marvellous variation knocked out by a Trinity boy and waiting ninety years for me to realise what it could mean, to be able to give the weirdness of the atom the beautiful simplicity of a wave.

But when they said, as a compliment: You are the successor of Hamilton, they had no idea what they wished on him, what failure cost. The students made him feel what was slipping away, and he thought of the girl at the party to which Quinn had taken him. He could see her strong-boned face and her dark, very young hair. The warm tension rose in him, making him blush as though with embarrassment at the strength of his instinct. There had been a spark between them, and he was already listening to the speech of blind need, as if he could argue with it and prevent it from drowning out

24

any other language. He thought of how confident she seemed in the knowledge of her own agile presence as she talked to him, and the graceful gestures she made with her cigarette. He pedalled hard again, the humming of the wheels rising and describing smooth curves on the road as he glided over Butt Bridge in the hard easterly wind off the sea. The river was high, with a heavy swell, a grey-brown soup. In front of the Custom House a Guinness boat was tied up, a gold harp on its bow, riding low and heavy in the water. One of the few things they have that Britain wants: he thought of a torpedo hitting her, of black beer mixing with salt water. It was the only ship in the river.

He cycled around the Custom House, built for a world that thought it could be healed by trade, by ships coming up the river, the lighted windows in the long pavilions muffled by the fog. That English gadfly Ashman called it the finest thing in the city, but emptied of itself, the façade an illusion, indoors nothing left, a room here or there, no more. Then he was up Gardiner Street and onto Summerhill. He liked to vary his route, and this was the worst. Some of the pillared doors were open on dark hallways, on stains of fire and dirt, on a smell of piss he could detect from the street as he passed. The fanlights of these old houses were broken. No men were on the street, only a few girls with thin, wasted faces. The young woman, Sinéad, had talked at the party with tranquil anger about the tenements. She spoke about lost opportunities for rebuilding the city, great schemes pushed into drawers and forgotten. She was working on an article for Quinn's magazine; 'I've discovered that my difficulty with writing', she said, 'is controlling my temper.' Her heat moved and aroused him. She worked in the Department of Justice, so near his office, and he thought, I must be careful; but he wanted to reach out and touch her hair. When he asked her lightly whether they might meet again, knowing she was drawn to the aura he could still pretend was his, the genius and the scandalous rumours, the Nobel Prize, she said yes, but impassively, and looked steadily at him through the smoke rising from her cigarette, and told him he was too old for her. Yet she spoke with such reluctance that he left the party calm and dumbly happy.

A motorless tractor with large rear wheels passed him, drawn by a pair of old horses and hauling a trailer full of hay. He crossed the bridge over the Tolka at Ballybough. There was the Jews' cemetery behind a narrow grey building; an embossed plaque merging with the grey wall bore the number 5618. Grey on grey, like a small bird in winter undergrowth. The eye skips it as it would any other dreary north Dublin house. 'You'd never have seen it, would you?' she asked him when she told him where it was. 'They'll build over it eventually, and after a few years no one will remember it was there. They used to hang robbers by the bridge,' she told him, 'it was where the city ended, and bury them where the sea came in, and they put suicides in the waste ground just above high tide. It was the only way out to the north shore of the bay. You'd never know', she said, 'that the land east of that bridge is the sea filled in; no one wants to remember.'

'Yes', he said, 'we have this urge to improve the sea. There's an awful human need to wall it out and cover it over. We have a distrust of water. But why do you care so much about these lost bits of shoreline?'

'We're forgetters,' she said. 'I don't mind the building, it's the forgetting I can't stand. The first language of this country is supposed to be Irish, but it's not. It's silence.'

He rode on over the reclaimed land and under the railway bridge. The sea appeared now on his right, where the Tolka flowed into the bay, where Vikings and Irish had slaughtered each other. He wondered if they left the bodies in the water. Tonight he could not see the manure works overlooking the channel, but the nitrous smells came strongly over the water as he cycled past in the fog.

Yet the bleakness that he entered each time he rode under the bridge had nothing to do with the stories she told him. The sadness of the place was formed out of its own light. The grey sky enlarged and emptied as the bay opened out, drawing warmth and colour from the houses facing the water. A quiet disappointment had condensed on them, a disappointment as palpable as the salt in the air. He could see it more clearly the longer he spent here, as his own body slowly revealed its weaknesses, and the light here was pitiless on skin and hair. Even the solid red-brick houses looked washed out; that little crescent of older grey houses, behind a thick hedge and gates on which sphinxes faced each other, had the look of a place where Victorian mistakes once were buried. The new bungalows with their garish Mediterranean colours and glassed-in doors seemed already to have lost the struggle with the damp and the corroding air. The sky appeared unmoving over the choppy water. It was a light that suited creeks and marshes, for the shoreline that it was before they built the promenade. The trimmed grass along the sea wall was withered. Green monkey puzzle trees with branches that wore sleeves of outward-facing thorns leaned away from the sea. The air was mild enough for them, but they would never grow tropical and glossy here. He felt that no one would come here if they did not have to; this place was still outside the walls, with the taint of waste ground.

He passed the bridge out to the Bull Island, and level with the centre of the island he stopped and stood over the crossbar of his bicycle. Behind the wall of the Guinness estate at his back the big pine trees intensified the darkness, their branches creaking in the quiet wind. Tonight the creek between the roadway and the island was heavy and calm, the high-tide fullness of the water barely moving. It seemed still to be rising. He could see at the limit of the fog thousands of wading birds on the near shore of the island, like tiny etchings, moving silently, picking and probing at the mud. Shitebirds, Quinn called them; the north-running tide carried the entire city's ooze up this channel, the green slimy weeds a sure sign of organic nitrogen: why, he supposed, they called the mudflats slob lands. The water formed a continuous mass three miles long from the northern tip of the island to the wooden bridge that joined it to the mainland. The piles of the bridge looked thin in the failing light, barely holding the planks above water. Faint glimmers came from the few cottages near the bridge. The dunes had already become invisible in the fog and even the outline of the island was fading into the night.

For a long moment he did not move, and then shifted onto the saddle and pedalled back to the bridge. He thought he might say later that he had not come home when he had said he would because he wanted to think, but all he wanted was for this moment, in which the tide seemed neither ebbing nor flowing, to continue for as long as possible, and to merge with the stillness of the sea. He wanted to postpone seeing his child a day older, and thinking about what that might entail; to forget for an hour the increasing disorder of his life.

On the bridge he felt the gaps between the tarred planks through the frame of his machine, and was aware of the mass of water very close beneath him. At the end of the bridge, past the cottages, where it joined the wall that ran out into the bay, he turned onto the beach. The golf club he saw was dark as he picked up speed. As he rode on the hard sand above the high-water line, the ground seemed to interact with the wheels in a single field of energy, and the cadence of his pedalling grew faster until he was flying along in the diminished light between the dunes and the water. The wind moved the rough grass with the sound of small pebbles in a gourd, and gulls whimpered from the dunes. These were the only sounds, other than the waves breaking with a soft, drawn-out clash in the background conversation of wind and sea, their energies exchanging as the waves broke, moving heat and gas from air to water and back again in the unending cycle. The light from his bicycle lamp took on a definite shape, a luminous hollow cone curving through the cloud hovering over the ground. The strand ahead of it was solid darkness, and he wanted to imagine the island's point as infinitely far away, so that he could keep moving so fast on a surface that offered so little resistance. He had always loved the feeling of moving suspended so near yet safely held just above the earth, eking out the inertial energy of the turning wheels to which an action much like walking can give such elegant motion, the small effort that allows you to glide over flat ground and then the heaviness on the upward curve of a hill, the world reminding you that it is there. It is so simple and so ingenious, he thought, the angular momentum of the wheels maintaining equilibrium and direction, on and on; a promise of eternity in a pair of linked wheels. It's the machine of the connecting field, of forces acting on forces in continuous space. Like the one Boltzmann made, when he was in Graz: a model of what really happens. So much of what is good about the world is about riding a bicycle, and doing it well. He wondered what the brown-shirted stocktakers would have made of that bicycle when they found it in the stores. They might like its humble folksiness, but they'd prefer a model truck, or a tank.

He heard a distinct reverberant crack from the far end of the island, where the high dunes were. He stopped and stood looking at the water and the turning light at the end of the wall, where the black lighthouse was. Perhaps it was not a shot; or perhaps it was a keeper culling rooks on the estate just across the channel. Here on winter evenings he was usually alone, the golfers in their clubhouse drinking gin, though at dusk when the tide was low he would sometimes see a man digging for ragworms far out on the exposed sand. And shooting was forbidden. The island had a close season all year round. For the birds it was a feeding ground and a place to stand when the water was high, waiting for the turn of the tide. He felt the countless sleeping birds behind him, their heads turned backwards, resting on their wing feathers, thousands of them standing on the short grass between the marsh and the dunes, safe and alert.

He felt protected here. The island was a tongue of sand folded back against the throat of the bay. It had grown in a few years when they built the southern wall to stop sand from drifting into the river; the sediments were driven inward, swept along the shore by the great clockwise mechanism of the tide inside the bay, and began to lodge on a sandspit below the water. Seeds blew onto the mud; grasses rooted and held the sand; insects colonised the grass. Birds came. In a generation there were mice in the sandhills, falcons hunting them, marshes and alder trees. Some said this land emerging out of the water was a sign of a new beginning for a sinful country, the recent union between colony and mainland; others said no engineer could prevent the waste of history flooding back, that the island was the tongue the English tried to silence.

Darkness closed in as the surf moved up and down the foreshore near his front wheel. The water left ripple marks on the sand: the imprint of waves, the ridges of the berm forming under the breaking point of the waves, their neat crests and troughs. The simple mechanics of the world. Out in the cloudy dark, the field of Dublin Bay merged with the ocean, a continuous turbulence that was infinitely various yet regular, the restlessness of water under the force we choose to call gravitation, undetectable and enigmatic.

He had come so far because of his equation, one single perform-ance of such concentrated power that it had changed his life. They knew so little before, could not describe what was going on when an electron orbited a nucleus like a planet, and even that was a childlike picture that gestured at the scary immensities deep within the world. His equation worked for matter inside the atom, a space so small that we cannot picture it in our gross heads; it imagined the total energy of this obscure thing and gave matter almost a familiar form. In it a particle was figured like a wave, and it was miraculously true. The equation allowed him to detect a particle anywhere in the vast darkness of the atom, allowed the mind for a moment to capture something infinitely elusive, as a bat can snatch a fly inside a lightless cave. But no one has ever seen a wave inside an atom. It was a form of the mind, like yet utterly unlike a wave of light or a wave in water. It was a vision of the world as a continuous field of energy, deterministic and predictable, without the quantum jumps he hated, a beautiful way of explaining how atoms were so strange. And anyone could use it. But it would not work with particles moving near the speed of light, particles of great mass and therefore great energy and speed. And when a burst of radiation hit a piece of matter the electrons shaken free did not behave like waves at all, more like jagged discontinuous fragments. His was a theory for matter bound in atoms: the stuff of chemistry and of life. It was not a universal law. He wanted to repair it with a greater wave equation, an expression true for both the daft behaviour of particles and the orderly turning of galaxies – a wavelike form linking all the forms of matter. He could see it as he could trace the movements of the water chased by currents of air in the foggy dusk, but he could not say it mathematically. If he could, he thought, it would be a form of language adequate to the sea.

He had that obsession from the first, needing to know how things melted and why, the transition states from gas to liquid to crystal: a fluid is the same in all directions and has the same elasticity; it can be measured along all axes and is always the same, a medium of flows and pulsations, and the world can be thought of as an immense field like an ocean, with laws that work for all of it. This is what held him, the image as much as the logic capturing his imagination: matter as the unfolding of a disturbance in a medium, a propagation that disturbs what it passes through and is a form only, a thing that does not itself travel yet can carry so much, as a wave lifts a swimmer onto a beach. Even now, after these fruitless years, he thought the wave the most beautiful idea of oscillation in time, moving from point to point while the points themselves do not move. It connects the whole of what it disturbs. And consequences flow from action to action like ripples moving outward in a pool or along a vibrating string, as the world plays its harsh music. I see in the world the forms I desire, he admitted; it was like the feeling that came with swimming, the sliding through dark water that became his substance and parted for his limbs and yet was so dense and enveloping. But the utterance he so badly needed would not take shape in his mind.

And the failure was bitter, the failing again and again to mend the failure. The anger and permanent hurt, the feeling that he was the object of intellectual contempt, a defeat as sharp as the worst humiliation an enemy could deliberately inflict. He knew that the image he found beautiful was disgusting to others, to Bohr, to Heisenberg, though mine is the equation that works – 'Works for *chemists*,' an acolyte of Heisenberg's once sneered so that Schrödinger could hear it. For them I am an embarrassment, Schrödinger thought, a reactionary nostalgic for a lost unity. There were days now when he seemed to live in rage. Heisenberg with his cult of uncertainty, his discontinuities, his endless room for manoeuvre. He wants the world broken. He looks for the position of a particle and its momentum becomes uncertain to the point of absurdity; he tracks its momentum and the thing can no longer be given a location, it smears across space. For me it's a ghastly mess waiting for a better explanation and for him a state to wallow in. If we could find a deeper meaning he'd no longer be able to say the real is what you make of it. No nature, only our relations with nature. The observer disturbs what he sees: the century's latest great cliché, swelling like a balloon as it feeds the gut of newspapers and fashion.

The tide was leaving cockle and razor shells and weed in a ragged line along the strand. A stoppered bottle rolled in the suck. He noticed that other regular shapes were there, resolving out of the subsiding waves. He could see what looked like a coat out in the surf. Closer to him, where the waves decayed on the edge of the backshore, there was a loose page with some dark image catching the remaining light. He laid down his bicycle and went to pick it up. It was a photographic print, on thick stock, drenched in salt water but still coherent. The paper felt sodden and cold in his hands. It showed a girl sleeping on a waste of white cotton. Her hair was very black, her skin dark-hued, the features strong. The photographer's erotic longing could be felt in the nakedness of the shoulders above the clean sheets, which were just caught in the frame. It could almost have been Hansi's face on the wide white pillow in her bed, in the apartment near the Hofburg. This woman had the same determined gaze, brown eyes looking up at him with the wiry curls of her hair spread out around her, as though it was always heavy and wet. He thought of the prints she had made of atomic particles at the moment of destruction, strange patterns of black spots and traces, and wondered what had happened to them, and who had taken this photograph. In the shipping lanes of the Irish Sea, the technicians were travelling gently just beneath the surface with their tubes of compressed air. Somewhere between here and Wales there would be oil burning on the water, flames undulating on the surface. The size of waves, their power and danger, has much to do with the fetch, the length of sea and the time over which the wind has been blowing. Now their reach was so long, their fetch so great. He had an image of a cruel mouth in a cherubic face at the corner of an old map, puffing cold air across a thousand miles.

His eyes were more tired now, and the fog thicker. He could feel the sweat of his ride from town cooling on his skin, but the stress and scraping anger would not lift. Perhaps they should run again, anywhere: some university in Chile or Argentina would surely take him.

Suddenly he cried out, so frightened that instinctively he choked the sound mute, and started backwards, almost falling over with his bicycle as it toppled onto the wet sand. A tall, heavily built man was walking slowly along the line of the dunes, out of the dripping fog, coming from the left, the northern half of the island. He was wearing a suit and a flat and rakish hat, a dark tie over a white shirt and an immense dark coat that flapped around him as he walked. He had his hands in his pockets, and carried a shotgun broken open, resting in the crook of his left arm. His course was steady, but he seemed to be ambling randomly, or perhaps searching for something, bearing now closer to the water, now back towards the dunes. He was shrouded in the fog and no more than twenty paces from Schrödinger, who thought that the cuffs of the man's trousers looked darker than the rest and that his boots – great polished things laced up to the ankle – must be soaked through. He has been in the water, paddling, he thought, but this is nonsensical. The man's face had a pale flagrant look, the look of strength and health applied with greasepaint. Schrödinger could see the mouth gaping open, as though he were an expected guest smiling at his host.

Schrödinger bent at the knees and picked up his machine without taking his eyes off the apparition in front of him, and pulled the bicycle around so that it stood between them. He was not sure that the man had seen him, but managed a placating kind of grimace, even as he felt the incongruity of two men grinning at each other in the darkness on a deserted island. The cold air around him seemed to be holding fear in suspension, condensing it on him so much that he felt drenched. He was intensely conscious of the lonely place he was in and the harmful power of the night all around him; his skin was hypersensitive, the hairs on its surface alert, as though brushed by a charged comb.

The man came to a stop under the dunes, the wet air shifting gently around him. He removed his hat, wriggled his shoulders and then his legs one at a time, spray fizzing off him. Schrödinger could not make him out for long, but the man looked familiar, though there was nothing reassuring about this. He has come out of the water, he thought, he could imagine him leaping from a boat out in the shallows and loping onto the beach like a great black dog. The man's face took form for an instant and was half erased again by the mist, losing its tone and shape. He seemed to be looking straight past him. As the face cleared like smoke he thought of the man who had accosted him in town before Christmas, perhaps it was the overbearing size, but whatever was there was gradually losing definition in the fog. Schrödinger kept still. Any sudden gesture would drag him into worse territory, grounded as he was with one knee braced inside the frame of his bicycle. Nor could he speak:

anything he said might encourage or provoke the stranger out of whom mist seemed to spool in the worsening light.

It occurred to him that his only way out might be to wade into the sea and swim towards the light. He might make it, he was a strong swimmer, but was the lighthouse manned? *And yet he must swim on through the cruel sea, where every inch is death* – lines of Grillparzer learnt by heart in the last century coming back to him, *poor wretch, exhausted by the waves and love,* this armed lunatic, if that was what he was, would give him a poetic death. Leander swimming for the lamp in the tower and the waves bringing him down in the darkness when the light goes out. A body on the rocks. He could feel the pitiless hardness of stone on his limbs, and shivered in anticipation of the freezing cold water, but he could not move, could not obey his instinct to step further back. His life seemed to depend on standing his ground.

He was still holding the wet photograph. The waves sent a light film of water underneath his bicycle wheels as the tide rose up the beach in tiny fluctuating increments. The other man was stamping his feet from side to side, a walker keeping warm on a sharp night, waiting for a companion to catch up with him. His hands were still in his pockets. The shotgun, in this light, could have been a walking stick. Every object seemed tenuous to Schrödinger, even the sand just in front of him was indistinct. The stranger started to laugh, took off his hat and threw his head back, his hacking exhalations deadened by the fog. He laughed again, and Schrödinger standing yards away holding a heavy black bicycle upright, between the dunes and the sea, felt helplessly alone and mocked. The man reached down and squeezed his trouser legs and scratched his head.

Schrödinger felt his vision blur, and closed his eyes for a few moments. He wanted to keep the other man's face and hands in view. He sensed his physical power, his capacity for lunging and beating. The nearest houses were the cottages at the end of the bridge, a mile and a half away in the chilly darkness. He was shivering with cold.

The stranger shook himself again and cocked his head, listening, then hunched over and turned to the south and the periodic flash of the light on the sea wall. Schrödinger was sure that the man was about to walk off into the shallows, returning to a boat. But instead he snapped to attention, a violent drawing in and up that made Schrödinger's heart spasm and his body jerk back, and he saw the man's large hand jam his hat back onto his head. Schrödinger tensed to defend himself against the violence of those fists; but the figure made a sweeping turn with his long coat and walked on, then out onto the hard sand. The fog enveloped the man, dissolving him.

Schrödinger waited, breathing shallowly. After a while he pushed his bicycle up the beach, and just short of the dunes tossed the machine onto the tall sharp grass rooted in the soft sand. He sat with his arms around his knees, straining to hear something other than the breaking of the slight waves. He sat there until he felt the cold sand chilling his hips. Picking up his bicycle, he brushed sand off the leather saddle-tongue, feeling the harsh calcium powder on his fingers, the uncountable mollusc lives in this beach. He stared unseeing after the creature that had burst in on him. This is my sanctuary, he wanted to shout, who the hell are you to interfere with me here? As easy as that, to walk out of the sea into this country and bring who knows what contagion into it. Schrödinger pushed the wheels through the finer sand and shell hash until the firm corrugated surface of the foreshore allowed him to roll the machine easily. He began walking, slowly. He did not want to catch the man up; the thought scared him, and he was glad his machine was well oiled. After he had walked some distance he heard from up near the bridge the sound of a car engine, distorted by the wind and fog so that it seemed to be driving out into the bay. Then he heard faintly the percussive give and spring of wooden planks under heavy wheels, a baffled drumming over the water. At the end of the invisible wall the light went on wheeling and blinking.

As he turned off the bridge he felt a toxic surge of anger, worse than any he had felt since Graz. There seemed no escape that was not as bad or worse than staying where they were. 'We could always go to South America,' he said once, and Hilde said acidly, 'Where the monkey puzzle trees grow.' He knew she would never risk the child on the Atlantic. And this dumb-show on the beach brought to a head something that he still could not name. It was as if someone was focusing on him. Then he thought, I terrified myself. Some eccentric poacher who thought he was alone, raving on the beach, has scared me out of my wits. But he could not control his shock at his own humiliation.

The night felt even colder as he pedalled his way along the road by the sea into a rising wind, and the glow from inside the pub at the bottom of Vernon Avenue made him hesitate and slow down. He dismounted and threw the bike against the concrete wall of the pub. Once he pushed through the door the promise of warmth became sad and human in the smell of malt and hops, the dense tobacco smoke trapped under the brown ceiling, the warm and unwashed bodies. In the narrow room there was a crush of men in dark suits, many of them also wearing their outdoor coats. He asked for a whiskey. He took a large swallow and felt the harshness of the taste turn soothing on his nerves.

He felt a touch on his arm, a muttered greeting, and turned to find a small dark man with rimless glasses low on his rodent nose. His eyes were calm and amused, but Schrödinger always saw flickers of a more turbulent sensitivity in them. Quinn worked as a sub-editor on the *Irish Times* and edited a journal in his spare time, a quarterly of essays on subjects that were once untouchable, 'the Victorian aspic in which we jellify ourselves, to show how free we are'. The pieces had a tone of prudent mockery: how ridiculous it is, that this is how we live. He lived in a flat above a butcher's shop nearby, and he lifted Schrödinger whenever he saw him. Quinn paid nothing for the stories and mild polemics he printed and seemed to gain nothing from publishing them. Schrödinger at first found it baffling that Quinn was so hated by people who were his, Schrödinger's, protectors, but he had learned that Quinn was disliked as much for what he could say and didn't as for what he actually said. He hinted at darker secrets in reserve. He had a knack of knowing how far to go, censoring himself before he provoked too much and harmed those who had given him their confidence, this the worst that could happen in a city hung like a colony of bats with sensitive ears. 'You're my quantum priest,' he said to Schrödinger soon after they met. 'Your confessional is secure.' Only his work on the Protestant paper saved him from the quiet destructive word, the rapid collapse that begins when aversion seeps into all the compartments of a life.

'I've a new theory of alcohol,' he said, looking solemnly at Schrödinger. 'If you don't observe the swallow, is the whiskey ever drunk? It's in his gullet but I can't tell you if it's being gargled or swallowed. If I tell you where it is I can't tell you where it's flowing. It could hover there, which would give it great value as a drink. According to the quantum theory of malt you can't measure two things at once. Or do them. Like whistle and chew oatmeal, for instance.' Schrödinger laughed, but he was aware how false it sounded. He liked Quinn's parodies of the pious, hardened phrases in the reported speech he had to edit on his long night shifts. But his mind seemed trapped in the mimicry of those who had won, and he seemed to feel had beaten him, with ideas that were already dead. Schrödinger knew he had written a novel that he never hoped to publish, and that it had been consigned to the attic of his digs. He imagined the manuscript in a file tied with string under the water cistern in the roof space, resting on the beams of the ceiling, next to a box of withered apples and an old suitcase. A complete thing with no existence. Quinn had never talked about it; yet the very thought of it increased Schrödinger's affection for the man.

'Are you all right?' Quinn said. 'I'm sorry if I've hopped a ball on your toe.' As he heard the question, Schrödinger saw in the mirror behind the bar that his hair was standing up like a duster, and his wild look. Madness and physics, he thought, I'm grist to the mill tonight. He tried to find a reason for his state. 'No, no,' he said, 'you've not offended me. Yes, I'm really very well, I've just had a narrow escape out on the road, some fool almost knocked me over. Before that I rode along the beach, a little too fast for my own good. I'm winded. Can I get you . . .?' But Quinn's black pint was barely touched.

'Oh you'd see some strange sights at night down there,' he said. 'The Later Greek tolerates cold that would freeze a lesser man.'

Schrödinger felt a moment of unsatisfactory relief. Was that what the man's strange behaviour was about? Had he been looking for a few minutes of anonymous love? But not with a shotgun under his arm. He had been shooting duck, and missed, and yet the thought of telling Quinn what he had seen was impossible, though he could not explain to himself why he was so unnerved. It would seem ridiculous. He did not want to appear more neurotic than he looked.

'And as for the roads,' Quinn was saying, 'I was nearly run over by a young brat going like a racer the other night, but what can you do? The guards will stop a man for wobbling or not having a light, but in the end there's something comic about summoning a fellow for dangerous driving on a bicycle. Was anyone ever fined in the old days for being drunk in charge of a horse? It's the state of affairs we're not allowed to define that's doing it, there's insanity coming in on the wind, and boredom and fantasy building up inside. We're bottling ourselves up. And it's not looking at all good, is it, this quarrel that's none of our business. The bad hats are winning, pardon the expression, your kith and kin after all . . .'

'You can say what you like about them, as you well know. I don't feel like a brother to assassins. Remind me what *kith* means, by the way.'

'Neighbours you'd die for. It's near enough an anagram of 'thick'. I suppose it depends on who the assassins are and what you think of them. We have experience of the matter here. The only safe principle is that they're all gougers.'

Gougers is right, he thought, fingers in the sockets of the eye; the ultimate cruelty, put out your enemy's light and let him live. 'And dropping bombs on us now.'

'It's supposed to make us think, of which there is precious little danger. Maybe you can explain to me now, if light is bent towards a dumb mass why doesn't it swerve up Kildare Street and cling to Leinster House and Government Buildings? The rest of the city should be in total darkness.'

Schrödinger laughed, the strain he was under easing a little as the whiskey took effect. 'Sometimes I think it is.' He wanted to be diverted from all this. 'But tell me, what of more local news? I've been in my ivory tower too much.'

'I hope I'll understand what you're meditating, but I know I won't. Still, there's no reason why a great idea can't be thought here. Your long friend is right about that. If Einstein could discover relativity while he was stuck in a patent office, half the fellows in this pub should be working with you instead of counting paperclips. Maybe they're fooling us and the Civil Service is a conspiracy of geniuses. We'll wake up some morning to find that Breen over there has discovered a way of getting coal from seawater. But Einstein wasn't that kind of bureaucrat, was he?'

'Not exactly. And I do a lot of paperclip counting. It does seem to crowd out thought, and we all fight for time, even in a quiet place like this.'

'But we're not disturbed around here by anything too exciting. No bohemians here, vegetarians, no adepts of free love. They'd wilt on this side of the bay.'

Schrödinger felt the doleful compliment, if that is what it was, without resentment. He was not even sure that Quinn knew how he lived. He assumed that no one really knew, or would believe that anyone living here could be so blatant, but tonight he felt how paper-thin the deception was and how much the casual glance could penetrate. If anyone cared to know they must know, even if they had no need to acknowledge the observation as a fact. And so far no one had crossed the invisible barrier they had thrown up around themselves, as though a protective hand made them immune. Even here, he told himself again, private life is sacred. Quinn said, 'There's always room for surprise, having said that. Nothing stops the ordinary sadness. Take your neighbour.'

Schrödinger waited. The family across the road had a lonely integrity that disturbed him. They fascinated Quinn too, who knew them slightly through a remote cousinly connection, and he seemed to find some desolate significance in them. Mrs Flaherty was a small handsome grey-haired woman, who never dressed in anything but black. 'She looks like an Italian widow who's had to stay on because of some awful shipwreck,' Hilde said once. Her son was a large, slow man, unmarried and still living at home. The father dead, the mother clung to religion and her grief. She was certain that her listeners shared her sense of the terrible loss she had suffered. Mourning had become her claim on the world, and it was impossible to rally her without offence, as easy-goers in the parish had tried to do and never been forgiven.

Dr O'Reilly told her husband he had slipped a disc. Flaherty lay for weeks on planks stretched out on the parlour floor downstairs; he could not move, and read the paper on his back. A bonesetter sent by the doctor made the pain worse; Schrödinger had heard his calvary recounted by his widow, each agonising step lingered over like a passion. Then he had seemed to recover, and Schrödinger remembered seeing him that first winter cycling down the road each morning, a small man made smaller and thinner by the heaviness of his thick blue coat. By the time the cancer became too obvious for even O'Reilly to miss, his patient had weeks to live. Mrs Flaherty never forgave the lazy golf-playing doctor who had lived well for twenty years on the stoic caution of his patients in these respectable streets. Yet none of them went elsewhere, a fact that no longer surprised Schrödinger: they would not wish to make a fuss about illness and death.

The son ministered to her. He was sullen in her company, almost derisive in a mild way, resentful of her but more resentful of the world for what it had made of her. Flaherty had been brilliant as a boy, lively and attractive. He had studied to be a lawyer, and Quinn had heard that he made insincerely passionate speeches at the Literary and Historical Society, facing down a mob of drunken students. Schrödinger could never see the glib young orator in the awkward man he knew. There was supposed to have been a girl; they had an understanding and marriage was assumed. Then he was bruised by something that no one could ever explain; he left university and his light dimmed. He went on living at home. His mother seemed to consume him, her heat draining his, praying and remembering. But it is the place that pulled him down, Schrödinger thought, the atmosphere of it; a fatalism that is contagious.

Schrödinger sometimes saw them walking to Mass, the son towering over his mother in his best suit. On weekday mornings he wheeled his bicycle silently down the short garden path, his thick home-knitted socks turned out over his trousers, swung his leg over and set off slowly, a cap on his bent head, to his job in the Department of Defence. He pedalled with a silent, hopeless discipline, as though the journey were a sentence that he was condemned to endure for the rest of his life.

Schrödinger had seen inside the house once or twice, the first time when he asked if the son would take delivery of a chair that Hilde had ordered from Clery's. Flaherty shook his hand. He had always seemed awkward, making dry and cynical and not unintelligent remarks about politics in an unanswerable sing-song way, and beyond that his conversation dried up, as though he had prepared certain responses and could not improvise any further. Yes, he said, he would be in, grand, he would do that. He held himself rigid, smiling kindly, but his smile was one of discomfort at this intrusion. They talked a little about the shortages, and Flaherty burst with surprising bitterness into a story he had heard of how his Minister's chauffeur had driven up in the big state car in the middle of the day to the Minister's house and carried in, in one gloved hand, a half-pint of cream for the Minister's wife. 'The rest of us haven't enough petrol to bless ourselves with. They put a stop on salaries as long as the emergency lasts but do they stint themselves? And this is the same crowd who won't give the schoolchildren lunches. They're all hooks.' He fell silent again, and as they stood close together in the narrow passage, the walls papered in dark green nearly touching their shoulders, Schrödinger could see through the doorway at the end of the passage a few plates, an ashtray and a cup on the table in the little kitchen. An image in needlework of the Sacred Heart impaled on a cross and bound in thorns hung on the wall over the cooker, Christ holding the heart perfectly still, radiant, exposed: a trance of blood loss and oneness. The hallway floor was dusty. Every glimpse he had of the house confirmed the postponement of action – the unmended bicycle in the back garden, the frames of a greenhouse half built. Nothing was complete; nothing prepared for a future.

'Limbo,' he had said to Anny that night. 'I think that Limbo is across the street. Mrs Flaherty and her boy. They're the innocent dead.'

Without looking up from her book, the same Irish novel she had been reading for days, she said: 'You forget the story. They would have had to die before Christ ever came if they were to get into Limbo. Or be infants, which they are not. Or not the kind we know.'

'They're certainly ghosts, wherever it is they live. Too late for Christ or any other saviour.'

Anny smiled, but her friendliness had been repelled by her

41

neighbours' shyness too often for her not to find them distressing. 'That poor man. Do you think he has ever been held in anyone's arms? What happened with that girl he was supposed to be in love with, I wonder? But you realise, now that I think of it, that Limbo is next door to Hell. Are you sure that they're not already condemned, and that it isn't we who are waiting to live again? To find out what's going to happen to us?'

It was as though she had flicked him casually in the face with her book, and though she hadn't meant it unkindly, when the work was blocked, as it had been all winter, he felt shabby and useless, a refugee. He realised that Flaherty left him with a fear of contamination, of sinking into torpor. And I live here, he thought: I breathe the same air.

Flaherty seemed to have no vices except a discreet weakness for whiskey, his large soft body held in its braces under his clean, worn suit. On Sundays he went out on his bicycle. Quinn knew that he cycled to the city stations or north on the country roads near Malahide to a footbridge under which the Belfast trains sped with a blast of noise. This was his hobby: noting the classes and occurrences of engines. Now fewer and fewer trains were running, though he would still cycle out as usual, in a long coat buttoned round a paisley scarf, his mother complaining from the door. Schrödinger saw him return one Sunday with a large package in brown paper balanced on his crossbar and another in the basket on his handlebars.

'He's not even got a piece of land or the company of animals. Cities were not supposed to be like this, living as though we were waiting for a father to die to start living, not even living when the father is dead.' Quinn was strangely passionate about his story. He said that the other night the mother called the son into the back room where they usually sat around the radio in a silence that only she had the authority to break. Schrödinger wondered how he knew, but Quinn described her interrupting the slow disembodied voice of the announcer to berate the governing party. Schrödinger felt the force of these subtle hatreds all around him, but imperfectly, and knew that ignorance made him safe. When he spoke to his elderly neighbour she did not seem to understand that he was the hobby of the man she hated, or perhaps knew it well and hoped that her curse might reach its object through him. The tall half-blind man had become for her evil, at once pious and demonic, the cause of all the disrepair in the country and their lives. 'Would you listen to him soft-soaping us? The language, how are you. The language never put meat on the table. It never stopped the boats leaving the country full of our young men. There won't be anyone left to speak it, the way he's going.' She struck a mock-saintly pose and intoned, '"We must save from death our own sweet language."' But her imitation of de Valera's incantatory alto was spoiled by her reduction of it to a jeering sneer, her indignation not drawing breath long enough even to mimic the voice she hated so much.

But that night, Quinn had heard, Mrs Flaherty had switched the radio off and told her son that she had something to discuss. She announced that she wished to be cremated and scattered over the sea, not buried in a coffin. 'Like a Viking,' Schrödinger murmured. Quinn nodded eagerly. 'She is afraid of dissection, you see, that she will be dug up. She's heard rumours about bodies being sold to the College of Surgeons, about the living being buried. She wants to be sure she's dead, and not in some fatal trance. She has more imagination than you'd think to look at her,' Quinn said, his porter-breath up close. 'You wonder what she reads. Buying corpses. Dissection. Anatomy lessons, Burke and Hare. And of course she wants your man to do the same.'

'I think it is because she distrusts doctors. I can't say I blame her very much.' He was aware of how careful and pedantic his English sounded. He wanted to enter into the spirit of this, though the sadness of it was too apparent, and he felt a little ashamed at witnessing the old woman's distraction. And he had no resilience left after the day's strange turns. 'She blames them for the death of her husband. Perhaps it is her protest against their complacency, some odd way of telling them that they are hopeless, that they can't be trusted even to confirm the fact of death.'

'For a woman so devout she's become a little hazy about the funeral rites. The Church, as you may have noticed, doesn't bury jars of ash. Not here. They want the body in position for the return of the soul, they like the solid thump the coffin gives when it is lowered into the hole. There's something about the killing weight on the bearers as well: the way it presses down mortally on the collarbone. She'll be *admonished* if she isn't careful.'

'What did the son say?'

'He was so shocked he walked out on her for the first time in his life. Came in here and talked to me consecutively, in more than monosyllables. He was in a state of shock.' Quinn had dropped any pretence of finding the story amusing, and shook his head briefly before drinking from his glass.

Schrödinger had heard their front door slam late one night a few days ago, an unheard-of sound in a road that was always hushed. He thought he had heard a voice cry out; perhaps that was the night.

He put his glass on the bar. He had drunk a second whiskey after catching the barman's eye and now felt a euphoric gas in his head, but the turmoil created by that scene on the island was also heightened by it, and the easy explanations he had found were not reassuring any more. He needed to eat and then to sleep, to forget about all this. After a few tired exchanges he bade goodnight to Quinn, who raised his glass and said, 'Until the Quarter Sessions.'

He came out into the cold wind, his coat pinned to him in the winter night. The tide was ebbing now, but he could still hear the waves massing under the sea wall. He had to stand on the pedals against the wind as he turned up Castle Avenue, past the kitsch gothic castle and into Kincora Road. It all seemed to fight quietly in his mind tonight, unbidden images of slaughter at low tide, the bodies of strangers. The Protestant church was an indistinct mass behind bare trees, and its spire rose into the mist. It was once visible from the sea and from the hills to the south of the city: a beacon for an England that was now too far away, its own churches smashed and burning. The lights in the Flaherty's house were off, except for a glimmer behind the curtains on the ground floor. The curtains should be heavier now, all their curtains should be. These faint lights have a different meaning four miles up in the sky. He thought of Flaherty and his mother silent in their parlour, smoke rising around the son's impassive face as he read the thin newspaper. Schrödinger imagined him in bed later, his longing rising like sour milk. His mother would be sitting near the radio, her fingers twisting needle and thread through pieces of cloth saved from old garments so that nothing might be wasted.

What happens to the souls of the unburied dead? he wondered, as he wheeled his bicycle into the garage beside the house. He thought of his neighbours, homeless, driven out of doors in the piercing dark of the sea wind, their coffins empty, their souls living after them as they found their way to the shoreline and the old pagan ghosts.

The hallway was cold, but it was full of a warm smell of cooking vegetables and meat. They were sitting in the room at the back with the curtains closed, the wood and turf fire banked and glowing red. It was stifling after the night air. They sheltered here in the evenings as though they were in a cave, on opposite sides of the fire, Anny knitting, Hilde reading a book, her brown hair pulled back tight and high by a silver clip. Anny was making a sweater for her friend's child. Both of them were smiling. When he thought about it, their arrangement seemed impossible, and the guilt rose in him when he thought about ruining this gift of their tolerance of each other, and of him.

Anny looked up at him from her wool and her needles with hollow, tired eyes. Her face had become heavier since they left Austria; middle age was forming and thickening around her, and she seemed to find the change more and more difficult. But her smile widened when she saw him, and she rose as he approached the fire. 'You look terrible,' she decided. Hilde followed her gaze. 'What's the matter? You look as though you've had bad news. What happened?' He sensed that they had been sharing a joke, and was aware of his set face chilling their good humour.

He shrugged irritably, his disquiet still working in him, making it impossible to articulate what he felt. There was something looping and complicated about what had happened on the beach that he couldn't disentangle. He knew that if he did not share it with them now it would become more difficult to describe with any precision, but he could not bear to touch the dregs the day had aroused in him. Not even the relief of speaking German, of slipping into a language in which he did not have to make an effort, was any comfort tonight. 'No, it was nothing. A lorry almost ran me down, that's all. The driver may have been drunk, or maybe the fog made me invisible, I didn't have my lights. They are the worst drivers in the world. Thank God there are so few cars now, or they'd make their own war here on the roads.' He knew he sounded petulant, the stuff he was hiding coming out in unruly gusts of emotion. He went back into the hall and let the rucksack fall to the linoleum floor like a careless boy, and walked up the short staircase to the bathroom.

'The gas is nearly gone,' he heard Anny say from below. 'Come and eat.' He turned on the hot tap and inserted the plug in the sink. The geyser lit up, and a slow trickle made a shallow pool. He washed his hands with the hard, unlathering soap and splashed his head up to the line of his hair, the warm water washing away the feeling of the night on his skin. The bathroom was the size of the vestibule of his father's apartment in Vienna, and it was always cold. He longed tonight for the gush of water from huge faucets in a deep bath instead of the thin difficult hot water, the damp, the cold rooms, the tiny spaces and thin walls, and the parlour where three adults had to sit so close to each others' knees.

He switched off the light, removed his shoes and stepped across the few feet that separated him from the bedroom that he shared with Hilde. The child's room was at right angles to theirs. Her door was ajar, and he looked at her as she lay in the glow of a red nightlight, her head turned to the side, her arms raised and bent at the elbow, both fists close to her head – an almost infant sleep of blind trust. She calmed him, for a moment, by making him long for her safety, but there was also the postponed decision sharpening its edge as time wore on. Perhaps this year he would tell her, when she would be seven, the age of reason; and from seven times seven a man begins to die. I should act my age, he thought.

Downstairs, when Hilde looked enquiringly at him he began to talk quickly about O'Hogan, one of his colleagues at the Institute and a known family demon. Anny asked, 'Is he drinking too much whiskey again?'

Schrödinger said, 'Probably, though he's not much better sober. There's a tribe of cheap corrosive sceptics out to ruin his world and I'm their local representative. If only he knew that my tribe is nearly extinct. But it's ghastly and I can't take any more of it. It has become disgusting.' He spoke the last word with real heat, anger so overt it repelled further sympathy. He sat at the table and removed a notebook from his jacket pocket, opening it and seeing nothing, then dropping it onto the table. In the silence Anny said, 'For heaven's sake stop being so tense and miserable. You're not in Graz any more. Let's eat.' She went into the kitchen and they heard her moving pots on the dying gas in the stove. Hilde stood up and moved close to where he sat at the dining table, his head now in his hands. She reached out and took his head, folding him close, his cheek pressed to her belly. She kissed him where the fine hair thinned out on his head.

'How was your day, really?'

He made an effort to loosen the knot of anger that was so tight he could barely speak. 'It was no worse than any other. I waste so much time in petty institutional squabbles. Endless, endless deferment of real work. But nothing to worry about. And you?'

'Shopping, waiting in lines, then we walked and read. By the time Ruth came home the day seemed to have been used up. She did her homework so neatly and so well. They're strict, these nuns.'

'For now it's probably good that she has these four-square disciplines. We can teach her what they leave out.'

They talked for a while about their daughter, and in the brief silence that followed she asked, with an effort at lightness that pitched her voice a little higher, 'Do you think we should be worried? We feel so safe here, but these bombs, and there are rumours, so many rumours. Mrs Flaherty and the old ladies say that the British are preparing to invade, and that will give the others the excuse they need.'

'No, of course not, and we are safe, safer than we could have dreamed two years ago. Although nowhere is really safe. And what is happening here is like a magic act. Nothing is quite as we see it to be. They may not be able to keep the illusion going, but the Taoiseach is a clever man. He has never survived worse times than this, but he is a survivor.'

'When you say nowhere is safe – why would they want this place? What is there here for them?' She spoke as if arguing against herself. 'They can't get blood out of a stone.'

'I was speaking loosely, and I'm tired. Please don't take me so seriously. I don't know what they want until I see what they actually do. Hold me; for God's sake hold me. I am so sorry.'

She squeezed him tighter as though his head were indeed a stone, a thing she despaired of. 'You have been so preoccupied lately, so strange. I know the work has not gone well for you, and that it is very difficult. But give it time. The distractions should not frighten you away from it, and there is nothing better that you can do here. You have to be ruthless if you are to find something that can live after all this horror has gone by.'

He closed his eyes against her warm stomach. To hear her speak for him so well only increased the stir of self-disgust.

'I know. But I have been restless, I admit that I've been agitated recently, I feel a certain . . .' He trailed off, the half-formed thought impossible to recover, one more unthought-out stupidity at the end of this stupid day.

She pressed him closer still, then asked, 'Is there someone else? Is that *also* what is happening?'

His silence was enough to tell her, but after what must have been half a minute – during which he stared at the dark-red curtain with its scrolls and spirals a yard from his face, as though he might find in its intricate forms a shape that he could use to explain himself – he said, 'I don't know. Perhaps.'

Her body became very still. The pressure of her arms did not lessen, but all the rest of her seemed to relax into passivity. She said, 'I see.' Then, with a smaller voice, 'If that is what you want. Now of all times.'

'Please, not now, this is not the time. I should have said nothing. I can't take it now. But you know what I am. We have spoken about this so much, endlessly. We agreed we would be honest with each other. We cannot be divided now if what we have been to each other changes for a moment, if it does at all. What we form together can't be taken from us, not ever, even if we sometimes need to express ourselves in different ways. Why should it change anything? And there is nothing happening.' He spoke as though from a text that was tired and overused and had become garbled, and was aware as he did so that she would remain unseduced by it; and still less by the painful erotic animation his conditional fidelity had once aroused in her.

'I know all that. I know what you said. But it isn't easy living up to what we think is beautiful, this world in which we can dream we are connected to everyone else but actually only to those we care about. I haven't forgotten quite as much as Anny has, not yet anyway, though I wonder whether she has really forgotten anything. She is young, no doubt, this one who is not quite there yet.' Her voice was now defensive and sharp. 'You will do as you wish. You are insatiable, and I admit I'd hoped you might become less so. Sometimes I even wish I had not come with you. And there is something else we must resolve, which you will not face and which goes on and on. When are we going to tell her? When? She will be so confused.'

He threw out his hands to either side of her in a gesture of denial and exasperation, his face still held to her body. 'I don't know. I think about it all the time, but I don't know what is best and even whether we should. You wanted to wait, after all, and we've gone on with it. I do know that I would not know how to deal with the consequences if we told her now. It would be unfair to her. There is already so much – I don't know what to call it, nastiness? – in the air, one can almost taste it. Let us wait for everything to calm down. Not now, please. I *beg* of you.'

'When will be a good time? This nonsense won't let me breathe normally. I have given in to so much, but I can't take much more. Everything we have done has been for you. I went through hell in Oxford after she was born, you were useless, I would have died, I think, if it had not been for Anny. I treated the man I loved, the man I married, like dirt, and he accepted almost everything. I wish I had not left him. Perhaps we could have mended things and at least he was not a compulsive child. We could have kept our heads down and survived it there instead of following you here where I can't even be myself. I lie awake at night asking myself why I came. All this way for – what? And now I am trapped here.'

Her arms slipped down and she jerked away out of the room, leaving him sitting back, torn out of her embrace, his arms still opened wide. Slowly he shifted forward in his seat and pressed his fists to his eyes, moving his glasses up into his hair. He remembered her frightening stillness in the months after the baby was born, not speaking, not eating, not so much as looking at her child. He had felt helpless, and what did her husband know about babies? Anny truly had saved them; taken the child away and fed it, and carried it on her shoulder when it cried at night, as if it had been her own. He dreaded the thought that Hilde might break down again. Confined in this house the effects would be so much worse; there would be no escape for any of them.

Both Hilde and her husband were in awe of him. The affair had begun in the year when intense vehement urges were set loose on the world, and he was part of it, loathing it but infected despite himself by the wildness around him. The aura he had then, the radiance of his Prize, made any craving seem easy to satisfy. She was tall and strong, and she had a warm and open air about her, and he told himself he was in love. There was a beautiful kindliness about her face, which seemed to regard him almost with pity. He caught her once looking at him as though she wanted to take him aside and calm him down with good humour and common sense. To make me better, he told himself. He had watched her skiing down a slope, cavorting and dodging like a deer, and after that he could not stop thinking about her, pursuing her for months, the obsession growing after he left Berlin. His charisma was enhanced by walking out on the thugs. She could not resist his heartfelt promises, his urgency and glamour.

And when, later, the child was born it had entered the world as hers and her husband's, and Arthur pretended that normal life went on, treating the child as his when half of Oxford knew the truth. He had taken the job there for her sake and tolerated his wife's nights in London; he heard of her at parties where she had turned up on the arm of his friend. Genius has its needs, and none of them admitted to petty jealousies. Sitting at the kitchen table hearing her footsteps on the upper floor, he thought, I was in a delirium, lust and celebration, drifting from one success to another, one erotic frenzy to the next. There were no limits, I was invincible, and here I am falling out of love with a woman who has never really loved me.

She did not reappear for dinner. They ate in the kitchen, husband

and wife sitting at the small wooden table. Anny's exhaustion seemed to lessen in response to his anxiety, and she spoke about Ruth's delight in playing hopscotch on the pavement, and her friends from the convent school. Almost as though the child were her own, which never ceased to amaze him. They laughed at the irony of sending her to a school founded by women who burned to preserve the faith, and about the girl's Dublin accent, in which they heard a hard, resigned sadness. They talked about money, about a winter coat for Hilde and shoes for the child, then lapsed into silence. She touched his hand lightly. She seemed unable not to care for him and was, he sensed, almost relieved that whatever had happened made him turn to her, as he always did. But there was also something in her self-denial that reached down and came up as a silent reproach – against his failure to have ever found her enough, while never ceasing to need her. She had watched the ebb and flow of his absurd sensuality long enough to know that it had a rhythm, and that there was always a return to a point of rest. For now she could try to lead him away from the edge she felt he was drifting towards. He was aware of this, and refused nothing that she offered. She diverted him by talking about the small acts of scavenging alertness that the Emergency called for every day. 'There is a place selling wood on the South Circular Road. It sounds good: ash, oak and beech, cut into blocks. They'll deliver it on a cart. We could put it under that tarpaulin in the back garden. But there's no good tea to be had, not for gold.' Later: 'Shall we go the cinema this weekend? I'd like to see something silly and happy. A musical. We could all go.' And he found himself calming down, and taking part once more.

Later he helped her to dry the dishes. By then she was so tired she was moving slowly, and said as she put a fresh towel out that she was going to bed, brushing a hand on his shoulder as she went towards the stairs.

In the living room he put a sod of turf on the dying fire. The dormant energy in a half-burnt log blazed up in a last flare of heat. *We light up from the dead.* That old Greek fragment. We are one; these plural selves such illusion. But we light up from each other, he thought, staggering from desire to desire like burning torches in the dark. I can't rise above it. There are things I cannot surrender. Stuck in the vortex. And he felt the old anger return. He wondered if the Greeks ever banished a thinker for using the wrong metaphor, for saying the world is fluid in a city devoted to particles. Your image stinks, like that archer's gangrenous foot. Go live on an island and rot. They needed the archer to fight at Troy. Who'll come and rescue me? He poured himself a whiskey from one of the bottles on the sideboard that also held the big radio. The fabric grille beneath the sunburst fretwork hummed and vibrated when he turned the knob. The glass panel etched with the names of cities illuminated slowly as the bulbs behind it heated up, the world arranged as a linear grid. The deep hiss of static rose, and out of it a supercilious voice invaded the room, praising the Englishness of English music. The languid tone that modulates the banal into profundity, a received pronunciation of received ideas. Music washed away the voice, dissolving it in sugary pastoral resolutions, reminding him of why he hated this hedgerow twittering, reminding him too much of Oxford, his first bolthole. There had been no agreement there not to see what did not need to be seen. His motives in persuading them to give Hilde's husband a job were transparent, and he did not help by making a show of loathing High Table, the dutiful talking with bishops and generals and dons serving a life sentence of Thucydides. He spun the dial and from the surf of buzz the clear metallic voices hardened out. Hamburg 352. Bremen 396. Vatican City 48.4. Moscow 25. Berlin 19.74. Flat lies, sneering contempt, voices with uncannily precise diction announcing their inversions of each others' truths. Their vicious misery churning the atmosphere, waves of low energy propagating and interfering in the air. Parts of a torn body that do not add up. A German voice said, 'Those who mewl for peace are the worst hypocrites. The law they dream of has been written for themselves by the plutocrats and imperialists.' He turned the knob back and off, and the light in the dial faded. He sat and watched the last log until it turned a brittle red, a delicate carbon thing holding its form for an instant before it crumbled into ash.

Hilde lay under the covers, her immobility almost that of sleep. He spoke her name, but she did not answer, and he could feel her hurt in the unheated room. He removed his clothes in the dark, the air cold on his arms and legs. He laid his glasses on the side table, then slipped under the blankets and tried to lie still. At first he thought he could sleep, but the pounding of his mind against the day's memories began, like a hammer hitting a nail stuck on metal under wood. That uncanny meeting on the beach, but the old quarrel bored at him, the jumps without continuity, the grinning positivism that believes only what it sees. As though to say until you see the cat it is neither alive nor dead, it is only a smear of probabilities. It lives in a blur as they want us to live, in a permanent fog. If they could see me here they'd be proud. His horrified, wakeful irritation could not help interfering with the image of the girl at the party, looking so thoughtfully at his smiling face, but it could not drown her out.

Yet much later he reached out and touched the rise of his sleeping companion's hip, then her neck where it joined the curved bone beneath the softness of her shoulder. Her fingers rose and stroked his, barely, the slight brush of her fingertips enough to flood him with relief. He must not lose this. After that he was taken by sleep.

His bladder woke him when the room was light and icy. He came awake not knowing where he was, panicking, and feeling that everything he had known had been taken from him. He pulled himself from under the blanket and without his glasses stepped to the wardrobe, groping for the handle to the door of a room he had left twenty years before, his body helpless in its memory. The light hard rattle of the wardrobe woke him fully. He felt the whiskey dull behind his eyes and in his stomach. Reaching for his glasses, he crossed the room and found the right door and his dressing gown hanging from it. In the toilet it was so cold the white porcelain blurred as his relief steamed around it.

He stepped very carefully on the outer treads of the stairs until he felt the lino under his feet in the hallway. He had always hated its austere chill, reminded of the waste of his father's life in that factory where burlap was impregnated with linseed oil and pigment, the feeling that he owed to linoleum his own freedom to think. The floors of Ireland seemed to be covered in it. It had come into his dream, he realised, an endless corridor of polished linoleum down which he ran towards a single black crucifix, with nothing but cold and emptiness behind him.

In the sitting room he shivered in his thin robe. He drew back the curtains, and the leaden air and the stir of rain on the patch of grass and the apple tree in the little back garden made the room feel twice as cold. A platform on a square post held breadcrumbs and a few scraps of food. Up above, enormous grey clouds were holding perfectly still. It was a raw, final sky. Beyond the low stone wall between the gardens, his neighbour's house showed no sign of life.

He twisted the previous day's *Irish Times* into rough paper fuses and raked the clinker from the grate onto the fine ash in the tray beneath, which he withdrew and poured into the bucket by the fireplace. He stacked turf and a couple of logs on the paper twists, then struck a match near a loose end. The paper consumed itself in yellow flames, licking at the hairy fibres of the peat. He wondered whether there was any tea left, and whether Quinn might know someone who would sell them some that was not dusty and bitter. He stood, feeling very cold as the fire began to take.

He had reached the furthest place he could go, he knew that now; this chaste suburb with its forsaken air was where he would have to come to terms. It was Hamilton's ghost that had brought him here; he owed him, but the man's unhappiness felt contagious now, the prodigy obsessed all his life with a woman he could not have, dreaming of her while she bore children to a dull clergyman and he had two loveless marriages, feeding his grief with drink all day in the 1840s, half conscious as peasants in the west dead of hunger were thrown into mass graves, while the vast orderly crowds of the Catholic poor walked to their outdoor meetings, torches flaming, their orator O'Connell telling them that they would soon be free. In their heavy tread and the massed chorus of their rosary voices Hamilton heard the massacre of everyone he knew, but O'Connell cancelled the last great meeting at Clontarf, the village of lost causes. Yet this was a mind that could predict, purely mathematically, how a single incident ray of light might shine through a crystal and become a hollow cone inside the mineral and emerge from it as a beautiful cylinder of light, and later it was proved that light could do exactly that if it were beamed the right way through a piece of aragonite. Light into form, light and matter unfolding in a space that is thought and is also the world. But for Hamilton it did no good. He wrote enormous unreadable books about quaternions, imaginary algebras that would transform the world. And then the game, the board game for travellers that he thought would make him rich, and no one wanted to buy. Schrödinger wondered if a copy had survived. Nothing worked, not in the only life Hamilton was given, but at least he was allowed to see his beloved once more when she was near the end. They kissed – once – in ecstasy before she died. He worked out the mathematics of ascension, calculating the time it would take her body to reach heaven on the last day, how it would trace many possible routes through space, seeming to cover so many of them before arriving at the point of destination, the path of least time under the principle of least action, as good for immortal souls as for the strange paths of light. And Schrödinger thought of Mrs Flaherty's bodiless soul rising, a puff of ash and smoke, and wondered how Hamilton would have tracked such a weightless sorrow.

He could smell his unwashed skin; he was overdue a bath, and he should wash his hair sometime this week. Perhaps the back boiler behind the fire would have enough tepid water this morning. As he looked at the winter state of the garden he felt that he was waking from an illness and expecting someone to arrive who would tell him what he should do, and how he should recover. He prayed he was not waiting for someone like the man he had seen last night. They were all waiting, he and the Irish. He stared at the white bloom of ice on the grass and the hardened brown potato skins on the bird table, and wondered if it was true about the cats in the old houses. Quinn told him it had once been a Dublin custom to bury a cat alive in the walls of a building, for luck. He searched the man's face to see if this was some joke at his expense, but there was no sign of it in the sad eyes behind the wire spectacles. He wondered at the uses of cats. How long would it survive, and would it scrape its claws on the inner face of the brick, the small powerful muscles launching it in a frenzy up the narrow space between the walls until it broke its claws and wore its body out, or would it lie patiently, an inert form waiting for a human to come back, remove a brick and look into the cavity before deciding whether it was alive or dead? The shape of history: someone comes and looks, and the past is agreed upon, measuring out the darkness, suffering and fear.

At eight the next morning the Institute was quiet. The dark branches of the leafless trees and the hedge across the road cut off the view. He rubbed his aching eyes. Those who lived here before, who knew their world was finished, did they long for an end, some way of stilling that feeling of worse times coming? Perhaps after all their heirs should turn the garden into a dump for statues no one loves any more. Wilde the Surgeon Oculist, the old queen's eye man, would have liked it, the collector of monuments and mummies. He had lived across the square, an expert on cataracts; he went to Vienna to learn the latest techniques. My God, Schrödinger thought, an Austrian cure for diseases of the eye: the blind leading the blind. He resolved to stop nursing the fear that came over him at the thought of a knife cutting through the egg-white lens, and ask Dr O'Reilly for the name of a specialist. It would be for the best.

He had taken the North Strand road this morning, and as he went through the crossroads by the Five Lamps among the other cyclists and the occasional car he was reminded of the absent cattle. Sometimes he rode away from the office at lunchtime, bored and impatient with himself, in order he would say to work at home, which often was the truth. He was held up every week at this crossroads by the cattle flooding down the hill that led to the docks, as the drovers flicked their sticks at them, the animals lifting their dark heavy bodies on frail-looking legs, spittle trailing from their mouths. The drovers in their muddy boots and brown coats and soft hats called to their charges in a guttural twang he could never understand, trotting clumsily but easily alongside them, smiling and laughing, coming to the end of a tiring journey that they and their beasts had made together, without hard feelings or passion. This final stampede brought them down to the waiting ship; Schrödinger wondered if the men made the cattle run to tire them out before they were packed into the hold. The great eyes of the bullocks rolled back in their heads, and some turned their heads to the side, staring at the waiting cyclists, and he believed they knew what was coming. The sight lingered with him after he crossed the road and cycled on through the piles of dung left on the roadway. The oxen, it was said, cried out when a new theory entered the world, the awful light striking their eyes, because they knew they would be sacrificed in thanksgiving. Pythagoras slaughtered a hundred when he got his theorem right. They scream anyway, he thought, the cattle in their shambles won't be any worse off because of me.

He had become hardened to seeing this frightened rush, but for weeks now the carts and bicycles had gone through the crossroads without being made to wait. At first he thought that the sailing times of the ships must have changed. There were so few ships now, it was said as few as ten a month. So little coal and oil was coming in, perhaps the British were making difficulties over cattle going out. A little squeeze, and the country's heart slowed. But he paid no attention to the missing cattle, as he ignored much that did not immediately affect him in the boring censored newspaper, until his neighbour Flaherty muttered one morning, to cover his embarrassment at having to talk to him as they wheeled their bicycles down their garden paths, 'The foot and mouth will ruin us, it's the last straw. I wouldn't put it past them.' And the butcher had run out of meat last Saturday morning. 'It will contaminate every animal in the country, blast it, excuse the language, madam,' he said to Anny. 'There's tinkers and the like spreading it, who knows what's going on.' And on Sunday he had taken the child for a walk past the farm called Geoghegan's Field, near the edge of the Guinness estate. There were houses near enough to make the mound of burning corpses in the pit obscene. The dead cattle looked so bulky pressing down on each other, and the long necks of those on top hung helplessly as though they had been broken. The wind changed so that the smoke followed them with the smell of roasting flesh and burned hair. Ruth turned her face against his coat and cried, holding him around his legs with her thin trusting arms. 'Uncle, it's horrible.' He felt helpless to protect her. I should read the paper more carefully, he thought. I should be more alert.

Though he was early this morning, the stoker and porter were at work before him and in his office the fire was already burning, and not giving off too much smoke. His secretary and the first graduate students would not be in for an hour. Yesterday's basket of brown sods was almost empty. It had not looked too dark with water, and he hoped today's would be as good. He pressed shavings of plug into his pipe with his thumb and lit the tobacco with a reddened lump of turf on the end of the tongs, then sat at his desk staring at a sheet of equations, the first page of a new notebook. The tobacco smoke hung low and sweet around his head, mingling with the peat smell from the fire. The stir of arousal, the first flicker of belief that this attempt might lead from the field equations of general relativity, from the bending of light by mass back into the heart of the atom, had faded into a mild disgust with himself. The equations did not work; their construction was fanciful and hideous. The lightness he needed to achieve a suspension of will, to imagine a perfect expression of what he could nearly see, was once more crushed out of him.

He thought of the girl and her watchful, intelligent face. She was strongly with him, pushing back his immediate memory of Hilde. He told himself again that he must not go any further; that it would complicate all their lives, and that he did not want to hurt Hilde again. And there is an air now of tense expectation that something is about to happen, and I don't want to be involved in their lives in ways I can't control. The more he tried to suppress the thought the more he was swept into a helpless state that left him facing her alone, imagining their speechless regard of each other. He felt no arousal: it was a dull, trancelike state softening the memory of last night's bewilderment, and the demands of the body even seemed loathsome, an addiction to be foresworn. He was aware that he felt desperate, as though this might be the last time, his last chance to feel his own radiance and to forget himself, and also that it had as much to do with his conscious mind as a plant turning light into sugar. He drifted with his body's dumb will, to which he knew he could only surrender. His body seemed to grow heavier and more irresistible. He felt suspended in a heavy fluid that also surrounded her, in which their attraction for each other was protected from every other force. And she might give him so much. He wanted just once more to be in that state where the world stands out whole and clear, a fleeting glimpse of peace, the striving cancelled out – an observer freed from the demands of the body and able to perceive serenely, the pure eye of the world. If he could phone her now he would, but she would be at work just across the square in a room full of typists.

O'Hogan appeared at his door, staring into the room. After a pause he came in as though he were dragging his soft flesh along with him in order to be goaded, a bear trailing its chain. His fat white stomach trembled through a broken button on his shirt, a dark woollen tie pointing to the gap. Schrödinger tried to check his abhorrence, but he found the sullen mass of the man's body unbearable, like a reproach: this is what you've made of me.

The man had a way of understanding the most trivial conversation with Schrödinger as an insult. He liked to show a wide-eyed deference to learning, and had cultivated the part of the honest doubter for so long it had become a mask: the bearded face turned mildly to the side, and his eyes filled with wonder at the things he had not known and which he now discovered were not so impressive at all. He was the common man seeing through the conspiracy of the cute, an artist of the small obstruction, the nails placed under his enemy's tyres. 'Ah yes, Professor, I will indeed. Now the only thing is the porters expect their overtime, and for that we're in the hands of those blackguards over in Finance. But I'm sure knowing the Taoiseach is interested . . .' – the hurt light in his eyes when he used that phrase, touching his great paunch as though his resentment had settled there, like a bag of stones – 'they might look favourably on a request for extraordinary expenditure over and above the allocation.' This old revolutionary could improvise Civil Service jargon at will. He could turn a waste-paper bin or even an inkwell into a sump of impossibilities. He invested objects with deep, fearful meaning: could a larger basket for turf be placed by the professor's fireplace, to save the stokers coming in so often? Of course, but there were difficulties, the basket would have to be ordered specially, the Board of Works might take exception, and would it fit, and might the stokers object to the extra weight? The colour of chalk for the blackboards. The purchase of a typewriter. Memoranda on the payment of a visiting speaker's travel expenses, their current dispute. After weeks of inaction he had suggested in a voice laden with sincere regret that because those so-and-sos in Finance would not authorise the money, if the Professor himself were to write a memo to the Secretary of the Department outlining the reasons why a travel voucher should be issued for Professor Reese to come from England, then perhaps the Secretary might relent.

O'Hogan had been out with the Taoiseach in the heroic year when the country rose up, and from his room at the Institute he overlooked the Dáil at an awkward angle – a short walk but a long way from power. Schrödinger sometimes thought it was a calculated punishment, so that O'Hogan could see from his window his old friends walking importantly out of the parliament building and the government offices. A careful, shambling man, he looked as bland as a kindly uncle, but the rage beneath the thickened surface could be drawn by the slightest hint of unguarded cleverness. He was a fat man who despised the roles that fat men are given to play, and his drinking darkened him. Schrödinger had never seen him laugh. Irony for him was a conspiracy of the fake and the glib. And he had an impassive unyielding conviction that whatever Schrödinger knew, there was something about it that could not be right.

Now they discussed, with exhausting politeness and futility, the purchase of four books on cosmology. While this went on, a dark-uniformed stoker knocked on the door and carried in a basket of brown turf, which he placed beside the fire. As the man brushed the tiled fireplace O'Hogan remarked, with his most thoughtful, kindly expression, how terrible the bombing was. 'Who knows whose planes they were, they're gone before anyone can see them. Still, we can make an educated guess: who wants our ports? They blame us for their lost ships. They'll be tempted to cross the border, their yellow press is howling for it. It's revenge they want. The bishops gave General Absolution in the barracks before the Christmas. They wouldn't do that if they weren't expecting something. The Church is not rushed, it is very careful about that kind of thing.'

The stoker walked silently around the desk again, not looking at either of the two men, and passed through the door he had left ajar. 'And why would the other crowd do it? Though if they were to drop bombs it might well be up there on the canal. They've no friends anywhere, I think. Their punishment comes again and again, God help them. Causing friction wherever they go.'

Schrödinger felt the oblique stab, as close as O'Hogan dared come to the suspicion that clung to him, the Austrian blow-in. The taint.

Why else would he be here? He had a sudden desire to lash out that he recognised only when the words were out of his mouth. 'But resistance at the boundary where two substances meet is not a bad thing, Mr O'Hogan; the ship needs the friction of the water, the train wouldn't run without the sliding of its wheels over the rails. A little heat in the process, what harm does it do us? The alternative is to sit and move as little as possible, until we rot.'

O'Hogan's grey jaw slackened. He looked over the rims of his glasses the better to see the man lounging on a chair with his back to the fire. O'Hogan's face struggled with a sneering smile as his hand crushed the paper he was holding. His mildness is the skin on boiling milk, Schrödinger thought, and wished he had said nothing. O'Hogan's mouth was trembling with the effort to contain his anger.

'You misunderstand me. I think you know you do. I try to see things as they are. We live in the real world, do we not? I did not mean to be uncharitable or to offend you.' The sheet of foolscap in his hand was crumpled so that the top half flared like a bouquet. Schrödinger knew that whatever he might say now would draw him deeper into this floundering combat, two senseless figures pawing each other in the mire. He backed away. 'My dear Mr O'Hogan, it is I who must apologise to you. Let us not quarrel. And let us try and get a ticket so Professor Reese can visit us.'

He sat tense with anger at his desk, reading, smoking, almost drowsing, looking at papers for the sake of moving them aside, their meaning lost on him. A comment on electron spin. On the quantum theory of solids. Memo on Porters' Overtime. Browne passed his open door, carrying a rolled-up newspaper. He stepped in, hesitating until Schrödinger smiled at him. He was an enormous man with disorderly, greying hair, whose body seemed to fill whatever room it entered. But his face was often stubbled and brooding, like the face of a much thinner man – whether from the rigours of early-morning prayer or his inconceivable abstinence, Schrödinger could never tell – but he had enjoyed the priest's largesse and shrewdness from the moment he met him and was ready for him this morning, if for no one else.

'How are you, Erwin, if I may ask?'

'I'm well, if a little discouraged.'

'Who could blame you? We're regressing nicely, I see.' He gestured with his paper baton. 'A bit of a spree just to remind us we're at peace with them – whoever they might be. Those poor souls up off the South Circular must have been terrified. I suppose if I squeeze this very hard,' and he held up the paper, 'I may get a few drops of something out of it. It's like drinking tea made with used leaves.' He shoved the paper into the pocket of his black jacket and rubbed the lapel for a moment. 'Any news of our distinguished visitor?'

'I think Reese will come. It's worth it, because even if he is a little mad, he may be on to something with his cosmical number and the rest of it. He has been right before, seeing patterns that none of us dreamed were there. He'll make us sit up, and maybe think.'

'I've no doubt he will. But these big numbers of his scare me, I may as well tell you. The number of particles in the universe, the size and age of creation, this airy familiarity with units of ten to the power of forty. He really believes we can deduce all knowledge from the relations between them. Isn't there something inappropriate about this obsession with huge numbers when we're slaughtering each other by the million? This is a flight into numerical fantasy, surely.'

'Not quite, but he does believe something like that. What happens in the present, the present of stars and atoms, is an effect of the large number at the heart of it all, the ratio between the electron and the proton, the relationship between the electrical and gravitational force. He does believe some odd things: for example that the constants of nature change with time; gravity is decreasing as the world ages because things are getting further apart.'

'So the step of our ancestors on the earth was heavier than ours, so to speak? Who's he fooling?' The priest sat down, planting his big feet apart. 'Well anyway, let him come. Is Mr O'Hogan of one mind with us?'

'Of course not, *a priori*. He is driving me mad, Patrick. I can't work in a place that has to tear at itself every time it needs to spend a penny. He seems to need this angry state of mind. I am too cowardly – I should flounce out, refusing to return until he is removed.'

Browne took a cigarette from a tan packet that had appeared in his hand and lit it with a quick flick of a lighter, with very unpriestly dexterity. The brief petrol stink mingled with the fug of Schrödinger's pipe, and then the acrid smell of Virginia drifted into the cloud already hanging under the discoloured ceiling. The priest's fingers were yellow, the nicotine stain so deep that his nails looked like smoked mussels. 'I know. But really the important thing is that we are secure, and as long as he is here it helps our patron over the road feel secure. Never underestimate his loyalty to anyone who carried a rifle for him. His whole system depends on that kind of faith. He will never sack him. They will be together now even if they never see each other again until one of them sits in the front row of the church behind the other's tricolour-draped coffin.'

'It's politics, that's what is so depressing about it. I'm convinced that if there is a Hell it will consist of smoke-filled rooms,' Schrödinger said. 'A politicians' club where they can intrigue against each other for all eternity. This need to dominate and conspire, even in tiny spaces like ours.'

'That's true enough. Living in and seeking out the darkness, looking for men equally preoccupied with anger and revenge. The darkness that is contempt for others.' Browne lifted his unfiltered cigarette and looked at the burning tip while he exhaled a stream of smoke towards the window. 'We'll have to live with him, but we will survive him. I'm looking forward to your mad English genius, now. The beautiful fertility of the unguided mind fascinates me. Always glancing at the truth, glimpsing only part of it. Heresy is the uncontrolled insight reaching too far.'

Don't underestimate him, Schrödinger thought, this priest who knows mathematics and the classics and reads heretic visionaries to improve the fine orthodox filter of his mind. And he heard the touch of regretful disapproval and the hint of a warning, felt the mild tug of the reins and wondered what he would have to do to make his friend jam the bit into his mouth. He said now, 'You spoke of the evil of contempt. Then good is the degree to which we turn towards each other, in the light? Not feel contempt?'

'You could say that, as a definition of charity. It depends on what you mean by turning, of course. But why these strange preoccupations?' Browne seemed so relaxed and good-humoured, but he was never less than alert. Schrödinger knew that the monsignor gave a faint clerical sanction to the audacious guesswork he was paid to do. And there were others watching them, listening for the tiniest shifts and settlings of a small country.

'I wonder how safe we are, that's all. Our openness is so great.'

'If either of them wants to come in, they will. We can't deter them. The only useful thing we have is our harmlessness. We have to work on our harmlessness.'

Schrödinger said nothing. In his state of exhaustion, the night's lack of sleep already making him light-headed, he could not be sure precisely what he wanted to confide in the priest. He veered onto safer ground. 'Have the philologists established yet what exactly it is that I do?'

Browne inhaled and waved his cigarette over his head in little circles of delight. 'What letters we've had! You wouldn't believe what heat this subject has generated. The Dáil translators themselves are working on it, the final arbiters of the language, men so fluent in Connemara Irish that each one's accent is a dialect in itself and their own children take years to understand them. They argue about which village has the purer Irish. They guard the passes where the language meets the modern world. Well, the translators think the nearest term for "theoretical" is an old word for the study of medicine: *teoraic*. Is what we do therapeutic? Are we healing old wounds? I'm not so sure. "Physics" falls into the same trap. The nearest equivalent is *fisigeacht*, the art of medicine. So you could if you liked be a *fisigeach teoraiceach* – a physician skilled in the concepts of physic. Not quite right, perhaps.'

'And who'd heal the physicist? I see what you mean. I have been thinking about Irish – I've been using my *Aids to Irish Composition*. I think the Bishop of Copenhagen, the Blessed Bohr, the fount of orthodoxy in my profane church, would love the language: especially the lack of single words for yes or no. Is the particle there? Not there is the particle, the Irish says. Did you see it? I saw it. Or, I did not see it. But never a straight no.'

'Isn't "*Ní fhaca mé é*," I did not see it, definite enough?'

'But doesn't it open a space of ambiguity? A delay. Is the particle there, yes or no? If the answer is simply no, it is not in that definite location. If the answer is that the particle is not there, which *there* is being referred to? It slides away from us. Still more if the response is not yes, but "I saw it." There is a "yes" – "*sea*" – but your yes is really "*is ea*", it is. And you know how ambiguous I find your Irish "it is". Is the situation good? Oh it is, it is. There's always a but coming. You have two forms of the verb "to be" and complicated ways of expressing the modes or qualities of what is. Four sentences where English would have only one to say that a thing is a particle. *Is páirteagal é*. It is a particle, not something else. *Tá sé ina pháirteagal*. It is in the state of being a particle, it has become one. *Páirteagal isea é*. It is emphatically a particle. *Páirteagal atá ann*. That thing there is a particle. Irish could be the ideal language for quantum theory. You have to live with its uncertainties.'

'If it survives at all. *Deo volente*. I'll leave you to your work. And we'll come up with a term that's not too bad, don't worry.'

He sat at his desk after the priest had gone and stared again at the built-up equations with their packed density of expression. Unless it could be refined and made to refer to a reality that would confirm it, the equation would remain a hermetic, incommunicable poem, and for now it was more unreal than ever. It would be useless to try and work on it today. He closed his eyes and let out a low cry. When he looked up he saw that his door was still open. This is not good, he thought, the staff will hear my involuntary groans. Like Boltzmann before the end. Across the road the trees rose up, perfectly still and bare. The feeling came over him, as it had done earlier that winter, with an indefinite shape, cold and sullen, a dull promise of relief.

He remembered Hagen telling him what Boltzmann looked like when it was already too late, when no one could have saved him. Hagen was a shabby and not very bright lecturer at Jena after the war, half starved like the rest of them because of the blockade still going on. He entertained them in the faculty dining room with half-believable anecdotes, and it took their minds off food while they ate the daily cabbage soup. He had been one of the students, Hagen claimed, and everyone pretended to believe him, it was his version of a story everyone knew, who had gone to the darkened villa on that hot August morning and walked in single file through the empty house to the study where the great man sat huddled behind his desk, his huge head lowered against his chest. He was dressed in a heavy wool suit despite the blaze of summer in the garden beyond the French windows, and barely looked up as they entered. The sun came through the slats of the wooden blinds, making even parallelograms of light and shadow on the surface of the desk. 'You could smell him,' Hagen said; 'he seemed to have been up all night and not to have bathed for days. He spoke in a voice thick with melancholy, his eyes as gentle as always when he looked at us, but glazed over as though he'd been drinking, yet there was no smell of alcohol from him. He listened to our papers on thermodynamics gravely. It must have been agony for him,' Hagen said, 'such immature rubbish, yet he responded carefully to each of us, he could never be anything other than courteous. I'm ashamed to say I don't remember what he said. At a certain point, and this is why I don't remember his response to our green essays on his theory, he began to speak in a low voice about suffering and pain, rambling and disconnected, about the torture of not sleeping and not forgetting. We were rigid with embarrassment. This revered man was breaking down before our eyes. Then he said in a clearer voice, "This life of ours is a war, no one will tell you this, but it is. Only the luckiest remain whole. Silence can kill you. You don't know how strong you have to be to come through it. Most of you will discover you're mediocre and have to live with that for the rest of your lives. There will be no second chance. No late flowering. By twenty-five you'll be good for teaching in a school, no more. Some of you may get much further and find you have nothing to say. But the worst is to be right and ugly, to be found intellectually repellent. Then there's no quarter. All you can do is take a position and hold it as best you can. We're all dispensable. Science may look like a temple of pure thought, but there are heaps of skulls under the temple steps that no one ever sees."'

Hagen said he sat staring at that puffy, sleep-deprived face, his long beard and wild greying hair, the darkness in the armpits of his jacket, and was embarrassed: all he wanted was for Boltzmann to faint so that they could lift that overweight body onto the couch and let it rest. But Boltzmann sat gazing at the wall of books opposite and muttered, 'Thank you, gentlemen,' and the students in their pale linen suits rose and passed again in single file down the hallway to the front door. As Hagen opened the door they heard in the silent house behind them a loud, sustained moan, an inconsolable lament for a loss that could not be made good.

Soon after, on holiday near Trieste, Boltzmann's wife found him hanging in his room when she returned from the beach with their children. Schrödinger remembered the look of that headland in the sunlight, the castle outlined against the grey sea. It was not far from the limestone heights: a different kind of war. When he heard that Boltzmann had killed himself and knew that he would never meet him, never hear him talk, he could hardly credit that such anguish over a theory was possible. The intensity of that suffering from an argument over the way atoms behave, Boltzmann holding to their reality, his rivals insisting that they were mere constructs of the mind, exchanges of energy, that what we cannot see does not exist. It was the pain and shame of defeat, he knew that now. The equivalence of mass and energy worked out by Einstein had finished off his atoms, so he thought, but if he'd waited a month he'd have heard that Einstein had also seen the evidence Boltzmann longed for in pollen grains dancing in water, agitated by the water's molecules, and Einstein saw that the fluctuation of the particles could be measured. The idea of atoms took unanswerable form.

He gave such precision to our disorder. If the fluctuations of the molecular energies seem to promise little gains of heat, cunning reversals of time, Boltzmann reassured us that the average of the tiny reversals of entropy leads, after all, to the cooling down of heat, leads probably to death and history grinding on. The bowl won't mend itself; the body won't grow more springy or rise again. The relief, Schrödinger thought. No wonder he was loved. He showed us we were human. And because we are, there is the longing for rest, the letting out of terrible groans. When Schrödinger wondered how he would do it, if it came to that, if he ever went under and could not reach the surface, he thought of cycling down the black wooden bridge at the Bull Island, then along the breakwater to the point where it seemed to peter out and the rock wall was hidden by the tide as it ran on out to the lighthouse, on a day when the surface of the sea was tranquil, so that the water stirred rather than moved, with barely a ripple, with each undulation shifting light and shadow as delicate cross-hatchings. Imagined becoming part of that calm.

He must, he knew, take hold of himself, drink less and try to sleep. *Poor Schrödinger. He couldn't see that the world had changed.* He would not give them the satisfaction of saying it over his body. An equation captures part of the real in a single line, yet it's still a work of art that can be sent overnight to a museum no one visits, discarded for a form that catches even more of how things are. No one measures Bach against reality, but it's the only measure we have. And it would still be something, he thought, to restore the continuity of the field, to conjure in the equations a great wave carrying so much – Boltzmann would have loved that, he loved images of the way the world works, this stutter on the verge of chaos. We struggle to speak, to reach the predicate without a spasm of incoherence. To stop now would be to admit that they had the last word, that an underlying reality could never be imagined that would make sense of all the weirdness they glory in, the quantum jumps, the permanent uncertainty and unknowing. And the role of the observer, he who makes the measurement and decides on what is real. And he wondered again how much de Valera knew about how he lived, and how much his knowing mattered.

Physics killed the odd man, he thought, but also his time in Graz. They did for him there. He was never the same again after that, as I am not. The bottomless rage of that frontier town, like gas lingering in a trench: the squat hill with the ruined fort above the green copper roofs facing down the Balkan tribes, the horse cultures, the peddlers and nomads. Behind the plain beautiful palaces and retired generals' villas a dark stew thickened. Three hundred years ago they burned the Protestant books, 12,000 volumes, with Kepler's book, the displacer of God, on top of the fire.

'Were you really so stupid? To go there in thirty-six when they already had their own puke-coloured little fascism and Hitler had his maw open underneath their tree, the fox waiting for his cheese? Could anyone be that naïve? We gave you refuge in 1933 and may as well not have bothered.' Lindemann had made no effort to hide how furiously he despised him.

'You bought us for a song, that is what you did in thirty-three.'

Schrödinger grinned at him, so angry that his teeth ground together. After that Lindemann cut him dead in the Magdalen dining hall whenever they met, once making sure that Schrödinger heard him say: 'He made his bed and should have lain in it. A weak narcissist. Let the Irish have him. They deserve each other.' Those were dreadful weeks, his tail between his legs, camping in the rooms he had left to go to Graz, waiting for word to visit Dublin and hoping they would keep the promise made in Geneva. It did not help that Lindemann was right. There was a hard man, working now if the rumours were true on the simple physics of mass death: given so many tons of explosive, so many bombers, how many German workers' houses can we knock down in a year? The homeless don't wave flags, or the dead.

Lindemann would have taken one look at the University in Graz and wondered how quickly he could turn it to rubble. Schrödinger arrived on a hot summer day and as he was conducted up the steps, before the welcoming speeches, a group of young men wearing red, white and black armbands over mud-coloured shirts came down in a military rush, jostling him as they passed. One of them stared at him, and laughed to his friends: *Der weisse Jude*. The white Jew. An elbow struck his arm and they were gone, strutting off like lovers in a jealous rage. Their flags hung from the windows; their banners were draped in passageways; twisted wooden crosses were nailed over doorways and noticeboards. The daubs of scarlet gave a celebratory air to the old academy, as though the university were the site of some strange local carnival and the students were jolted by a holiday into defiance and buffoonery. They seemed possessed; many wore permanent clownish grins, as though they had been eating an ergotic fungus and walked around staring at visions inside their heads. He could feel a lust for disaster in a flood of violent language. The Professor of Physical Chemistry lectured in brownshirt uniform under a giant portrait of his leader, and doubled as the local party chief, strutting through the campus flanked by bodyguards, followed by the students' admiring eyes.

They added a sinecure in Vienna: he had two chairs and very little work. He had a pretty house with a room for Hilde and her daughter to stay whenever she wanted to come from Innsbruck, where she was living with her long-suffering husband. The Austrians had bought him, he knew that, his Nobel and his reputation, but he had had enough of Oxford, its certainty that it was the heart of the world and its boring male rituals. At Christmas the previous year he had gone skiing in the Austrian Alps. He had spent a morning sitting on a terrace staring at a blazing mass of snow and cold rock. Life is better here, he found himself thinking, I want to be near the mountains and to settle in what passes for home; there has been too much wandering in the last twenty years. I want to speak my language where my accent isn't strange. And I've done my best work here, in this landscape, in this vast icy indifference. He spoke to Anny about the reasons and the money, and believed what he was saying, holding the other truth closer. He had Hilde already; he needed her tranquillity and honesty. Despite her breakdown she was drawn to him, and the others went along, as they always did. But it was not those arrangements that mattered; they had become part of the ordinariness he was driven to escape.

I went back because I wanted more, he thought, I can't pretend anything else. Hilde was never enough; especially not in that demented year when the world was at his feet after he thumbed his nose at Hitler. Almost at the moment he possessed Hilde, after months of longing, he had met Hansi Bohm in a grocery store on Lake Garda. He and Hilde were cycling along the western shore while Anny remained at the hotel in Brixen looking after Arthur. They could no longer contain themselves; the friendship between the couples had become too charged, and all of them knew what was building between him and his friend's wife. They wheeled north on the narrow lakeside road, dazzled and lazy in the sun, to a village where pink and yellow villas hugged the shore so that the rich could have their perfect view of water. Walking along the cobbled main street of the old village on the hill, the tension and the anger with which Berlin had affected him began to recede. All he had said was *I resign*. It was turned in the telling into a gesture of which he was not capable: the only non-Jew to throw his job in their teeth, striking heroic attitudes as he left the stage. But it was so much simpler. He had meant what he said: This politics bores me. Enough.

She was a photographer, an acquaintance of a friend. Nothing had ever taken him like his first impression of her. She stared at him with unembarrassed interest. Her body in her light summer clothes was completely present to him. He remembered the dark smooth skin of her neck, and the clean white shirt that folded around it. Her eyes were very brown, her hair thick and black, falling heavily over her tanned shoulders. She said, 'I have read about your work. And you were very brave in Berlin.' He knew that she meant not simply his refusal to be employed by them; but he was so struck by her that he had said nothing to diminish her enjoyment of his legend. So he had not replied, No, that is not the way it happened. I don't have that sort of courage. He had said nothing.

That night in Berlin, he should have stayed at home. He had already decided to leave because they repelled him, and he could not stand their racket. Instead he went out into the noise for a walk, and in front of a department store found his path blocked by a crowd of grinning drunks in uniform breaking windows and stomping on plaster mannequins, whose beige plaster heads, gashed white, littered the pavement among splinters of window glass. He lost his temper and shouted, what exactly he could never remember, so unexpected was the rage that made him do it, and their faces went heavy and quiet, lingering on the pleasure of the focus he had given them. They began a slow shuffle towards him and then he was aware of a rapid commanding patter from behind him as someone he barely recognised took charge, a graduate student dressed in a darker uniform, the young cosmologist ordering him home after telling the others that he was a good German when he was sober, and a friend of his. 'You're lucky I was here,' he said to Schrödinger.

But as it passed from mouth to mouth, the story of what happened made him more than lucky. So when Hansi stood looking at him with admiration in the half-darkness of the store amid the smell of cured meat and spices, he could see himself in her eyes, pushing in, standing over the body of a beaten Jew. They talked about the lake and Vienna until Hilde had bought their bread and cheese, then said goodbye, and he watched her walk down the village street against the backdrop of snow-capped mountains on the other side of the lake. The water was chased by small unbreaking waves, like eels playing on its surface. He thought about her almost every day for three years, thought about her that very afternoon as he and Hilde made love in the shuttered room of the *pensione* overlooking the lakeside road. She saw me, he told himself, and I saw her, there is a flow of energy that unites those who are open to it, sounding together like strings tuned to the same pitch. That was the afternoon, Hilde told him later, that she became pregnant.

Anny had always known and had given up, long ago, in the twenties. She had even fallen in love for a while when they lived in Zurich. She had taken a friend, a kindly mathematician, to bed when the sheer compulsion of Erwin's craving was clear to her and she had to make a choice between him and a semblance of happiness. She accepted the grand fiction that each new encounter was part of a web of oneness, that nothing could change what was truly essential to their friendship. The worst part of it, she told him, is that you are nearly right.

Once they were in Graz Anny saw her mother in Vienna as much as she could, attending the high secular masses, *Fidelio*, *Elektra*, *Tristan*, sitting in evening dress among the other dark-clad worshippers as doomed lovers went down amid annihilating chords. She returned to be with him as much for her own comfort as for his.

And Hilde knew, could not have been unaware if she tried, though he did not at first tell her, that now he was back in Austria his post in Vienna was an excuse to couple with the glossy animal of his fantasy, to lose himself in her calm enjoyment of her body. He was in a state of permanent heady arousal; he felt invulnerable. He walked to her flat past his grandfather's old building, where his family had lived; from her windows he could make out the walls of the Hofburg. He had not seen these streets since the last hungry winter of the blockade. They drank wine and she would prepare some food, but the eating and drinking were no more than a restraint that forced them to talk a little before they reached for each other with sighs of astonishment.

The bed was in a large, airy room whose walls were lined with framed prints of spectral tracks, the dark silver and black-and-white traces of shattered atoms and alpha particles. Wavering lines, streaks, spirals, faint star-like impressions emerged out of the darkness. Different emulsions gave different effects. Some impacts looked like blackened grains on the surface of the silver halide; others like the vapour trails of aircraft; and one seemed to have been etched onto the emulsion, a particle track resembling an old pale scar. There was what looked at first like a photograph taken in bad light of distant clouds, through which something with an indeterminately regular shape was falling. Their pale bodies lay surrounded by these images of subatomic catastrophe.

She knew a physicist, a woman who had begun to record this evidence of things previously unseen by using a radioactive source to generate the particles that struck the emulsion, and these were her treated prints of the experiments. Schrödinger lay in bed in the half-dark on the first morning he woke in her apartment and saw protons recoiling from unseen neutrons, dying atoms, disintegrating forms registered on thin layers of light-sensitive film. The trails were of different lengths and energies, some so enlarged that they resembled phosphorus shells exploding. Some, where the emulsion was too thin, were barely fixed latent images, very faint impressions of things passing, lost somewhere between exposure and development. They reminded him of images from the spirit world, half-formed shapes in doctored photographs taken at séances in the winter after the war, when half the houses in Europe were visited by gentle entities hovering in the light entering darkened rooms.

They were beautiful to him, much more so than the flicker of a particle as it hits a scintillation screen. All we can do there is count them; we're supposed to be content with that, he thought. We're not allowed any more to want pictures of our theories. They think my need to see, as we once saw orbits and interacting forces, is indecent. I'm a pornographer to them. But why not think of the most beautiful analogy and see how much reality can be caught in it? I'm sick of the ugly metaphors, the thrown dice, things that are here and nowhere, both dead and alive until we look at them. Her prints are snapshots of what we can't yet see clearly, like photographs not quite focused. He thought of the first photographs of children printed on silver nitrate a century ago – so fragile that the light of day made them fade. He was half afraid that if he opened the curtains these images would react with the sunlight and disappear, erasing the evidence.

She lay on her side watching him look, and said, 'It's difficult for us. She has to adjust the emulsion so carefully to catch their tracks. When the grains of the emulsion are too fine the particles are barely distinct. But it's compulsive. I hardly understand what she's trying to do, but the images have a strange truth for me, of things caught at the moment they vanish. We're two Jewish women trying to see the world more delicately and more clearly. We've become ghost photographers.'

He had told Browne once, in a confessional moment he regretted, that carelessness had ruined Austria for him, even saying that he deserved what had come to him. But he could not admit to Browne that he had been in an erotic trance. And he could not stop seeing himself through his own eyes when he wondered how others saw him, and finding his own brilliance irresistible. He was still the beautiful boy who could solve the hardest problems with casual mastery. The sheer purity of his calling would save him in the end, that and the Nobel. Part of him thought that they all still shared in the cult of great men's minds, the handing down of wisdom, the festive rituals like that banquet for the vast throng of German scientists in the summer before the war.

At the congress banquet all the men wore full evening dress, their decorations iridescent, their gold medals heavy and silky in the mild light of the thorium oxide gas mantles. Bodies were held in a field of slowness, the energy of light diminished, and they moved with great deliberation, hands reaching out punctiliously to each other in the warm haze. Even the electric bulbs gave a soft uncertain light, an illumination that was almost part of the darkness. Thousands of cut flowers scented the great hall of the Rathaus, where candles played on the white silk and black wool of the formal garments. Franz Josef was very far away, at a high table with his titled physicists, who sat rigid, waiting for him to lift a spoon.

The speeches promised a future that was radiant and secure, and very near. Cities will be illuminated by power stations. The more light there is, the more creative hours there will be. The darkness of the soul will lessen. Light will be clearer and harder. From his table far down the hall near the kitchens, the faces of the grave bearded men were softened by distance. They nodded their heads, Exner, Lorentz, Planck: councillors to one or the other Emperor. I will never be like them, he thought, and felt crushed by the sheer numbers placed above him. Then Einstein spoke, ironic, modest and plain, those amused and curious eyes looking out over the vast congregation. He talked about what they all knew. That we can only talk about relative motion, that there is no such thing as an absolute measure of motion, only situations related to each other by the speed of light. But now the force of gravity itself looks strange. The inertia of bodies influences other bodies; mass and energy take different shapes, and gravity should influence the propagation of light. Light passing near the sun should suffer a deviation from its straight path. In the shimmering light of that enormous room the professors sat with straight backs as the candle flames bent in the draught of the doors opening and shutting for the waiters carrying bottles. They sat still and self-controlled in the soft haze of the old clean air, the aether, which filled the universe like a sea through which light waves undulated and electricity moved; it was the frame of everything, the invisible, subtle, material thing they had never found and that they knew was gone for ever, but that night they sat and listened as if drugged by a whiff of cold volatile stuff breathed in with the smoke of their cigars.

Once, during the second winter in Graz, he opened his office door to a loud knock and found four perfectly clean shaven-headed boys in brown uniforms. They filled the doorway and the passage outside. 'We are collecting for the families of our oppressed brethren in the Sudetenland where, as you know, Herr Professor, the Slavs deny them the most basic rights and treat them with unprecedented cruelty.' *Unprecedented*. It was like hearing a truncheon speak. The young body was hard, the shiny pink face beamed with satisfaction at lines so well del'vered. He muttered that he had no money about him; he could not meet their eyes. He was aware of his thin, ageing body, and of being a coward and a liar. 'Very good, then we will return another time. Heil Hitler.' He said nothing, and could tell that they noted his failure to echo them.

He told Mark about their visit. He had known him since they were at school together in Vienna. He was a chemist, a Catholic, and an

Austro-fascist by convenience: grey-green uniforms, blunt untwisted crosses, paternal order. Better this than red or black, he would say, though he seemed not to care. He had money; Schrödinger envied his gleaming nonchalance. He always seemed just to have bathed in dark oil. 'I could not confront them; they were so menacing and confident. They're the true face of our youth. Ardent apes.'

'The genius of these people. They make the insecure youth feel that he needs to be a hooligan in order to prove what a good boy he is,' Mark said.

He asked Mark: 'Why do you bother still to work as a chemist, to put yourself through all this? With your money, you could live as you wish.'

'You made it interesting for us again,' Mark said. 'Interesting but vulgar. There's no mystery in it any more. Your damn equation took over the periodic table. Now we all have to speak the language of quantum numbers. You think you're so detached and high-minded, but you're an invader, you disrupt, you have large effects on the world. The only thing you haven't colonised is life, the central thing that can't be broken down, the force that tells the proteins what to be. Maybe that's where God has retreated. But it is fascinating, and so I go on. What I really can't figure out about you is why you felt the need to come back to this leftover scrap of a country when you could be drinking port with the English dons.'

'I wanted to get away from all that, very urgently. You have to sit next to some bore at lunch every day whether you like it or not, and talk nonsense. There was never a woman in the room. And they don't have high places, snow and ice, where politics can't reach.'

'You can't be serious. The true believers climb cliffs so that they can have visions of their leader's face as the air thins. They're at their purest facing a wall of ice.'

'They'll contaminate anything, I know, but my reasons are simple. The accent, the way we speak German, the food, some feeling of being at home. And it has other attractions.'

'I can't believe I'm listening to this tourist guff from you. The "other" attractions, now that has the ring of truth. They had better be worth it.'

It was the week the Chancellor went to see Hitler. The blaring in the controlled newspapers repelled him so much that he barely glanced at what they had to say. All that cacophony had begun to seem like so much weather to be shaken off as he retreated inside to the things that mattered.

One night Hansi said, 'It is coming, isn't it? I should leave now, should I not?' and he said that he thought it was still all gestures and theatrical alarms. The British would not let him do it, nor the Italians, who would feel threatened if he came so close to the Alps. How can they let him take over another country? Where would it stop? But she said that if they did take over she would lose everything: 'I don't want to leave, you or Austria.'

They were lying in bed, in the dark. 'There is no question, you must stay.' He went on in a babble of wishful thinking, quoting half-remembered editorials and conversations with well-meaning men who guessed and knew nothing. My desire, he thought later, took such articulate form to save itself, not her or me. It was the most uncontrolled persuasion, made easier because she couldn't see his face. He told her that the country could not be thrown away so easily. The League, Halifax, France, America would all be watching. 'You believe seeing changes things, all of a sudden?' she said. He did not plead with her, but the tone of his voice did, and his hands, touching her shoulders while his body moved against her hips. 'We will see, won't we,' she said. 'But without you I'd go.'

On the last day of Austria the weather was cold, the streets wet from an overnight thunderstorm and the sky drawn down by grey cumulus heads charged with more rain. Beyond the town there was a haze that made distances empty, but the damp streets were suffused with the colours of blood and shit. All day cars full of uniformed men cruised without urgency, lazy with anticipation, while from the speaker tubes on the car roofs voices clamoured metallically. Speakers of the same shape had been torn down the week before from lamp-posts by brownshirts and turned into flattened bells when the government tried to address the crowds. Now the ridiculous policemen in their tall hats and epaulettes stood aside, like operetta soldiers waiting for the singers. There was a convulsive grinning, a delirious lightness in the air. Flowers were heaped round lamp-posts and hung on railings. A public ecstasy he had never seen before, housewives dancing, tears streaming down the faces of prim men in shirts and ties. A panic of joyful surrender. Thousands upon thousands of copies of the Führer's image, balding, unhealthy, the furtive face and breath drawn in to give his chest the drum look of a breastplate.

Schrödinger was sitting with Mark in a café when a brass dirge erupted from the avenue a few blocks away, underpinned by the roll of bass drums, a sluggish marching rhythm amid the crescendo of trumpets blaring. Every few bars cymbal-crashes scattered the melody like breaking glass. After a long noisy measure, the brass stopped playing, abruptly, leaving a silence filled with the beaten skins of animals, unison strokes on the big tuned drums now mingling with the stamping of massed feet, the slight variations in the sound waves rippling around the central beat.

'One of my students came to me yesterday,' Mark was saying, 'and said he would try to help my family. Not me, mind you, just my wife and daughters. I'm past saving. He likes me though; he stood there quite stricken, almost blushing, but he was also very proud of himself. I knew then I was sunk. His human gesture. He knows that he'll soon have some power of life and death over his betters. His mercy will be worth more than any law. And he's just a nice boring boy from a Styrian farming family. As for you, you should go now. They won't have forgotten Berlin.' Mark drank off the coffee into which he had tipped a glass of brandy.

'Why should they care about me, even if they know I can't stand them? What can I do to them? I'm not, I can't be, a political animal. I want to live here and do physics. Is that so impossible? I left in thirty-three because they made too much nasty fuss, I despise all that – listen to this ghastly noise – but I don't want to run any more. Do you know how many cities I've lived in? Three alone in the first year after the war, when we almost starved. Then Zurich, Berlin, Oxford. The English loathe me. I'm a bohemian, a cad. I know they make it impossible for Jews, but this madness will pass – how can any civilisation go on at this pitch? They haven't when it comes to it murdered many people. It could have been a lot worse. Perhaps expelling all their hot air has tired them out. And now they've got what they wanted so badly, almost all the Germans under one roof, surely they'll calm down? They can't want a war.' He went on and on. He knew even then that to Mark he was like a child who turns his face to a dark corner of the room in the hope that those he doesn't see can't see him.

Mark said, 'Damnation. God forgive me.' His eyes closed, and his groomed face set in an anger that seemed to surprise him. When he spoke again his voice was low and emphatic. 'They may not even allow you to run. No one will remember me for long, but for Christ's sake, and your family's, try to ensure that you're not remembered more for your idiocy and blindness than for your wretched equation. Don't you realise what's happening? When Schussnigg met him he's supposed to have said, "I will piss on you like a spring shower. You won't hold me up for an hour." That's what you're dealing with now.'

Mark's face had gone pale, and his hand was tight around his coffee cup. Schrödinger heard a rustle and saw that Mark had grabbed his newspaper and was rising from his seat. Schrödinger had an impulse to throw the water carafe into the sullen handsome face, but he could not move. A roar of voices washed over the street.

When he found his own voice it was almost pleading. 'This is fine, really fine. They've already won if they've reduced us to this. Blast you, stay where you are and tell me what I should do. It's complicated. There's my wife and Frau March and – well, her daughter, and I may as well be frank, another lady too. It is not a simple matter.'

'Yes, I can see that.' Mark remained standing. 'Harems rarely are. You do fill up the energy levels, don't you? How many erotic states have you room for? Well, I'll tell you what I'm doing, because I know you won't betray me, and you'll have your work cut out looking after yourself. I'll be arrested, but I've already bought the friendship of a man who'll remain a police official after they come in. I've known him since he was a dunce at the University. He isn't so fanatical that he isn't corrupt, thank the Lord. The rest of the money I've turned into platinum and had strung into coat-hangers – we won't be allowed to take any money out. I'll drive to the border, if this all works, with my family in our largest car, with suitcases full of neatly hung garments. I should have gone long ago, but I took the country seriously, a bad mistake. As for you, just go, while you still can with your wife and your brain intact. You won't last a year if you stay. Have you ever been inside the museum over there? No? The stuffed birds have their skeletons mounted beside them. The ostrich is a particularly striking display.' He turned his cup upside down, rapped the table and walked away.

In the streets Schrödinger seemed to be the only person who was not as festive as a drunk hailing a storm as though it was the cure to his miserable life. There was something about the feeble, reeling crowd that reminded him of insect lives, of termites bursting from their clay towers, flying ecstatically for a few metres and then falling into the dust, helpless and crawling, their wings inert. A middle-aged man was running up and down stone steps in front of a school, his face inflamed, his eyes dilated. At the foot of the staircase a youth in a brown shirt kept turning him again and again. 'Run up Jacob's ladder, you fucker, you might meet an angel.' The sky over the rooftops was blue, with white clouds rising as soft as clean smoke. It was already spring. The young man who spoke as he grasped his victim's hair and turned him about was blond and sweet-faced, his expression tranquil. The churches rang their bells from steeples flying the black, white and crimson flag.

By the time Schrödinger reached the house he was sweating profusely. He pushed open the front door and rushed into the kitchen, hugging Anny, his long-lost lover. He cried against her shoulder while she held his head. Later, they sat at the kitchen table and drank a bottle of wine. By ten he was so spent that she had to help him to bed, making sensible consoling noises as she would to a child.

He read the note again. *Dublin. Yes or no?* His mother-in-law, having delivered it, was staring at him, holding her handbag on her knees, ready to run from the room and the house but curious enough to enjoy the effect she had made. He looked up at her and tried to breathe normally, enough to say, 'Who is this Dutchman? What did he say?'

He had spoken too loudly. She burst into prolonged sobbing and began to scream at him, if he had not been such a louse they would never have been in this situation only so that he could be with his married mistress, how can you live like this, both of you? And everyone knows, banging her fist on the glass table so that the pot fell, spilling hot black coffee onto the wooden floor, that you are sleeping with a Jewess as well. You are faithful to nothing but your *cock*. Her face was bright with anger and shame and it was this that calmed him, his outrage irrelevant. He wanted to say to her that she was right, but even that seemed like the language of a life they had already lost. But in the silence he did say that he was sorry. Sorry for the pain he had caused her. 'But we must know, please, I beg you, tell me who this man is.'

'He said he was a friend of a friend of Erwin's in Zurich, and that the man in Zurich had a telephone call from Herr Professor Born in Scotland. Herr Born was calling on behalf of another professor, a Catholic gentleman who is a Papal Knight and is very trustworthy. I know you are a Papal Knight too, but if the Holy Father had known the way you live you would never have been honoured by him.'

Erwin wanted to up-end the glass table to bring this branching trail to an end. The Irishman Whittaker and the Pontifical Academy of Sciences for Catholic savants of impeccable moral character. One of the honours he barely remembered. He took a deep breath.

'It seems that the gentleman in Scotland was asked to see if you would consider going to Dublin.' She pronounced the name of the city in two stressed syllables, as though it were a remote and doubtful place.

'And who asked him?'

'*Der irische Führer.*'

The dead weight of surprise shifted his equilibrium again and he could feel the blood draining from his head. He stared at her for a moment, then walked into the kitchen and laid the note in the sink. He found a box of matches and lit the edge of the paper, turning on the tap to wash the black scraps away.

Later, he found that the Chief's followers believed him capable of supernatural foresight. Browne told him that on the day before Schrödinger was dismissed from Vienna de Valera wrote to his old teacher Whittaker, saying he had heard a rumour that he had been sacked and wondered how they might reach him. Some impossible vibration of a string, moving faster than light; that or destiny guiding his hand. 'We'll put it down in the book of miracles,' Browne said, 'and if they ever want to canonise him, God forbid, the devil's advocate will have fun.'

Anny drove to Munich and crossed the border into Switzerland. She met the young physicist who had become a link in the chain that led from the other side of Europe. They ate lunch in the sunshine in a café under gaudy umbrellas. She remembered him as a playboy who took them on cruises up the lake, and took nothing seriously. But now he confirmed that this was not a bizarre joke, and agreed to pass their message back along the line. She said that being there made her think of her lover, her one real experiment in the free life. 'I feel so used up when I think of it,' she told Erwin later; 'you do this again and again, I don't know how you bear it.'

From then on they thought about a country they had never imagined seeing. Ireland to me is like the Black Sea to the Romans, he thought, the limit of the world. Hamilton was marooned in the Atlantic, lost in a fog. Twigs for a nest seemed the right image: him clutching the sheer face of a rock plunging down to the sea. He could remember photographs of lakes behind which were low bare mountains, pictures of men and women with pinched faces wearing dark rough clothes in front of white cottages, and pitch-covered canoes drawn up on a beach. The patterns of light and dark made up a bleak landscape. He imagined the chill wet weather, a city of empty eighteenth-century squares. The revival of a language, the great German philologists codifying Celtic grammar. He had seen a photograph in a newspaper once of young men in trench coats, rifles dangling from their hands. There had been a war there, twenty years ago, and then silence.

In one of those fragile black boats, in a story he had read as a child, Saint Brendan had sailed west on the great ocean. The saint had read reports in an old book of magical islands, but had thrown the book into the fire, refusing to believe in wonders that he couldn't see. God commanded him to sail in order to discover what is true and what is not, because a part of the truth had been lost through his lack of faith. This Brendan saw many marvels, and once found a land where physical laws were suspended and entropy was negative: candles burned till the sun rose and none of them ever melted, though the wax dripped from them all night.

'He was wandering for many years, if I remember how it went,' he said to Anny and Hilde, who had come to Graz when she heard. Anny welcomed her with her unfailing tenderness, and he realised then that she had already spoken to Hilde. 'But he came home to die in the end.' They were looking at the atlas, too excited to listen to his self-indulgent irony. The tiny island floated off the side of the immense mass of land like an afterthought of the mapmaker. 'I wish I could see that far ahead.'

'You can't see beyond the end of your nose,' Hilde said, but not without affection.

'How is life at home?' Anny asked her, as they ate dinner.

'It's not good,' Hilde replied. 'We're living in separate parts of the house. We barely speak. He is, after all, angry with me. If he had been angry in 1933 I would have understood more, but this bitterness is terrible. It's as though he's waited to pay me back for all the hurt I've caused him. The little one reminds him every day of what we took from him.' She held Erwin's eyes. Her brown hair showed the first streaks of grey, he noticed, but her eyes had lost none of their steady directness, and he felt a stirring of his need to animate her placid self-absorption. 'He feels drained. And it is miserable for both of us, to be honest, and I don't know what to do.'

'You must come. Erwin, she must come. It is as simple as that. Why should we leave Hilde in this awful mess? Have the child brought up in this madhouse? It is dangerous for both of them. Ask them, ask the Irish. You are persuasive, and they need you.'

'I'm not so sure of that. We need *them* very badly.'

Hilde was silent. It came to him that Anny knew what he would think, and that he did want them near him. It would repair some of the damage he had done; and it would be less painful than leaving this thread dangling, which would tug on him and never let him be at ease. And he realised, to his surprise, that he needed to have the child who did not know she was his as close to him as possible when he ran away once more.

Anny said, with heated emphasis, 'There can't be any argument about it. *I* want her and Ruth to come, if humanly possible. I will not come if they don't. The thought of that little creature at the mercy of these animals!' Her face was flushed as she sat back and folded her arms.

'Is this what you want?' he asked, turning to Hilde.

'The truth is, Erwin, I don't trust you, but at least you will speak to me. I would prefer to be with Arthur, but I have ruined him for me. Perhaps for ever. Certainly for now. I love him but I have hurt him too much. So I will come with you for the child's sake.'

They agreed that when the Irish sent word again they would leave, Anny and Erwin first, Hilde later with the child, when they had convinced these people he had never met to let them all come.

Even after they had made the decision, which elated him more than he could have imagined, he still felt astonished at the way the familiar order of books on a shelf, his papers scattered on a table by a window under a shaft of summer light, even the sheen on a cold glass of beer, could make him doubt the need to leave these quiet arrangements, which had begun to feel like home. But then he would remember that Mark was gone, his English suits shaped around thin fabulous wire, and that time was closing in.

He had met Hansi in the mountains one weekend. The wooden shutters and eaves of the houses in the village were polished and gleaming in the sunlight reflected from the glacier. She was wearing a scarf and dark glasses when she drove up, and looked pale and shocked when she took them off. He tried to explain the letter; she waved his excuses aside. 'You're weak, Erwin, but the jails are full of strong people. You thought they believed in the old routines. But I'm glad you're still here.' They drank wine on the terrace of their hotel and she said to him in a pensive, meditative tone, 'Let us go to bed now.' Hours later he was still engulfed in the quiet urgency of her voice, her body confident in its power over him. 'Please let us not lose this,' he said to her. Wild schemes flitted through his mind, of the two of them hiding, surviving by private tutoring, concealing her identity. Surely there had to be a way. She lay with one arm around his neck and the other on his stomach and spoke slowly, as though she'd been sent to explain reality to him once and for all, telling him what had happened to her friend. 'None of them lifted a finger to save her. She was sacked straight after they came in. She flew out with a ticket for Sweden. At Hamburg her bags were searched. They took her notebooks, her microscope, her halftone plates: all her work. The plates and chemicals don't matter, she can buy them anywhere, but the notebooks can't be replaced. Her colleagues have stolen her notes, that's what it comes down to, and are passing them off as their own. She told me all this on the phone; she sounded so serene and tough. She said you can photograph radioactive decay wherever you like. All you need are plates and a source and a darkroom. She may go to South America, she thinks. As for me, it's all up. They have inventoried my things: the apartment, everything in it, my cameras and books. They stared at the prints on the walls with frowns on their faces and I saw one of them write something down in his notebook. They probably thought they were photographs of dirt. My neighbours pass me on the stairs without seeing me. My butcher refused to serve me last week, but at least he looked apologetic. My bank account is frozen. I have no rights here. That's the end of it. I am going to London as soon as I can. Please don't even think of not going to Dublin. The fact that this is a crime' – she touched him with her thoughtful fingers – 'is the worst for me.'

He still had no departure date and no escape plan, and the anxiety made him sensitive to dangers he had never seen before. The fear of being trapped built on itself, grating on his nerves. He began to think of all the unguarded comments he had made or written down, in language that was now criminal. He imagined dire consequences, his letter to the Rector squirming around and polluting everything, making him feel how vulnerable he was to his own voice. So he wrote a letter to Hansi. He did not work on it nearly as hard as on that other letter designed to save himself. It was merely a precaution. We should all travel lightly, he thought, strip ourselves of incriminating paper while we can. Yet the next day it lay unposted, and for two more days he saw it on the hall table each time he left the house and could not pick it up.

On the third day she called him at the house in Graz. Walking into her building that morning, she said, she felt a light soft mass strike her coat and turned to see two boys she recognised running off down the street. The smell reached up and nauseated her, a sweetly rotten meaty stink. Some pet dog's doings were sliding down her coat. She threw the coat out into the gutter. 'You know the one,' she said, 'the light red coat, the one you like.' She said she was looking down as she spoke from her apartment at the coat crumpled in the drain curve of the street, the white silk lining showing inside the red wool. He was outraged and sympathetic, and sobered by the control she had over herself. As they talked he found fragments of the sentences he had written in the unsent letter come fumbling out, broken and clumsy out of context. Instead of the wary request he had meant to make, his guilt loaded the words with innuendo. When he was finished she was silent. She repeated what he had said, and paraphrased it for him. 'I have got that right, have I,' she asked? 'No,' he said, 'that is not what I meant, but we must be careful,' and as he stammered he heard that she had broken the line.

She called him again very late that night, her voice hard and remote. 'I have one thing that I must ask you,' she said. 'What really happened in Berlin? Did you save a shopkeeper?' He tried to project a small note of self-respect into his reply. She had never referred to the incident after their first meeting. When he spoke his voice was abject for what he knew was irreparable: 'No. That is not what happened. There was no shopkeeper.'

'So it's true, then. You saved a few Jewish *dummies*. That is what you did, and you deserved what you had coming. You are delightful, you goyim, there, that's a word I've not used in a long time. You make me think and feel as I have never wished to feel, as my family has not had to feel in its worst nightmares for a hundred years. We thought we could resolve all difficulties, tragically maybe, but always sweetly and humanly. And now this horrible howling, this brass farting, and you step up at the last moment to add your little piccolo's worth. Your shame at what you're asking is so raw I can taste it down this phone line. You fear them, I think you fear me even more for the loss of respect you know you've earned. Burn the letters you're afraid they will read and find out you love to fuck a Jew. I will, don't worry.'

The second thin brown envelope came a week later, like a response to the letter he had written and not sent, a reaction to keep the energy of the transaction whole. It was delivered during the hottest and most humid week of the summer and was in its way more expressive than any of his had been. The writer mentioned a numbered decree; out of its provisions a conclusion emerged, blunt as a truck. *You are dismissed, with immediate effect. You have no right of appeal. The reason is your political unreliability.*

Later the same day, two policemen arrived and searched the house. In a trunk they found a heavy pistol his father had bought for him when he was called up in 1914. He had forgotten he still had it. He had kept it only because it represented his father's awkward care for him. The policemen took it away with them, but not before making him sign a form that confirmed he had surrendered his weapons.

They were at the end of their rope. Eighteen hours in a second-class carriage had exhausted them. They left Graz with ten marks in their pockets, a few suitcases of clothes, a few books, and two return tickets to Rome. When they arrived, they allowed themselves two espressos at the central station and threw the remains of their overnight picnic into a bin. They took a taxi into the Vatican, to the Papal Academy he could hardly believe existed, but it was there in a villa in the Vatican Gardens among the statues and fountains, swarming with moulded reliefs. The bursts of stone ecstasy all over the façade were too feverish for him. He was morbidly self-conscious about not having the money to pay for more than this cab journey. He felt like a petty criminal, dishevelled and dog-tired, and imagined how they must look to the porter walking silently ahead of them up the curving marble stairs. I'm a confidence man with one trick, he thought: if you give me money I'll find the key to all reality's secrets. Neither of them could speak when they closed the door of their room. From the window he saw cypress trees standing like folded green blades in the lingering summer heat. Everywhere he looked there was the business of the celibate, the women with lowered eyes, the men walking in confident swirls of robes. He closed the wooden shutters and they lay side by side on separate beds in the thick heat.

The Irish consul came and took them to lunch, cheerful, portly and quick. He oozed piety and cynicism. His English had, to Schrödinger's ear, a kind of lilting derision, yet he recited the Yeats poem, from which the cryptic message had borrowed the final line, with a real tenderness. 'The ones who opposed the building of a gallery for modern art infuriated the poet into this great polemic,' he said, 'and you'll find that the argument isn't over. And this *is* an imaginative idea of the Taoiseach's, I must say, founding a college in such unpropitious times.' A vestige of something droll flickered across his well-fed face. He became earnest, as though he'd noticed his mask slipping, and said with great seriousness, 'Now Europe is set to destroy itself again, perhaps we can conserve the modern forms of learning for the times to come. As we did long ago.'

He poured them all another glass of chilled Orvieto, and the baking heat of the afternoon outside the cool restaurant seemed to recede even further. They talked on, the consul telling mildly satirical stories about Irish scholars he knew. Then he said, 'Did you know that Bishop Berkeley founded a college in Bermuda to civilise America? He shipped thousands of books over to the island to radiate, as it were, Christian learning from six hundred miles offshore. Do you think America existed at all, though, since he wasn't looking at it? He was a lovely man. God, but the Irish have had some strange notions.' Strange notions like me, thought Schrödinger as the consul laughed but it was difficult to tell how comic the man found his latest diplomatic chore. Stepping back into his role with a speed that caught them off balance, the consul said, 'Well, now, the Taoiseach would very much like to see you. He is in Geneva, where he is chairing the League.'

'We must leave again?' said Anny. 'But we have no money, and no papers.'

The diplomat bustled, his feet shuffling invisibly. He withdrew a thick envelope from the portfolio beneath his chair. 'Swiss and French visas. And Spanish and Portuguese, just in case. Even a British document. His Majesty's representatives thought you were a goner, if you'll pardon the phrase, so they will let you through, though they were not too happy about it. You seem to be a loose end for them. And rail tickets. It's not allowed to take out money, but here's something for emergencies.' He reached into his pocket for his wallet and, with a thoughtful expression on his face, placed two English pound notes in Schrödinger's outstretched hand. So this is what it means to dole out money, he thought, and for a moment wondered if he would be asked to sign a receipt.

Their first-class carriage on the train north was stifling. The windows would not open. There was a faint reek of sweat, and Anny found a soldier's forage cap in the rack above her seat. The traces of the hot force of young male bodies kept them alert and sleepless during the first hours of the long journey, but the carriage swayed like a great cradle as it plunged on, enough to make her close her eyes and slump into a corner of the leather banquette. For hours he churned his mistakes around, stirring them uselessly. They felt thin and sour. He thought about his father's books and with a sudden piercing regret remembered one leather-bound octavo volume of Grillparzer. He felt bereft of that one book as though it had in it all the consolation he would need for years to come. At that moment he yearned more for this sign of all the irretrievable carelessness of his life than he did for Hilde and Ruth waiting for his call.

At Domodossola an official came on board and checked their passports. He let Anny sleep on. Erwin began to relax, leaned against his wife and closed his eyes. It was already nightfall. In a little while the train slowed again, he assumed for the Simplon Tunnel, but there was a decisive movement in the passage and the compartment door shot back on its grooves with the snap of a rifle bolt. Two young carabinieri in tight blue uniforms and beautiful riding boots stood looking at them. They had the angelic look of bowmen murdering a saint, and gazed down at the two bewildered travellers as though they found their slack bodies morally repugnant. One of them plucked a sheet of paper from a folder he carried and the liquid Italian sound of their names woke Anny. Afraid and disoriented, she clutched Erwin's hand as they walked down the suffocating passage, asking where they were. Behind them a porter dragged their cases out and the whole group stepped down from the high train onto the platform. No other passengers had been removed. Their cases looked pathetically shabby on the great arc of the platform in the harsh station light. One of the policemen told them to follow him. He spoke in a mildly insolent way, as though he was familiar with unflattering summaries of their lives.

At the office they were separated, a woman taking Anny into an adjoining room. The room was dominated by a bulky machine. 'What are you carrying?' one of the officers asked, in German. 'The change from ten marks and an English pound. Apart from that, nothing. I wish it were otherwise.' He had replied in Italian, but the young man did not smile. He pushed the first suitcase under the flaps into the machine. It went through with a deep hum, a quiver in the field as the short waves of electromagnetic energy pulsed through leather and cotton and wool. The policemen examined the skeleton of each case on the flickering screen. They had not removed their peaked hats. One of them searched Schrödinger's pockets, and tranquilly patted his legs and genitals. He was motioned behind the large machine where another device stood in a corner, a low pedestal with two arched holes cut into the base. They told him to insert his feet into the cavities. A screen flared into light on the apparatus, livid, showing the complicated bones of his feet, the flux of fields stripping him of flesh. I look like the remains of an extinct ape, he thought, an array of metatarsals and phalanges, and he was overcome with pity for himself and for the long past and the animal weakness that could come to this, dragged so easily into the harshest light, waves that nothing human could turn back. One of the policemen said to another in their own language: 'No rings on this one's toes.' They smiled a little to each other and sent Erwin back to the train.

They had X-rayed Anny's teeth. 'I was a bag of bones to them. We've become a sad pair, you and I,' she said as the train crossed the border into Switzerland.

He stood waiting for them in the drawing room of his suite at the Hôtel du Lac. He was wearing a fine black evening suit and white dress shirt, and wore a silver and enamel order low on his chest. A red sash set off the boiled dazzle of his shirt. Immensely tall and erect, he had a face like a great alert bird's, with unmoving dark eyes. Schrödinger wished that he had had time to bathe, but they had been brought straight from the station and he hoped that he was meeting a man who could see past his exhaustion. The statesman held himself perfectly still, he noticed, his upper body unbending and watchful: He might stoop fast as a heron and impale me, Schrödinger thought, but he had never wanted to believe in anyone so much. Their lives depended on it, and he felt he was being inspected very carefully. If the man did not like what he saw they would have nothing but their collection of temporary visas. But de Valera was being gravely courteous to Anny, and Erwin felt he should perform a little, rise above his travel-stained appearance and show what a catch he was.

'I cannot express to you my gratitude, sir, for the kindness and far-sightedness of your proposal. It does me great honour,' and on he went with a few polished sonorities that he hoped were appropriate to the moment. The tall man listened gravely, but after a few sentences he interrupted with an inclination of his head. 'The honour is mine. I am more pleased than I can say to meet the author of the great equation that brought the work of Hamilton to a glorious climax. You will be, I hope, if all goes well, an illustrious guest in our small country. That the same language can be used to express different states of a thing has fascinated me from my student days; the idea that the solid and the incorporeal could be given the same mathematical form seemed sublime. Forgive me, I state the obvious, but you must indulge a failed mathematician. I hope that we will be able to talk more freely later. I am forced to be brief now to the point of discourtesy. Mr McManus will show you to your rooms in a moment. I must be elsewhere tonight. We are trying to come to a harmonious solution of the Sudeten crisis. A tragic case. The claim of the Sudeten Germans is largely just. All artificial divisions of national territory are terrible, as we ourselves have cause to know. Meanwhile, we support Mr Chamberlain's efforts. War will come otherwise.' The long face with its great re-curved nose bent forward again. 'May I ask what you need to work? What facilities?'

'Almost none, except peace and quiet, and a comfortable office. And a good blackboard.'

'I cannot tell you how inspiring it is to me to hear that.' Without altering the solemn ferocity of his expression, he added: 'But at least now you are safe. We will meet again very soon. After the Council meeting here I must visit the oculist at Zurich. My eyes are not what they should be. For now, goodbye.' He shook Erwin's hand and Anny's, bowed, and turned to his assistant. Speaking in a language Schrödinger did not recognise they left the room, the tall figure stalking forward and the young man deferential beside him.

He and Anny lingered for a moment while another official told them how they would travel to Britain, where they would have to wait. From the high windows of the room they stood in, they could see the edge of the lake. The brightness of the city interfered with the long signals from the stars, and the sky was dark over the barely stirring water. He was so tired that the heavy furniture – the claw-leg sofas, the polished tables, the mirror over the fireplace – receded into a mild haze, as though the objects in the room were wrapped in gauze, stilled and distanced by this film drawn over them and their surface coherence troubled by a strange inner light. In a state of muffled apprehension he moved with Anny towards the door to find their bed.

Oxford was more like the Coventry of their English silence, especially in the cold November weather with the rain on the pale-red college walls. He was there on sufferance, waiting for the call from Dublin. Lindemann was only the most openly hostile. Schrödinger could not make himself justify anything he had done, but the letter followed him, like a scroll pinned to his back. 'You must have been threatened terribly,' someone said encouragingly. 'No,' he said, 'but you don't understand what it was like.' There are worse things to be ashamed of than pleading for your life.

When the telegram came he went down to London and caught the night train to Holyhead and the mailboat to Dun Laoire. The second-class passengers disembarked with their thin suitcases. He heard the train shrieking quietly near the ship, then it snuffled off and the dock was silent again. At six-thirty, he walked down the gangplank to the long open shed, as he had been instructed to do. He had spent the crossing walking the enclosed deck amid the smells of urine leaking from a toilet, of spilled beer and stale tobacco fumes. He wished he had slept more, and hoped that he could soon, rested and full of vim, meet his benefactor on more equal terms. He has yet to see me as I once saw myself. There were a few customs officers and policemen standing around in the dim space under the iron roof, and a young man walking towards him wearing a dark coat, with a hat in his hand. 'The Taoiseach has sent his own car,' he said, and gestured to a porter, who carried Erwin's small case towards the steps up to the street.

It was the first border he had crossed that year without dreading what he would find. If you are looked at hard enough by hostile eyes, he thought, you become something other than the person you thought you were. I don't want to be tested again, earn more contempt, and discover more weakness in myself. Let this be the moment when I start seeing clearly once more. As they climbed the stairs he felt the cold wind from the harbour and saw the choppy sea beyond the grey pier walls. On the nearest wall an empty bandstand lay open to the weather under an iron pagoda roof. This is an island, he thought with a thrill of relief, cut off as nowhere I have lived has ever been. Rain began to gust along the pavement. They reached the street, where a black car was waiting.

They drove into the city under a dull sky that turned to rain as they left the harbour road. Schrödinger could see very little through the streaming car windows. The young man pointed out the Taoiseach's old school behind gated walls, but all Schrödinger could see was wet playing fields and a dismal house. Later as they crossed a bridge over a canal the official said that they were on the site of a battle, near where the Taoiseach had led a company in the rebellion, barricaded in a bread factory overlooking the canal. Trams and buses moved quietly on the main roads. They were in an old part of the city by now, undamaged but a little derelict, the paint on some doors faded down to the wood. They passed through an austere square where the doors were flanked by thin classical columns. The garden in the square looked dense and private. He was struck by the stillness and composure of the houses, and the lack of traffic on the smaller streets. They turned into a guarded gateway and a short drive leading to a domed building.

At lunch he was flattered by the heads of two universities and ministers and a group of professors, and charmed them all. Most of them drank a glass of wine, except the Taoiseach. When the guests had left, Schrödinger was taken into a private room, reached through a darkened lobby where plain-clothes men sat about. In the inner room he was invited to take a leather chair in front of a desk on which a single sheet of paper was positioned square with the edge, illuminated by a single reading lamp, and in the shadow to the side a pair of compasses lay. There was no other light in the room. A globe on a stand stood to the side of the desk. A marble clock ticked audibly on the high mantelpiece and a coal fire burned in the grate. Schrödinger, sitting in the shadow outside the cone of light, noticed the size of the print on the page under the lamp and realised that all his fervent handwritten letters of the past four months must have been copied and typed with double spacing in a large point size, stripping his writing of its personality. This reduction to mechanical characters was a small blow to his pride. He could not read what the man was now scrutinising with a pained frown. Schrödinger noticed again how big the face was, how the nose was like a billhook, slashing down through the features, and how the eyes behind the rimless glasses were magnified by the strength of the lenses. He detected a clamping hardness in the lines around the thin mouth, a careful holding in check of emotion. It was a face rigid with caution. The long torso held it up in the way a priest holds a monstrance, proclaiming its integrity. A light embroidered ring was stitched into the left lapel of the dark suit.

De Valera spoke with immense precision in a clear high voice, to which an odd keening soulfulness gave the character of a lament. It was less like speaking than intoning, as though a carefully prepared utterance were rising from the tragic depths of the soul. At lunch his formality had had a friskiness to it, and he had revealed a real passion for mathematics, a more than passing familiarity with Riemann and Gauss and Hamilton, for whom he seemed to have a feeling at odds with his impassive manner. That levity was gone now. He wished, he said, and his right hand adjusted the paper in front of him as though to perfect its alignment with the desk edge, to give a clearer outline of his plans for the Institute, and hoped his guest would bear with him.

Schrödinger felt, as he had in Geneva, the impulse to gush, to say how incapable he was of giving appropriate wording to his sensation of gratitude, but de Valera once more cut him off, and he fell back, remembering how easy it is to say too much. 'Without you there would be no Institute.' He was suddenly more truly happy than he had been for years. The smile that came to his face felt foolish, but the Taoiseach raised his eyes and seemed to stare unblinkingly at his guest. It is as though he is fixing my position, Schrödinger thought, his sight is very bad.

'I will speak frankly,' the Taoiseach went on. 'Our country is poor and defenceless. It is divided. A quarter of our territory is denied to us. A third of our people remain under British rule, and two-thirds of those do so willingly. Our nation is recovering from centuries of oppression and servitude. We have barely recovered the use of our naval ports. If war comes the British may be tempted to take them back. The power we have recovered is partial and illusory. Our young people are still driven to Britain like our cattle, their servitude and degradation terrible to behold. But we are beginning to reverse the dilution of our sovereignty, emerging like the crystal of a new form from a watery solution that has kept us weak and diffuse. Our state can't even be called by its proper name. We would be a republic, in logic we are, yet we can't afford to declare that it is so – not anywhere, not even in our Constitution. We are bound by an unjust treaty with the former power. On so many subjects we must be careful what we say.

'Partition might seem to be all that stands between us and nationhood. It is indeed a great crime.' He stood up abruptly, looming in the shadows and the wavering firelight as he crossed to the far wall. Schrödinger turned in his seat, wondering whether he should also rise. On the wall hung a large map of the country with the twenty-six counties in a dark green that looked almost black in the late-afternoon light. Above them, the six counties stood out in a sickly absence of colour. He thought it resembled a dead white head on a rotting body, and de Valera seemed to sense his unspoken revulsion. 'It is like the picture of a monstrous unfinished being, neither alive nor dead. This child born so incomplete . . .'

He returned to his desk without finishing his sentence, and settled back into the bright light that illuminated its surface. 'But the truth, and the reason that we are having this conversation, is that the removal of partition would not cure us. I can say this to you because you will understand the higher significance of what I wish us to do together. My friends would disown me if they heard me saying what I am about to say, though they hear me say it all the time and do not grasp what it is that I'm saying.' He paused and looked over his guest's head. 'You may find us strange. I should warn you of this. Things that the free thinker accepts as normal are alien to our country.' Schrödinger was aware of a chill tingle on his back. 'But for us compromise is fatal. We must remain what we really are if we are to survive this onslaught, this modern flood.'

There was a silence. Schrödinger nodded, wondering how much his host could see of him, unless, he thought, he has the bat-like trick of finding his way in the dark, the sound of his own voice echoed from the bodies of his listeners. Still staring at some point on the far wall, the politician began to speak once more.

'Language, in the end, is all that matters. Our very survival depends on it. What we say and how we say it, the symbols that we use to represent reality, these are the things that will preserve us. How can a symbol inspire if it cannot call the truth into being? It is like your equation. Without that beautiful utterance would the truths it discloses ever have been perceived? Would we even have known that they were there?

'And unity without our language would come at too high a price. It is nearly dead, in all honesty, so it is like demanding a resurrection, but we can revive it or at least preserve it. There is a chaotic archive of old Irish manuscripts. We need good editions of the poems and the sagas. Proper grammars. We must record the uncontaminated language while there are still people alive who speak it. In the deluge that is coming the kernel must be preserved at all costs. War destroys the seed, bears down with its terrible pressures on the possibility of new life. We are like that tiny animal the tardigrade, the water bear, a barely visible creature in a world of large hungry animals, which can close itself down, dry out, and endure thirst, extreme heat, and vast pressures of water. I am told this by my daughter, who is a biologist. Well, we are also strange creatures, and we must shrink and be extraordinarily patient.'

Schrödinger was mesmerised by this cascade of lapidary English in the service of a language of which he knew nothing. He groped for some response, snatching at traces of ideas he half remembered from Herder and Fichte. In order to say something polite and deeply felt, he murmured his approval of the admirable programme of revival of which he had read, and the importance of language to national identity. He was feeling the lunchtime wine irritating his bladder, but did not dare do more than flex his right leg.

De Valera still stared, with eyes that looked black above the cone of lamplight, at a point above his visitor's head. The pale face and unmoving eyes did not seem to have changed expression since he began speaking, and he did not seem to need a response. He reached out and touched the dull globe with his long fingers. The reedy voice went on with a discourse so finished that Schrödinger wondered whether it had been learnt by heart.

'That will be the first purpose of the new body. But there is so much more. We can become, as we were long ago, the teachers of the great teachers. The British Empire may be destroyed, and some would say deserves to be. And we may, just may, be left alone. We could become the nursery of the highest scientific learning, of which you are among the greatest exponents. All other sciences depend on yours. Look how you and your peers have transformed chemistry, so that now we can calculate the energy states of the elements and their combinations.

'It does not matter if there are few in Ireland who can fully understand your work. The work can be done and you will find students. And the Irish have a genius for it. This is the country of Hamilton, and you completed what he had begun, seeing matter and light flowing in the same beautiful movement. You are his true successor. It is a miracle that you might come here, a miracle. You speak the other language that we really need.' Erwin's bladder burned more painfully now. *Might?* It had all been agreed. This invocation of mere possibility made his face go numb. De Valera was almost chanting now, his hands gripping the desk, knocking the sheet of paper gently out of alignment. 'When you said in Geneva that what you needed most was paper and a board I knew you could do it. That is the attitude of pure thought. We do not need expensive machines and elaborate equipment. Hamilton, you know, though a convinced Unionist, hated the industrial world of the British, their factories and mills. He believed that imagination could flesh out new forms. He was right. He preserved the true idea. So can we, in our time. Do you see what I'm asking you to do, while the world is preparing to set itself on fire? You must help us bring our imagination to its full radiance.'

In the silence that followed Schrödinger felt an uncanny serenity and unreality, and in it he recovered himself, even as he dreaded that he could lose everything in this strange man's incredible scheme. He had to learn to understand and even to like this benefactor on whom his future now depended; he was the only protector he had found. He understood, with a giddy anticipation, that when he came here he would be stepping out of the flow of ordinary time, and that there were paths through the world which did not resemble any he had known before. And it occurred to him that he was after all an artist, and that he was being asked to live in this little state to give its ruler pleasure. 'I never dreamed that I would one day work under the protection of a statesman who cares about physics. I will be honest with you, I long for peace. These last years have been dreadful for me and my wife. But I wonder how much I can contribute to your great scheme, which is so visionary. Perhaps all I can show is that science may be beautiful as well as useful.' Then he asked, regretting the suppliant tone that he heard in his voice, 'How soon can I come?'

The stately animation of the Taoiseach's face cleared, replaced by a more cautious expression. He began to speak more briskly and rapidly, his note of lamentation gone. 'We must proceed carefully, of course. My political enemies will oppose this idea. We must first draft a bill, and have it passed by both houses of the Oireachtas. We will immediately prepare a memorandum which will, which may, serve as a preliminary scheme of a bill. But of course I cannot commit the government to a course of action yet.' Schrödinger now sensed a certain scrupulous wiliness in the man looking solemnly at him across the desk. He was speaking a language which Schrödinger could not follow, except with a redoubling of that feeling of panic that he had felt a few moments before. This was very like the sticky lingo of the time-server, full of traps and promises made with qualifying conditions that nullify them in advance.

'How soon, Your Excellency? I must ask you again how soon. I trust you implicitly, but our situation is difficult and further ambiguity would be terrible.'

'I have no wish to alarm you. I might assume that a majority of my own colleagues will support me' – here Erwin was certain the ghost of a smile flickered over the long face – 'and enable the bill to become law. But I cannot assume such an outcome. We are among the last of the democracies. You must keep calm, and in the meantime it would be best to stay in Oxford.'

'They do not want me there. I have not been as grateful as they would like. I do not seem to fit in. Perhaps I may be able to get a temporary fellowship elsewhere. Perhaps at Ghent, where they have asked me to give some lectures.'

'Take it. We will stay in close touch, and you may write to me whenever you wish. Mr McManus will contact you. I promise that if I am spared we will soon be inaugurating an institution more important to me than anything I have achieved in politics. There is, however, one other matter.' He was staring again at the single sheet of paper, which he restored to its previous alignment. 'Your wife's – friend . . .' Had Schrödinger imagined that beat of hesitancy? 'It would be appropriate, yes, if you were to call on Mr Duff of Justice – the Department of Justice, that is, and have a talk with him. I hope that will not be inconvenient for you. McManus can walk you over.'

The young official in the black suit appeared in the room at that moment, summoned by a buzzer or a fine sense of timing. The conversation was over. As the courtesies of parting were chopped and scattered, Schrödinger wondered whose hands were being washed here. This was a twist he had not foreseen. They walked down a hall, down a staircase, with the civil servant's hand poised a few inches from his buttocks, then out into the yard. They turned and turned again and he was ushered into another entrance hall and up a flight of stairs into a tiled corridor with high ceilings. Young women passed them carrying brown files tied with green cords. From rooms on either side he could hear the rapid tapping of typewriters. They came to a closed door, on which McManus rapped; when a voice called out he pushed it open with one arm and touched Schrödinger's elbow with the other, announcing the visitor with an encouraging tone that reminded him of a nurse delivering a patient to a specialist. He could do without these reassuring modulations; he did not even know where he was, and wished he could go to his hotel and sleep.

Mr Duff was small and dignified, and had thin white hair combed close over his wide skull. He seemed very benign, like an ageing tailor who is himself a little moth-eaten, whose only concern is that his customers should have the right shade of black or grey. He smiled unceasingly. Schrödinger noticed that his lips were thin and delicate, so that his yellow teeth were exposed like bone. This vulnerable ugliness made him pity the man a little, while Duff jostled a sheaf of papers on his desk. After he had enquired about Schrödinger's journey he said that he understood that the Professor and Frau Schrödinger might be joining them in Dublin. Could he be permitted, he said, to add his congratulations and to express his pleasure that such a world-renowned scientist might be gracing Ireland with his presence? 'Of course, in the light of the Taoiseach's interest our Department is prepared to look favourably on a request by the Taoiseach's Department for visas for yourself and Frau Schrödinger, and of course there is the matter of residence permits. But all of this will be taken care of when the request is made officially.'

'It has not been made – officially?' Schrödinger was again touched by a slight nausea at this devious prudence. 'I had rather assumed that it was under way. I mean, that the process had begun.'

A look of profound concern softened the rictus of Duff's painful smile. 'Ah, but before the bill has been drafted, let alone presented to the Oireachtas, while it is still a gleam in the Taoiseach's eye so to speak, it would not be proper for us to act.' His voice grew brighter and more expectant. 'Now perhaps if I could just take note of a few details concerning you and your wife.' As he spoke he unscrewed the top of a black fountain pen. He asked questions about their ages, their original addresses, their effects, as though he were about to apply to the authorities in Graz for a reference. He asked what religion they professed, and when Schrödinger explained that he had been baptised a Protestant, but that his wife was Catholic, Duff's smile widened as he bent over his white memo pad making notes in a careful script. Schrödinger realised that he had made a deprecating gesture as he replied, an unconscious waving-off of any significance in the question. But Duff did not seem to notice, and went on writing. When he raised his head again and tilted the dark barrel of his pen so that the nib was poised just above the cap, his smile was at its widest, like the retraction of flesh on a corpse. Schrödinger felt guilty for thinking this and for the slight repugnance it induced in him. 'Was there anything else, Professor?' Duff asked.

'Well actually I thought you knew, as His Excellency is aware of it. There is a lady, a friend of my wife's actually, and she – my wife, that is – is most anxious that she should join us in Dublin. She would be enormously helpful, especially to my wife, as we set up house in a new country and discover a new culture.'

Duff said, yes, he seemed to make an effort to remember, the Taoiseach's Secretary had adverted to something of the sort. He had not closed his pen; the gold nib hovered like a needle over a sheath. 'So this lady,' he asked, 'is a family friend?'

'Yes, indeed, an old friend.'

'Of your wife's particularly.'

'Indeed, they have known each other for many years.'

'And her name is –'

'Frau Hilde March.'

'She is not by any chance related to your wife?'

'No, not at all, no. But she is as it were part of the family.'

'And is she living at present, now, in England?'

'She lives in Austria.'

'In *Austria*?' Duff's kindly tone skipped to a higher key. 'And what is her situation there, may I ask? You see it's important to have all the facts at our disposal in cases of this sort. Why, if I may put it like this, does she wish to leave Austria?'

'She is not terribly happy with the new government.'

'Like yourself in that respect, Professor. Understandably so. She intends to become a refugee, would I be right in saying?'

'I suppose so, yes, in a way she is on the verge of becoming a refugee, in the same way that my wife and I found ourselves in that unhappy situation.'

'Now if I could just ask in addition what are Frau March's personal circumstances?' Duff's eagerness was almost endearing, and he seemed so caught up in his questioning that he laid his pen down, cap and barrel separated by the papers in front of him.

'She is living in Innsbruck with her husband and daughter. Her husband is a former colleague of mine.' As he said it Erwin was aware of nearly stepping out from cover, and that the threadbare story was pathetic, and of how cold he was. He realised that the room was unheated; the coal was stacked neatly and untouched in the grate. He noticed a small blue-and-white statue of the Virgin on the mantelpiece, the woman treading snakes on an icy globe, her right arm raised in blessing.

'She is a married lady? With a child? And she is proposing to leave her family in order to help set up house for you in Dublin?' Duff, it seemed, could register within his affable tone a fine shade of incredulity.

'Not entirely – not leave them I mean. She would like to bring her daughter with her.'

'So we are being asked to consider four visas, not one. I see. Frau March wishes to remove herself from her husband and to come here. And she and her daughter would live where?'

'Oh, with us, in our house, with my wife and me.'

'In your house?'

'Yes.'

'I see. I think I see. So. Well now.'

'I am sorry if it is inconvenient, but her presence is imperative to my wife's well-being, and indeed to mine. There is, after all, nothing improper or unusual in it.' He reddened, knowing that he was floundering, that every word was in danger of making him stumble from the path of blustery confidence he had marked out before he came into the room.

Duff leaned back in his chair, as though he had heard a blasphemy uttered. 'Professor, you must forgive me. I was not suggesting that there was anything remotely *improper* about the proposal. Improper, please, I apologise if that construction could remotely be placed upon my response. But you must bear with me. So that I can draw up the matter properly, may I ask when Herr – I assume Doctor? Professor? – March will be reunited with his wife and child?'

'That I'm unable to say. You appreciate how unstable the European situation is at present.'

'Indeed, it is terrible. So Mrs March may have to stay here indefinitely.' Schrödinger was aware of a slight chilling of the atmosphere with the change of title. 'There are certain difficulties implicit in such an application, I should explain to you. You may not be aware that as we are a very small country we have allotted a quota, a quota of twenty persons who may be admitted as refugees provided that they are guaranteed. Guaranteed, that is, to be maintained by others, by families and relatives, but not in any way to be a charge on the State.'

'Twenty?'

'Yes, that seemed a generous number in view of our own great difficulties.'

'But I assure you I would guarantee absolutely that my wife's friend and daughter would not be a burden. They are entirely my responsibility.' He imagined that there was a gelling of shrewd insight in Duff's eyes as he heard this, but he refused to acknowledge it.

'Oh I am sure, but that is not quite what I meant. Because we are a very small country it is most important that we do not admit, especially at this time of great international tension, that we do not permit to enter aliens who may by their presence stir up animosities, whose presence above the very smallest number tends to alter the character of the country, who may even contribute to rendering the State itself unstable at a dangerous moment.'

Schrödinger could not help a nervous laugh. 'These are surely dramatic consequences, Mr Duff, to draw from the possible admission of one woman and her daughter. One would think they constituted an invasion!'

'Of course in themselves they are harmless. But harmlessness accumulates. Each case breaks the heart, but there is a greater duty of charity to our own nation. The outcome of tenderness in individual cases is worse than the distressing cause of their plight. We have twenty places, as I've said. You wish to take up two, or I might say four except that your case and your wife's come under a different heading. One tenth of the country's entire allocation of refugee places, nonetheless.' Duff frowned for the first time, his smile shrinking as he contemplated the proportion.

Schrödinger fought back, clawing at the handholds he thought he saw in order to wrench this conversation off its lurching, downward course. He wanted to snap, We wish to be together. Where is the harm in that? You must accommodate me, *he* wishes you to. He said instead, 'Frau March is not a refugee, not really, that is not the aspect under which I expected this to be discussed.'

'But you indicated that she was unhappy with the government of Austria, and one would assume that that government has reason not to be happy with her.'

'Yes. No, not really, she wishes to come of her own free will, that is the point. My wife wishes her to come, and they are as I have said dear friends. And her husband would, I know, prefer to see her safe in a neutral country. They are sure there will be another war.' The stupidity of saying anything, of making even the smallest admission. He looked at Duff and could not help seeing in him a sexless innocent smelling out a truth that he could not quite describe, but which was for him unspeakable, and which could ruin them all.

'But she is essentially, in virtue of her position, a refugee? You would say that, surely? You see there are important matters at stake here. Living in such close proximity tends to sharpen and highlight different points of view. Differences on matters of profound import. Your wife is a Catholic lady, you are you say of the Protestant faith. You see that the household you are proposing to set up will make the regular observance of religious duties more difficult, and then there is the question of example, of the danger that if such a mixed household were to become widely known it might have a tendency to raise scandal, though all might be arranged perfectly properly between its members. When those of different faiths live at such close quarters there is an inevitable tendency for one faith to resent the other. For one even to corrode the other. A certain ingrained obstinacy, on the part of some. The selfishness of ancient habit.'

'I don't follow, you must forgive me, her position – I don't quite see the problem. I am very tired indeed. The train from Oxford, then the night ferry, and the last few months have been relentless.' His only chance was to be obtuse, to continue on his chosen track and to ignore the obscure drift of the man's intrusions.

'I am sorry if I press you. My responsibilities give me a less than diplomatic sheen. I am a mere guard dog, when it comes down to it. The point is this. We are vulnerable. We are exposed. We cannot afford to add one on one to make an effervescent yeast. Or if I may use an equally homely analogy from my mother's kitchen, to allow the buttermilk plant to grow unchecked. Feed it a little every day and the harmless culture becomes a blossoming white parasite. Matters of faith are so delicate. And the situation you describe is irregular. I have to say, Professor, and you'll forgive me if I speak frankly, that this is a most unusual request. I am tempted to say, if I may so put it without offence, that it is a most peculiar request. Certainly the most unusual application ever to have come before me in my time in Justice, though of course the application strictly speaking has not been made yet. Because of the Taoiseach's close interest in it, we must of course view the case of your wife's friend with the utmost sympathy, but it is also my duty to present the facts of the case to my Minister for a determination. Certain people who come here do not become fully settled. They are stubborn with a stubbornness thousands of years old, refusing to accept that the world has changed and always wishing to adapt society to their needs. As head of the Aliens Section it is my duty to refuse them as often as possible, to say no. It is best for all concerned. If their numbers were to increase there might well be a definite agitation against them, and there is already a feeling that there are undue numbers of them here, with undue influence. Even for the sake of those already here, one might say, no more should come. Charity in the profoundest sense begins at home.'

Schrödinger said, his face blank with comprehension at last, 'You mention matters of faith. I don't fully understand, but as far as faith goes, and of course that is deeply important, Frau March is a Catholic, like my wife.'

Duff's smile went out as though a muscle had been released under his ear. The face became a watchful grey mask, and dark-red patches flushed high on his cheeks. He sat watching Schrödinger with a look almost of hurt. It was difficult even now not to feel an impulse of pity for him. Duff said, 'I am sorry. The misunderstanding is mine. Excuse me for just one moment.' He picked up his pen and wrote. The soft scratching of gold on paper was the only sound in the room. Duff's fingers danced in place as he reached a conclusion and the pen jabbed down a period. He capped the pen, at last, and looked up, his damaged smile restored. 'Thank you, Professor. You have been more than patient with me. I wish you once more a very pleasant visit to Dublin. I trust we may have the pleasure of meeting again.'

The officials recorded and proposed and amended drafts; Minute answered Minute. They sent condensed and neutered reports to him on the Belgian coast, where they had taken a house. Schrödinger woke in the early mornings knowing that when it was exposed to the cold light of day the entire project would be derided as insane and killed off. He had seen what had happened to the Habsburgs and their dreams. It ended with starvation, bad soup and freezing rooms, his father dead in an apartment he could not leave because he was too weak to climb the stairs. This Irishman with the Spanish name thinks he can save a world that is going to hell with a centre for cosmology and philology. The College of Atoms and Verbs. They will put him behind high walls and that is the last I will hear of it. And yet the anxious letters he wrote to him brought measured replies, though every fastidious ambiguity in the phrasing brought new anxiety and as he scrutinised each utterance he drove himself senseless finding evasions in the courteous formalities.

Until the law was passed in their assembly he would not believe it; until he saw it, yes, he said, I'm a positivist now, Heisenberg has beaten me after all. Their goodwill is not enough: the event won't happen until it is observed. He went out for long walks in the dunes. Strong grasses, low hazel bushes and tiny beech trees grew on the thin topsoil. He watched a buzzard climb higher and higher in the enormous sky. The dunes trickled and shifted slowly and visibly, their faces hollowed out where the wind and their own weight were making them unstable. He liked to lie in a cavity protected from the wind and read, but often he would simply lie flat and try not to think, closing his eyes on the quiet void above him. Anny found him there one evening, when he failed to come back for dinner, with the light nearly gone and the sand growing cold. She suggested they spend a weekend across the border in Amsterdam and look at the paintings they might not ever see again.

They walked around the Rijksmuseum. Each of them stood in front of paintings that they remembered. They ate lunch in a café, then walked counter-clockwise around the Singel, enjoying the sun on the water and the stones and the polished curtainless windows which opened onto careful interiors, where the burnished surface of a grand piano next to an arrangement of flowers looked to them like a dream of money and security. Before dinner they drank a glass of cold *genever* in an old pub. They walked on, but the mood Schrödinger had hoped to leave behind on the coast would not lift. The light played at a lower angle now on the glass in the windows, as dirty tarpaulin-like clouds moved slowly east. Along the canal the tall houses lit up, the rich dark paint on their surfaces concentrating the remaining sunlight. There was a chill of imminent rain, and the sky grew darker: it seemed to be full of smoke, as though the city's oil and coal were burning out of control and falling as smut and ash on this clean stone and brass. An iron hook jutted from the gable ridge of each buttressed house. The air felt warm and raw and impure, and seemed to have some unpleasant suspension in it that should not be swallowed. He put a hand over his mouth. There was no unusual smell, yet it felt to him as the night came on that the intricate hydraulics of the city were clogging up, and that something foul was settling in the canals. He stood on a bridge unable to move, and Anny got him back to the hotel by taking his arm and forcing him to walk. He was tense, sweating, his face pale and rigid. She felt his pulse, and made him lie down. He stretched out with a pillow over his head and slept after she had held him for half an hour. He had begged her not to call a doctor. From the hotel window she watched night finally come down and the air outside fill with rain. Yellow leaves floated on the canal, the surface of the water defined by their light cling.

Later, in the early morning, he woke to find Anny sleeping on the covers beside him. He rose and went to the window. On the other side of the canal a door stood open, a rectangle of light in a dark wall. A small child played on large flagstones in the hallway of the house, tottering and then sitting and laughing, clapping her hands. He could see an inner door open to the first sunlight, and the corner of a large heavy table. The child could, he assumed, be watched from the inner room. The safety and order of the arrangements entranced him. But he was looking down on the scene from outside and infecting it with his mood, as though his was the despair and scorn that might ruin it and all the safe places of the world.

When the news of war reached them, the four of them were eating lunch in a restaurant near their house. The mussels tasted of garlic; they drank cold beer. Hilde and Ruth had arrived a few days before, travelling via Switzerland and France. The Irish had come through, voting after bitter argument to indulge their leader's whim, though Schrödinger had the impression that none of them was happy. No more was heard from Mr Duff.

'So that is supposed to have been peace, was it?' Hilde asked. 'I hope they have a better one where we're going.' They sat and ate, glad of their affection for each other and of how they had survived their own crushing and unfeasible needs. 'We are together and safe, in our strange way, that is what matters,' Anny said, draining her beer. She kissed Hilde on the cheek.

They were given twenty-four-hour transit visas and sailed for Dover from Ostend. They travelled that whole day, and the three adults forgot their stiff backs in the need to amuse the child. On the boat a frozen silence built around them when she called out in a clear voice, in German, *Why is England so far away?* They were driven across London to Euston station, and a train that seemed to have only one very deliberate speed dragged slowly north into Wales, hour after hour. They were not allowed to get down from the train until they reached the boat terminal. A policeman wearing a raincoat stood in the corridor of their carriage, and did not speak to them. They saw houses from the train that were small and closely packed, terrace after fragile terrace. The train hauled its string of carriages through the evening. The deep cuttings laid bare the age of the rocks as a knife exposes old injuries to the body. As they chuffed along the north coast they crossed the head of a small bay where the waves folded white crests on a grey and dirty field. The beach was the colour of coal. The sky was dismal, the smoke drifting out over the black waste. It's as though this coast has been at war for years, Schrödinger thought, this was Hamilton's bad dream and it's now de Valera's, the thing he wants to escape: ripping the land open so it can give passage to any force that we let loose.

Their train was full. Men in cheap suits carried cardboard suitcases along the platform and up onto the boat. Some of them had a woman and young children with them, but most, both men and women, seemed to be travelling alone. They were poor and rough-looking, with weathered faces and strong bodies, and Schrödinger could barely understand the English that they spoke, but he could see that they were going home for a visit, rather than fleeing the war, and this October night seemed no different for them from any other. Groups of policemen called out one young man or another and interrogated him. He had heard about the bombs in English cities. How desperate, he thought, to put a bomb on a bicycle. They were never meant for that, he thought, but he remembered the fragile, silent machines climbing that hill in Italy. There is nothing we won't use to kill.

A man asked him, 'Have you been in Ireland before, sir?' 'Yes, once.' 'Have you got work there?' 'Yes, I do.' 'Well, that's the main thing. You may as well stay there, then.' 'I hope so,' Schrödinger said.

They sat together on chairs in the lounge and ate sandwiches and cured herring. Ruth finally slept, under a blanket of coats stretched out on a bench, and they all dozed off. When he woke some time later in the early morning Anny was gone and the ship was shuddering around its engines. The lounge was silent, full of people slumped on chairs sleeping in their clothes. He went out to the open deck where he found her standing in the lee of the funnel, in the wet and cold, as the ship drove on. The vessel seemed to pause for a few seconds after each collision with the swell, which was visible beyond the rail as a turbulence of shifting hollows, an infinite dark rolling and breaking. Her face was cold to the touch of his fingers and she barely responded to it, or to his musing on what was waiting for them over there. She held herself in her good coat, one of the few things she had been able to take with her from Austria, and shook her head silently. The gesture frightened him, because it seemed to be part of the cold wind and the emptiness around them.

'This life that you have chosen for us.' She shook her head again. 'Of course it's you who can make the choices, even though I'm glad that we're getting away from the terrible things that will happen now, but have you any idea what all this costs?' She was not crying, though it was clear from her inflamed eyes that she had been, and she did not seem angry; but her voice was clear and cutting, and it rang through the noisy business of the sea all around her. 'You go on and on, and I follow. But you know, just because I live with it doesn't mean that it suits me. I've tried to live like you, but it was like working at being in love, though I really was for a time, and then you end up with the cold leavings, and it isn't enough. I prefer the remains of you to the companionship of another man – I won't pretend anything else, but can you see how it makes me feel, even now, when I wake in the middle of the night and try to remember who you are sleeping with at the moment, where exactly we are in the great meeting of souls and bodies in which we're all one? I lost much of you a long time ago. One gets by, even in happiness, but I do sometimes feel that that is all I am doing. I'm sure it will be all right once we get there, but it feels like going to the end of the world. Do you know what I mean?'

He held her shoulders, damp with the wind and spray, and said, 'Yes, I do. But they are very kind and enthusiastic, and they will let me work, and we will be fine. And you haven't lost me.' He tried to say it with loud urgency, but his voice was weak against the sound of the engines and the waves. His hair was wet and flying around his face, and his glasses had misted over with salt water. 'You can never lose me. We are friends beyond anything. That has always been what mattered. You mean more to me than any other person in the world.'

'I know that,' she said, barely audible now, and touched his hand on her shoulder. 'But I did lose something when we stopped being lovers. Something had to give and it was never going to be you. We exist to reflect you, all the women in your life since you've been a little boy. But there it is. If it was not worth it I would have stepped overboard, and long before tonight.' She smiled again, to his intense relief.

When the backwash became heavier they went in through the bulkhead doors and down to the lounge. Young men were getting drunk, swaying with inflamed faces as they stood at the bar. From the room with its moving tide of beer on the floor there was a raw smell of bitterness and defeat. A man vomited quietly near the stairs, the expression on his face one of agonised shame.

Early the next morning they walked onto the pier among the returning emigrants. Another civil servant in his long dark coat and wide hat stood waiting for them. He lifted his hat solemnly and came forward when he saw them. The two women chatted to him as they walked up the stairs to the street where two cars stood waiting. The end of the crossing seemed to have startled them into happiness, and they laughed like passengers relieved to be among old friends after an unfortunate cruise.

A week later they took a bus out to Clontarf. It was another day of rain and of toppling white clouds over the city and the hills beyond it. They went up the metal steps to the top, and sat at the front on the hard plush seats so that Ruth could help drive the bus and watch the road rushing up and feel the tree branches scrape the upper windows as it rounded tight corners. Behind them a few young men sat talking and smoking. The bus seemed to run in the same direction as the railway and then north out by the sea, which was flat, the colour of wormwood, stretching out beyond the harbour until it became a pale line on the horizon. Soon the conductor left his bare niche under the stairs and told them that they should get off. The seafront promenade was deserted; the rain was not heavy, but the wind drove it into their faces. A few isolated palm trees stood on the promenade; their leaves had withered brown tips. They walked up Castle Avenue in silence under their umbrellas.

A young auctioneer met them at the gates of Clontarf Castle. Hilde said: 'That is the ugliest house I have ever seen.' It was a crude grey mansion with crenellations and mock battlements. 'It's where the Vernons used to live,' the auctioneer told them. 'They owned all this land.' 'Is it haunted?' Ruth asked. The young man glanced at her merrily. 'A lawyer lives there now, so I suppose you could say it is. But you have to be Irish to see the ghosts. Maybe if you live here for a bit you'll get to know them.' He walked his clients a hundred yards to the house they had come to see, which was part of a terrace in a tree-shaded street. It looked new and cold and suburban. The auctioneer was brisk and realistic. 'It's not quaint, it's not old, but it's a quiet street in a very respectable area. Very respectable altogether. It's well built and it's not damp. Good school nearby, the Holy Faith for girls. The sea is a few minutes' walk away and there are fields to the north. Lovely walks generally. There is the sea-bathing pool on the promenade, around the corner. There's the old Guinness estate, the Corporation own it now. And of course you have the island. Miles of strand, empty at this time of year. Well, that's an attraction for some people. And the house is going cheap.'

They wanted a roof there and then, to move their bags out of the overheated hotel and to cook a meal and eat it together. The street was, as the auctioneer had promised, very quiet, but it was the closeness of the sea that decided them. From the back window upstairs they could see the tide combed by the wind moving in small unbroken waves towards the coast, wrinkles on a shaken grey-green surface. In the small back garden the air was chilly and clean. The two women ordered furniture and bed linen in a department store in the city. The child helped, carrying and dropping small boxes and supervising the delivery men who came with the furniture and carried her down the garden path on the mattress of her own small bed. Schrödinger was happy to let the women organise it all, and worried about the arrival of his desk.

That afternoon, after they had unpacked their small collection of books, clothes and cutlery, they walked along the promenade and across the frail-looking wooden bridge. The tide was out, and the long sandbanks were streaked with clear sheets of glittering water. Instead of turning left onto the beach they stayed on the sea wall and walked to the end of it. Schrödinger saw that this was not, in fact, the end, that there was a line of massive rocks stretching away to a black lighthouse. The water licked around and between them, their tops uncovered. He picked his way out onto the jagged blocks and began to jump from rock to rock towards the lighthouse, balancing himself on his hands when he had to cross a larger gap. He concentrated carefully because the weed was thick and slippery. He heard Anny and Hilde shouting his name. He saw the waves rushing onto the piled-up rocks, pulling and sucking at the seaweed and limpets. Sea lice scuttled in the cracks on the stones. The spray wet his shoes. Balancing on a square block, he raised himself upright and looked north along the curved blade-shape of the island towards the dark mass of Howth Head, near which a couple of sails stood motionless on the sea. In the other direction he saw the harbour entrance and the southern sea wall with a red lighthouse at its tip. He waited long enough, thinking of nothing except the changing face of the water, so that when he looked down his boots were almost covered. He turned back and saw that he was standing in the midst of a cold, grey and restless sea, with a tide sweeping in over the line of rubble put there to drive it north with its silt and refuse and empty shells, and that he was in the way. The higher solid wall seemed further off than he remembered. The two women were yelling angrily at him now, and he saw Anny run back and take a lifebuoy from its post, trailing its rope behind her as she returned to the edge of the wall. He stumbled towards them, his trousers splashed and hanging heavily around his legs. His coat sleeves were soaked when he leaned forward to get a grip on a stone. I must not let my glasses fall off my nose, he thought, and tried to keep his head upright. By the time he pulled himself up onto the wall again he was wet and cold and Anny made to hit him with the lifebuoy. Ruth was pale and near tears, but when they were back on the springy wood of the old bridge, the three adults walked arm in arm laughing with relief, and she began to jump over the gaps between the grey boards, fascinated by the sea which she glimpsed between the planks, moving underneath them and slapping heavily against the piles.

Part Two

Spring 1941

The confident whistle of a blackbird entered his dream at the moment it broke down. He had been trying to cut intricate figures – spirals, scrolls, festoons of fruit like the ones on the cornice of his room in Merrion Square – into a stone pillar with a knife, an ordinary kitchen knife. All he had been able to do was make scratches on the glittering surface, which seemed to be made of reddish granite, and he was weeping with frustration, shaking his head and pleading with someone standing behind him for more time. The knife was blunt. The scoring it added to the rock crystals would come off with the rub of a cloth. Then the knife turned into a fountain pen, which fell apart in his hands, the gold band around the barrel first, the clip breaking off at the top of the cap, the black lacquered barrel cracking, the nib splaying and bending as it was forced onto the stone.

The return of a dull morning consciousness, of being awake and safe, brought relief so deep that he felt he was breathing again after choking under water. His body relaxed. A mock-solemn voice addressing the child filtered up from the ground floor. He heard her call out in response. He could not read the clock face until he found his glasses on the side table. It felt too early for the house to be so awake, but he remembered that yesterday, Easter Day, the clocks had gone forward an hour. Since Hilde was saying as little as possible to him, she had kept her own time and left him behind. She had fallen asleep again last night without speaking to him.

The nights were the worst, because when he woke in the early morning, as he always did, he often thought that he heard engines in the sky somewhere out to sea. The direction of the sound, if it was there at all, was impossible to determine, too far away, damped and dispersed by wind and air pressure. One dark morning it came to him as an angry whine, the Doppler of a huge bee, a whacking buzz overhead and then gone. Once he heard a clapping burst from a direction that made no sense at all, as though a ship were firing a gun way out in the bay. Yet the sound left no trace on anyone else. Hilde and Anny slept through the strange noises, or maybe their origin was far away, over Liverpool and Bristol, and this was a trick of the atmosphere for the sleepless with bad consciences. He was hearing things, that much he knew.

He thought about the cheerful sadness of the day before. In the morning, dark-suited men and women and neat children in their brushed once-a-week coats had passed along the street with their black missals in their hands. This was the life that he thought he could observe from a distance, but they were being drawn into it, all three of them along with the child, as the nuns at school made their world compelling to her. They had grown used to watching their own reactions carefully, avoiding any sceptical note that would hurt her if she imitated them outside the house. At school she sang the hymns and recited the catechism, call-and-response certainties from the green manual that had its own cosmology. Who made the world? God made the world. How many persons in the Trinity? Three: Father Son and Holy Ghost. Prayers for black babies and orphans, medals of the Virgin with blue enamel facings, white pearl rosary beads, scapulars. A mother sewed a relic into her communist son's jacket and he was saved. Now there were the preparations for First Communion, and complicity with the fathomless belief of their neighbours was unavoidable. It was too late to announce that she was, like him, a kind of Protestant and to send her to another school; he would have to admit in public what had not been said in private. The white dress and shoes and white glazed missal were wrapped in layers of tissue paper in Hilde's wardrobe. The child's excited belief was contagious.

They even went to the Easter parade, another step closer to the life around them. Their shell could not afford to be so roughly handled: he knew that a tiny fracture would make it easy to crush.

But the girls in her class were going, and it was important because if too few people went the British would come back, and it was the twenty-fifth anniversary of the Rising. They would know we didn't care. Even he gave in; he had heard the congregation singing woeful hymns inside the grey church on the seafront as he passed it on Good Friday. He knew that they were kneeling in front of the bare altar, the tabernacle locked, and the spell of death was present in the closed shops and silent streets. He wanted to be with them when it lifted, even at a military parade. They set off after breakfast to walk to O'Connell Street.

As they left the house, Anny looked around and said that spring was coming in the trees along the road, and even in their garden. They noticed the smell of mint that had run wild, and in the tiny borders of the lawn, straggling daffodils and bluebells appeared, limp survivors among the dandelions and nettles. Anny said: 'The shears and lawnmower need sharpening. I can't cut anything with blunt tools. The garden is tiny but the grass is so thick. I must ask the knife grinder to stop when I see him next. He could sharpen the cutlery as well.'

Along the coast road thousands of people were walking or cycling towards the city, avoiding the packed trams that whined evenly as they passed. The dark hills to the south seemed very close. The tide was out, and the bare flats stretched off to the channel of the river flowing into the bay. Close to the shore, dinghies lay canted over on the mud near the jetty that ran out from the seafront road. Some of the men seemed to be in drink, and laughed with desperate relief at jokes Schrödinger could not hear and would never understand. One man rubbed his hands vigorously as he walked, scrubbing at something he couldn't wash off. The crowds grew thicker as they crossed the Tolka at Annesley Bridge and walked along the North Strand. The streets to the side were tiny cul-de-sacs, blinded by the railway embankment and dwarfed by it. The traffic and the crowd broke against a barrier at the foot of Talbot Street, where people were locking their cycles to the railings beneath the railway station. They moved slowly up towards O'Connell Street. At the top of the street they could see that barriers fenced off the General Post Office, the thick columns of the portico picked out in green, white and orange flags. The blackened granite of the building dwarfed the reviewing stand of crude white-painted wood. More tricolours hung from the lamp-posts above metal loudspeakers, and from the plane trees between the tramlines. Smiling faces crowded the windows of the buildings overlooking the street, it was a holiday, but the Army officers in ash-green uniforms and brown boots stalking around the stand had an air of grim purpose. High above it all stood the British admiral on his elegant stone truncheon, the slim figure missing an arm and looking away to the south.

The crowd behind them grew denser; young men pushed in to the barrier. Schrödinger edged back from the railing. The crowd was good-humoured but settled and serious now, and was ready when the parade began, moving with a steady tramp of feet, cornets and trombones playing brassy versions of patriotic tunes under which the tubas belched out deep percussive notes. Armoured cars cruised by. They looked like grand saloons of the twenties to which turrets had been welded. Lorries rumbled past in strict order. A voice made nasal by the tannoy announced the different units. He held the girl up until his arms grew tired. Soldiers eight abreast in field green, their rifles shouldered, marched in long columns past the stand where the Taoiseach and other men now stood or sat in their black suits. The new bishop was there, with his purple vest under his dark coat. Schrödinger watched him for a minute, struck by how thin and fierce his face looked, but then a bicycle squadron rolled by, hundreds of saluting soldiers keeping their machines stable and turning eyes right, while their legs trod the pedals slowly down and around. 'They will rush to the front,' the commentator said, and for a moment before he could suppress the impulse Schrödinger laughed, bluffing it into a cough when a man in front of him turned and scowled. There was a pause while medals were presented to veterans of the Rising, the announcer adding a soulful vibrato to his throbbing voice. Men younger than me, Schrödinger thought, looking old in their dark clothing as they stood with shoulders back and heads up while the Taoiseach pinned medals to their coats. After a long hush for the dead, a firing party, invisible on the roof of the GPO, sent volleys of blank shots into the air.

It seemed to last for hours. Then he heard the tannoys amplify and harden the plaintive rigour of his patron's voice. Schrödinger took in snatches of the speech. He spoke of the gall of political servitude, their impatience with the stranger's hand on their necks. Yet a few had made a choice, refused to endure slavery and impotence, and steeled themselves to die rather than submit. They seized the chance that might not come again, knowing that failure then would doom untold further generations to bondage. The awakening when it came was more complete than any the heroes could have dreamed of. The high keening voice went on, a ballad of defiant loss. 'Yet the gift they left us is imperilled once again. We may be called to fight in order to defend our freedom. We must look death in the face. We must be ready to evacuate our cities. Perfect our training. We must act as though we know the value of the only freedom we have had for seven hundred years.' The men and women around Schrödinger, dressed in their best hats and coats and scarves, listened in silence. A woman next to him raised a hand to shield her eyes as she gazed at the tall figure on the wooden stand, who was illuminated by the sunlight shining down on the massive Post Office. Her face was twisted nervously, her lips drawn back to reveal her darkened teeth. The speech was met by a vast wave of handclapping, the sound reflected back from the solid Victorian buildings and dissipated in the air over the wide avenue.

At the end the crowd around him and all along O'Connell Street sang the national anthem in Irish, the yearning qualification of the melodic argument in the bridge sounding like a ragged break in the song's marching beat. Confront our fears and leap into history, he thought, fling ourselves off the edge; make the decision, cut and run. The wisdom that has dug the pit we're in. His daughter sang the song from start to finish in this language he struggled to understand.

The crowd dispersed slowly, the people hunching their shoulders against a rain of which there was only a hint yet in the chilly air. The four of them lingered at the street corner. Anny said, 'I'd like not to have to walk home in this crowd. Why don't we have tea at the Gresham?' He could imagine the taste of good tea, not the bitter stewed dust they had drunk at breakfast, and the heavy fruit cake that would come with it. As they made their way up the street to the hotel, thousands of wagtails began to gather in the trees, their quick sweet chirps scattering over the quiet throng. On the branches the birds made their constant nervous gestures so that the trees seemed to flicker. Hilde moved closer to him and said: 'I'm glad she enjoyed it, but all this talk of soldiers, they seem so helpless it breaks my heart. Our poor little one. We have to put her first, whatever happens. I have such foreboding dreams, I am sure we all do. But let's try to be good to each other.' He was moved that she could rise above her anger; their conversations had been terse all winter, relaxing into affection only when they could centre on something that the child had said or done.

'Yes, of course. You must know that I will always put her first, and you and Anny. Please don't work yourself up over this.' After a pause he went on, more hesitantly, 'I hope we can be as we really are with each other. You're too important to me for this tension to persist. We must talk, or our fears will get worse. Can't we be honest with each other without this endless suffering?'

'You don't seem to realise that everything here is so much more charged. It takes place in a smaller room. We were supposed to stay together in order to survive, but you've already weakened the bonds. You know that we're dependent on you, and it gives me a feeling of utter powerlessness. Sometimes I feel that we're just your servants. We look for good bread and decent meat, we try to find wood and turf that isn't soaked with water, but all you've noticed is that tea is hard to get. You can do what you like, as you have always done, but I left everything to come here and already I feel that I am about to be retired.' She was serenely bitter, but she was still smiling, and even gave his arm a playful caress.

'But I have done nothing. At least wait until I have.'

'It is a matter of time, nothing more than that. I don't want to be surprised, that's why I assume the worst.'

He had nothing to say to that, nothing that would not sound hollow and dishonest. When Anny caught up to them with Ruth he filled the silence by telling the child how the birds in the trees fed all day on the island near their house and flew here in the evening to roost in the trees. 'I suppose it's safer,' she said, 'but it must be uncomfortable sleeping up a tree.'

'I don't know', said her mother under her breath, 'we all seem to manage it.' But no one else seemed to hear.

A few minutes later, his wife and his lover were laughing about something as they passed through the doors of the hotel, and Ruth ran ahead of them into the dining room and the smell of warm pastry.

In the kitchen the next morning, as he ate the egg Anny had boiled, Hilde barely spoke to him. Her moods were quick to change; the thaw had not lasted long. She had closed herself off again by the time he had joined her in bed. She told Anny that she and Ruth were going to the National Gallery, and half an hour later he heard the front door close. He went into the living room and, parting the net curtains slightly, watched the two figures in their black woollen coats, perfectly matched, turn left along the tree-shaded street and walk into the light that waited in the open space before the castle gates. Hilde's stiff intentness and her smiling attention to her child were so painful to see that he wanted to run after them and lead them back with an arm around each of their shoulders, but he did not move from where he stood, his nose almost touching the glass.

Watching them go, his mood sank a little deeper. The ceremony the day before had left him feeling pity for this little free state with its tin-can armour and gawky infantry, its grand words and thin skin. Their bicycles rushing to the front. And before the holiday he had received another anonymous letter, an odious mixture of denunciation and flattery and obscure threats. He told himself that if he looked from a different angle, perhaps he would see himself for what he really was, and he had been struggling for months to avoid the sense of a quiet observing gaze in the margins of every conversation outside this house, though he insisted to himself, over and over, I am harmless, there is till such a thing as privacy, even here; let them see. I answer only for my work.

And yet, the week before, the shell had been cracked. Not since seeing the poacher on the island at the turn of the year had he felt so infringed upon. He had been working at the table in the back room when Hilde pushed open the door during the hours when he was never interrupted. She made no apology. 'He has come, he has just turned up,' she hissed in a half-panicked whisper. 'He's sitting downstairs like a great Zeppelin as though he owns the place. For God's sake, what shall we do? He hasn't seen me. Shall I stay up here?' She was almost laughing, and for that he was oddly grateful to the visitor, whoever it was.

'We aren't expecting anybody, are we?' he asked. 'Who is it?'

'Parish priests don't have to make appointments, we should have known that.'

He felt a weird shoot of pleasure, as though he had been expecting this moment, and a vague unease. This was not meant to happen: the unspoken contract between him and them was that they would leave him alone.

He doubted if the big man in the enormous black soutane with the red sash around his stomach would have taken much notice of any agreement, even if it were written down in Civil Service prose. He occupied two-thirds of the sofa, and his arm rested on a soft leather-bound breviary. He was austerely dignified but jovial with it, a grand hotelier putting guests at their ease. There was a fragrance of some mild masculine spirit around the huge head, with its short grey hair and pink and violet skin. Anny said, 'I don't think you have met Archdeacon McMahon.'

The priest rose and stretched out his hand. Schrödinger almost bowed to kiss it. 'You must forgive me, Professor, I was out for a walk – I stroll on occasion through St Anne's, it is quiet there while I say my office.' He patted the book lying beside him. 'And since I was passing I was inspired to remedy my discourtesy in not welcoming you to the parish long ago. I have of course had the pleasure of meeting your wife on occasion. We are so privileged to have a visitor such as yourself amongst us. I once met Professor Whittaker at a function in Maynooth – it was connected I believe with the Eucharistic Congress, it seems such a long time ago now – and he gave it as his opinion that you were, with Einstein, the greatest living scientist.'

Schrödinger shook his head. 'You are too kind. If only my friend were not such a terrible liar. And everyone knows you shouldn't believe what physicists tell you.' He joined in the rousing laughter as their two bodies swayed like trees.

'You'll stay for a cup of tea, Father?' Anny enquired, catching her husband's eye as she played the flustered housewife caught off guard. The large smooth head turned to her, ah well, yes, walking had given him a thirst, if it was not too much trouble. He had such an enormous mild confidence that Schrödinger felt the pull the man exerted, the residue of others' deference absorbed and adding to his presence. Anny withdrew to the kitchen. The two men sat looking at each other.

'We owe a lot to Whittaker's kindness. Were it not for his word in the Taoiseach's ear I can't imagine where we might be. And we are privileged to have found such a delightful place to live, with such fine neighbours. You are lucky, it seems to me, to be posted here.' He felt instantly that posted might be the wrong word, but the priest showed no offence. They exchanged niceties for a very long quarter of an hour. The gas was so weak on certain days that watching a kettle boil seemed to slow down time. What patience we learn, he thought, we could live without gas if we had to, but then the door was opened by Anny backing in with a tray tipping over with the china that they never used, silver sugar tongs, an almond cake that she had baked for Easter. And a good share of their rationed tea, to judge by the scent from the pot.

The priest's calm flirtatiousness moved up a gear. 'You will spoil me, dear lady, a cup of tea would be more than enough – and may I say how lovely you've made the house. It's always a pleasure to see such pride in family life. I'm fond of this shady road. And you could not be better situated, Professor, for your Sunday Service.' Schrödinger smiled and nodded for a few dizzy seconds. 'The Rector and I are old friends', McMahon said. The daring edge that he gave this assertion allowed Schrödinger to discover where he was: the Rector he had never set eyes on, the church he had never entered. Why not just say so? he thought, and at once drew back because it would hurt the man's feelings. He seemed as blind as a child to any optic other than his own.

'Yes, it is most convenient. We are fortunate here in many ways. I must ask you, Father, you say you like to walk on the old estate? You must have known it in its heyday.' He plunged down the nearest side road he could find. 'It is as big as a royal palace. Brewing in this country must have been like mining gold.'

'Indeed. Drink is more reliable than a crown these days. And the cathedrals we could have built with the money washed down in porter. From the river to the river, so to speak, if you'll pardon the vulgarity, my dear lady. But I'm not long enough in the parish to have seen it as it was. I saw it at the very end, before the Corporation bought it. In its day, indeed it must have been a wonderful sight. They brought the stone to build the house from England, you know. It was like a fairy-tale castle set down here in this quiet place on the sea, even quieter then. But that's the trouble, these stories of building paradise on earth never end as they're meant to. They must have thought it would last for centuries, but when you think about it all they got out of it was a few summers. The war, I mean the last war, the rising, and then the Tan war – well, everything changed. They sold all the furniture and the pictures; it was the week after this war broke out. I couldn't resist going along. There were lovely statues, good imitations of antique sculpture I must say, some fine profane pieces. The most beautiful piano I have ever seen, made of rosewood. They even had an organ built into one of the drawing rooms, a huge thing that must have made the walls shudder if it was ever played. It was like a big jumble sale, and there was a terrible air of hurry. I felt a great sadness that day, though it was for the best.'

It struck Schrödinger that this cleric had in him less iron, less of the magisterial stuff he ought to have; that McMahon would like to have been lifted for a moment into that gorgeous fantasy before it was brought to earth. He asked, 'I wonder whether they knew their time was up, when they built the place. I believe they did, they must have, but why spend so lavishly before losing it all?'

The priest did not reply. Instead he looked past Schrödinger and rose from the sofa, bowing slightly. 'Ah, but who is this, I don't believe I've had the pleasure?'

'You have not met Frau March, my wife's old friend, a friend of the family. Her daughter attends the Holy Faith.' He was surprised to find his tone encouraging, almost appeasing.

'Is that right? I am pleased to welcome another parishioner, I confess I was not even aware . . . and how is your little girl getting on? The sisters are wonderful teachers.'

Hilde smiled. 'Ah yes, very good. The nuns are wonderful. She is happy there. I am so sorry, you know, but my English . . .' Her diffident appeal to her friends showed a sense of timing that Schrödinger had never known she had. He took his cue. 'Frau March has not learned as much English as she would like, Father. It takes time to adjust to a new life.'

'Mrs March's daughter will be making her communion soon.' Anny flourished this evidence of conformity, smiling winningly at the archdeacon.

'Beautiful, beautiful. Is there anything more wonderful than that innocent discovery of the sacrament?' McMahon asked. He turned beaming from one to the other. 'You are bearing exile so bravely, and the Irish can appreciate that. How fortunate that Frau March has found a home with such a distinguished family. The world in our time uproots so much. One can't comprehend it in human terms. Well, I'll not keep you any longer, you have been very patient with an old priest. I am glad we have met, and I'll be sure to keep an eye out for these good ladies after Sunday Mass from now on.' The welcoming note with the admonition folded inside it could not have been more genial. Schrödinger saw a flicker of colder calculation as the priest's serene gaze touched Hilde. 'May your great work prosper,' he said to Schrödinger. 'Ireland is lucky that Germany does not value all her children.' There was that note again, not even a note, they had a strange harmonic genius for producing overtones, waves of subtly different frequencies interfering. All four of them crowded the hallway as the priest made his way heavily to the door, turning to Anny last and laying his hand on her arm. 'You're very good, my child.' He raised his hand to them and made a sign that was, Schrödinger realised, a form of blessing.

He was still amused and irritated when he thought about it a week later, as he set out in the late afternoon, after a few unproductive hours at his desk. He was dressed in boots and a tweed jacket, and his head was bare despite the chill wind. The sky was clear, with higher up a few long white tendrils moving slowly north. The lane beside the Protestant church was a space of filtered green light under the big chestnut trees, a shelter for the worshippers who seemed to enter and leave their church so quietly that he never saw them. Walking under the branches with their white pyramids of blossom he realised that it was spring again, and that he was leaving too much undone. At least, he thought, I saw the specialist. He had a surgery in Fitzwilliam Square. A former rugby player with huge delicate hands, he had a reputation as the best eye man in Dublin, and his manner was that of the clubhouse. He leaned in wearing a circular mirror perforated at the centre, and Schrödinger wished that seeing his own way clear were as easy as shining reflected light into his eyes. 'You have an intransparency of the crystalline lens; cataract, in short. The opacity is progressing.' And in every sense this was true. The work was blocked, confused; the late winter had not given him any new insight into the form the theory needed. He needed that moment of being given to, of an illumination that would allow him to find an equation that had a counterpart in the world of space and time. He wondered how much of his daughter's life he would see; and he flinched at the impossibility of telling her, each postponed month an intensification of bewilderment and hurt. After the operation he would tell her, whenever that would be. The doctor, whose name was Dargan, said to him, 'We'll eventually have to have those lenses of yours out, though it will be a while before they're ripe. Unless you want to become a blind sage, and we can't have that. Two in one country would be too much.' He looked at the man's thick fingers and wondered how they could perform so delicate a trick as cutting into his eye. He heard the shrill sweetness of invisible starlings. The birds' indifference, the heavy trees planted here when there was still a Habsburg Kaiser, the empty sky, and the fact that he was part of this cold unintentional thing elated him, as the thought of all the men who had seen this arrangement of light and matter always did.

There were no other walkers on the road as he turned north by the ploughed fields. He passed a street of new semi-terraced houses, which looked raw in the harsh light of the spring day, and he speculated idly on who had bought them. Civil servants, men with pensions putting down roots? Ahead of him was the screen of trees inside the estate. He could see the walls of Furry Park off to the left, another locked-up mansion at the end of a drive, and he wondered what it was like when these houses were alone out here, in their network of green roads before the wars started half his lifetime ago. Crows grazed the fields, pecking in the furrows. He approached a gate by the small lodge. There was no soldier on duty as he pushed the gate open. If he saw the parish priest walking in the distance, bent over his book, he hoped he could avoid him.

He walked up to the central avenue, as straight as a military road. Half a mile away at the end of it, the enormous white house closed off the perspective, drawing light onto dozens of window-panes. A colony of rooks uttered their metallic cries in the Austrian pines and holm oaks that lined the avenue. The parkland beyond the trees was bare and corrugated earth, sown with wheat. Stacks of turf closed in the road, stepped like defensive walls. The avenue crossed a kind of drain, a path in a tunnel under the road. He had once walked through it, dark and damp, reeking of urine: a grudging right of way. In heavy rains it flooded. Quinn told him that Guinness hadn't wanted to see the people from the villages round about crossing his grand allée. The pines spread wide umbrellas of dense green over the road. Each tree and its placement was thought out, each angle planned. He wondered if even the earth they grew in was Irish. There were giant yew trees near a walled garden, with an ivy-covered clock tower above the garden gate. Such artful vistas: money planted and shaped as far as the eye could see. A herb garden was laid out in a circle of ilex trees, and as he passed he caught the pungent smell of thyme and rosemary straggling among weeds and red poppies over paths made of crushed shell.

A wooden sentry hut stood on the forecourt of the mansion, and the two soldiers inside it looked straight through him. The house was shuttered and silent, its back turned to the sea, facing in to Ireland and the west dressed in its English stone. The elegant unwashed windows under the tympanum of a harp supported by lions had little pediments of their own, like sharply drawn eyebrows. He wondered again about the soil under the trees. Why not? Maximilian had a million tons of Austrian dirt carried to Italy to make a garden. This place reminded him of that headland on the Gulf of Trieste, where the Emperor's hopeless brother used to sit and watch the sunlight flood the bay from his great terrace over the sea.

The road to the left of the house sank through a rock grotto, and he followed it to the stream beyond, which was channelled between artificially rugged banks, the miniature sublime. He followed it down towards the seaward edge of the estate. To be this rich is to have your own point of view, your dream angles. Enclose the world you want to see. The stream emptied into an artificial lake choked with green algae, the miniature Pompeian temple on its edge scarred and blackened where someone had built a fire. A rowing boat was sunk up to the rowlocks in the water.

He sat in the low fork of a brown yew, looking at the pond and the wall. Beyond the wall was the coast road. Gulls flew over towards the island, their implacable calls the only sound audible in the stillness. Above the lake the builders had left a hill of brown earth tangled with exposed tree roots. On the edge of the hill stood a structure like a bell-tower with an open-sided top. He wondered if the tycoon used to climb up there to watch his ships steaming in and out of the bay with their shifting loads of barrelled beer. Now his rose alleys were going to seed and his lawns were planted with wheat, to feed people he would not have let pass his gate.

Labourers cutting road, planting trees and rocks, deepening gullies. There must have been thousands of them, an imperial workforce. He had gone out once to see Maximilian's house while on leave from the front, which was a scant few miles north on the limestone plateau. Though it was a hot August day he had walked along the road from Trieste by the beaches and hotels, under the shade of the palm trees. Men in white suits and women with parasols walked by the shore. The headland reared up, dense and secretive in its covering of green trees. Even in his summer uniform he was wet with perspiration by the time he walked into the park. The oaks were huge. Slim, graceful cypress trees bent towards the sea, as though the wind was pressing gently on their spines. Only Styrian earth would do to root these trees: the muck of resentment. Maximilian should have swept the streets of Graz for dung. There was a bronze statue of him as Emperor of Mexico in the park, a tall, greening figure with his hand stretched out, forever on the take. The house and its vast terrace were at the tip of the promontory. Schrödinger walked to the edge of the terrace and saw the gulf spread out, the water like foil shaken under a strong light. The prow-shaped stone base was built straight up from the sea, a dreadnought ready to sail. Power loves coming to the edge, he thought; the world's potential opens up in sight of water. The Habsburg dreaming of America over breakfast on the terrace, watching his navy play at war out in the gulf, studying his maps of the south, with all that empty land. Schrödinger could feel the lure, as though the desire were enough, coming to the brink and lifting your arms, with the wind around you and the sea breaking against the rocks; making the leap and deciding what world you wish to create. It reminded him now of Berlin, the sweaty vitality of feverish minds. Druid stuff.

He sat for a long time, his back resting against the trunk of the yew. When the tree felt cold on his thighs and the bark dug into his spine, he hitched himself off the branch and walked up the hill to his left so that he could return around the back of the house. A promenade he had not noticed before was cut into the hill, giving a view of the sea and the island. The back wall of the path was inset with arches and tiny grottoes. *Nelson. No more faithful friend ever lived. Here Zulu sleeps, his long day done. Jupiter. His tale is ended.* The noble snouts in profile. To dream a cat is to dream an enemy; to dream a dog, a friend.

Behind the house the cypresses and yews had trapped a warm amber light, and the brown needles on the floor of the wood damped the sound of his footsteps. He heard the beat of horses' hooves from far up the avenue. A conservatory was built onto the side of the house, made of delicate curved steel with glass walls, a broken promise of lightness. He went up the steps to the door and pressed his nose against the dirty glass. The plants inside were dead or rampant, and mould was scattered on the floor between the stone troughs.

Out on the avenue the sound of iron shoes on stone was now ringing closer. He walked around to the front of the house as a cart drawn by two giant horses rolled up. The drays slowed and stopped, blowing clouds of air and showing their teeth. The elderly carter sat looking at Schrödinger. His whip was a piece of rope knotted to a stick. He said, 'Fine day for a walk.'

'A very fine day. And you have two fine horses. It is such a beautiful park. It's sad to see it so neglected.'

'Isn't it? You should have seen it, though. My brother worked here for old Lady Ardilaun, the Guinness widow, just before she died, and it was already going down. Not even she could afford to keep it up. She'd walk around the park on her own, no one coming to see her. God help her she ended up living in this tomb, that's what it turned out to be. And thirty of them couldn't do the work – the gardens, the hothouse, the palm court – they had trees inside the house, I ask you – and the woods. The house is a shame now, all bare and piled up with boxes and dust. It's as cold as sin.'

'It's used for storage now?'

'Air-raid gear. Clothes for the LDF. Gas masks, that kind of thing. The Corpo has stuff here; I've come to pick up some tools. No one knows the half of what's in there, between you and me. But with boys like that, it's in safe hands.' He gestured derisively to the soldiers in their hut, who had not stirred since the cart drew up; did not seem to have moved in the last hour. 'It won't be needed, the way things are going. The English have had it now.'

'Who knows what will happen?' said Schrödinger with a lightness he did not feel. 'Well, I must not detain you. Good afternoon.' He moved off, feeling he had been abrupt with the old man, back down the avenue on which the evening was beginning to settle in a dull copper radiance. He was still the only walker in the park, as far as he could see, and it was so empty he wondered if he was after all trespassing in a forbidden zone, not molested because he didn't matter. Off to the right he heard two flat loud cracks, and the uproar in the trees grew worse.

The avenue focused the declining sun's rays down the long lens of trees. Perhaps they really didn't know they could not last, he thought, building this fabulous park and discovering too late that nothing takes or lasts here. He remembered something Quinn had said, that the tide is always out at Clontarf. 'And in a way it is, you know? The smell of slightly rotting seaweed is what I remember, from when I first came. A village where it always seems to be the off season. One water-polo team refused to come to the baths there on the front road near you to play a game. They said they heard the fertiliser plant across on the other side was leaking poison into the water. But I'm convinced it's the place that makes people uneasy. The back of beyond, and not because it's remote.' They must have made the best of it, gathering each day in the summer to watch the sun go down with the windows open onto the huge park. At least they knew what they were losing. But then, he thought, we also inherited a fine old house and look what we have done with it. We've made a mess of it, this old obsession with light.

As he came closer to the point where the avenue crossed the sunken road he saw to his right through the clamps of turf a man on a bicycle balancing a large brown-paper parcel in the basket on his handlebars. There was something familiar about him – he had what Hilde called bachelor hunch, she claimed she could tell how repressed men were by the way they rode their bicycles. But surely it was Flaherty, and he was freewheeling now along the old right of way towards the tunnel. He had not noticed Schrödinger through the trees and the turf walls in the fading light. Flaherty disappeared into the tunnel. Schrödinger kept walking, watching the hazy dappling of the sun through the leaves. He prepared a suitably jovial greeting for his neighbour, should he look up when he cycled out of the tunnel, but Flaherty did not emerge. Schrödinger halted above the exit, puzzled now, and heard indistinct voices below in the passageway. He was curious enough to hang back behind a pile of turf sods. After a few minutes Flaherty rode out, standing on his pedals as he rode up the slight incline, heading for a gate at the southern edge of the park. The package was no longer in his basket.

Schrödinger had gone less than fifty paces when he sensed movement behind him; it must be one of the soldiers, he thought as he turned around. On the road where it crossed the passageway a small, almost dwarfish, man was standing. Even with his eyes, Schrödinger could see that he was smiling, but the sight was repellent because the man's grin was at once threatening and buffoonish. His round little shoulders were squared back in some dark workman's jacket, his legs planted firmly apart, the arms down by his side aping a soldier's stance. For a moment Schrödinger thought the man was about to call out to him, and he knew if he did it would be some taunting insult, but no sound came. Some labourer on the estate, he decided, as he walked faster along the darkening avenue and the rooks made their raucous noise, slum birds crowded into Lady Ardilaun's trees.

As he walked down the hill from the estate the church spire on Seafield Road reared up into a dark-blue sky under low clouds; it looked like a bone cleaned in acid. He walked all the way to the coast road and turned along the promenade, passing the grey walls of the swimming baths. The tips of the branches on the evergreen trees, the monkey puzzles and palms, were withered brown, and the sight of them and the summery villas facing the sea worsened his mood. Above the hills to the south the low sun was firing up thick white cloud through the burnt wastes of Dublin. He was reluctant, as he often was now, to go home. Hilde would have returned and their common rooms would be stiff with tension. He crossed the road and walked up the lane by the Protestant church. He stood to look at the rectory on the other side of the lane, a large solid house with a gravel yard. I wonder what kind of man my rector is. The whole neighbourhood was dark and still, as though everyone had gone away for the Easter holiday, or was staying quietly indoors, taking seriously now the warnings about showing light. A slim young man, perfectly bald, passed the entrance of the lane wearing a heavy coat. He turned pale eyes on the man in the tweed jacket and heavy boots standing looking at the church house. '*Oíche mhaith,*' he said in a clear, high-pitched voice. Schrödinger ran through his inventory of phrases. '*Lá bhreá gheal a bhí ann.*' And the young man agreed it had been a fine bright day.

When he let himself in, Anny was reading in the back room beside a low fire; she still felt the cold at nights. She stood and kissed him on the cheek. 'You've been gone a long time,' she said. 'Where did you go?'

'Around the old estate. It's like visiting a museum that's been forgotten and abandoned. There is such a strange atmosphere there. And I saw Flaherty, on his bicycle as usual. He seemed to hand over a package to a man in the tunnel that goes under the road, you know the place I mean? A very unpleasant little creature.' He felt a bad taste even speaking about him and veered away by asking, 'Where's Hilde? Is Ruth in bed?'

'The little one was exhausted. They went to the Natural History Museum as well. She loves those old cabinets full of stuffed animals. Hilde is upstairs. Erwin, she is very unhappy, she's moved into the spare room. I'm worried about her. She sleeps so much. She goes to bed earlier and earlier and she's not eating well. You can see it, the slow dragging movements. When she is out she pulls herself together and plays at being all right, but she is becoming completely passive, expecting the worst to be done to her. I feel locked out. She is not even angry with you, I think, but the reality of the situation, the feeling that there is no way out, has as much to do with it as knowing that your relationship is over.'

Hearing it like this as a statement of fact unnerved him, and he struggled to find some way of denying it. Yet no guilt could penetrate the hard clear feeling that tomorrow night aroused in him, a source of energy that could not be touched by anything else. He had no conscious plan, only an instinct of warmth that grew around the thought of seeing the girl once more and a feeling that a change was coming, that there might be an escape from the evasions and unavoidable honesties he had to face inside this house, and from the morass of stale thought in which he floundered. So he said nothing that meant anything, but promised to speak to Hilde, to come to some new understanding with her, for he did not wish to hurt her. He meant this sincerely, but could not protect his goodwill from the blind force of the only impulse that now mattered. He held Anny to him, her greying hair and forehead resting lightly on his shoulder. Her shoulders felt soft in his hands and smelt of tobacco; and although he felt that only with her could he be truly himself, her body was a strange and faintly distasteful presence, more alien than if he had never known it. It was as it had been for twenty years: closeness without desire, the current passing through without harming them.

He ate quietly with her and went to bed alone. In the bathroom he turned on the geyser. The little boiler's thin jets exploded quietly into low flames. There was just enough gas left to heat a trickle of water that made a warm pool at the bottom of the bath. He undressed and sat in it and splashed himself until it grew cold.

The rooms were so close together on the small landing that he could hear the slight wheeze of his wife's breathing as she slept, and the sound of their friend's body turning in her sleep, or what he hoped was sleep, on the damaged springs of the mattress in the spare bedroom.

On Tuesday morning he woke early and in the kitchen drank a cup of tea so tannic that it numbed his mouth. He had a meeting with his patron later, and if he cycled to the Institute now he could work before O'Hogan's stewing presence began to make him restless. He had washed standing up with a flannel soaked in cold water and dressed in one of his good suits, and was wearing a bow tie. He rolled his socks over his trousers and lifted his bicycle out of the garage with a sweeping turn, feeling strong and efficient: he had slept well, and the next few hours held only the calm light-headedness that the attention of the powerful brings, a feeling of being drunk and in control. He looked forward almost with affection to seeing the politician who guarded himself so carefully. Beyond that the evening glowed. He thought of the pub where they had arranged to meet, and he sensed that a pattern was about to take shape, either that or his need for her would spread out formlessly.

Crossing the Tolka at Annesley Bridge he decided to turn down East Wall Road, which he had never done before because he thought it looked so bleak. He rode past factories and warehouses, towards which men in overalls and dark jackets were walking with their hands in their pockets in a rapid gait that was half defiant strut, half submission to the easterly wind. The docks closed off the view south; a huge crane rose high over the enclosed basin, squat and brutal, the colour of a warship in the morning light. The short streets under the railway viaduct were lined with rows of tiny cottages, one-floored red-brick houses with grey slate roofs, one window and one door. Terraces of these dwarf houses faced each other across the narrow streets, which smelled of decaying food and sewers. Men in small groups leaned against the walls on certain corners, talking and blowing on their hands. No ships, no men needed to unload them.

She wants to arouse them, he thought, and us to them, but I am frightened here.

A door to one of the cottages was open on a bare floor and a broken table propped up by a barrel, a few pieces of clothing hanging at the back of the room. Two young boys in thin shirts stopped whirling around a lamp-post on a piece of rope and took a look at him. Their faces frowned in concentration, neither hostile nor afraid, giving him their serious attention. He came out by the railway station and turned towards the Custom House and the river. He joined a stream of bicycles, all black, high and upright like his own. He passed a lorry hauling a wicker creel of turf on a flatbed trailer, and a pair of horses pulling a covered wagon painted neatly back and sides with black, broken crosses. *'You know you can rely on the Swastika Laundry'* read the legend under each.

O'Hogan's door was shut. Schrödinger's office felt oven hot and he reminded himself to ask O'Hogan to tell the stoker not to light the fire on such a mild day. An envelope of heavy creamy paper lay on his desk, addressed to Herr Professor Dr Schrödinger. He had not seen that kind of titulomania for years, not since Austria; it could only, he thought, be the flowery cover for something he did not want to know. Instead of opening it he poured a glass of water from the carafe on his desk, and after draining it half-filled the glass again and poured it onto the fire, feeling stupid as soon as he had emptied the glass. The fire hissed and released a cloud of bitter turf smoke into the room, making his eyes water. He took his glasses off and rubbed the lenses with a piece of silk he kept in his jacket pocket. The trees outside the high windows of his room were lost in fog until he put his glasses on again. When he did so O'Hogan was standing in the doorway, lowering and deferential, his face impassive under beard and black-framed glasses. Only a widening of the eyes and a slackening of the mouth betrayed his awareness of the smoke drifting past him into the colder air of the corridor. 'There are better ways of damping a fire,' he said at last, his head inclining thoughtfully, as though this were folk wisdom hauled up from the deepest well.

The way he said it made Schrödinger snap, 'No doubt, and better things to throw on one,' before he realised that the man was carrying a thin sheaf of papers. O'Hogan's soft flesh seemed to tense and quiver, the livid pale cheeks above the greying beard turning a darker red.

'Your mind is on higher things, of course. But you might consider, if you can spare the time, mentioning to An Taoiseach when you see him later that our budget is strained. And if you wish to fund these extraordinary visits by gentlemen from England in a time of financial stringency you can use your powers of analysis, which are highly developed as we know, to discover from which direction the money for their travel expenses is likely to appear. I said when this matter was first raised months ago that it would be difficult, and so it is. Perhaps you might ask An Taoiseach for a donation from the contingency fund for this professor who seems to have found God Almighty in an equation. These are things beyond the ken of a mere civil servant with his mind on finding enough to pay the porters and messenger boys and secretaries. And the *higher* staff.' He gave the adjective a trembling, sneering emphasis.

Schrödinger felt himself calming down. The futility of it was already so settled. 'You are, Mr O'Hogan, your own best judge. I'll say this though, because I wish us to work together, I really do. Not everything has an obvious purpose at first. The equations you deride may last. If this were not true, what would be the point of physical research, though it may be that you think such research trivial and abstruse? Can we not work together, Mr O'Hogan? Can't you pretend to be interested in what we do?'

O'Hogan said: 'I will carry out my duties, Professor, of that you may be sure.' He came forward and laid the paper on the desk, on top of the envelope, then hunched his shoulders and walked off with that deliberate painful trudge, carrying the weight of his neglected flesh. He did not close the door on his way out.

Schrödinger pushed O'Hogan's paper aside and stared at the envelope, his hand reaching for the blunt silver knife he kept in his desk drawer. He cut the envelope and unfolded the letter inside. The heading, on matching watermarked paper, announced the Dana Shoe Company, with an office in Dawson Street, Dublin and 'Copenhagen Paris Vienna'. The typed text was in German.

Dear Professor Dr Schrödinger,

Please forgive this intrusion into the affairs of an illustrious compatriot. I would quite understand if you did not wish to reply to this communication. The undersigned is a mere commercial, but in appealing to you as a fellow German I must trust to your goodwill.

I am the manager of the Dana Shoe Company, which – with very unfortunate timing – was set up just before the Declaration of Emergency to import fine ladies' and gentlemen's shoes into Ireland. Shoes of a craftsmanship that the most refined clients can appreciate. Since the cutting off of trade our company has faced difficult conditions. It is impossible now to conduct normal business with our Head or other Branch Offices. We have, in short, a large stock of the best and most stylish Ladies' and Gentlemen's Shoes, delivered to us just as the Emergency began, but without further injections of capital we are unable to open a place of business from which to sell them.

I am writing therefore to distinguished members of our community in exile with a view to offering them and their wives a special discount for our wares. Perhaps this may lead to a passing on of our name to other reputable members of the wider public and to a revival of trade when more normal conditions resume. Personal satisfaction is the best advertisement. I ask your forgiveness, distinguished Professor Dr Schrödinger, and beg to assure you that nothing other than quite exceptional circumstances would induce me to write a letter such as this to a great scientist. If it were possible, however, to be granted a few moments of your time so that I might wait on you and show you some samples of our shoes, I dare hope that our exceptional quality might appeal to even your exacting taste.

Sincerely
Erich Goltz

Schrödinger said: 'There is a great deal I do not understand. There is such energy here, among the young, the artists, but the city often feels as though it lives in the past. The old houses in which the poor live such difficult lives. And there are people who do not seem to wish the country to develop, who resent anything but the past and the grievance it brings. They appear to dislike what the Institute represents, for example.'

He was speaking more frankly than he had ever dared before. The question had, after all, been asked: I wonder what you think of the country, now that you have been here for a year and a half? He wondered if it was a test. The expressionless face of the tall man sitting across from him did not change, and his long body hardly moved. They had begun by drinking tea and with a solemn discussion about a postage stamp. He asked Schrödinger's view of the appropriateness of putting William Rowan Hamilton on a new sixpenny issue. And what, the Taoiseach mused, would be the right mathematical symbol to accompany the image of Hamilton's face? The formulae for the quaternion, or some version of the Hamiltonian function? They looked at the proposed designs sent in by the Post Office artist. A miniature Hamilton, already overweight, Dunsink Observatory sketched in behind him, Astronomer Royal of Ireland, gazing at the stars, his real work done in the half-dark of a gas lamp with a pen. The statesman's face was inches from his as they bent to peer at the drawings. Schrödinger knew the face was a mask of self-control, and he wanted to plead with the inscrutable man to relieve him of O'Hogan's dragging weight, but knew that it was part of the price he had to pay, the system that gave him a cleric and a bitter old drunk to dilute his own profane arrogance.

He waited as his host allowed the silence to thicken. When the Taoiseach spoke he even smiled a little, as though charmed by the implied criticism. Their teacups lay on the low table between them, the sketches for the stamp pushed to one side. The room was cool and airy, the fire-grate neatly swept and empty. He was, Schrödinger felt, almost relaxing. He noticed that the large globe he remembered now stood on top of a high cupboard, in the shadow of the corner furthest from the door.

'There are those even among us who can't accept that we exist, as we are, weak and wounded. The truth is,' the Taoiseach said, in a low voice, as though he wished to share a grave confidence, 'that we've not found our self-respect yet. We feel that we are illegitimate. Our enemies have a particular fondness for that concept. It is said, you may not know this,' and he gestured at the sketches with what was nearly a smile, 'that he was the natural son of Archibald Hamilton Rowan, a revolutionary, a leader in the Rising of 1798.'

'Yes,' said Schrödinger, 'I had heard that.'

'What an ornament he would have been to the new nation if the story were true and his father had been successful. But the conceit of illegitimacy persists, in relation to the country and to me. You've heard the tales, I have no doubt.' Schrödinger felt a hot unease reach his face. 'My mother's memory has been traduced, her exile in New York made the stuff of calumny. Worse, my father was a Cuban. They like to evoke the exotic taint. A miscellany of races. They conjure up a man in a white suit, a hot night. Unthinking blood and uncontrollable flesh.' Schrödinger realised he was blushing, wondering how much his host could see of changes in the surface of the skin. He remembered that he had been unable to read a note in his own handwriting that morning and felt a wistful pang at the slow atrophy of his body, wondering if his own eyes would deteriorate so much. The oculist at Zurich. I should have asked him who he consults at home. He thought of Dargan's brawny hands. The fierce gaze was holding his. Was this also some subtle warning? 'The Spanish tinge, as some call it, they hint that it will surely lead the country to disaster.'

'These notions of purity are so naïve,' Schrödinger found himself saying, unsure as he said it if it might mean more than he intended, but wanting to lift the pressure he felt in his host's look. 'It is the first resort of the scoundrel. Sadly, even here. Many suspect, I am sure, that I am not what I say I am.'

'I know. And indeed that too has been flung at me, a hard accusation in Ireland. My father can be made a member of any race they choose.' He said the words with dispassionate distaste. 'I admire them as a people, though I cannot in conscience condone their faithful stubbornness in error. I have had to deny it in public, in the Dáil. Well, we come to what we are by strange paths.'

'Yes, precisely. What makes a theorist? I cannot explain to you rationally how I found the wave equation so late and so fortunately. And by the time I did, my homeland, which it had seemed so natural should be an empire, had all but vanished. Never did I dream that I would find myself here. And yet I feel so at home, and in a way my life has prepared me for it. I really hope I can bring my work to fruition here.' He looked at the tall figure sitting so still in his chair. Their eyes met. He hoped that this would be the end of it, a moment of unspoken compromise. The statesman nodded solemnly. But after a short silence he leaned against the headrest of his chair, easing his back, and began to speak again.

'I feel sure that you will. Your gift is, I think, divine. It is important that you have the freedom that you need. And as to what makes us and forms our ideals, well, as you know, there is much nonsense talked about the influence of early childhood on our lives, but I can't deny that we have memories that come to mean something. I have one such recollection, I think. I was very young. My mother had just returned me to her relatives in Bruree. I remember nothing of the transatlantic crossing: the young uncle who escorted me, the sounds of the ship, and the smell of the great ocean. I can conjecture those experiences from later crossings, when I try to recall my younger self. But I do remember that when we arrived I was taken to my mother's family's house in the dark and put to bed. I awoke to find the whole house deserted. They had all gone to their new house nearby to move the furniture and crockery, but it was also a day of family excitement, and a near-orphan boy would have been a hindrance. The new house was an agricultural labourer's cottage built by the reforming English Liberals, that is how modest our circumstances were. What I remember is waking in the single large room of the mud-walled house, and seeing the ashes cold in the grate at the far end of the room, and a single window looking out at a clouded sky. Rain hung on the glass. The plaster on the walls was dirty with paler stains where a few religious pictures, perhaps also a picture of Parnell or O'Connell, had been taken down. There were smoke marks on the ceiling and brown tobacco stains on the walls. It was the first and only night I spent in that house. I was not quite four years old. I was, though my family were very kind, no family could have been more kind, a charity case. My mother was still in New York. Families can be cruel to foster-children, but my relatives never were. Still, you know that at the great events, the turning points in their lives, you are a little less than precious. The new house was never quite a home to me. So some might say that this is perhaps why I demand that our

142

people should at last have a proper dwelling place. There is no peace in a house that is incomplete, where we are not fully at home. These promises of our full sovereignty if we join one side or the other are so meaningless. What is the point in waking up half a century hence, bereft of what really matters?'

'That would be terrible,' Schrödinger said, 'I grant you. But you do have a home, if I may continue your metaphor, you have made a great deal of the house you inherited. One can improve on that, surely? You could make the house more your own; give it new windows and a roof.' In the silence he realised that he had voiced words he would not have chosen himself, before knowing her, and wondered if he strayed too far.

The Taoiseach said nothing, but stood and walked to his desk, where he picked up the compasses that Schrödinger had noticed on his first visit to this room, checking with his thumb that the pencil was sharp, and a sheet of white foolscap paper. When he sat down again he said, 'Bear with me, just for a moment.' He laid the paper on the low table between them and with practised skill drew a large circle with smaller circles within it touching its circumference, and an even smaller one outside, also in contact with the large circle. 'Think of it as a mass defect diagram. The large circle is Britain, the smaller circles its colonies. We are outside, but forced to associate with it. We pretend that our relationship is merely external, but we are in fact bound to this great mass. We know that the mass of the whole is slightly less than the mass of its constituent particles – two bound spheres, if you'll pardon the expression, I know they must not be thought of as literal spheres but as areas of probability, but indulge my geometrical image, spheres forced together reluctantly whose masses do not add up. The lost mass is the binding energy holding them together. That leaves something lacking, which is the cost of their association, and that force must be released. Think of the liberation of energy when that happens, the release when the spheres split apart.'

He had spoken in the same trusting voice, with a wistfulness that was headily endearing, and Schrödinger felt for a moment that he was succouring this powerful man, in an intimacy that he knew could not be real.

But what he said was, 'I think you and your people must have their home. Yet if you will forgive me saying so, the dream of perfection can defer living, any kind of living.' I must stop, he thought, I am presuming too much, but the words were out, and he felt a little brave.

The politician's face did not react. When he spoke again his voice seemed not to register any offence in what Schrödinger had said, had if anything become even less precise and didactic. 'You're right. And there is work that we can do. In my own constituency there are many townlands in darkness or half lit by candles, though even they are hard to come by now, or even rush lights. We can light up the houses so that people can read. And do much more in the longer run. Are you still thinking of going there, to Clare, by the way? It is the place where the past most survives, despite everything.'

They talked for a while about the remoteness of the county, and the limestone region that Schrödinger half-dreaded seeing. The past not lost was what he feared. Nothing is ever dead all out in Ireland, Quinn once said, just struck by a blast, a curse. Waiting to rise again, if the right words are said. 'Your friend, you know, he's half a dead man.' Quinn's voice was serious and unironic. 'You have to realise that about him. He reconciled himself to being shot in 1916. He was under sentence of death, and in some ways still is, so he feels chosen, and he thinks the past can be changed, that we can be reborn to a better life. Nothing must change very much in the present. I think your friend feels that if we do not move an inch our life will be better than modern, and we will be safe.' And Schrödinger recalled Mrs Flaherty's picture of Christ standing upright, with a mild look in his eyes, holding his heart in his hands. Then the Taoiseach seemed to rouse himself. 'I have made you listen to my tedious reminiscence and not asked you about your work, which is much more important.'

As Schrödinger answered him the long harsh planes of the older man's face actually softened, for the first time since he had entered the room. An almost yearning look came into his eyes.

'You know what I'm after: a continuum in four dimensions that has geometric structure with inherent laws, a model of the real world in the space and time we inhabit so that all the events – including quantum events with all their strangeness – can be displayed in it. I am sick of a world in which gravity and this thing we call quantum mechanics cannot be translated into each other's languages. In plain terms, as you know, I want to explain quantisation on the basis of a field equation for the entire cosmos and so get past the quantum discontinuities. The quantum particles will be incorporated into a grander field, in which gravitation and electromagnetism are linked. It must occur in real space and time, not in a zone of staccato events and unrelated forces. One side-product of my theory seems to be that the universe is expanding, and that new matter may be created out of nothing as it expands. But the number of electrons in the universe should be finite. This creativity is a problem. At the moment all I have are problems. So, yes, I want to restore the world to what I think it really is – a field of waves propagating in space. The universe must have in it energies that are discrete; they must give rise to what we now think of as quantum jumps. And matter may be the places where the field is strong, a density of charge in an infinite field of wave-like energy.' As he spoke he thought of an animal falling, a changing field where the states of greatest field intensity travel through space with the velocity of the body that lands lightly on four spread feet, its spine absorbing the shock.

The Taoiseach smiled. 'That to me is the beauty of your work – to dream forms that have never existed, and yet were always real. As Hamilton developed his quaternions, and gave us an algebra that gave real meaning to negative and imaginary numbers, he showed us that multiplying $a \times b$ need not give the same result as the product of $b \times a$. It comforts me greatly that the quaternions do not conform to the arithmetic of cattle exports. Four-dimensional numbers for a four-dimensional world. In the world of those numbers there is a wholeness we lack. Numbers that even when divided by each other always remain within the same order of fours. An ideal world existing alongside our own. This is the real poetry of the Irish race. What writer of verse has achieved as much?'

They talked for a few more minutes. Schrödinger found himself defending poets. 'There are times when the most beautiful equation is too cold a place to live,' he said, half believing it, wanting him to understand, 'and we can't always rise above ourselves and forget that we're here for the blink of an eye.' It was as if to this plea that the politician replied when he said, just as Schrödinger was turning to leave, 'May God bless and protect you, Professor.' And then, as he shook his guest's hand, and as though he'd left a delicate subject until last, to be touched on quickly, he asked: 'How is your wife? She must join us soon for dinner. And her friend, Frau March – all well?' Though he responded with the normal bright assurances, the leader's sombre tone and steady look made Schrödinger so tense that he calmed down only after walking twice around the square, past the handsome closed doors, as fast as he was able.

He met her in a dark wood-panelled pub. The bar was divided by opaque glass frames deep enough to conceal the bodies of seated drinkers, and the stalls were full. Many of the customers were already wide-eyed with drink; there were no women among them. The air was heavy with smoke. As he stood inside the street door he saw another door in a partition to his side and pushed it open. She sat in the snug smoking and reading a book, a glass of red lemonade on the table in front of her, ignoring the covert glances of the barman over the short counter that served the tiny space with its single table. She was delighted to see him, her eyes lifting and clearing. She reached out a hand for him and whispered vehemently, 'Get me a bloody drink, for God's sake. This stuff is giving me a headache. Why can't a woman order a whiskey in this *foul* city without being seen as a hoor? I need Dutch courage before I go on tonight.' He ordered two Jamesons and the barman repeated what he had said with the sceptical politeness of his trade. When he sat down again the barman kept away from the counter and the snug was a private room.

'Are you nervous about the play?'

'I should be, but it's just an evening among friends, in a way, so no, I'm not. It's no masterpiece, as I've told you before, but at least it's not another play about a disputed will and an alcoholic brother with the pox.'

'I'm sure you'll be wonderful. Have you finished your essay for Quinn yet? I saw – I should say I went to look at your slums today, down by the docks. I can see what you mean.'

'Mine, I like that. I wish they were, I know what I'd do with them.

I'm glad you're getting a bit of a conscience in your old age.' She stubbed out her cigarette and looked at him with a frank, vivid seriousness that alerted him to the shabbiness of evasions he had tried in the past, and shamed him into thinking that he never would again, though her tone was much lighter than it had been the night they met, when she said, after they had talked for hours with no awareness of those around them, 'You're too old for me.' She was saying, 'Some of those places have a family of eight in them. Anyway, I've finished it, all two thousand words. My first literary endeavour. It will be out in a couple of weeks, not under my own name, needless to say. And it will have as much impact as a flea on a dog, but maybe it will annoy someone.'

It was her anger that still stirred him up. He knew what she brought to life for him, and he wanted to touch it with her. She carried her own body like a strange, dangerous force that she was just beginning to understand. It had ceased to matter that she withheld herself from him; the slow deferment had become the brooding centre of every day during the winter that was finally coming to an end. They had been meeting in quiet pubs like this one, and at the end of each evening she kissed him passionately. He surprised himself by not pleading with her to sleep with him. She was a second chance, a last chance. Even the look of her was like Hansi, the dark hair and eyes, her apparent toughness. Because she had forgiven him, after she finally escaped, Hansi was all the more lost to him, and the memory of their time in her flat in London was bitter. He came down at the weekends from Oxford, while he was waiting for the call from Dublin. There were melancholy, blissful struggles with each other on the bed; he was kind and attentive to her, his gifts thoughtful, his conversation delicate. She had not done with him yet; there could be no cancelling her recognition of his weakness. Those last weeks were the dry remains. Her forgiveness was indifferent. He was already a bad memory as he tried hopelessly to reach her.

'I had a visit yesterday from our parish priest; he was like the local baron coming to check on the state of his tenants, though much more polite.'

Her pale skin flushed. 'To your harem. Your ménage.'

The first time she had slapped him like this he had been struck dumb. It was a secret that he thought he needed to unravel carefully, and she had ripped off the thin cover of euphemism as soon as she saw it. He had been speaking about the need for freedom and total honesty, the hypocrisy of denying the urge to connect at the deepest level with another consciousness, the most profound experience of oneness in all human perception. She had been so caustic about 'this Buddhist gunk' that he nearly walked out of the bar, yet in the way she said it, softly and regretfully, he could see that she did not completely despise him for using the timeless in order to seduce her. He had told her almost everything, nearly honestly – the withering of his marriage, what Hilde had been to him – and nothing. He realised that she was willing to make room for what had once been unimaginable to her so long as he made a different life seem real. She asked him one night: 'The child's father, is he still in Austria?'

Seconds passed before he answered, 'Yes.' She did not seem to notice his hesitation, but he was aware as he said it that he had lost an opportunity. An image came to him, of Ruth at a year and a half standing in the middle of a brightly lit room, covering her eyes with her little hands. 'Where's Ruth, where is she?' they all cried, and after an interval the child would lower her hands with a delighted grin. '*There's* Ruth!' they shouted, and she would whoop with laughter at how she had fooled them.

'To my home, my ménage. The very thing. He drank tea and talked about the Protestant aristocracy. He is fascinated by the old estate across the fields from where I live. So am I. Have you ever been there? Their animals were buried looking out to sea. There are little temples in the grounds. We should go there some day. I feel at home among dead dogs and broken greenhouses. And you, how was your day running the country?'

'I typed a lot of terribly important documents. That's what clerk typists do. I sat at my table in a row of tables beside another row of tables and typed onto the usual layers of paper and carbon, great wads of the stuff. I didn't look up for four hours this afternoon. I didn't dare, I was in disgrace. Miss McCabe sat at the head of the room like my teacher in primary school, a harsh old stick, except that we've gone beyond the age of learning anything, so a dozen girls clattered their machines and copied the wise words of the men who run Justice, never mind that they don't seem to have much of an idea what that means. It sounds like a factory when all of us are hammering away at the same time. I admit I love it for a few minutes when no one stops to change a ribbon or staple sheets of a memo together and it's just the pounding of the keys and the crash of the carriages returning. There was one day when we all hit 'return' together by a fluke, Miss McCabe reared up as though she'd been shot. But that wasn't the reason I was in trouble.'

'You inserted one of your parodies into the minutes of a meeting? On the immorality of transparent paper?'

'I wish I had. No, I was an occasion of sin. A temptation of the eyes for a Prince of the Church.'

'You are that, certainly, but I don't follow.'

'Miss McCabe rapped her desk as soon as we came in and stood up, coughing and rubbing her hands as though she were going to tell us terribly important news. I thought your friend had been hit by a lamp-post and died. It turned out that the Archbishop was coming to meet the Minister and the senior officials. She declared, and declared is the word, she was ready to pop with self-importance, that no female staff were to be seen on the front stairs or in the common areas between eleven and twelve. Well, I thought it was all a bit dramatic, but didn't think much more about it, then later she caught my eye and asked me to deliver some copies of indents to the travel section, and I ran down the back stairs. You've no idea how good it feels to get out of that room. I skipped down the two floors. I stopped afterwards to chat with a girl I knew, and I felt so good that I forgot what I was doing and walked back up by the front stairs. I was just stepping out into the corridor and there he was, coming around the corner, with his purple sash, the biretta, the cape and a train of high-ups in suits. He has a very hard face for a man who's not that old. I nearly fainted, to be honest. I was mortified, but I had to decide in a second what to do, so I cast my eyes down and walked as demurely as I could on the far side of the corridor past him, but I saw him stare, a real keen stare, I've never had anyone look at me like that before. Cold, looking right through you. One of the Assistant Secretaries, a right holy joe, was practically bowing to him. They swept past and on up the stairs. Well, about ten minutes later the phone on McCabe's desk rang. She was practically doubled over talking into it, grinning away at first and then very serious. She stood up when she had finished.' Sinéad's expression became severe, willing her face to look pinched, that of a panicking clerk. '"*Was* there a female member of staff from this department on the stairs just now?" I put up my hand, yes, it was me, I'm sorry Miss McCabe, I forgot. I wanted to die, but really to throw my typewriter at the old fraud. She told me in front of the whole room to heed instructions in future, the Secretary was not best pleased but was gracious enough to wish that nothing be made of the incident – the *incident*! So there, my cards are marked.'

She paused and looked at him. 'You haven't kissed me yet tonight. Don't you want to? No one is looking.'

Over the counter he saw the white shirt of the barman, who was rubbing a pint glass with a towel and examining it closely, not looking into the snug. They all look, he thought, as he leaned over the table for her mouth.

He walked up a staircase to the first floor of a tall narrow building, into a high room with wooden floors set out with kitchen chairs. A rough proscenium arch had been built out of painted planks towards the back of the room, which was concealed by black curtains hanging from the arch. From the walls at head height a series of pictures hung. They looked like woodcuts, heavy blocks of black ink and bare white space forming dour, swirling images of a city where the rain slanted eternally down, driven by a cold wind, and crowds trudged into the weather. Sombre Georgian buildings filled the background, their massive fronts rendered sparely, their columns dwarfing the figures in the streets. Schrödinger recognised Nelson's Pillar, the GPO, the Four Courts. The crowds walked in their sleep towards a desperate and collective fate. The images reminded him of Germany in the twenties, the monochrome comic-book intensity of history being made, the longing of an army for a reckoning.

The room filled up, until a few dozen people were sitting on the chairs, and then went dark and a spot beam formed a cone of light centred on the floor where the black curtain split. A small stout woman dressed in a dark wool suit and a tight circle of pearls stepped into the lit circle. Her voice was slow and her diction mesmerisingly perfect, her stillness – the low bulk she held so upright – trancelike. Her elocution reminded Schrödinger of actors reciting Grillparzer in drawing rooms at the turn of the century. '*Failte romhaimh, a dhaoine uasail*. The policy of this theatre club is to sponsor young writers. We try to look reality in the face. We present tonight the first performed work of one such writer. It is a trenchant piece, full of vigorous comedy. I commend it to you.'

The curtains fell back. A backcloth in the style of the dark woodcuts, black mountains, lowering clouds, the suggestion of a big house across a waste of moorland. Two actors entered stage left. Sinéad, dressed in plain black and white, her hair drawn back and tight in a bun. A young male actor in dark-green uniform. Both wearing heavy make-up, swarthy and lurid. They began an absurd, angry dialogue about violence and the cost of freedom; it was abstract and crudely parable-like. Two types caught in a stand-off, duty versus compassion, action against endurance. A hint that the young man has to shoot the well-guarded owner of the house whose beauty he describes, flowering out of centuries-old cruelty. Sinéad was restrained, playing her character without vehemence. She held the young soldier back, deriding the love that murders, the idea that starves, speaking for the smaller passions, the permanent needs. The drama was as static as the tableaux on the walls. Schrödinger expected the boy to break free and run to his death, leaving the girl bereaved. Instead a third character emerged, a one-legged tinker, speaking in a rapid babble. Only fragments of it made sense to Schrödinger. 'I'd die for Ireland if she knew who I was. The medal's lovely, but the wooden leg's the thing. Try walking on a medal. Or turning on a sixpence, though I'd manage on half a crown,' and he stuck his hand out with an inquiring leer. He sent them both up, courting the girl, making sly camp gestures to the boy. 'Think of it, the flute that once. Ah, the lap of the gods.' He glanced at the soldier's pelvis. 'The rising of the moon. The foggy dew. Nothing like it.' Sinéad became more like herself, animated, salty and mischievous. In the end the soldier boy died uselessly and the tinker went off after failing to persuade the girl to come with him on the roads. The audience sat very still. It was as if anyone who moved might brush against an exposed electric wire. Before the curtain fell, two couples and a single man rose from their seats and snatched their coats from the chairbacks and walked out, their shoes drumming on the stairs. But those that stayed clapped politely.

The actors came out. Sinéad walked straight up to him as though there were no one else in the room. Scrubbing off the make-up had left her skin pink and warm. 'What did you think? You didn't like it much, I can tell.'

'You were good. The play was unformed, but it has energy and anger. The tramp was excellent, though I missed half his point. But isn't it a little risky, in all senses? Won't the censors raid you?'

'We're a club. You're a member, in case you're asked. Well, at least you weren't locked into a country drawing room for three acts.'

The woman who had introduced the play came over, burnished and composed. 'You were so good,' she said. Madame Cogley. Sinéad had warned him against Miss or Mrs, she would not have the English forms and despised the Irish *Bean Uí*. 'She says she's not the "woman of" anybody.' Madame introduced a man wearing a black roll-neck jersey, short and muscular, brown eyes in a dark-skinned face alert and shrewd. His nose would kill him now, anywhere outside these islands, Schrödinger thought, but in the hubbub of people laughing he could not catch the man's name, heard Sinéad tell him the man was an artist. He leaned in and said, 'I'm honoured. I read a book of yours, a book of essays. For about a week I thought I understood the world.'

'Longer than I have, then. But thank you. These pictures are all yours?'

'Yes. It's the coming thing. Hard to say now how long in coming.' Sinéad hugged the small man around his broad shoulders and they moved off to begin stacking chairs with the actors and helpers, the artist giving him a second, appraising glance. Schrödinger noticed that a few of them had tight black hair and olive skin, and saw that this was a room in which to breathe, for her and others.

In the pub the theatre people and their audience formed a fluctuating mass, eddying and turning. The whiskey he had drunk earlier was fading inside him as he bought the first round; he knew he would pay for this tomorrow but he wanted more, exalted by her attention and the faces of the young people around her. She talked with great liveliness and clarity, and looked beautiful and mildly drunk in the smoke from all their cigarettes. The young male actors and Cogley and her artist exchanged friendly jokes and barbs. The two actors glanced with puzzled disdain at the old man towards whom Sinéad swayed on her stool, touching his arm and once brushing the tips of her fingers along his cheek. Schrödinger caught one of them looking at him, the one who'd worn a wooden leg and played such a brilliant clown. My God, he thought, the arrow in the eye, his light would kill me. The rounds of drink came faster as the clock over the bar neared ten, the men draining pints of stout in a few swallows and new drinks clustering on the bar counter. Cigarettes passed like offerings to ease the sting of stylised rudeness. The jealous actor baited a hook for Schrödinger about Lloyd George, old men and sex. In the hilarious noise, the frantic pulling by a barman at the tap a few feet away, the splashes of beer on the counter, and the fog of smoke in the light reflecting from the engraved mirrors behind the bar, he found he didn't care. As the barmen began to call time he said to her, 'I am full of you.' He touched her fingers with his, and then her face, her skin charged and tense. 'I with you,' she said. A heavy, drunken sincerity had taken hold of them all, the talk earnest and elaborate, even Madame speaking as though she were at last discovering an insight she had been longing to reach for years. Sinéad leaned over and kissed him on the lips. Those nearest to them looked carefully into their drinks. The artist turned to Cogley and asked, 'Are you going to offer us a nightcap, or what?' The older woman looked at Schrödinger with tolerant yet knowing appraisal.

The young actor who had looked so disdainfully at him seemed about to make some jibe when his attention was caught by someone further down the narrow hall of the bar. He lifted his glass in greeting and edged through the standing drinkers towards a short man dressed in a dark-blue jacket with leather patches on the shoulders. He seemed almost deferential to him, and ordered the man a drink.

Schrödinger pushed his way through the swimming unreality of the room to the door of the toilet to find himself at the head of a staircase, and had to steady himself for a moment. In the cellar, reeking and damp, a runnel overflowed with yellow urine and floating cigarette butts from which tobacco strands were loosening. He began to relieve himself. He heard the door open and rapid feet on the stairs. The young actor stood beside Schrödinger and undid his trousers. In the silence he seemed to be looking intently at the course of his own piss. Then he said, 'You know I'm well locked now, well locked, so I'll say it, but it's all very well coming in here and slumming it with the natives.'

'I don't,' Schrödinger said, eager for his urgent stream to dwindle. 'I assure you I don't.' In his sideways glance he could not be sure whether he had been threatened, though the boy seemed more melancholy than violent.

'Well that's good. I know what you're after, it's obvious. Good luck to you. But for the rest, even if it is all nonsense, and I think it is, none of them have the answers, they're all using words to keep us in the dark. My friend who wrote the play is a cynic, and the situation is absurd, yes, absurd it may be, but someone has to break out of all this. Just burst it open. We're suffocating, do you know what I mean?'

Schrödinger tried to placate what he could not understand. 'I think it is a difficult time here; but with so many threats outside perhaps nothing can change for the moment. It is a difficult time to be young, if I can say that without seeming patronising.'

'You can't.' The voice had hardened, and Schrödinger tensed himself in case the boy turned on him, but he stood holding his penis and shook his head slowly from side to side. 'They talk about democracy, your man's version of democracy, he wouldn't know it if it walked up and bit him on the arse. All this' – he gestured towards the dripping skylight and bare pipes just above their heads – 'all of it is just show, that's all it is. If the people stirred themselves again it wouldn't last a day.' Schrödinger, with the whiskey soaring inside him, imagined the bar upstairs, the wood and heavy glass, the solid house around it and acres of grey stone government buildings dissolving like mist. A shadow state vanishing in the burning unhappiness of this young rage.

The boy finished and buttoned his fly carefully, as Schrödinger was doing. He looked at the young face under its severely cut thick black hair, hair like Sinéad's. The blue eyes were wide and apprehensive, as if he was trying to believe in an idea but was still bewildered by it. Not yet possessed; not yet convinced that he knew all that needed to be known. The eyes softened for a moment. The young man almost whispered, swaying a little on his feet, and Schrödinger could not quite hear what he said. He shook his head apologetically. The boy looked straight into Schrödinger's eyes and repeated louder and pleadingly: 'You'd better look after her. She's worth it.'

Back in the bar, the servers were chanting, 'Time, come on gents, time please.' Sinéad had vanished. He felt happy and light-headed again, and in the lull as drinkers began to finish their glasses and put on outdoor clothes he looked down the bar through the crowd. He saw the man in the donkey jacket, and how small he was. He had a balding head and protruding teeth. The actor was talking to him again. The other man's face was full of a delighted, leering cockiness, a fixed aggression that was at once ludicrous and menacing. The staring face that was so familiar, that was taking over the world. And Schrödinger realised that he had seen this face before, looking at him up the driveway of St Anne's. He felt the heady charge of the spirit turning cold and thick, and for a moment he thought he might vomit. He placed his half-full glass on the bar. When he turned around again the small man had turned his back and was leaving, and Sinéad was beside him again.

Madame Cogley led the way up Grafton Street and around Stephen's Green. The night was cold and very clear, with a full moon. Over the green's iron railings the glittering constellations hung in a black sky. The streets were silent except for the hissing of passing bicycles, the engine of a distant bus, the birdlike ring of a small bell. Schrödinger lost his sense of direction, aware only of the girl walking beside him holding his hand. They reached the house with their hostess, who led them up to the first floor.

While the stragglers made their way up the stairs he and Sinéad looked at the drawings on the walls, images of rundown courtyards and lanes, of a street under an arch. Nothing happened: clothes hung from a first-floor window, a child waited by a doorway in a lane where the plaster on the buildings was cracked and the flagstones old and uneven. A woman carried a bucket towards a doorway, barely lifting her feet. The eye that had seen her was quiet, unpatronising, taking part in the hopelessness of what was there. The tragic swagger of the prints on the walls of the theatre came from a harder world, but when he said so she told him that gazing at squalor was not enough, and he wanted to say, 'At least look before you march,' but suddenly the room was full of a brown-haired, bearded young man, wearing a tweed suit and crushed hat, the flecked wool of a weight and cut better than any the men around him were wearing. Ashman positioned himself, his stance a swaying form of motion, leaning from one foot to the other, donnish and pugilistic. 'My dear Professor,' he said, 'a huge pleasure to see you. How is my friend the priestly polymath? I have not seen him for weeks.' His voice was a tenor instrument cutting through the local sounds with the confidence of a definition. The familiarity he assumed might have disgusted him, but Schrödinger tonight was too happy to care. The theatre people seemed to know Ashman, and laughed at the sight of him. 'What a *shame* I missed the play, though I'm a frightful fogey, as you know. A well-made melodrama reduces me to tears. Expressionist piece, I believe?' He mugged at them, round-eyed. 'We'll have all-day bicycle races next. Would you say,' he asked Schrödinger, 'that Dublin was like Berlin in the twenties, dear Quantumergo? On the edge of the abyss?' His eyebrows arched and he took a half-turn backwards from the people around him, admiring his own reflection in their eyes. 'Weimar without the naughty bits. But who knows what simmers beneath the surface of our Balya Awha Kleeah! The crust is so thin.' He beamed and swivelled, the eyes flicking from face to face, and even Sinéad was smiling at him. 'How are you, Tony?' she asked.

'Ah, the kawleen awling. You're as lovely as ever. A ray of light in a lousy world. Still, it's not all bad news. I found a splendid church today, with quite a beautiful metal rood screen, out near Bray, the purest Irish gothic. Still has the original box pews. The Descendancy's forgotten gems. There's my imperial melancholy, but no one enjoys being whipped in the desert, if you know what I mean. Well, unless you've been to Marlborough. They say this Rommel learned his flogging in Italy, I shall say no more.' He became solicitous and intimate in a flash. 'Did you hear from Lehmann? I think he liked your poem.' And a young man blushed and said, 'I did, and thanks for putting in the word.'

'Oh for God's sake, what else can I do? Apart from encouraging you all to think treasonable thoughts.' He darted close again, and swayed out to inspect the effect he made.

As the night wore into morning he threw out opinions and confidences, gleaned, he said, from less discreet colleagues at the Legation. The Pope is about to speak out. There has been a vision of Our Lady at Munich; thousands are flocking to her. There is panic among the Nazis. How will they hold Bavaria? His gossip filtered through the room like smoke.

'But you,' he said to Schrödinger, '*you* can imagine how much I enjoy myself here.' They were standing next to the kitchen, where some of the actors were laughing as they drank the rough red wine. Ashman glanced at the prints on the wall with cool disdain. 'Charming. Madame's a great friend of Israel, as you must have noticed. But England has become so tediously pagan. It is so relaxing here. There's a wonderful *innocence* about it, don't you think? The green paint thick over Victoria's crown. Adding definite Gaelic articles to our vulgar imprecision. *An Bus. An Post.* Paint and Articles, sounds like an affair between a dauber and a barrister. A pity the place is so undecided. It doesn't know what it is. Whatever one can say about Britain, and really I have nothing good to say about it, but I mean come *on*. Home rule's a lovely thing, but to try so hard to cut oneself off *altogether* . . .' He spread his hands in a gesture of mild despair, an invitation to share what urbane men know. 'Keeping house in a minor state. How can it be enough?' Even in this room full of the smell of tobacco and alcohol, and of talk that no one would remember in the morning, Schrödinger resented the complicity that Ashman took for granted. Rumours clung to him, his entry into every clique, his keen ears, that bustling connectedness.

'I could not care less about all that,' Schrödinger said quickly. 'All I wish is to be allowed to work; to be left alone. I think the Irish want that too. In that we are alike. Is it so unreasonable? To be allowed to find your own reality, make your own mistakes? It is not their war;

they have no quarrel with anybody. Is that not so? They want to go their own way. The country is full of people telling each other that the country is unreal or provisional. I feel it myself sometimes, I admit, but if we don't believe it's even living how can it be expected to survive?'

Ashman's eyes widened. 'Of course, of course, but I'll be completely frank with you, I know the English were beastly here, but we did give something back. If I can put it this way, they had the *Book of Kells* and the Chalice of Armagh. We gave them Shakespeare and the Magna Carta.' He was tremendously pleased with this formula; he weaved in and out again, and seemed to Schrödinger to be dancing, almost hugging himself. And as the evening wore on he was everywhere in the room, switching from one group to another, never causing offence or strain.

After midnight he came back. Schrödinger was talking to a drunken poet about Hölderlin, and Ashman began to speak about Austria, as casually as if he were turning a page. He had travelled Central Europe, and when he described the journey it was as though he had walked the whole way with his feet pressing a pump that inflated his own ego. He had met chancellors and generals, princes and a prime minister 'who happened to know my work'. And now that he was both drunk and serious, the unstoppable charm looked machine-like. Schrödinger had a glimpse of oiled cogwheels engaging beneath the warm dazzle. Ashman's essays, signed and sent round by messenger the day after they first met, were plummy and moderate, splashed with mild colour and aching with self-importance. He was the central character in them all. Statesmen confided in him, the ambassador of good sense. He had his own omniscient dialect. 'In a century, I said to His Excellency, let us hope there will be no need of conversations like the one we have just had: nationalism and the Transylvanian question will be curious antiques. "For us, my friend," he said, and his hand went unconsciously to the little bust of Goethe he kept on his desk, "that may be too late."' Now Schrödinger heard him say, 'Austria had, so to speak, Musil and Schussnigg, the unreadable and the unspeakable; the Czechs had Hasek and Masaryk, the incomparable and impeccable.' He fans himself with this punning air, Schrödinger thought, it cools him down.

Without missing a beat Ashman slipped back into the character of the wag abroad. 'I forgot, I forgot. One of our visiting poets – you know the one I mean – produced this *jewel* of Faberish verse before he tottered onto the mailboat, the worse for ham and porter.' He planted himself with his right hand in his pocket, his other hand raised and limply notching a cigarette, and declaimed in a fluting variation of his own drawl:

'"Wicklow".

'It's called "Wicklow",' he said, dropping his voice and looking innocently round the party of which he was the centre again. Sinéad was trying not to laugh, her hand over her mouth.

> North the limestone, the High Kings,
> Tara and the slow brown river;
> South the wild men, the eternal rain,
> Raids from the hills and rumours of gold
> In the streams and abandoned workings.
> North the plain and the cattle fat in the grass,
> The shipyards and the smoke of mills,
> Sunk in trade and the jargon of trade,
> A language as hard as steel.
> A stranger holds the bridge.
> And south the unforgiving tribes, the hidden arms,
> The unphonetic spelling, a language dying of exposure:
> A tongue parched in a granite mouth.

'No dear lady, really, it's marvellous, don't you think? There's much more, but you should savour it at leisure.' Madame Cogley's mouth was closed and her round cheeks were trembling.

Sinéad brought Schrödinger a glass of wine, which he drank without tasting. 'Has he been trying to convert you? You're wasting your time,' she said to Ashman, 'he's more neutral than the rest of us put together.' Then Ashman was drawn to one side by the young writer and introduced to people who had just found their way up the stairs.

Schrödinger asked Sinéad: 'Who was that nasty-looking little man in the pub just now, talking to your friend?'

'He's not someone you'd want to know. That anyone would want to know, if they could avoid it. He can get things, smuggles them across the border. Butter and meat from here, other things from up there. He's around quite a lot. He's supposed to be involved in some way, up north.'

He had a vague idea what she meant, but let it go by. Time passed, worse wine was poured. Conversation became effortless and flowing, one dialogue merging with another without apparent rudeness or interruption. He heard Ashman talking to Sinéad, with an urgency and edge that seemed to have slipped out from under his character, about small victories in East Africa, a force from every corner of the Empire, their differences sunk, men from England, India, Kenya and Nyasaland, all marching on Asmara.

The boy who had warned off Schrödinger laughed and pulled on a cigarette. 'A famous victory all right. I hear the camels they ride on die like flies. The road stinks from their carcasses.'

'My dear boy,' cried Ashman, 'is a few thousand camels too much to pay? The Eyeties gassed the blacks like rats. Still, I'm sure we'll protect your nostrils, for which I've the highest regard, as best we can.'

'I suppose they rape nuns too. Well, it's all a filthy business. The only safe thing is to believe none of it.' The boy took another angry draw on his cigarette and brushed past Ashman to the kitchen. Schrödinger wondered how he could have played the comic tramp so well. Ashman shook his lowered head and chuckled, the joke too private to share.

'Killing,' he said to no one in particular. Several others had overheard the exchange, and it chilled the fun. The room seemed quieter. It occurred to Schrödinger that perhaps even this was a stage whisper, a calculated indiscretion. Ashman sensed the change of mood; he raised his head and laid his hand on Schrödinger's arm.

'I do apologise, my dear fellow, it's the drink, the drink talking. You listen so well. And I shouldn't listen to the BBC, propaganda is so depressing. Well, I'm off to the country before my dear wife turns into a horse. O'Cogley! *Chère Madame, je dois partir.*' He flew into a round of kisses and goodbyes, eyes widened, every leave-taking a wash of admiration and flattery.

'It's not a good time for abstainers, is it?' said Schrödinger to Sinéad, as they watched the Englishman finally turn and leave.

'I don't think total abstinence is a good idea, do you?' she said. Her parted lips and frank eyes, a little bloodshot now, startled him. He wanted to touch her deep-black hair, but she touched his hand first, her fingers slowly brushing the hairs on the back of it. He realised that we are young in our hair as nowhere else, and his own felt like dry straw. A force seemed to be lifting their bodies, pushing them gently towards each other. He was intensely aware of her skin under the white linen shirt, and it was she who suggested that they leave.

It was the way the letter was phrased that made it so effective – the eagerness, the pathetic appeal to the elegance of European style, the commercial jargon. It can do no harm, Schrödinger thought, the man is reduced to near-begging. Later he admitted to himself that he thought he might get a bargain. Now, the day after the party, he asked Miss Nesbit to ring the man at the Dawson Street number on the letterhead to cancel the meeting, but there had been no reply. Suddenly it was the afternoon, and the appointment clogged up the hours ahead. He wanted to go home, but he waited, unable to work, lazy with memories of her, and swallowing water to ease his awful thirst. The dead in Belfast, hundreds blown up, thousands homeless. A mile of houses burning. The fire engines going north, that must have been the sound of the motors she had heard. He thought of the viaduct over the estuary at Malahide, as wide as a human body is long, the way they would come from the North, train after train bearing down on it. The machines suspended over the sea for a few moments on that narrow artery. But even this meant nothing to him now; he was light-headed with happiness, and the only shadow on it was his duty to return to Clontarf that evening, to the house with its cold silences.

Miss Nesbit rapped quietly on his door and glanced around it without looking in. She opened it wider, and a tall, broad-shouldered man took small steps, as though hesitantly easing into the room. He had an apologetic smile on his face, which was bold with weather and exercise. Whatever was submissive about him could not be sustained; as he came forward he bullied the air behind him.

Schrödinger had been expecting someone small and vulnerable, a dapper traveller down on his luck, not this man with the build of a sergeant major. His greying blond hair was brushed forward over the left temple, falling into his eye, and he had a moustache clipped neatly just above his lips. The nose was strong, the ears prominent and graspable. Schrödinger was struck by his washed-out grey eyes. They looked at him now without a trace of the deference that his body acted out, the slightly servile bowing, the awkward putting down of his leather bag as he took the seat to which Schrödinger pointed. It is ridiculous, he thought, surely it is not him. I am seeing things. It had been dark and foggy, and with his eyes as they were he could not be sure. And last night's alcohol was poisoning him. He felt sweat on his forehead and on his back.

'You are so kind, I can hardly believe that you have responded with such generous promptness to a countryman. And on such a tragic day. One feels so helpless. And you must be very busy. I will try not to take more than a moment of your time, Professor. And may I say what an honour it is to meet you?'

'Thank you, that is gracious of you. But I'm a little pressed today, unforeseen calls on my time . . . If you don't mind – you mentioned that you had shoes you wished to show me?'

And Goltz talked shoes, in an accent that wavered from south to north, but never quite the hard, flat High German his name implied. He opened his bag and took out two heavy green cardboard boxes, from which he removed a woman's court shoe in black and a man's brown Oxford, both solid, smoothly grained, the stitching close and perfect, the leather flawless with a dull rich shine. He described them with an offhand admiration, as though they were so good he did not need to sell them. 'Each pair handmade from a single piece of leather, all too rare, look at the craftsmanship, the stitching, the best cut of hide. You see, I'm lumbered with the stock and have no way of selling them. What is a man to do, walk from door to door? I am not a gypsy peddler. Besides, would they take kindly to a foreigner wandering about? It is not a propitious time, though good shoes are so hard to find here now. I need a shop front, capital, I am seeking backing.' He must have seen the closed look on Schröding-er's face because he said, 'Don't misunderstand me, from more orthodox capitalist sources, not my customers, but if you could mention me, if I can make so bold, to the distinguished gentlemen with whom you come in contact, whenever that might be appropriate, I would be grateful, most grateful, and who knows where it might lead? Would you like to try these on, may I ask?'

The shoes Schrödinger was wearing, lace-up low boots, looked scuffed and worn, poor in comparison to the dense glow of the new shoes. Good shoes were hard to find, and there was something in the man's performance that was irresistible, but it was like being seduced into mischief by an older boy who you felt could turn on you and beat you up. And so he rose from behind the desk and undid his shoes and slipped the new pair on, cool and heavy gloves soft around his feet. They fitted well; their flexibility was erotic, the sliding of skin on skin. 'And how do you find the colour?' 'It is fine.' Goltz pressed his fingers into the toecaps and asked him to take a few steps. He stood back, looking critically down. 'Yes, a good fit.' He said, without a trace of his earlier obsequious manner, 'As a small token of my gratitude, I would like you to have these shoes. Consider it a gesture of self-interest, if you like.'

'I couldn't possibly,' Schrödinger said, and Goltz insisted lazily, and Schrödinger stood there in his new shoes. 'What size shoe does your wife take?' the salesman asked. 'Six,' said Schrödinger, thinking of Hilde. 'I think these are a six and a half,' said Goltz, 'but in a small fitting. They might be suitable for her. If she likes them we can settle later. There is no obligation. You can change them if necessary. I have more in this style.' Schrödinger bent down to unlace the shoes but felt awkward and thought better of it, conscious that he would feel strangely weak in his stockinged feet, his hangover much worse now.

As Goltz packed the women's shoes away in tissue paper he talked about longing for home. 'I miss the mountains,' he said, 'the snow, wine. The language. Simple things.'

'Yes, there are things I miss too,' said Schrödinger. 'Including the mountain air and the wine.' He realised that the other man had not said where he was from.

'Ah, the wine, for you of course the clean sharp wine of Styria.'
'I do not miss the Styrian wine so much.' What did he mean by it,

this arch reference to the place Schrödinger could not think of without feeling dishonoured? You weren't there, he told him silently, what do you know?

'But there is something of the national character in what we drink,' the salesman went on. 'Don't you feel this? I don't understand how here they can drink this liquid tar of theirs by the litre. But home, yes, we long for what we can't have and we are not happy when we get it, and home is not where we think it is. So much has changed. And in the world, good Lord. Old empires fall in a matter of weeks. Weeks! Days even! Who'd have dreamed?' He went on talking, an easy patter. While he spoke he was very carefully repacking the shoes. There was something unsettling about him: his sheer size, the pale eyes, but he was so fluent and easy, and the set of his face and the slow movements of his powerful hands intimated that the voice would stop when it was good and ready. Yet the resemblance was uncanny. Perhaps, Schrödinger told himself, your head is getting bad for faces. If you had to bear witness against him for a crime, would you trust your memory and your eyes?

'What I really miss so much are my trips to Copenhagen,' Goltz declared. 'It was our head office actually, do you know the city? Beautiful. It has the right values. Clean, orderly. A city of culture, and as I understand it of science.' Schrödinger felt an odd prickle of disquiet, but at that moment the salesman finished and stood up straight with his neatly packaged box, a string tied around it to make a carrying loop.

'It is hard, here. I am not a success, like you, even in my lowly field. Indeed everything I've touched seems to have gone not quite right.' He said this with a kind of detached dignity, looking coolly round the room. 'The law, which I tried long ago, my marriage, my business ventures, though I fought well in the last war. I kept my nerve. Perhaps a man like me needs wars. You fought on the Italian front. Yes, one hears these things, you are a public man.'

Schrödinger shook his head. 'It was a violent waste. A scandal. Have you travelled much of the country since you have been here?' He meant it as a reassertion of his authority, a banal conversational switch, as though to ask do you like the scenery, have you seen the Lakes of Killarney, rowed on Lough Corrib? But it came out flat and nervous and interrogative. He felt he had to keep the conversation moving in shallow channels, since he dared not find the words yet that would end this unmanageable scene.

'Oh yes, I have travelled a good deal,' said Goltz, smiling broadly. His teeth looked white and even, unfeasibly so in a man his age. Schrödinger glimpsed for a horrible moment discoloured teeth in the same mouth, on a dark evening, a flickering of perception. I need to sleep, he told himself. 'I walk as much as I can, since it saves money and one sees more of the country that way. I move around at night, I am less busy then, but it's as though I'm not there, I seem not to be noticed very much, have you ever had that feeling here? The stranger who does not exist.'

He presented the shoebox formally, dangling from the string in his powerful hand. Schrödinger took it, and Goltz stood with his hands on his hips, a little too close now for comfort, appraising the man who held his gift suspended awkwardly by his side. 'They are a strange people in that way. They know, but don't see, and suddenly something happens that makes them see what has been under their noses all the time. It is in their character. This deep hiding. They hide from themselves, from each other. They look through what they decide they don't want to notice. It can lead you to believe that you're invisible,' he said, looking thoughtfully at his bag. 'It's the great Irish art, hiding in plain sight. Like their terrible Michael Collins, cycling around Dublin in a suit and tie when he was the most wanted man in the country. You live in a country of magical cyclists and you think that you have become like them. But what if all of a sudden they had to acknowledge what they see, to *know* it? To name it? A different situation, different results. One may live the way one wants for so long and then – boom! – one is an open book. And books, they ban so many for just a little word. If it were discovered that you were – as a book, I mean, excuse the clumsy metaphor – a whole collection of obscene verbs, where would you be? One in general, I mean, not you. A strange race. Yes, if you become too visible here you are finished. Nothing can protect you.'

Schrödinger was sweating freely now. The intimations danced and pricked, their slyness unrelenting. There was an unhappy energy about the man that made it more soul-destroying to be with him the longer he was in the room. Schrödinger thought, I wanted to be charitable to him, and this is what happens, though he could not define clearly what was wrong.

'You appear to know a good deal about the discretion of the Irish. They are hypocritical, they avoid scenes. There are worse ways of living, don't you think?'

'Yes, but there is something about the way they *stage* their willingness to look away! You are a theatre lover, are you not? I have heard of your support for young actors. And one question I have always wanted to ask. Forgive me for outstaying my time. You are famous for your cat. The cat sits in a closed cage of some sort, a device leaks a radioactive atom into the cage where a counter clicks and triggers a hammer, is that not so? and the hammer smashes a phial of prussic acid, or does not, because it might not after all leak, is that right? I remember the device, I must admit, it is so ingenious, so humane in its way, but I do not quite grasp the point of it.'

Theatre lover. Young actors. The innocuous phrases settling in him, but he was still too bewildered to respond. He answered the question in an effort to control himself. 'Some of my old friends prefer a blurred version of reality. I found it absurd that their philosophy would have the cat smeared out, neither alive nor dead, in an uncertain state until an observer opened the cage to look at him. It is as if they would have the cat defined by two waves interfering with each other, for the probability that he is alive is no more certain than that he is dead. Both states seem to cling to him. But the states of being alive and of being dead are different from each other, whether we are observing them or not. Real things are as they are, independent of our consciousness. This is no longer a fashionable view, however. Now if you'll excuse me, I have another meeting.' He turned, and laid the box on his desk. He wondered if he should hand it back, with some cutting phrase, but then he would have to remove the shoes that he was wearing, there might be a degrading scene, the porter would have to be called. He would return both pairs to the man's office tomorrow.

The salesman did not move except to lower his arms, which seemed to compact his bulk and to draw him even closer. 'I am so fascinated by this, please forgive me for detaining you. I will be gone in a moment. One last question. It is very powerful, is it not, this new science? We can change the elements, gain access to new energies, release powers inside the atom. I understand none of it. It is said that every grain of sand on a beach could be used for murder. Is that so?'

'In theory. The power of a machine that could harness such energies would be incalculable, even if it were possible, which I sincerely hope it is not. There would be immense problems – how to contain the energy, the calculation of the mass at which the enormous electrical fields in the nucleus could be captured and released, terrible instabilities. But one shouldn't even think about such monstrosities. There are limits beyond which the mind shouldn't go.'

'How interesting. How interesting though, now I think of it, that you chose a *cat*. Why not a dog?' When he saw Schrödinger shrug dismissively he smiled. 'An instinctive choice? Well. But no one healthy likes cats, you know. It's a dislike in every culture, ingrained, inherited. They insinuate themselves around us, sidle up to us, slink away, steal and exploit whatever they can, give nothing back. At night they indulge their bloodlust in secret massacres of birds. They are parasites, smarmy and elegant, but dangerous. They can't form real relationships with men, and they're incapable of bearing burdens. They have a grip on the weak, I would say, the lonely, the senile, women without children, who pamper them. They hold themselves apart. Even their physiology is sinister. All their teeth stab. They walk with their claws tucked in; their claws can't be traced in their footprints. Unproductive killers who leave no clues. Other animals are different – the bull, the horse, even the dog: potency, honour. Hunting and war. Loyalty, and the saliva that cures. No cat ever, like a dog, stood over its master dying in the snow. In New York before the last war they drowned a hundred thousand of them during the polio epidemic because they were thought to carry the disease, which I'm sure they did. They carry all kinds of diseases. And nobody missed them. So, your cat sits there waiting, mewling and whining as it waits for the gas to enter its lungs.' He paused. 'It only goes to show.'

His voice had become assertive, his stare bolder and harder. Who are you? Schrödinger wanted to ask, with as much arrogance as he could muster. He heard his own voice before he spoke, shrill and uncontrolled, and knew he could not face down this great strange thug. But *theatre lover*, surely he had heard right. The anger rose without thought, the words ripped out before he had articulated them to himself: 'Damn this, if you think you can come in here, making remarks, how dare you? Do you think I can be so easily imposed upon? This cheap stunt. Your innuendo is wasted on me. Take your shoes and leave!'

Goltz picked up his leather case and thrust out his hand and for an instant Schrödinger flinched and was back on a fog-drenched evening imagining the impact of a fist on his unprotected stomach, but he could not prevent the reflex of courtesy. The grip of the man's hand on his was light but hard, the touch of a vice before it closes. The German waved his hat in a tight arc and was outside the door before Schrödinger could say another word. The shoebox lay on the desk, a matt-green solid cube.

Later, as he drank sweet tea at his desk, fighting with nausea, he had a vision of that face with its empty eyes and jug ears hovering at the window three floors up, looking through a crack in the cheap curtains into the third-floor room of the old house on the street just off the Green. She had started a wood fire and they had clung together, standing in the cold, kissing and saying little. He was at last able to lift and stroke fine strands of her dark hair. She pressed her mouth to his neck. The fire scorched the backs of his legs when they sank onto the thin carpet. She said, 'I have never done anything like this before; nothing like it.' He said that he had never loved anyone like her, and meant it from the bottom of his heart. Her calm eagerness overcame her shyness. He had one prophylactic in his wallet and in his fumbling urgency, the drink making him clumsy, he worried in the moment he entered her that it was not positioned well. Their bodies became warm, helpless animals in a pocket of warm air at the top of an old rundown building. But now he had to live with this trickster and his veiled threats observing in thought their defenceless bodies. The pub, the company, the kiss. The jealous boys. An absence of discretion so extreme it made him feel faint at his own stupidity.

When he came to again they were in the narrow bed, and his head was thick and painful, his body dried out by alcohol, but it did not matter. He eased himself away from her and stood up. The room was cold. He could see the geyser over the metal bath, which had a hinged wooden board across it, the gas meter, her narrow table and two wooden chairs. Four shelves were filled with books on economics, the history of Dublin, plays and poetry. More books lay on the floor near the bed; one was a large volume open on a page showing lines drawn through a map of the city and around the bay. He felt a slither of silk on his bare leg, moving and curving around it. He looked down. The thin dark cat made a crying sound. It leaped onto the bed and sat on Sinéad's naked back. She turned, her fists pressed into her eyes. 'That red stuff was paint stripper, I knew it.' She picked up the animal and wrapped the sheet around herself, stroking the creature's back tenderly, her hair falling onto it so that the two glossy coats of black hair intermingled. '*God save all here, except the cat.* That's what they say in the west, according to my mother. But this is a nice cat. God save me, more like. Did you hear engines in the night? I woke up and there were motors going in the distance. Then it went quiet again.'

'It has been very quiet. I don't want to go out.'

'You don't have to, but I do. Are you going to stand there all day in the cold like a saint waiting to be flogged?'

'Where is the toilet?'

'Out on the landing. And be careful: I share it with the girl downstairs. I'll have to hide you till she goes to work. Then I have to go. Remember I work around the corner, so be careful when you leave. And put something on. You're not in Vienna now.'

They met under Nelson's Pillar, and he was standing by the door in the plinth watching a couple pass through the turnstile when she strode across to him, her blue coat framing her so well. Her warm face dazzled him. She looked at him very seriously and he had to resist embracing her. In the last few weeks he had learned restraint.

His mood lifted, and the anger Hilde had left him with began to clear. Just before he left that morning she had said to him in her calm way, in a low voice so that their daughter could not hear: 'You think you can conjure up your theory for the whole universe. Even the Earth is a speck of dust, and we don't figure at all. But we come into contact and you think we are forever connected. Well we are, in a way, but you act as if we were lifeless particles, not human beings, and you don't know the effect you have. I read somewhere that one glass of water poured into the ocean has enough molecules in it to make it possible to find one of them in a glass you dip in the waves an ocean away. I have probably misunderstood it, but it happens with people, even if it doesn't with atoms. A faint memory of what something was like. Maybe it's explained by some great equation, but we're not that easily unmixed. Yes, you hurt me by what you do. I am discovering how it is possible to love someone and to dislike them very much at the same time, even to despise them.'

They were in the garden watching the knife grinder at work. He was a small man who stood his bicycle on a frame that folded down and lifted the wheels off the ground and kept the machine stable. A round grinding stone was mounted on the handlebars, connected by a belt to the back wheel. He sat in the saddle with a knife in his hand and began to pedal, holding the blade at an angle to the turning stone. Sparks flew off as the knife was passed across the spinning grinder. He stopped pedalling and let the bicycle wheels turn free as he tested the blade with his thumb. The knife looked freshly scored and the blade had a dull silver edge. Ruth watched, fascinated, just out of range of the sparks. The man dismounted and picked up a pair of shears. 'Can I cut the grass when they're sharp?' she called out to her parents standing side by side.

Waiting for one of the trams drawn up beyond the pillar to move forward, he glanced up and saw the word Copenhagen engraved in elegant letters on the pillar's base. Was that where Nelson lost his arm, or his eye? No better place to go half blind. Or was it where he put the glass to his bad eye? Making a virtue of not seeing clearly, another quantum specialty. Heisenberg nearly failed his doctorate because he knew so little about the resolving power of microscopes; seeing well never mattered to him. He and Bohr, the admirals of physics. He wondered how Bohr was coping; no doubt he would have some suitably quantum-jumping thoughts about invasion. In Denmark it had taken all of twelve hours. About occupation being complementary to self-determination, dictatorship to freedom, shame to dignity. Choose your qualities and see only them. You can't measure momentum and position with equal accuracy, or have your cake and eat it. He could hear Quinn: 'You can lose your arse when you find your elbow.' But that slow decent man doesn't deserve any jibes where he is now: yet Schrödinger, thinking this, still felt the anger rising at the dogma that had beaten him. But if it took half a day there, how long would it take to wipe this state without a proper name from the map? Six hours, an afternoon; perhaps the holy hour would be enough, a country erased in the time it takes to walk home from the pub.

Sinéad followed his eyes up the grooved channels of the high Doric column. 'It's a stake in our heart. I hate it; it ruins the view from the river, gives the city a dead centre when we could have made the north bank so great, this blind sailor lording it over us instead. We could have changed all this and we did nothing.' A dog cart drawn by a fine-looking horse rolled jauntily towards the bridge, a tram sliding behind it with an even whine up to the stop by the pillar.

They sat on the upper deck at the front of the tram. Riding towards home with her added a destructive thrill to the outing. Hilde might be waiting at a stop along the road, if she had been shopping, if her bicycle was broken, if she had been walking and was tired. And if she mounted to the upper deck – normally she would not, but if she did and had the child with her – no polite conversation could manage her shame, but he felt reckless and indifferent to consequences.

Sinéad talked quietly and compulsively about things he couldn't know. She told hi n that there were roads on the old maps called after things they once intended to build, roads never reclaimed from the sea, what they called wet lots. 'Owning a piece of the river: you could step into it, I suppose. Paddle in your property.'

'You might find more than you bargained for if you did,' he said, but he was thinking of something else. 'Nothing, I'm sorry,' he replied to her puzzled look.

As the tram glided under the railway bridge and the bay spread out to their right she tried to get him to imagine what had vanished without trace, to understand that in choosing to live here on the north shore he had taken on obscure responsibilities. 'We mark nothing,' she said; 'we just let it go: there isn't anything to say that the sea was where those streets are now, or that a disaster happened here. There was a small island near the mouth of the Tolka over there. They put a house on it in Cromwell's time, and people sick with the plague were rowed over and left to die. You could hear them crying out on the old coast road if the wind was from the south. Later the island was torn up and the stone dumped in the water to make the sea walls.'

'You're fascinated by loss,' he told her; 'you and Hamilton would have got on. I wonder if he used to walk out here.'

She shrugged her shoulders, dismissing the thought. 'It's always the same,' she said, 'things are not finished, or they're built at the wrong time or in the wrong place. There was a lead mine under the sea along there near those cold-water baths, but it went broke and it was flooded. Everything seems to fail and shift; the land on the edge of the sea drifts and changes and then the sea is covered over and no one remembers what the shore looked like. There's such energy here,' she said, 'and it's doing nothing. There's dreams of new houses, we imagine old slums being torn down, but none of it happens. The houses are never built, and even the books aren't written or ever published. Look at poor old Quinn. It all feels so heavy and sluggish. We're standing still while this goes on, wages frozen, nothing growing. It's as though we're weak from loss of blood. And after this war? More of this? You should have seen the future twenty years ago. There were such lovely maps, plans for wide boulevards, a grand square at the top of O'Connell Street, an opera house. For a while they thought they could make Dublin like Paris. But none of it will ever happen, no matter how much we talk.'

He glanced sideways at her face. Beyond her he could see the water surging against the promenade a few yards from the road. She was looking down, her eyes focused on the metal shelf under the front window of the tram. 'You're supposed to be irresponsible at your age. What makes you care about such things? Is your family as

172

passionate as you are?' It occurred to him then that he had never mentioned her parents before, recoiling from the thought of her talking about a father who might be younger than he was himself.

'They aren't passionate at all, not about how we live or where we're going. Not a bit. I have nothing to do with them, most of them, one of my brothers still comes to see me when he's up, but in secret. They wouldn't let me go on with school after the Intermediate, so after a year I applied for the Civil Service and got the job and left for Dublin. I stopped sending letters home after a while and they started to imagine I had something to be ashamed of. One year I wouldn't go down for Christmas. My father came to Dublin and demanded I come home and give up the job, and I said no. He wouldn't allow them to speak to me from then on. He's a hard man, very strict and stubborn. And now he does have something to be ashamed of, so he was right in the end.'

'It must be upsetting. I'm sorry.'

'Don't be sorry. I got over it. Think of the arguments I don't have to have, and I don't have to introduce you to my mother.'

The tram moved on, the clear note of its bell warning cyclists away from the rails. They passed the bottom of Castle Avenue, falling silent as they did so. He realised that she knew exactly where he lived. She looked straight ahead; the wooden bridge and the island came into sight, and she said nothing for what seemed like minutes. He had no idea how to break the silence. The lagoon was nearly empty and the mud was covered with small wading birds. She spoke at last, to his relief, but her voice was tight, with an edge of aggression.

'Danger over, I suppose.'

He hesitated, then said, 'Yes.'

After the stop at the bridge, the tram picked up speed and ran fast close to the edge of the water, not stopping for a good half-mile. The enormous windbreak of trees inside the walls of the estate shadowed the road. 'Now *this* would be the place, right at the arc of the bay, to put new houses. All this green out here when the poor live in filth. You could even have factories here.' She was speaking with an edge of provoking mockery.

'You want to turn my village into a Manchester. It's a very

peaceful place. It has the lowest death rate in Dublin, I have this on the best authority.'

'That's because no one here is really alive. And the island there – thousands of families come out to it every summer and there's nothing for them except the sand and water and a few ice creams. You could have concert halls and cinemas for them.'

'Maybe these poor people just want peace and quiet and to look at the sea, and to swim a little. And your amusements would drive out the birds.'

'I'm more interested in human beings. The birds would find somewhere else.'

'I'm not so sure,' he said.

'Talk to me for a change. You must be bored with hearing me rave on, and I love to hear you talk. I try to imagine Vienna and your life there. All that music and art, coffee shops where writers can work. I'll even believe what you tell me, at least for a while.'

'You can believe what I feel for you, you must know that I have never felt like this. This is like a miracle for me, to have found you here. I don't have to strain or pretend. I can be myself and we can speak clearly to each other. You've given me such energy. I can't begin to tell you how happy I am.'

'I trust you while you feel it, but how long will that be? Those women back there in that house' – and she jerked her head behind her as though pushing to clear some constriction in her neck – 'you thought you could be trusted then too.'

'We must be absolutely honest. Our truth to ourselves includes accepting that the world is ours so very briefly. Being in love, as we are, is the most powerful way of being fully part of it and astonished by it, and you are the most astonishing thing I have ever found in this world. Those women, as you call them, are my dear friends whatever happens. I know this is strange, even scandalous in Irish eyes, but I am loyal to them in my way and they knew the terms on which we started this journey together, and would not change them now.'

'I doubt that, somehow, I really do. Why should I last longer, a simple Irish girl?'

'Simple indeed. I know that I feel at one with the world through you, that's all. You must believe it.' He meant, if you believe me then it will be true; the impossibilities will come right.

'I will try to, so. But tell me about your family, I want to know.'

As the tram hummed, steady and undeviating, past Kilbarrack and across the narrow neck of land onto the head of Howth he talked to her, and kept talking as they slowly rounded the hill.

'Father ran a linoleum factory, I told you that; the less said about it the better. His real passion was the study of plants. He spent hours hunched over his microscope cutting open the lidded seed-pods of the low trailing potherbs that were his specialty and I was forbidden to disturb him. He was a vigorous man, he hiked in the Alps whenever he could, but what I remember of him is stillness and narrowness and caution; and he would never have made the mistakes I've made, never.

'I was girlish and blond, quite delicate, very spoiled. There's a photograph of me being held up by my grandfather, my hand resting on his head: an Infant of Prague carried by an old Joseph. I was frowning unblinkingly at the camera. I was told later that my mother, her sisters, the maids and the nurse were all behind the camera, trying to make me smile.'

Sinéad moved closer to him. 'It's always the same. The future genius. The hero. You know, I always thought those Greek boys in the plays were brought up like that. It's what made them such fools: too many adoring aunts. What was it like for you as a child, then?'

'They would have been happier if they'd been sent out to break their backs working the fields, no doubt. But we did live well. Our building was of pale stone studded with big blocks of red marble. The third-floor windows were flanked by two big naked atlases, who looked like well-fed thugs. I could see their shoulders below me as I looked out of our window on the top floor. The cathedral lay to the west and between me and the spire, really very close by, was the Hofburg, the streets coming right up to it, the centre of the Empire. What else do I remember? The elevator in our building had a black wrought-iron cage that clicked as it reached a floor, which I loved. My grandfather owned the building and I had two rooms of my own, each larger than any of the rooms in the house I live in now. I remember the light of that time, it seems that I'll never see that kind of light again, rooms glowing with stained- and well-cut glass. There was a purple glass lamp in the drawing room: lily-pads formed the base, and steel strands reached into the mouth of the bell, and ivory blooms hung from the stem. The rooms seemed to be full of those rich, festering colours; they used uranium pigments in the glass.'

'You really have come down in the world. Do you feel you've been banished here, is that how you think of it?'

'At first perhaps I did. But I don't think that now.' He had his arm around her, enjoying the motion of the tram and the softness and strength of her shoulders. 'Anyway, my father was absorbed in his seed-pods, but my mother was lost in her music, and I remember the sound of the piano as she played Chopin nocturnes and the adagio passages of Beethoven. I would drown in angry exclusion as she merged with the music, the mouth of the piano seemed to engulf her as she bent over it. She played the violin too, the fiddle tucked hard against her breast, I hated that, and I blamed it later for her illness. I've loathed most music all my life, even though my work is saturated in it. Waves have amplitude, frequency and pitch. Matter is like the nodes of a vibrating string, the points at which it vibrates and is most dense; and the way a string vibrates resembles how a wave moves, so that matter has different frequencies, tones and variations, as voices are distinct and unforgettably individual. I seem to find the variations of ordinary music too banal. Real music can't be heard, the waves of energy that move deep within reality, these sound tones are the kitsch of the world by comparison.'

'*Let no such man be trusted,*' Sinéad said.

'You see? I can't talk about Mozart. That Vienna means nothing to me. I remember all the wrong things. But back then I was the centre of the world and I was given whatever I needed, tutors in Greek, Latin, mathematics. I found I could manipulate numbers and symbols. I could understand the relationship of shapes, recall solutions to geometric and algebraic problems and sense how they could be extended. I began really to see when I learned how to solve differential equations and felt I was looking deep inside the world and visualising how it moved, the inexorable increments of motion brought to life. Following through bleak assumptions about nature that at first seem unreal. And then the equations of electricity and magnetism, equations of such enormous power, a vision of energy unified and unfolding in space and time. The equations spoke more forcefully than the evidence of the senses, and yet you could visualise the world they formed, and everything in that world connected to everything else. It was like a bicycle, that sounds crazy, but the bicycle is an image of the unity of the world, of interacting flows of energy. That world that was so good to me is gone, except here of course. A city full of silent bicycles where nothing is ever decided.'

At the East Pier in Howth they got down to wait for the tram that would take them to the summit of the hill. Small trawlers were moored at the pier, their nets piled on deck, and open boats lay on their keels in the mud at the back of the harbour. Grey-and-white gulls floated over the little quay and the lighthouse, making their unself-pitying cries. There was a biting wind from the east.

They walked to the end of the pier while they waited, sheltering from the wind under the lighthouse. A few hundred yards offshore a tiny island rose from a narrow beach to a high slope thick with green ferns. A trawler was under way, moving against the swell through the narrow gap between the granite piers. The sea outside was full of dark waves, and the boat looked stubby and awkward against the restless assault as it passed the harbour wall. They were close enough to look down at the grey curls of the man at the helm, the nets ready in the bow and a tin bucket hanging on a rope from the wheelhouse.

'What happened to them, your parents I mean? What was it like after the war?'

'It all fell apart. We had lived so well, but I came back from the war and the blockade went on and on, and it was like a tap being turned off very slowly over the face of someone dying of thirst. First the light itself went. The gaslights that my father had kept in our apartment because he liked their mild aura became weaker and weaker and were lit for fewer hours every week. They did at least soften my parents' faces, which had become thin and lined like the faces of the very poor. My mother was in constant pain. She refused to visit the doctor and when she did of course it was quite far gone. She had pressed that violin against her breast for so long: I'm sure it made the cancer worse. Then fuel for the stove and the oven ran out. The gas ration was cut again and again and we would sit in the dark

177

at night, around candles on a low table. I tried to read; I think I was reading Schopenhauer. Overcoming the urgent demands of the flesh and the will. I didn't have much choice that winter.' But it was very like happiness, he thought, that freezing winter, writing page after page on the analogy between mechanics and optics: to have the glimmer of a form that might capture all the states of a physical thing, even a thing as ugly as the quantum.

She batted him with her gloved hand. 'You've been making up for lost time.' She said this with a kind of affectionate derision, yet he knew she meant it as a defensive blow, warding off the consequences of her recklessness. I must try to protect her against me, he thought, resolving sincerely that he would measure up to her.

'I think I damaged my sight that year. And cooking food on so little gas is difficult, as you well know, and the food was not there to cook. We didn't have beer or butter, bacon and bread, as we do here now. There was some horsemeat in tiny amounts; I suspect it was the carcasses of the beasts that were dying at the front. The potatoes were often half black. Shrivelled dry beans. We had a powdered-vegetable gruel that had a smell like vomit when hot water was poured over it.

'And even after the army surrendered, the blockade went on. It was the most relentless, self-righteous punishment. The streets filled up with soldiers in dirty uniforms wearing medals, swinging on crutches, or just sitting staring at nothing. They had walked from Carniola, from Trieste and the Isonzo. They told stories of the Italians shelling them as they moved towards the passes in huge processions. It was said the Italians would soon be in Vienna, but no one cared by then, as long as they brought food with them. My mother, even when she was very ill, walked for miles out to farms where she knew the people. She used to wear two coats and swap one of them for eggs or meat, and she'd take a few rings or brooches for barter.

'Then the Emperor went, just like that, the old man's son who'd only been there for a moment. One morning I walked to the university and the centre of the city was just a collection of museums and palaces. The statues were there – I wonder if you know what I mean, perhaps it was the same here twenty years ago – alone in the squares of which they were once the centre, but suddenly a duke on a stone horse had no more meaning than a tedious old book about a forgotten campaign. By then we were eating at soup kitchens, waiting with the ones who had always been poor in long lines outside school halls. The soup was always grey and scummed with oil, cooked too long, full of onions and turnips.

'The strange thing is that my mother survived, for a time. It was my father who was destroyed. He couldn't climb the stairs to our apartment without great effort, and his lungs burned, he kept saying that no breath would come. This was a man who had loved walking in the Alps. The elevator sat in its gilded cage between floors, where it had stopped one day. I was barely thirty, but the climb was tiring for me too, because we all had so little energy. He had nosebleeds, there was blood even in his eyes, and his legs became swollen. By the end of the winter the cold was so horrible that bodies shut down. He lost control of himself one day on his way home, "an urgent call of nature", as he put it, at the door of the building when he was almost safe. He was terribly humiliated. After that he refused to go out and stayed sitting or dozing in the apartment in the cold and darkness. He had a choking fit one night and we called a doctor. "I have looked into the valley of death," he whispered up to me later that day. He was just lying there, looking emaciated, his face wasted, his eyes wide and staring, his voice hoarse. He said it as though he were confiding a secret, something he had been tempted by and pulled back from at the last moment.

'I was earning two hundred crowns a month. We needed twice that to survive. The government stock my father owned was printed on heavy expensive paper, like huge banknotes, watermarked with eagles and signed by committees of important councillors. Now the paper itself was worth more than the money it promised, like the plenary indulgences my neighbour buys, not cashable anywhere on earth. On Christmas Eve my father was sitting in his leather chair with a book on his lap and a candle on the table beside him. I was by the window making notes and fell asleep, and when I woke it occurred to me that he had been silent for a long time. His sleeping head was resting against the wing back of his chair. He had stopped breathing without a sound of regret loud enough to wake me. I sold his books and microscopes, his plant specimens, the silk rugs, his suits – it paid for his funeral and my mother's doctor's bills. You have no idea how stable and orderly and refined his life had been, how careful he was. War comes into a life and turns it to shit. I can almost feel it lurking on the seaward side of that little island there, under those cliffs where I'm sure no one ever looks.'

'Don't,' she said. 'I don't want to think about that. I'm so sorry about your father. It must have been dreadful. What did you do after he died?'

'I had to work,' he said, and turned with her out of the wind and back under the shelter of the wall. In the village on the hill above the harbour nothing moved except the smoke from the chimneys of the small houses. 'I was married by then. I took one job after another and resigned if another post offered a few marks more, or seemed to promise more interesting people doing physics. The first job disappeared when the Empire vanished; the town became Romanian. No room for strangers after that. Then I went to Jena, which was miserable. I moved to Stuttgart where the pay was better and everything else worse. The inflation meant that twelve thousand marks there were worth less than two thousand six months before. My mother was weakening again, and came to stay with us, but it was awful, the coal fog, the sulphur in the air, the smoke trapped under the clouds. After a few days, her coughing sounded as though a liquid were choking her. Anny took her back to Vienna and she died soon after we moved to Breslau, where they made me a professor, but the value of money shrank as it expanded in volume. You had to spend it the morning you were paid, turn it into a few pieces of meat or cheese. The miners went on strike and marched through the streets under red flags. The police had armoured cars. There was shooting at night, people were killed. We were close to the Polish border, too close for me. You could feel the Russians coming towards us across the plains. Then my mother died, and I heard about a post in Zurich. All this in a year, more or less.'

'Did you grow tired of moving?' She asked this calmly, though he could hear some great significance in what she was asking.

'Yes, very. It was unutterably wearying. And I want to be here now, certainly as long as this war lasts. I never again want to be swallowed up by people who think blood is a cure for sickness. You are here too, which is very important to me.'

She lifted her face and touched her lips to his, brushing her hand along his lapel. He clutched at her and held her. 'But you look out to sea,' she said, as his head rested on hers, 'like someone expecting something terrible. It is the most helpless place you could think of to be, isn't it?'

'The country is more water than land, that's what makes it so beautiful. But it's the only place I can imagine being now. And it is safer here than anywhere I have been for years, as long as they leave us alone.'

'But Zurich, you felt safe there, surely?'

'Very safe. I felt we had passed through a high fence and back in time, into a world like the one before the war. The cleanliness was dazzling. The wooden parts of the houses always looked as though they had been painted that morning. We had a house on the heights, looking down on the river and lake. You could see the white mass of the Eiger if you walked a little way up the hill. We ate veal again, as though it was the most normal thing in the world. We had friends. That time was the start of our friendship, Anny and I, and the end of our marriage. She fell in love with a good man. I think he could relax with her, he liked her warmth and decency. She could go with him to the opera, which I could never bear. Those damn plaintive vibrations propagating in the air so self-importantly.'

'And you had a lover too,' she murmured into his neck; he could feel her lips on his throat, and the tension of jealousy and desire animating the surface of his skin. The urge to know, to see what should not be seen; he could feel her need to be told.

'Yes,' he said, in a voice as low as hers. 'Everyone was unfaithful; the air made everything thin and inconsequential and took the sting out of every hurt. It was the war, partly, everyone wanted to live. That winter my lungs became very bad. A doctor thought it might be tuberculosis, so I went to the mountains for a cure. From the veranda of my room there was a view of nothing but great folds of white rock. I was exhausted and depressed; I had been for most of that year, despite the pleasures of Switzerland. I realised then how alone I was. My parents were gone, my marriage breaking down, it had not yet become something else. My death would barely have been noticed. I was an artist who had failed the test of his twenties, with no beautiful utterance to my name that would force the minds of other young men to think through it and humble those older than me. A bad poet and a mediocre physicist are much the same. I was wrapped up in blankets and staring at the gigantic, crumpled surface of the earth, and I thought people have been seeing this, like me, for thousands of years and I am part of that perception and I will live on in that, but it is still for all that unrepeatable for me. I thought I must find the thing I need, the mountains don't give a damn, just for a moment to speak in a language that will outlast me.'

She held him and kissed him with a lingering solicitude that made him giddy. When she released his lips from hers she seemed to shake herself, and looked over to the island. 'It looks so quiet, doesn't it?' She held her face up to him again, her eyes open and at ease, with a look almost like trust. 'I should not be here.'

He held her against him. Later he would think of this moment as his last chance, and he held her tighter and said, 'There is nowhere else you should be.' He felt insatiable desire for the part of her that still resisted him, needed the kick of her intelligent doubt, while longing for her to merge with him. To have said, yes, you were right, I am too old, we should not be doing this, would have diminished his obsession to a piece of sordid dishonesty, a bitter mistake. And less than consciously he thought, if you stay I have a chance, a chance to find that state again, and remembered sitting on the glassed-over heated balcony looking up at the snow and then not looking at all as he wrote at the little table with pearls in his ears to shut out the sound of glasses clinking, of waiters bringing coffee and apple cake to skiers and convalescents, the background chatter. It was suddenly there, the whole numbers of quantum theory arising from an equation for a wave, forming as though in a continuously propagating thing, a miraculous entry of probability into an unfolding curve, a ripple that is also a grain. It was like watching a breaker about to foam and vanish on the beach and being able to give it an identity and a name. When he removed the pearls his ears were full of the hushed noises of the hotel, as though he'd never heard such sounds before.

When they turned back they saw a magnificent tram rolling sedately down the hill, and cruising to a stop near the pier, its varnished mahogany livery so highly polished that it gleamed. The windows were tall and elegant, in delicate frames; the brass lamps were burnished and shining. It brought a glow of lacquer and wealth into the cold salt air, like the bridge of a tycoon's yacht.

Inside they sat upstairs on a slatted bench. The tram moved slowly back up the village street and out onto the hill. Through the large windows, in the sunshine, they saw the green ferns and the yellow flowers of the gorse on the slopes, with the water glittering across the bay. In the foreground, the Bull Island looked flat, barren and white. As the tram climbed along the viaduct below the summit they felt it sway slightly, as though thrown off the iron steadiness of its momentum. They were aware of the cliffs plunging away, and the waves breaking below them. White birds circled the lighthouse on its long promontory. Another place for a last stand, he thought, these coasts are full of them.

At the terminus they got down and drank a glass of warm beer in an empty, silent bar. They left quickly and walked up to the summit; they had time before the tram looped around again. At the top they had a view of the whole bay in clear light. Below them the long headland stepped down to a narrow rocky outcrop and a stack shaped like a rounded fist on which the lighthouse stood. Thick gorse and scrub covered the slope. The sea crinkled in pale gold, the waves barely marring the surface. A three-masted schooner under full sail was making for the river mouth across the bay.

They went into the undergrowth, until they were waist-deep among the ferns. After a few yards they saw below them a gun emplacement camouflaged with stalks of fern strung through a net, the gun itself painted in patterns of grass and hay. A soldier stood near it with a rifle and a long bayonet. Her fingers played inside his hand. 'Do you think you'd dare?' He looked at her, astonished. 'But I haven't any . . .' 'I have,' she said, her face turning a warm pink. She handed him a prophylactic, laying it on his palm carefully with two fingers and a look of modest triumph on her face. They sank onto the dry grass and tore at each other, pulling their coats aside.

*

The hall was full. There were students, but also journalists and a scattering of priests, and men in well-worn suits who greeted each other with immense pleasure. Browne was sitting in the front row with a theologian from Maynooth. O'Hogan sat at the back, his head sunk on his chest, and Quinn came in, taking a seat in the same row. Reese sat at the centre of the table facing the audience with Schrödinger to one side of him. He had the narrowest shoulders of any man Schrödinger had ever seen, and he sat in silence with his hands resting limply on his knees. The table between them was empty.

On the way in from Clontarf, Reese had said almost nothing, walking quickly with his head bent and a slight smile on his face. Schrödinger made an effort to register for him the existence of the places they passed, but the Englishman stepped doggedly forward, uttering low polite sounds. The walk became a mute slog, with Schrödinger feeling embarrassment press in, not for the first time with Reese, a liquid closing up around them as they moved through it. In the silence after they crossed the Tolka onto the North Strand Road Reese said: 'The fine-structure constant is very important, you know.' And so as they walked past the entrances to cul-de-sacs of low houses under the railway they talked about a dimensionless quantity, the numbers that define the strength of gravity and the force that holds the particles together.

The night before, Anny and Hilde had flattered and attended to their guest. The impassive face attempted a smile as though under a terrible compulsion to remember his manners. He seemed to have forgotten how to speak. He said, at last, like a formula he was trying out, 'Your village is charming. In Cambridge we miss the sea.' He did not elaborate, but he did thank Anny for the food. He ate slowly and carefully, sipping on a glass of wine which he did not finish.

He had asked that morning after he arrived if he might bathe. Schrödinger explained about the shortage of gas and that it would be best to wait until night fell and the water in the boiler was hot from the fire. Reese murmured, 'I mean in the sea.'

They walked down to the front road with rolled-up towels under their arms. A palm tree leaned close to the outer wall of the baths. The concrete terrace of the pool was rough under their bare feet.

The attendant who admitted them was the only other person there on a bright and windy day that did not make cold seawater inviting. Reese undressed with the same blank remoteness that cloaked everything he did. He stood naked in his cubicle with the wooden door open, looking at his feet, his hands by his side. His body was pale, without a trace of muscular development. Schrödinger, who had changed quickly, thought Reese had forgotten why they had come, or that he was about to emerge as a gaunt nudist, and kept an eye out for the attendant, but the man had disappeared into some shelter out of the wind. Reese at last removed from his towel a pair of loose trunks, which he put on with great care, tying them with a draw-string. They hung shapelessly on him. Schrödinger walked with him to the edge of the pool, which was the sea fenced off by a low wall from the choppy waters of the bay. He removed his glasses and laid them on the ground near the rim of the pool. Without them the day was full of shadows and fog. Over the mountains to the south hung a dark mass of cloud, all a blur to him. He jumped and the salt water shocked him with a jolt of freezing cold. He splashed and shouted, flailing for a moment, then plunged outward, arm over arm in a fast crawl.

As he turned at the edge he saw Reese lower his thin body slowly into the water. No gasp came from him. Once immersed he began a prim breaststroke, his arms close to his sides and his hands dabbing fussily at the water. After many slow lengths he lifted himself out. Schrödinger followed him, his body feeling warm and strong as rain started to fall on the roof of the changing rooms and stippled the water. The waves that he and Reese had made reflected back off the sides of the pool and interfered with the waves still coming on, so that their crests and troughs seemed stationary, their ripples dancing in place. Reese, wearing his spectacles now, and still in his trunks, appeared before him. 'I think I shall walk to the house to dress, Schrödinger, since it is raining.' He turned back to his cubicle and as Schrödinger pulled on his trousers he saw Reese drape his suit and shirt over his arm, and his towel over the clothes. He held his shoes in his right hand. Pulling on his shirt and closing a few buttons, Schrödinger picked up his shoes and glasses and followed the skinny figure through the turnstile. The rain came down now in heavy freezing sheets. Reese's almost naked body had turned very white. The two men crossed the road together and turned up the quiet street. Schrödinger saw a curtain in one of the bungalows move; some neighbour seeing an almost-naked Englishman walking past her gate. They lowered their heads to the rain until they reached the top of the road and turned left under the trees. When they came into the house, Reese rubbed his feet on the mat inside the door and walked upstairs, while Anny stared after him from the hallway.

Now Reese stood up to speak, his arms by his sides. In a nerveless low monotone that the audience had to strain to hear and in the accent of the English upper class he spoke without notes, in a voice uninterested in persuasion. His lips barely moved. Schrödinger could sense the deep, fascinated hostility of the audience, and he remembered a remark that Flaherty had made about the English one morning. 'Hypocrites, look at the way they treat the Burmese and the Indians, they've locked up Nehru and they lord it over the coloureds. Never trust a word they say.' He found himself trying to defend Reese as that affectless voice and all it stood for murmured on.

He said that he wished to describe briefly and without mathematical elaboration the results of certain cosmological speculations. He wished to stress the importance of relating the constants of nature to each other. He asked them to consider the quantity that we use to measure the strength of the electromagnetic interaction. It unites certain irreducible physical circumstances – the speed of light, the electronic charge, and the constant of energy. That quantity simplifies them to a still more fundamental relationship. It is the fine-structure constant. In numerical terms the relationship may be expressed as 1/137. 'And let us not forget', he said, 'the ratio between the masses of the proton and electron, the very stuff of matter. Here the number to bear in mind is 1836. Meanwhile, the force of gravity, compared to the electromagnetic force between the electron and proton, is 10 to the power of 40 times weaker, so very subtle. And there is what may be called the cosmical number, the number of protons in the universe, which Reese believed to be 10 to the power of 80. There is an inner harmony between these ratios and numbers that has less to do with the observation of nature than with the relationships between the numbers themselves. The most elementary particle we observe is inseparable from the entire universe; the equation we use to describe it must hold good on a cosmic scale. And we seek,' he said tonelessly, 'in the numbers that our minds impel us to find most beautiful, a general expression that will unite all the forces and all the constants of nature.'

He mentioned an equation that linked the fine-structure constant and the permutations of numbers and directions that made up our four dimensions of space and time, and that the solution to the equation gave a similar number to the ratio between the masses of the proton and electron, or 1836.

The large numbers were also linked. He urged them to notice that the cosmical number was very nearly the square of the ratio between the gravitational and electromagnetic forces. And he predicted that the age of the universe would be shown to be around 10 to the power of 40 times the time light took to travel across a proton. And that the size of our universe would be of the same order of magnitude.

'These are surely not, ladies and gentlemen and reverend fathers, mere coincidences. These numbers are not mere facts of nature, but the defining characteristic of the universe: they enter into the laws of nature. The numbers may be deduced from each other. The speed of light, the quantum of energy, the charge on the electron, and the ratios between the atomic particles, the gravitational constant and the cosmical number: these are notes that vibrate in the cold emptiness of the space that surrounds us and in the darkness of our minds. Their combinations give the world its defining tonal centres, they are the true music of thought. They are a universal scale.

'The real world is the world that God has established in the harmony of fundamental numbers. There is no other. We do not require more than knowledge of these figures of thought to reach a profound apprehension of the world that has been given to us, that moves according to harmonies that are themselves the product of a Mind. It opens to us, however dimly, the rational process that is the thought of the Creator. Through the numbers, God speaks.'

The audience shifted and coughed after Reese sat down. Then there was a hesitant clapping, which swelled into a brief round of applause. The Maynooth theologian's hands made no sound, and he stared at his shoes as he said something sidelong to Browne.

It was not until he had been standing for a few moments that O'Hogan made any impression on Schrödinger, who had called for questions. There was a fixed smile on his face, a lopsided sneer made more angry by his beard and moist eyes. His tie was askew under a red cardigan and dark suit. Once he had caught Schrödinger's eye he began to speak. 'Listening to our distinguished speaker has been an uplifting experience. To think that we know how God thinks now, and all from a few numbers.' If the listeners had been awkward when Reese stopped speaking they were profoundly silent now. 'I would like to suggest if I may that there are other numbers, in their way equally profound, numbers that inhere in a people, in history. There are patterns there too.' Schrödinger gulped water from a glass and tried to clear his throat. His nervous 'I think' was drowned out by O'Hogan, who raised his voice almost to a shout. 'You see there are waves in nature, we're already familiar with our esteemed colleague Professor Schrödinger's waves of matter, but also in history. The energy of a nation comes in peaks and troughs. It is uncanny, how regular it is.' He belched, and swayed as though about to keel over, but did not stop speaking. 'I'd argue that it has to do with human generations, the energy of youth. I could show you this over the whole course of our history, but we haven't got the time.'

Schrödinger took his chance and said in a loud bland voice, 'Indeed, that is unfortunately true, and our guests would I am sure welcome the chance to join the Professor for some refreshments in the common room,' but O'Hogan was too massive and belligerent to be deflected by embarrassment. 'Take the nineteenth century alone, you have the rising of ninety-eight and a generation later, exactly twenty-five years in fact, the Catholic Association is founded to fight for Catholic Emancipation. And the Young Irelanders rise up in eighteen forty-eight in the midst of the worst disaster ever to strike our people. Then the Fenians hardening our character, warriors and poets, and then you have the revival of the language in the early nineties, a generation after the Fenians seemed to have been crushed. The Celtic and national idea comes into the world again. The rope is cast anew. And the next generation discovered what to do with it in nineteen sixteen. History is cumulative. The energies superimpose themselves on each other. And now there is the uncanny coincidence, which I cannot think is really a mere coincidence, that this is the twenty-fifth anniversary of that miracle. I think history is unlikely to have gone to sleep. The page will be turned. Twenty-five. There's your *historical* number.' O'Hogan sat down heavily, waving his hand in a gesture that could have been self-deprecating or derisive, or that of a drowning man.

Schrödinger noticed someone turn to look at O'Hogan. Duff. His teeth bared as he turned back and smiled at the speaker's table, but his face was pale with anger. The lecture ended in a round of mannered thanks. Reese sat expressionless, as though nothing had happened or could ever happen to disturb his tranquillity, yet Schrödinger still felt the need to apologise: 'It was such a dreadful outburst, the man is not well.' All Reese said was, 'His remark was irrelevant. He was not speaking of physics.'

At the reception Browne engaged Reese and Schrödinger about the closed nature of the universe and what it would mean if the equations indicated that the cosmos was expanding, and suggesting that neither outcome would preclude the ineffable creativity of a divinity. 'Perhaps both solutions are true in the mind of God; the ambiguity in our calculations, our groping among the pure numbers, is his way of reminding us that we are fallible.' Reese and Browne talked quietly to one side. Browne could make the dead speak, Schrödinger thought as he left them, watching the priest work his man.

Duff's presence was jarring, though Schrödinger noticed other high officials here, and diplomats from the legations. Duff was talking to a small, indignant-looking Italian. The handsome press officer from the German Legation talked to the wife of a minister. Ashman charmed the Papal Nuncio while Ashman's chief, a huge man in a chalk-striped suit as full as a mainsail, condescended to a Pole.

Duff came over, a glass of green cordial in his hand. 'And you have settled down comfortably? I am so pleased. A lovely area. And your wife is well? That is marvellous. And Mrs March, how is she finding Dublin? Delightful. I am so pleased. Our Department is always ready to help if there is anything we can do. Yes. Well, Professor, it has been a pleasure meeting you again, what difficult times we live in, those poor souls above in Belfast.' Quinn appeared from behind him, signalling to Schrödinger and avoiding Duff's eye, and Duff's smile vanished. He turned to safer ground, barely nodding to Quinn.

Quinn looked dishevelled, his white shirt greying and his shoes dry and worn. The whiskey on his breath masked the faint smell of unwashed skin that rose from him. His deterioration was frightening, and Schrödinger felt embarrassed and guilty for feeling it. 'You don't look at all well. What on earth is wrong?'

'That blackguard and his like want to ruin me.' Quinn spoke in a furious mutter. 'I've had a visit from the police, for God's sake. I've been blacklisted from the radio. No one has told me, of course, but they never ring me or write to me any more. No more little talks on poetry. I'm not neutral enough to discuss a sonnet. I haven't slept a good night's sleep in weeks. It's not fear, nothing like that. You know what fear is, I could not imagine being threatened by the secret police.'

'Neither could I,' said Schrödinger, so low that he was talking to himself, and Quinn did not seem to catch it.

'What gets me is the way you come to loathe yourself for your inability to find an audience. It's their calmness, their silence. I try to prick them and they don't bleed, they pretend not to notice. They turn their heavy smiling faces to me in the bar of Buswell's Hotel if I dare go in there and shake my hand warmly, their eyes lazy, how are you now Dan? and out the door they go, their big dark coats keeping out the cold. They mime ignorance the better not to see because they know in advance what's worth knowing. They only have to look at the form of a sentence and it no longer has any meaning for them. They don't read what they know will disagree with them, but for all that they don't like the thought of you writing it. There's an image in their heads of the likes of me sitting at a table writing, and it's as though they can hear the scratching sound of the pen on the page, and that very faint sound from far away annoys them. And for that they have ears you wouldn't believe. You've no idea how touchy they are underneath their thick skin. Our young friend's article on the slums in the current issue did not go down well, thank God they don't know who she is, her pen name seems to have worked. They've banned another novel, a book about nuns, this time because of a single sentence that reveals the heroine's father was a queer, and we'd have been banned too if we hinted what the sentence said.'

'But why are you letting it enrage you so much? It is no worse now than before. You are making yourself ill.'

'Don't I know it? But it is worse. I'm a ghost in my own country. My income is drying up. I'm waking at four in the morning full of rage at men I know, men I was at school with and in the IRA with twenty years ago, who've never written an honest sentence that is not sneering or derogatory or second-hand. They have the vocabulary they need and that's all they want. Was it for this the wild geese spread? Who fears to speak? No man can set the boundary. Mindful of the dead generations.' Quinn's face was contorted with nausea, tasting rotten food in his mouth. 'Their memoranda to each other are real works of art, all scorn and brutality for the eyes of three or four like-minded souls, destroying lives, and after that the dark, into the files. Pious in public and salty and venomous in there where their real energy is. I'll go home tonight and I'll wake again, my head dry and heavy, with a raging thirst, and I'll want to kill them. I'm not joking. You can see them here, look at them, they're beginning to be sure which way the wind is blowing, quiet little adjustments here and there. That's why they're so furious with your old hack tonight. Never say what you're thinking. The two lads who came to see me were polite, you'd tell us sir now if there were any loose talk, it's important that we don't publish anything that would give any outside power the excuse. Oh quite, I said. As if I've ever written anything about the Emergency except in language so coded I forgot what I was trying to say myself.'

'Do not get so upset, I really implore you,' Schrödinger said. 'This is the way you have to live until it is over. We all have to grin and keep our noses clean, and stay out of what does not concern us. This is easy for me; the political is torture to me, a complete distraction from what matters. But don't allow them to devour you like this. I can't believe that her little article on the poor and your comments on censorship have brought you to such a state.'

'It's not only that.' Quinn looked around the room, which was full of enemies staring urbanely past each other, His Majesty's representative stopping to light a cigarette to cover the awkward closeness of Mussolini's, and their hosts smiling warmly at them all. The air was full of smoke. He wished he could open a window, as Quinn's voice sank to a hoarse whisper, for the room seemed too close to contain the mass of his depression. Schrödinger could see that Browne was steering Reese towards him, his face mild and untroubled. Quinn went on quickly, 'I broke my own rules, all the rules. I saw something I should not have seen. Somebody slipped me a few sheets of paper I could barely read.' Schrödinger raised his eyebrows, but Quinn looked down and shook his head, then gestured with it to the side. 'Do you know what "duff" is? It's the fuel you burn when you are really hard up, when even turf is a luxury. Dust and pitch moulded together. It has the foulest smell. It's horribly smoky and gives very little heat. That man has a lump of it in his chest.' Quinn turned away, brushing against Reese's arm as the cosmologist said, 'I had hoped we might leave now, Schrödinger. I am very tired.'

Waiting for Reese to say a stilted goodbye to Browne, he looked around the room full of warring gentlemen in dark suits. The Taoiseach had not come tonight. As he thought about his last conversation with him, his oracular turns, his careful admissions of weakness, Schrödinger had a clear image, as in an enlarged photograph, of men behind the leader deep in the shadows, vague shapes in the apparently empty air of a darkened room. Their indistinct pressure disturbed Schrödinger's image of the man. If the picture were developed differently these ghostly figures behind him might come into the foreground, changing the picture in an instant. Safety is dependent on a breath, he thought, a trick of the light. Reese came up again and they walked out onto Stephen's Green, where the dark garden was shut behind its heavy iron railings. The two men trudged in silence towards the river and home.

At first he was sure that the sound that woke him came from deep underground. It seemed like a pulse that shuddered and broke against the brick and wood of the house. But when he came awake, alone in the double bed, it was already fading and the source of the shock seemed to have been further off and on the surface, a merging series of heavy crushing blows. He could not have said where the centre of the impact lay. The wind was playing its usual tricks, and though it was twenty-five years since he had heard that form of disturbance in the air, the sudden drastic change in pressure, he was certain this morning that he was not mistaking one kind of sound for another. He sat hunched over in the bed, feeling cold despite the pyjamas he had taken to wearing, and his body felt thin and unprotected. The stuff of the room was so thin, the cheap plaster walls and hollow bricks. A swung pickaxe would break through the walls of these houses. Only the deepest shelter survives. Perhaps it was out at sea again, but this seemed close, somewhere around the curve of the bay. He turned to find his glasses and when he put them on he noticed the ripples in the glass of water by his bed. I am so tired, he complained to himself, please not this. Sirens began to howl, rising and falling.

He heard a door opening. It was like the opening of adjacent cupboards, the rooms were so close. He pulled the handle of his own door and saw Hilde on the landing in a dark nightdress, tall and upright, her face white and serious. 'Jesus Christ,' she said, 'there is no hiding place.' He stared at her thinking: she is right, and searched for a reassuring phrase, but she shouted, 'There is no cellar!' Her whole body was alert. He stood confused and tongue-tied as she walked into the room they had recently shared and pulled a shirt and a woollen sweater out of the wardrobe and drew them on, and then a heavy coat. She found her walking boots and pulled and crossed the laces, and hampered by her sudden bulk she stepped across to the child's room, from which there was still no sound. She looked shapeless in her motley dress and he realised that it takes seconds to make a refugee ugly; and he was conscious as he dressed of his own matted hair, his unshaven face, his pyjama legs inside his trousers. A cardigan hung loosely around him under his coat. Anny was up too, rubbing her eyes and moving hesitantly. The sirens went on wailing. Hilde said, 'They may come back, there may be more. We are so close to the docks.' Anny reached out to her and they embraced each other. 'We should go down to the island,' Anny said over her shoulder, 'there are no houses there beyond the bridge. Hilde is right. Just in case.' She reached out to him too. He took her hand

and put his left arm around Hilde's shoulders, and though she did not shrink from his touch she hardly yielded to it, her body seeming to say: we can stand together, but no more. The three of them stood on the dark landing like that for a few moments, uttering wordless reassurances to each other. Then they broke apart, Hilde going into the child's room making high-pitched reassuring noises, and the other two downstairs, gathering blankets and food.

They walked along the front road in the dark in a pale, watery mist that veiled the trees and houses. The city on the other side of the channel had vanished. Ruth was excited with the notion of an adventure outing to the beach. 'Will we hear the bombs when they fall?' she asked. 'Can I have new clothes if one hits our house?' Nothing moved on the still, dark water as they crossed the wooden bridge, but they heard the curlews crying further out on the mud. On the strand they could hear the grass on the dunes rustling in the breeze and waves breaking softly at the edge of the mist. The tide seemed to be withdrawing. The wind blew sand streams along the beach that eddied and vanished ahead of them.

They turned after a mile and walked into the dunes, where it was silent and sheltered from the wind. The marram grass was tangled and bushy, and they laid down the sleeping bags and blankets they had brought with them on a level patch of moss. Schrödinger lay on his back, his hands under his head. He noticed a trickle of fine sand falling from the hollow lee side of a nearby dune, and closed his eyes.

He woke again in the pale dawn light. The others were still sleeping. He felt stiff and chilled, and needed badly to urinate. He climbed out of his bag and walked into a small valley between the dunes, where it was perfectly still. Their surfaces were covered with a mat of short grass and moss, on which tiny white and lavender flowers bloomed. He walked up the slope of a high dune, feeling his calf muscles work in the deep sand. The landscape of pale-grey dust folded and repeated itself in subtle variations as far as he could see, though he knew he was less than a mile from the bridge. He came to the top and looked down the steep inner slope, a soft grey cliff, out over a marsh in which there was a stand of low alder trees. A family of hares cropped the short grass at the edge of the marsh. They ignored him when he unbuttoned his flies and pissed off the top of the dune, his urine arcing and making a wide dark stream on the fine sand, puddling for yards at the base of the slope. He felt like a rebellious boy. It may be all right after all, he thought. The world felt so clean again. As he buttoned up he caught a face looking at him, a grinning owl face with long ears on the branch of an alder tree, brown and immobile. He could swear its face changed in the uncertain light. 'What are you laughing at?' he called out in English, and turned back to rejoin the others.

As he walked around a dune he saw a small, elderly man crouching in the grass, facing the marsh. He had a pair of binoculars around his neck and a large notebook lay on the sand beside him. At Schrödinger's approach he rose timidly and bade him good morning. His look of bewilderment was endearing enough to make Schrödinger slow down and return the man's greeting gently.

'There's a bit too much excitement this awful morning,' said the man, caressing his binoculars with one hand. 'For the birds, I mean. They've gone to ground.'

'I'm sorry to hear it. So have I, in a manner of speaking, but I'm sure they will come back.'

The other man looked alarmed by this flippant speech and nodded solemnly. To ease his embarrassment Schrödinger tried to flatter him. 'You must be one of the naturalists who preserve this island for the birds. An admirable thing. Are you out here a great deal?'

'Every day, since my retirement, unless the weather is too cold,' and the old man's face lit up. 'I have the touch of rheumatism.' He spoke earnestly, explaining a regrettable weakness. 'But if I can, I come down and observe and I draw as well. You see some great species, people don't know the half of the species that visit the island.'

'I'm sure they don't. Well, let us hope we see no more of the savage new bird that passed through this morning.'

The birdwatcher looked nervous again, as though Schrödinger were threatening to hit him. He held up the thick notebook in an appeasing gesture. 'I try to record as much as I can. It's important, you know, to have an accurate record of sightings.' He opened the book and Schrödinger took a horrified step backwards, then saw that it was not a tiny bird carcass embedded into the cavity cut into the pages but something dull and jagged. Around it the sides of the open page were covered with neat lists of dates and names on the left, and to the right with crayon sketches of black waders standing in a pool of blue water. The old man flicked the pages. On some he had drawn the flat sand stretching off to the horizon, covered in minute birdlike forms, or the granite headland of Howth rising up in dark green and black. Images of single birds – a miniature kingfisher in ice-blue and russet – were surrounded by careful notes. The drawings were spare and competent. He noticed Schrödinger staring at the wound in the centre of the book.

'You'll be wondering about the bit of metal. That was an accident to begin with. I found it on the beach, stuck in a plank of timber. It's from a bomb all right, my nephew told me. It must have slipped into the notebook when I moved some things at home, and then I put the notebook under a pile of heavy books. I collect bird books, you see.' Schrödinger wondered if he ever read any other kind. 'It was sharper than I thought and dug into the pages, and there it was, I thought of throwing the book out but I sort of made room for it. It reminds me of what's going on, if you see what I mean. It's a bit of a diary as well. I find it gets things off the chest.'

The page the man was holding up listed, in his minute script, the names of ships. Schrödinger felt a spasm of helpless pity for this observer who could make only lists and notes of what he'd honestly seen. Beside each name was written the date of the ship's sinking in the Irish Sea. He wondered if the man would record the bombers too, if they came more often, and he thought of Flaherty and his trains. 'That is very – impressive,' he said quietly. 'I hope you have better mornings here. There was an owl just now, on a tree back in the marsh.'

The man beamed, his glee serious and childlike. 'I've heard there's a long-eared owl passing through. That's a rare sight.'

Schrödinger walked on, thinking of delicate coloured sketches worked around shrapnel, and found his family in the lee of the dunes. They were all awake now. They picked up their bedclothes and walked down to the beach, from which the tide had drawn all the way out. Other families were walking on the shoreline, looking across the flat wet sand to the harbour and the city. Beyond the north wall, the buildings looked tranquil and unchanged, the spires intact, the cranes and chimneys still standing.

When they returned to the house his exhausted lucidity would not allow him further sleep. They breakfasted listening to the wireless and he went outside again. The road was completely quiet. A figure moved away from behind Flaherty's glazed front door. He felt a desperate need to see Sinéad, and knew he could not because it was a Saturday morning and she would have to work. He was overcome by anxiety for her. He opened the garage and wheeled his bicycle out, pushing and mounting without conscious admission to himself of his need to see where it had happened. Cyclists were strung out along the front road, and he passed three young women talking and laughing in line abreast as they pedalled towards town. The light was clear and mild now. The palms had lost their dreary winter look, and for a moment seemed gay and sunlit, part of a warmer climate.

As he rode under the railway bridge he smelled smoke; another hundred yards and he seemed to be cycling through a dust in which there was a heavy, bitter odour of burnt timber, of minerals and rubber. From the bridge over the Tolka he saw the men in workers' clothes walking along East Wall Road towards the docks, and further on at the humpbacked bridge over the canal he had to stop at a small silent crowd standing at a barrier manned by Guards. He left his bike against a wall and eased through the crowd until he could stand at the side of the bridge and see past it. The roadway with its thick grooved tramlines ran on ahead into an area of blackened, broken walls, piles of brick and splintered wood. Between the roadway and the canal the small low houses had disappeared or were turned to wreckage. Here and there tables, legs of chairs and pieces of white porcelain stuck out, clean things that had become dirty with a sudden thickness of grime. One house looked like a torn cardboard box with its lid ripped down and the contents emptied. Others had been eaten by something that reduced their forms to a grey, rotten dust. He imagined the instant between explosion and propagation when the houses, which were such tiny buildings, still stood and retained their form. Then shape and structure vanished in the release of energy, the shock wave travelling through them. The sound would have spent itself over the river and the bay after the dead were already lying in the ruins, and reached his ears as it did so.

Soldiers wearing heavy gloves, their faces filthy, moved slowly through the rubble, lifting and setting carefully aside fragments of ruined furniture and clothes. Men in long black coats stood on the edge of the rubble field, their hats in their hands. They looked trapped, waiting as though a burst pipe had blocked a street that they wished to cross. An army officer was pointing upwards for their benefit and spreading his arms wide, describing the pattern of the explosion. Schrödinger could see that by some fluke most of the kinetic energy of the blast had travelled one way, and the houses on the far side of the road were nearly untouched. Is this it, he thought, the end of waiting? War is the surprise we feel that shelter has ever been allowed to exist. He longed to hear her voice. He felt how quickly it could end – how delicate and perfectly organised she was, how close to not being there at all.

Someone said, to no one in particular, 'How many?' 'No one knows,' said a man behind the first speaker, so that they seemed to have arrived together and were continuing a conversation they had started as they walked along the street. 'Hundreds it must be, there isn't a house left standing.' 'Who was it?' Schrödinger turned to look at the strangers talking. The first man said: 'No one knows that either. No one's got a clue. And they'll say no one did it.'

On Monday night as he rode home, cycling around by Ballybough and the old road, and after a dreamlike day at the Institute in which people had exchanged fragments of information in low, almost tender voices, giving each other estimates of the dead, he saw the railway bridge at the Howth Road outlined against a low sky, and long grey clouds full of smoke from the air driven west across Europe, drawing up by convection the particles of ash from burning houses and factories, water drops forming around the dust and now ready to fall. Yet the upper part of the Presbyterian church by the bridge was flooded with summer evening light, leaving the body of the chapel in shadow. As he passed it the light seemed to turn itself into fine particles of water, and the air became wet and chilled. The rain came down seconds later in a vast drench of cold water.

He had fallen asleep at his desk late that afternoon and woken with a start, unable to see the door of his room properly because his glasses had slipped off. He had dreamed of his spectacles disassembling themselves, a screw reversing on its thread, and then the delicate organism of wires and lenses and fine steel cracking and disintegrating, the facets of the lenses visible to the naked eye falling to a stone floor and being crunched underfoot. He stared down at the desk-top and could not read what he had written half an hour before. He picked up the spectacles, feeling intense relief that they had not broken. He felt that his room was tainted now. The menace of that weird visit remained, despite the silence in the weeks that followed. He had walked down Dawson Street a few days later with the boxes in his hands and rung the bell at the address on the company letterhead. The rooms at the top of the building were empty; they had been vacant for months, the woman who answered the door told him. She took him up and showed him a disconnected phone sitting on a desk in a bare room. Perhaps I scared him off, he thought; he may have taken my anger for confidence.

O'Hogan came in soon afterwards and gave him the latest casualty figures, thirty or so, one whole family wiped out, all seven of them while they slept. 'The German Legation has put out a statement that there were none of their planes in the vicinity. I wouldn't be surprised if it was the other crowd wanting us to think it was the Germans.' But he said this with a lack of conviction that was dismaying, and spoke like a man reciting a creed whose words he could no longer believe. He had been quiet since the night of the reception for Reese, avoiding Schrödinger unless he had to see him, and when he did he was almost submissive and helpful. 'God help us,' he said now, 'we had a few years' peace before this started, that's all. There is nothing we can do.'

Part Three

Summer 1941

Since the late spring, the Flahertys had seemed more restless, their unhappiness less contained. The son came home later and later; when he wheeled into the road, tea time had been and gone. Schrödinger saw him awkwardly dismounting one evening as he opened his own door to go out. Some devotion or other, he could not keep count of them, had just ended at the parish church, and neighbours were passing quietly along the road as Flaherty wobbled up and snatched at the brakes and tried to stabilise it with his feet, but too late, so that the bicycle fell under him and he staggered clear, grabbing at the oblong hedge that fringed his mother's garden. A branch tore off in a burst of small green leaves, leaving blood on Flaherty's hand. A parcel on his back carrier fell off and burst open, spilling clothes onto the pavement, what looked like dark folded shirts, and steel tools that struck the concrete with a dull ring. At that moment his mother opened her door and saw her neighbour watching. Her smile was bright and unseeing as she stepped back into her hallway while Flaherty picked up the disordered clothes and implements, laid them across the handlebars and wheeled his bike up the garden path, an untidy middle-aged man with clips around the cuffs of his trousers. And his lurch had other witnesses, who walked by with their prayer books in their hands and their eyes turned away.

Anny said that she felt the adjustment in the Flahertys' stock at the bakers as she queued for bread, which was much denser now, and lay heavily on the stomach, a sedative weight. The talk in the shops was always commiserating, ah how is Sean Flaherty, and is he better? Oh that's good, his poor mother has been through the wars, her husband going like that was a terrible shock, I do hope he's all right.

Flaherty was aware of it and kept his eyes averted when they met in the street, muttering 'Good day' but no longer stopping to scratch at the government and the world. Schrödinger wondered whether the man was not glad to be relieved of the burden of small talk. He felt this as a small, nagging loss. His neighbour's sadness had something formidable about it that would not let him alone, as though the man had to be appeased, and now Schrödinger had no way of doing so.

Since Easter he was often so late himself that no one on that road, with its regular hours, was about to see his return. But he knew that dark curtains were gently adjusted, a little more light escaping from cracks between fabric and window as he reached his gate after cycling from Sinéad's flat in the street near the green. He was aware that Mrs Flaherty was one of the silent observers who noted his odd movements: her shadow moved one night behind her bedroom window. His body's tired happiness on these warm nights allowed him not to care.

She came to the door one hot afternoon in early August when he was at home, lying aching and sweating on the sofa, the book he was reading revolting him because he could barely see it through watering eyes. He heard the brittle cheerfulness of her voice, enquiring after him, the words 'summer cold' and Anny responding in a tone of jaunty optimism. Then he heard Mrs Flaherty end a sentence in a higher, firmer voice: 'a grand cure'. He lay with an arm over his eyes to shut out the light, wanting the voices to stop and the house to be silent again so that he could be miserable and sleep. When the old woman's voice continued to insinuate itself through the wall next to his head, full of an exaggerated concern that he found almost mocking, he rolled upright and opened the living-room door without any conscious intention of doing so and found himself in the narrow corridor facing his wife and his neighbour, only then knowing that he could not slam the house door shut in her face. She smiled up at him. She was dressed in black, her grey head bare. Her hands, wrapped in a tea towel, held a white jug capped by a saucer, beneath which steam escaped. *It hides dread secret flames.* In his mild fever the line came to him, as though he had perfect recall of everything he had read forty years ago.

'Mrs Flaherty has brought you a drink to help your cold, Erwin.' Anny's voice encouraged him to play his part.

'It's only an old Clare remedy, Professor, but you know it always worked when I was a girl and I still give it to my boy whenever he has a bad dose. He's had some terrible colds this summer, sometimes he's unsteady on his feet, but he won't rest though I beg him to.' She said this confidingly, with a resigned sprightliness, as though this was a truth that Schrödinger already knew.

He found himself drawn into polite acquiescence. 'Yes, these unseasonable illnesses reduce us so much. I feel quite useless.' He could not take his eyes off the white china jar. Revenge on the ingrate guest: old women bearing gifts. 'How kind of you. I must thank my wife for telling you I was unwell,' and he looked at Anny.

'I *did* mention it, yes, but who'd have thought our neighbour would be so thoughtful?'

'Not at all, not at all. Well listen, I have a cup here.' Mrs Flaherty's left hand moved swiftly downwards inside what he saw was a black apron over her dress, and came up holding a blue-striped white cup. For an instant he was about to utter a brusque refusal, then controlled his temper as he found himself carried along on the current of politeness, and thought, why not? and even warmed to the poor woman as he stretched out his hand. She lifted the saucer covering the jug. The surface of the liquid looked white, hot and oily, and among the grease bubbles there floated specks of fine powder and silvery-grey skin. Wisps of steam rose from the jug. It must have been boiling when she left the house. She poured a measure into the cup and handed it to him. 'Better drink it down while it's hot.' He inhaled sour, savoury fumes. It was like a broth, but with a strange bilious sweetness in the smell. The cup was hot. He lifted it to his mouth and swallowed as much as he could get down, but the liquid filled his mouth and throat with a vile mixture of tart and sugary flavours, none of them letting each other be, a mad soup in which none of the ingredients fused with any other. His revulsion sent some of it into his nasal passages. He clamped his teeth shut and bit on a tiny piece of wood that released a dusty root taste, overpowering the milk and onions and sugar. Enough sugar to clog a pot of tea, he thought, and was grateful for the analgesic spiciness of the clove. But as he gagged he completed his swallow, his eyes watering: how much white pepper did she put into it? She has poisoned me.

'Finish it off now, it will do you good.' She raised the jug enticingly, as though for a refill. He moved backwards, shaking his head. 'No, really. I must let it work, I will drink the rest in the kitchen, thank you. I can see how it might well kill a cold. Thank you so much.' While Anny rounded out the ritual of parting he walked into the kitchen and shut the door, and drank a glass of water from the tap, then another. His throat burned with pepper. He poured the remainder of the cure down the sink; some onion skins and a clove lay on the plughole. She knows, or thinks she knows about me; she thinks that her son and I balance out, and as she sits in her darkened room with the curtains ajar before she goes to bed she thinks that I am worse than him.

If these were the folk remedies, he must not fall ill in Clare. Sinéad wanted to be alone with him, even for a few days, and he had escaped before on cycling trips to the west coast. But he knew that this journey would make the cold silence worse between him and Hilde. They seemed to be holding either end of a wet sheet which they could not fold or shake, and so they stood there, feeling it sag between them. Most of the time she ignored him, and if she did speak to him she was remote. When he said that he was going to walk for a weekend on the Burren, she said without looking at him from the cupboard where she was stacking linen, 'It is all so familiar. You behave like the Kaiser with his mistresses. We have to defer to your ungovernable needs. But they and we are all cooped up in this tiny bloody house where we can't even swing a cat, can't breathe without hearing each other. I hear you fart and piss. If you cough it comes through the wall. Your secrets are as threadbare as your old drawers, you stupid miserable genius. It's pathetic. All you are is a randy old man.'

The more contemptuous she became the more Anny grew back to him. Her kindness and tolerance seemed inexhaustible, and it was she who ate with him and sympathised with him over the Institute and O'Hogan. She even listened to his ecstatic admission that he had fallen in love, and did not laugh at him.

And Sinéad was with him all the time, her voice, the feel of her hair on his skin. When he was holding still with her in her narrow bed, he thought he knew at last the meaning of inseparability. She had changed; she was not as brittle or as quick to lash out as she had been at first. When he ran up the three flights of narrow stairs to her flat under the roof of the old building she would be waiting for him at the open door; in the beginning he had to knock and wait, but now she would throw her arms around him and cling to him, her body searching his with subtle movements while she looked into his eyes, smiling at him, saying nothing, fathoming something that she found worthwhile. He was exalted by her readiness to see the best that he could imagine of himself, and immune to the anger crushed out of rejection that was all Hilde had left for him.

The closeness he experienced with her felt enormous and joyful. It was there in the dingy room on a Sunday afternoon that was grey and cold down in the silent street. Her passion was overt, and she crouched over him in a private conversation with her body. She seemed to be discovering herself almost despite him. She was unabashed about her need, and even took care of what she called the precautions. She said, 'I don't want to leave it to you, you'll forget and come up short, and I won't be able to restrain myself even so.' He asked how she arranged it and she said, 'I told you there were people crossing the border all the time, some of them make a profit from it, with butter and eggs going up and other things coming down.'

'I'm a party to smuggling,' he said, laughing. 'A respectable teacher could be ruined. I'm a civil servant like you. I will be dismissed and arrested.'

'Only if you're caught using the goods. They'd have to be quick.'

'Seriously, is it risky for you?'

'No, no. The worst thing is having to deal with Eamon. He's the little creep who supplies the arty crowd. You saw him that night in the pub, after the play – when we first gave in to temptation.'

'Not that repellent little man?'

'Yes, him. I remember you making strange when you saw him. He has a finger in all kinds of pies. And he'd like to have his fingers in more, but he's such a runt he's easy to shake off. But I have to endure his ramblings about bringing the whole rotten set-up down. It's as if he's on the verge of something, maybe just his own craziness, but you'd swear he was the centre of it all. He goes on about the need to be hard, never wear the glove again, never again make the mistake of trusting them. He hints at a big change coming. I don't know what to make of him.'

'There is probably nothing to make of him. The times we're living in are made for men like him. I've seen them given their heads. I don't think that will happen here.'

'I hope not. Perhaps they just tolerate him, if he has anything to do with them at all. He belongs in a county home. But I'm sort of frightened of him as well, I have to admit. There's a mad light in his eyes when he talks about the Tan War, he lights up in ecstasy when he describes some great ambush, and even when he's talking about the terrible things the Free-Staters did in Kerry, men blown to smithereens, shot in bogs before they had made their confessions, he seems to get a thrill out of it. He leans in on you and won't stop talking, you know that kind of man?'

'I think I do.'

'There's never a gap, he never allows you a moment's silence, so you just sit there numb. The way he talks about the hard men is nearly like a lover, you know what I mean? There's a lilt in his voice when he describes so-and-so shooting a tommy in the head. Almost adoring something he can never be. Then he leans in and says "You're very beautiful, you are, did ya know that?" It's only when he's made a pass at me that he'll hand over the stuff. He's never dealt with a woman before. He daren't say anything too direct, but he thinks I'm a right hoor. He is so unhappy and twisted. I don't think he'd ever do anything dangerous himself, but you could imagine him egging on a weaker man to do something stupid.'

The thought of her consorting with this figure from the underworld, the two of them in some sordid pub, his hand sneaking towards hers, gave him a shock of disgusted jealousy. He remembered the grinning insult of the man's face and now this creature was brought even closer. He thought of Flaherty sleeping yards away, the houses crammed against each other, contagious and inseparable.

'I'll take care of it from now on,' he said. 'I should have done so anyway. I can ask a friend in England.'

But she said, with a bright confidence that he would remember later: 'Don't worry. I have enough. More than enough for now.' She folded herself around him, lying half on top of him, winding her arms through his.

As the weather grew hotter and the dust and smells of the city more intrusive, the sheer completion of what he was sure was their love made the routine of life at home bearable, but this feeling also took on a mass of its own when at first it had been so light and unbounded, and as it did so it shifted internally, testing the strength of his desire. It was still as perfect as it had ever been, and he was excited by her need for him, yet as the weeks went by he found himself wishing, as he had never done before, to lift her gently from where she lay on him, as if she was putting almost too much weight on his yearning heart. And he sometimes felt, at the moment when Sinéad reached for him as he came to the top of the dark stairwell and saw her books on the table, the worn carpet on the floor and the bed waiting, neatly turned down in the corner, a pang of regret as his notion of her fierce independence faded a little, like a transfer that has been peeled from a child's hand, losing its vivid colour when the ink dries. There were times when her happiness began to press on him, so that he felt she was almost too ready to listen to him without giving back the sting of resistance that he had found so exhilarating. He caught himself wondering if there was not something almost too restful about these long erotic afternoons in the little flat, and asked himself where her tougher self was hiding. It did not help that he sensed she wanted to tell him something and felt she couldn't. Once or twice she seemed to be bottling up speech, and he felt her second thoughts. These rare moments allowed him to imagine, almost as a remote, abstract possibility, how he might be impatient with her, and resent her making claims on him.

The work was no further advanced than it had been at the turn of the year. He covered pages with field equations that yielded nothing satisfactory or elegant. He had taken to reading, for relaxation, stray papers on genetics that he found in the Institute library. They were an escape from the crushing difficulty of making his field theory work, or at least taking a form that would please him. As he lay beside her on the last Sunday before they left for Clare, he heard the faint sound of children's screams from the Green a hundred yards away and wondered what it could be, this dumb will to grasp and eat and make love, which he was so unable to master as men of his age and stature should, what it could be reduced to and what made it so stable and tough, generation after generation, the same physical form so devious and persistent. He thought of a badly printed photograph in some paper he had read – an image of the dark bands on the fibre of a fly's chromosome – which might be the very image of the genes. But what gives this design such strength, what carries it so far through thousands of generations with so few monstrosities and errors and still allows for variation? Somewhere in the atomic distances inside the gene there is something unnebulous and hard, a few thousand-millionths of a metre long, a kind of molecule, the substance that lets this strange predictable thing endure yet leaves us open to change. And he felt a disappointment that he knew was shameful, that she had not inspired him more. He had done nothing real, and as the year unravelled he was speculating idly on a subject he knew nothing about, as far removed from the grand concert of the forces as he could get.

The summer heat made petty irritations worse. O'Hogan, the permanent shadow: as soon as he loomed in his doorway one morning in August he spoiled the sweet, contented mood in which Schrödinger had walked from her flat to his office. In the same moment that he saw O'Hogan he noticed that some papers he had left on the floor the previous evening were missing. The blood rushed to his head, and he suddenly felt merely tired. 'The cleaners have thrown out my notes,' he said loudly. 'Days of work swept up like rubbish. How often do I have to ask you to supervise them properly? Only paper in the waste basket should be thrown out. Is this really so complicated, may I ask?' And under his breath in German he snarled, 'A disgrace.' But O'Hogan heard him and with his hands clenched and a furious smile on his face hissed something in Irish that Schrödinger could not catch.

And Quinn helped least of all. The day Schrödinger saw him there was a lurking smell of decaying rubbish on the streets, and the memory of that weird shoe salesman or whatever he really was, the restless, shifty menace he embodied, was eating at him with a parasitic energy of its own. Quinn looked exhausted; his cheeks were drawn in and he had not shaved for days. His lack of sleep and food was so obvious that he looked incongruous in the low, prosperous light of the hotel bar, and he had a large whiskey in front of him, not his first, and talked uncontrollably.

'I've been ostracised, and that feels the way it's supposed to feel. My printer refuses to take any more work. He wants to be paid in advance when he used to give me credit for months. The bookshops are returning all their stock of the magazine. My floor has towers of copies with their edges brown from being on shelves in the sun.' He took a mouthful of whiskey. 'They've given me sick leave at the paper and told me not to come back until I'm well, so I'm going to a cottage in Wicklow that's three miles from the nearest pub. I'm not really here any more, in a way, your friends have seen to that, but now I'm not part of it, this staggering on having it both ways, I don't have the consolation of feeling that this is normal, worrying about turf and fags and soap from one day to the next. I've started seeing things. We've convinced ourselves that if we don't make a noise we'll be all right and avoid the worst. Hold still and no one will see us. But now I feel there is some muffled, dirty stuff going on, I can't define what it is. Little hints and shifts. Rumours of contacts and conversations. Feelers waving about in the dark and being stroked in return. We've started to move and it feels horrible, like we're about to tip over into a cesspit.' Quinn was hunched over his drink, his eyes locked on his friend's, but it was obvious that anyone sitting near him, any stranger, would have had to share his fever of disgust. He seemed to have taken all the anxiety he could absorb into himself, raw and undiluted, and to be possessed by it. 'We're whistling past a vicious dog who's not chained up. We don't know what we're dealing with, though we should. It happened here in Elizabeth's time, the people were already nothing to them, it was just a little step to kill them. That ash-grey head of hers staring out of her portraits, the face she turned on Munster. The lucky ones ate grass, some gave themselves up to be killed to stop the pain of hunger. Heads in sacks, bodies hanging thick as apples on the trees.' Quinn stared at Schrödinger, insomnia burning in eyes that had no amusement left.

Schrödinger resisted, allowing his impatience to show in his voice. 'You're making yourself ill about nothing. These are vague speculations, you don't have the slightest ground for feeling any of this. They're going further east every day, forgetting we exist. Snap out of it, for God's sake, you have friends, and this atmosphere of suspicion and rumour will pass, you shouldn't take it so seriously. Laugh at them, as you used to do.' He meant what he was saying, but a small leak formed around his own doubt as fast as he staunched it, and he was uncomfortably aware of how warm his feet felt in the handmade shoes he had not been able to resist wearing.

'Sorry,' Quinn said, 'I'm sorry.' He sat back, letting go of his drink for the first time. His eyes closed and he passed a hand over his face, which relaxed into the appearance of sleep for a few seconds. 'We are all going a little mad, I suppose. I know I am. I hear the worst in what little news we have. Maybe I'm seeing too much, though I'm really hearing things. But it's all because no one dares say what they really think. There's a fear of saying the wrong thing to the wrong person, flipping the coin and not getting the result you want. And you never know who's listening, I swear to God. Best to say nothing, the line of least resistance, and never show you're afraid.'

Because Quinn was drunk and so unguarded, Schrödinger felt that he had nothing to lose by asking the question, though he shrank from the answer. 'What was it you saw? The document you talked about.'

'I saw a copy of a paper I should not have seen, I've told you that.'

'Yes.'

'It was a minute, that's all I can tell you. A carbon of a carbon. From the Department of Justice to the Board of Works. What a biblical ring that has. Justice to Works. The good word made flesh. Well, this voice of justice spoke of certain contingencies. The author's name was blotted out, but it had the track of a certain hatchet. You'd recognise the voice behind the ink. But I'm not going to say more, I've said too much. You shouldn't know.'

But you told me it was Justice, Schrödinger thought; you have told me too much. 'Was it very faint, this copy that you saw?' The question formed before he was aware of it, and was spoken in an almost pleading tone that surprised him.

'So faint that letters on worn keys did not strike through. I had to recognise words by their first and last letters, like an archaeologist reading an old tomb. I had to hold it up to the light. At least a fourth carbon, I'd say. Though what it said was clear enough. And of course I can't do anything with it, and no one else will. But then a week after it showed up in the post in a brown-paper envelope, an invitation came from our friend. He met me in his office, which was cold as a bloody cell. He was a lot less polite than the Branchmen who came to see me before. All very civil and oily at first. We talked about poetry and the language, our language. We agreed about Dante and Shakespeare. We disagreed on Yeats. Then he unburdened himself on modernist delusions, agnosticism, the wretched heirs of Rousseau and Zola, the anticlericals who kept the Pope a prisoner for sixty years. All this noise will pass away, the war is a war of heresies, let them fight it out. So much hurry, he said, none of them can explain a mystery that they cannot see or touch and they turn away, cold and dejected. They're baffled by apparitions to the poorest of the poor in the mountains of France or the bogs of County Mayo. Such things cannot be proved like the existence of oxygen; the proof lies in the hearts of the innocent. I asked what all this was about: "Are you warning me?" I asked "The censor hasn't gone to sleep," I said, "I'm not aware that we've been sailing close to the wind." I tried to be polite, not to provoke him if I could help it. He said, "Don't worry, why would anyone stop you putting out your sheet, Mr Quinn? We are democrats, after all." He called it my *sheet*. "But I see nothing that is serious and sincere in it, nothing that is grounded and will last. The trouble is that certain people may draw the conclusion from it that there is more sympathy for them here than there really is. Temptation, Mr Quinn. You must be careful. Too much clarity is always dangerous. We can't afford these certainties of yours, they might help external forces define us. But we know what we believe, so that if there were, God forbid, a catastrophe, we would at least know how to behave. This is your war, Mr Quinn, not ours." Then he said: "We are a few hours from Belfast. A word away. It would be a shame to harm the country for the sake of a little sheet a few hundred deluded people read."

'The fucker. He lorded it over me and never even mentioned what he knew I'd seen and would never dare use. Then he threw me out.' Quinn's tears streamed down his cheeks. 'His confidence, his complete confidence. That is what I couldn't stand. The sheer weight behind him.'

Schrödinger stared at him, murmuring reassurance. But the image that crowded out all else as he sat there while Quinn composed himself and went to the toilet was of young women typing at rows of desks, the keys of their machines hammering through the foolscap sheets, never quite puncturing the flimsy black carbon paper. He gulped the remains of his whiskey and prepared to leave as soon as Quinn returned, hoping he would not be hurt by his eagerness to escape. He would mumble an excuse about a dinner at home.

By late August the city felt inert and suffocating. There were days of sprawling heat when the young civil servants and shop assistants eating their lunch on the grass in Stephen's Green lay on their sides, stunned and listless, the men's white shirtsleeves rolled up and the girls' summer dresses spread around them. On the Clontarf road when the tide was out the sun baked the drying seaweed and drew the iodine smell onshore. Ice-cream barrows waited at the landward side of the bridge for the families walking out to the island with dazzled frowns on their pale faces. The river was the colour of grey tea, and had an odour of bad drains. As he crossed the bridge under the railway one afternoon, he saw something he had not seen at the north wall all year: a big tanker painted grey, no name on the stern as far as his eyes could make out, being towed downriver by a tug, with another nudging it from behind. A red flag flew from the mast. There was a gun on the tanker's deck. The tug in front cast off with four woeful blasts on its siren, answered by four from the tanker. The rear tug let go and the long ship steamed down the empty river. Up near the bridge a Guinness ship was moored by the Custom House. Two

214

white-skinned boys were standing on the prow, baggy drawers on their thin hips. The smaller of the two took a step and a jump and fell standing into the river, his arms by his sides. The other boy screamed down at him when he surfaced, laughing, his tough little face delighted. He swung around a stanchion on the bow as though he owned the ship. The thought of that cloudy grey fluid entering his mouth nauseated Schrödinger, but he felt a pang of envy and impotent affection for the diving boy, who was dog-paddling his way to the anchor chain.

Dublin was choking with small fears. He could feel them as he rode past the Georgian slums with their doors gone and their fanlights smashed and saw the hollow faces of the women sitting on the doorsteps, in the crowds on the quays waiting in the heat for buses to take them away from the smell of the river to Portmarnock or Clontarf. And the cattle were back, the lumbering herd being driven to the ships past the Five Lamps where he stood over his bicycle and watched them pass, lowing and gibbering. He could see the fear in the grimace on a woman's face as she pushed a high pram across the bridge to the island, snapping at her older children to come on, as if they were running from danger. Whatever was out there was as indistinct and menacing to him as the vast, dark sky he saw from the dunes one morning rising straight out of the sea, a griminess in the air all the way to the cold region where the gases thin out and nothing can breathe.

He was remembering how war smelled. The images in the paper he could not bring himself to read were blurred, all the tones crude and grey. They seemed like copies of copies with no sharp definition left, drained of colour and heat, the closest we get, he thought, to the truth of what is happening. The prose of the reports was censored into vacuity, battles described so blandly that they might have been taking place on the moon. He could imagine the smells when the photographs were taken; but they showed only the naked legs of the young soldiers, the grinning blond heads, a wisp of smoke in the distance and wheat stretching to the horizon, towards which a tank was setting off like a badly made toy. Sunburnt Russian faces contorted against the sun, abject and thirsty, looking up from the ground at the camera and the light behind the cameraman. They knew well that being looked at isn't good. Images of another summer, when the first newsreel was shown in Vienna after that war began. It flickered for a few minutes in the silent, crowded cinema. Tired Russian soldiers came shambling forward, faces dark with the sun and dirt. Their stony-faced officers rode in carriages, and the wounded in open carts, jerking along as the reel of film unspooled. Now half his life later there were still trains of horses pulling wagons down a track whose vanishing point seemed infinitely far away. He remembered the smell of the huge dray horses on the Karst as they lowered their heads and strained their shoulder muscles, taking one deliberate step after another as the enormous weight of metal in the gun wagons pressed on them and abraded the skin under their harness. Their bodies lay about on the rock swollen by gases after they were killed by shells, and were safer than a wall because they did not splinter. It occurred to him that animals were never counted. Ashman and his camels. And perhaps the Taoiseach was not fit for office. The story was that he freed the cats and dogs from a pet sanctuary on the canal near the bakery which he seized during their Rising. Why should a dog die for a country he can't imagine? But a serious man would have let them burn, or drowned them in the canal.

And Ashman, that conversation in the hot sun among the flowerbeds in the Free French consul's garden. He watched the young Englishman lean in and release a little gust of irony, then stand off to admire the effect on a straight-backed Frenchman and his wife. All three were wearing white linen, looking as if they'd come from a tennis match, and as Ashman swung back and balanced on his toes Schrödinger could imagine him serving a ball or striking out with the glass in his right hand. But the Frenchman lifted his own glass and bowed, acknowledging some graceful hit, and Ashman turned and saw Schrödinger. He sidled across the lawn, mugging impish delight.

'You are looking so well. And how is our young friend? Still no one's fool, I trust?'

The assumption that he would know. Schrödinger played along. 'I think not. But you must ask her yourself.'

'I wish I could, but she has dropped all her old friends. No more expressionist soirées. Besides, she doesn't really approve of me. I talk about naval matters too much, dead sailors and submarines. It doesn't do around here. You are a lucky man, if I may say so.'

He pulls the covers off so neatly you barely feel them lift, and then you're facing him as good as naked. Schrödinger found it tiring to be offended by this young poseur staring around his bedroom door, and though he wished he could provoke the man, the effort felt too great.

'I'm not quite sure what you mean,' he said impassively, 'but I am lucky, in many ways.'

'And so fortunate to be *here*,' said Ashman at his most eagerly winning, 'to be able to work under such conditions. I hear that many of your old pals are shackled to desks, dreaming up new ways of smiting the foe. What a lot you turn out to have behind those noble brows, speaking collectively of course.'

'Speaking personally I think it was better when we were sent off with our regiments, as we were in 1914. I don't think the old Emperor liked us very much. He didn't care much for typewriters or electric light. Perhaps he had good instincts. The more we're put to work the more horrible war becomes.'

'That was a different world, a better one. I suspect you're nostalgic for it behind, if you'll forgive me, that bohemian façade, as indeed am I.' Ashman beamed at him, his round cheeks above his beard glowing with goodwill. 'But yes, everyone's knuckling down and working like the devil. How fortunate you've never had to make the choice.'

He said this with such comic relish that Schrödinger felt as if he were waving that letter mockingly in his face. At least I did not want to do it, he told himself, sit in an office like a good boy, doing the homework set by his masters. Saving German physics, or English. Ashman stood there with his openness and guile, so sure he was in the right and all the more free to crush, Schrödinger now saw, whatever stood in the way of the imperfect decency for which his England stood. He was looking at him steadily, without any of his prancing or shadow-boxing. Schrödinger had never seen him so at rest. He wondered was this what made Dublin so safe, the secrets cancelling each other out, dying of exposure, and he could not think of anything to say.

'You don't know what you're talking about,' he snapped, though his anger was without heat. He turned and walked out of the garden, handing his half-full glass to a waiter so roughly that the man's white glove was splashed with wine.

The day before they left he was told by his tobacconist on College Green that the plug he smoked was finished. 'We just can't get it, sir, there's no more coming in, so little coming in at all.' The man sold him instead a cake of dark, hard tobacco that Schrödinger knew would taste bitter on his tongue.

He visited the oculist that afternoon. After the examination Dargan said, 'It will be a while yet. And it could be worse. Think if this was a century ago. In those days to cure cataract they'd push the opaque lens down into the eye, which would clear a passage for light through the pupil. Well, it would, but not for long. I can see, the patient would say, dazzled by the light. But soon he'd lose the eye altogether when the thing became inflamed. I always think it must have been almost a religious experience, a vision, that brief moment of illumination. A sad kind of miracle, anyway.' The doctor observed him with his mirror dangling from his hand.

I would prefer the ecstasy, Schrödinger thought, but I will settle for your stitches. He could feel the thin knife coming closer, cutting through the cornea, the pincers feeling for the lens, and left the building wondering what the failure rate for cataract operations might be, and promising himself, with a happiness he had not expected to feel, that while he could he must look carefully at the world.

The house that evening hardly seemed like the place he lived in. Hilde looked through him with a bright disdain, a wide-eyed accusing wonder that left him no mitigation for what he had become.

As he lay sleepless at three in the morning the images of Duff and Quinn and the German bully came and went as he tried to put them out of his mind. He lay on his back and relaxed his limbs one by one, trying to drift on a black canoe through calm water among islands of rock and moss. Empty mountain and bog rising up. But it did not work, and he turned and lay on his back, thinking of affinities between gravitation and electromagnetism, forms that change as their co-ordinates change. I am too tired, he thought, there is no point in this. I cannot sleep and could not force myself to get up and write something down even if I saw a way through. His mind churned on and on. Gravitation and electricity could be treated as variations on a geometric structure, transforming themselves as they shift between one co-ordinate system and another; but they cannot explain each other. Matter as a special kind of geometry. Gravity as a geometrical property of space-time where nothing follows a straight line, the path a particle traces already curved by the space of the rotating earth on which it moves, our given frame. We are all bent by where we are, our every move constrained. What if she did it? Her conscience is so strong, and she would follow it. He lay for hours thinking hopelessly, his mind going round like a millstone grinding on nothing and making only dust and splinters, and then thought of her again, the silky rustle of the carbon, how three layers of it and four sheets of paper would make a thick, soft sheaf. The roller would scarcely feel the keys. The layers of writing would be aligned with each other, yet weakening the further they were from the typist's fingers. The copyist as reader, stealing a ghost document in pale-blue letters that barely cut the page. No longer a mindless pair of hands. And each copy is an enduring image of the previous one but there are subtle variations, as there are with us, this is how we become strange to each other; we think we can read what is there, he thought, but then the small mistakes accumulate and we are lost.

Goltz leered over him, holding his hand in a tight cold grip. He could not move. His body was completely rigid. I have had a paralytic fit, he thought, and at that moment came fully awake and realised that he was safe, and took a deep, gratifying breath.

When he came downstairs it was not yet six and the house was still silent. He made himself a cup of dusty tea. This morning the west felt like a forgotten place where it might be possible to start again, though he wished for a moment they were going to some other part of Clare, but it was too late to change their plans without upsetting her. An insect was flying in slow patrols over the sink by the kitchen window. His instinct was to swat it with the book he had picked up from the table. Instead he placed the back of his hand a few inches beneath the tiny articulated body and blurring wings and lifted his hand slowly, noticing the hairs and thick veins, the spotted skin sunk between the canal system of his own blood and small bones. I have old hands, he thought. Slowly he continued to draw his hand upward, rising past the level of his chest. The silently moving creature kept an even distance from his skin. When his hand was above his head he moved it slowly forward towards the crack in the window. The insect's wings never stopped moving. The pull of cooler air at the sill seemed to lift it from its trance and it turned and took off, flying slowly into the bright air of the garden.

Early the next morning she was waiting for him at the station in Westland Row, carrying a loose rucksack and wearing a white shirt and blue slacks. She stood behind her bicycle, her stance slightly crouched, as though to apologise modestly for her body, yet ready to stretch and spring. He was aware of the tense strength of her neck and shoulders. She reached out to shake his hand, laughing at him across the gap between their bicycles. 'I believe we're going the same way. What a coincidence.'

'I hope not many other civil servants are visiting their grandmothers this weekend.'

'No, I think they're saving their leave days for something really important. You seem a bit on edge. I hope you're not having second thoughts. After all, I'm the one taking the risk. If someone did see me, my goose'd be cooked.'

He said that he was sorry, and that he had not slept well, making a conscious effort to move closer to her mood. And because he was entranced by her once more, he found it easy to mispronounce the Gaelic on the station signs so that she could mock and correct him. *Iarnród. Slí Amach.* 'The way out – isn't that what we're looking for? Isn't it a wonderful sign to have at a railway station? I think they should have days when all they offer are ways out. You would take the first train and not know where you were going. A random distribution of destinations.'

'You might end up in Belfast, that would teach you to gamble,' Sinéad laughed.

He produced two first-class tickets that he had bought on the way home the day before. 'You should save your money,' she said.

'Oh, this is honestly earned Irish money. For cutting the mental turf in Merrion Square. I have to spend it somehow.'

The carriages were coated with a film of black dust, and inside the smoking compartment the seats were clean but faded. The air in the corridor reeked of burnt tar and nicotine, reminding him of the night mailboat that had brought him here, the smell of human weakness shut inside a public room. They sat and smoked and waited for the train to move. His tobacco was not as thin and harsh as he had feared. A half-hour after the scheduled time a keener soot-laden smell penetrated the carriage with the huffing sound of the engine raising steam. The smoke grew thicker and more sulphurous. She slid the vent in the window across.

They talked about the theatre as the engine made its first great snatch at the weight of the carriages and the shafts turned the wheels. Fine particles of soot drifted through the closed window as though it were not there, and he watched them settle slowly on her shirt. He spoke about a production of *Medea* he had seen before the last war, the rage and jealous pain set against a backdrop of white and grey walls framed by golden columns broken in half and twined with ivy leaves. In such a stark setting the woman's violence seemed more terrible, digging up her lethal jar and turning its magic against the girl who had displaced her, burning her alive and butchering her children. Jason never seemed more callous or arrogant, drawing the horror down upon himself. At the end Medea, wrapped in the Golden Fleece, meets him, a homeless vagrant in the wasteland outside the city, and tells him to endure. 'It is almost like forgiveness,' he said, 'this terrible woman who's killed his children explaining to him that there's nothing to do but go on.'

She said little, but drew on her cigarette and watched him speak with an expression that made him feel omniscient and vulnerable, as though he were onstage himself and needed to keep holding his audience at the right distance. She leaned forward and kissed him, then sat back, still looking at him, calmly determined to discover something that she needed in him. She seemed about to speak, but then the trembling of the carriage lulled them, and the train moved at a steady shuffle that rarely increased, making sounds like an old man blowing his nose. After a while, she said, 'I reckon this is as fast as it gets.' The train went on with its slow hammering, and they could not say very much that made the rocking rhythm and the torpor it induced worth disturbing. He tried to read some notes, but he felt as if a strong light were being reflected onto the page, blurring the lines of his own handwriting. He lay back, trying to rest his eyes. She was reading a book of poetry and read two poems to him, without the vehement intonation of importance he hated in actors, but even her colloquial statement of the lines – 'It is as though you are reciting a mad rant reasonably,' he said – could not attract him.

She made a face at him and he leaned back to stare at the flat green fields, the cattle standing stock-still watching the train pass. The sudden wide flood of the river at Athlone as the train crossed the bridge surprised him when he woke. In the station they halted, doors clunked shut as new passengers boarded, and the train stayed where it was. The engine made quiet steam. An inspector passing along the corridor called out that they were waiting for coal. This coal that makes no steam.

They wheeled their bicycles out of Galway station and found themselves part of a Friday lunchtime crowd. The town might just have been liberated, and a great happiness entering the world. Young men laughed and rubbed their hands together, in that way they had, as they strode along filled with gleeful purpose. In the square outside the station a fort of turf sods had been built, with walkways between the piles. On the edges of the square bicycles were balanced in layers of black bony shapes. He recalled, as he had before, a photograph of crutches hanging in clustered bunches over the grotto at Lourdes, which he had seen once in a shop window near the Pro-Cathedral. The discarded machines seemed to be tangled together, twisted into slotted concrete blocks or leaning casually against walls.

'There is something pitiable about so many bicycles in one place,' he said in a low voice, speaking as if to himself.

'Why do you say that?'

'I'll tell you another time,' he said, though he had no intention then of doing so.

Two hours later they cycled into Ballyvaughan after a half-turn clockwise around the bay. He was aware of the higher mass of ground to their left, rising sharply from the road that ran along the ocean, which was burnished and sluggish under the afternoon sun. The wind off the bay chilled them, though in the hollows of the road it was still a warm late-summer afternoon.

At the hotel they told their barefaced lies. The woman at the desk welcomed them and smiled brightly at Sinéad as he signed in, before turning the register fastidiously back towards herself. 'Well, now, I hope you have a pleasant stay, Mr and Mrs Haffner. You will be walking on the Burren, is that right? The weather is still very nice for it.'

While she splashed her face with cold water Sinéad said, 'She saw through us in a second. She must be desperate for the money. We're as transparent as glass.' But he was gazing at the elasticity of her neck as it bent over the tap, and resolving that nothing must endanger what they had found.

Downstairs at the bar they ate sandwiches and drank small glasses of stout. Quiet men smoked at the small tables in the back of the room. Through the open door into the yard, they saw the rain come down. 'At least mud won't keep us off these hills,' he said.

Wearing boots and with sweaters around their shoulders they walked up a rising track through alder trees and hazels. When they reached a level place they stopped and it was what he had expected, yet not like anything on earth. Already the larger rounded blocks of stone, darkened by the rain, were drying to their true harsh colour as the water ran off and vanished into the ground. Beyond them, to the south, all they could see was bare grey limestone hills, an empty ruination in the warm afternoon light. The rock looked bone-clean, picked to an aseptic rawness, scrubbed and abandoned. It seemed to have nothing living on it; the interchange of earth and sky had gone wrong, as if the chemistry that made the fields green and earthy to the east was lethal here, the land making its own carbonic acid as the rain mingled with the limestone, etching the rock into furrows and slabs.

They walked across a sleek block of pavement, and as the ground sloped they came to a low wall made of stacked shards of grey stone, a fragile barrier that seemed to keep nothing in or out, not even the light or the wind, and was joined to a maze of similar walls dividing a narrow valley into rough squares. The walls enclosed empty rock. Fields without a blade of grass, a place that did not look as if it could feed a rabbit parcelled out: division for its own sake. They climbed over the wall and walked across the valley and up the other side, on stairways that made their calf muscles work. In places the rock formed concertina patterns of weathered grey leaves, thin enough to break and twist underfoot. There were ulcers in the stone, like the holes that form in melting ice, as if the rock were being eaten away in the time of a human body. The woods on the hills above Trieste had been so easily destroyed, but here there were no trees. It was as though a bomb of unbelievable power had burnt away the soft parts of the world, leaving the stones balanced strangely on each other. Perhaps, he thought, there were trees and soil once, but humans scratched it too hard, and the rock cast them off like an old coat, leaving the useless walls. But he was certain that there were caves and galleries under his feet, and that water flowed underground from these hills into the bay. He knew this place he had never seen like the back of his hand.

He could not tell if it was accident or piety that had tipped a massive oval stone so elegantly at the centre of a square of rock, but for much of the time he felt that he was walking in a cemetery, the horizontal beds of stone graves from which the names had been erased. The rock was marked with wave patterns, memories of the slow clouds of shell drifting down in the warm sea that rolled from here to the north of Italy: the beat of time so subtle it can't be detected, millions of generations as well attuned as we are turned to rubbish on the ocean floor. Who would miss my blind need to live? he thought. It is already forgotten here.

They walked west for another hour, wandering around without seeing another human being. Once she saw a fox, far away, small and furtive out in the open on the grey waste. To him it was a copper smudge. They found what was left of a nest of ring-shaped walls, an intricate masonry of wedge-shaped stones stacked like books leaning on a flat shelf of bigger blocks. It felt like the way everything would end; the back of beyond, she called it. 'Behind the moon,' he said.

She was a good walker, with a steady stride that he could tell would last all day. Her feet made sense of every uneven rock. After a long, comfortable silence he told her that her crazy Berkeley – 'Mine?' she said – thought that the sun drew heat through hollow hills like these from the old star at the centre of the earth. 'Berkeley was fascinated by caves, I suspect because inside them he felt the darkness of the world, which was a mere idea in the mind of God, even with his eyes wide open.'

'That's the way he and his like ran the country too,' she said disdainfully. 'As though we weren't really there.'

A little later they had to walk around a small herd of lean cattle that seemed to be grazing the rocks. He saw that there were, after all, grasses and lichens in the cracks between the sheets of rock, and plants with tiny, fat green stems, and miniature blue and purple flowers. Mountain plants, adapted to life in the cold. Enough water to make even this forsaken place worth picking over.

Climbing up the side of a small valley they came out onto a flat hilltop. It was split into long narrow courses with clefts like drainage channels, and resembled the floor of an excavated city. The sea came into view, its westerly infinity glittering and crawling away under the reddening light of the sun. Where the hill broke off there was a low circular wall that seemed to have emerged from the rock as one of the forms it took, a fort with the Atlantic at its back, but around it there was nothing, a flat space on the edge of a cliff. They walked to the edge and looked out at the three islands. He wished he had brought his binoculars, but he could see that the waves around the nearest island made great calm swells, and further out the white turbulence bursting up and fading and breaking again, the waves moving massively through their own spray. There were areas of unbroken roll, green and enormous. He could feel the pull of that surging and flowing, the planetary mass of water drawing him to the edge. He stood in silence, lost in the illusion of merging with that vast continuity, while a red-legged crow threw falls in the wind where the cliff dropped away. She interrupted him. 'The light is fading, we should head back.'

As he turned from the tremendous sight he could not restrain himself. 'Think of it, the Atlantic spreading as the plates shift. These cracks are the lines of stress. See how they run north-south? The bias of the force that tore this place from America. People have stood here witnessing this for thousands of years and will go on doing so after us. This is the part of us that will survive, the mind that sees and can't forget. We discover something that we knew already. It feels like the end of the world here, and yet those who have gone before us are not lost, nor will we be. Don't you feel that?'

She shivered and pulled on her sweater, and as her head emerged she said angrily, 'For God's sake, one year is what matters, not this thousand-year thing of yours, this mind we're all part of when we're dead. It's like looking at everything through the wrong end of a telescope. In a few months the world has gone to hell. And what will happen to us? Anyway, let's get on. I'm cold now and the light is going.'

She walked off abruptly, her hair shifting in a dark gentle mass on the back of her white sweater. He followed, shaken by her anger. He had almost to run to catch up with her. After a strained silence he told her that he had seen a place like this on the other side of Europe in the war.

'I forget you're an old veteran. I'm sorry,' Sinéad said, 'I don't mean to be glib. I'd like to ask you what it was like but you are so enigmatic, when it comes to it. And stop being so hard to reach. You've got all you want and it's a lovely day. Do you think I have ever done anything like this before? I'm young enough to be your daughter, but I'll be damned if you treat me like a child.'

'Forgive me. There are things I can't help thinking about, though I would prefer not to. Much of what was my science has become unspeakable to me, and I hate thinking about it. As to what the war was like, it was stupid and cruel. I had an easy time of it, safe in charge of a ridiculously large gun. But it was a bad place, so very like this. We had all the high ground, hills of naked rock, and the Italians had to come up so that they could take back Trieste. Can you imagine a war on this wasteland? Fighting for it?'

'Yes, I can. Dogs fight over a bare bone.'

'It was utterly pointless. All the things we were told we were fighting for just vanished overnight; even the places we fought over ceased to mean the same when they were given new names and the languages changed. No one remembers the war I was in, unless they were there.'

They fell silent again. He knew that he had told her nothing, and her pace showed that her anger wasn't appeased. The tension between them felt too highly charged to reduce with plausible words. She kept to the edge of the hill as they headed for the village a few miles to the east. The sky over the bay was already shifting from light to dark. The road along the edge of the sea was empty: the few houses he could see below him looked empty, and several had lost their roofs. They found themselves after a while walking along the closely packed contours of the hill, stepping and jumping on knife-like flakes and leaves of rock. He had to pause and test each vertical blade with his foot, feeling his ankle bones twist. In the failing light his eyes were troubling him. The hill became a wall of shards, sticking out like the scales of a dry pine cone. He was following her doggedly; her legs seemed sure of their position for each new step. He could barely keep upright and had to crouch, looking for handholds. When he grabbed at a slice of sharp stone to prevent himself toppling over he yelled to her, 'Please, let's go down to the road, we will kill ourselves up here. I can't even see any longer what's under my feet.'

'It would ruin the day for me to go down now. We came out for a walk in the hills and let's go back that way.' She spoke as though she had had enough of weakness and self-indulgence.

He felt exhausted, unable to argue with her, and he was scared of the rotten, sliding wall on which he was being forced to walk. The slope ahead looked almost vertical, but after a rest on his knees he got up again, determined to keep stumbling along behind her. He was also stiff with rage and even clumsier now, immediately cutting his shin on the edge of a rock. He wanted to rush her, grab her shoulders and push her off the hill. We've no one but ourselves to blame, he thought, if this ends badly, my neck broken on this godforsaken hill. Even in the half-light he could see that his boots were cut and scarified with lime. If my glasses fall I will not survive. The silence between them was broken by nothing except the scattering of loose splinters under their feet. Now even she was reaching out for handholds and balancing on the thin sheets of stone.

Out in the bay, three cormorants perched on a rock, their stillness a part of the stillness of the water. They were holding their wings out to dry, watching the road, black against the setting sun that was flooding the sea with copper radiance all the way to Galway on the opposite shore. She stopped, finally, balancing on a narrow piece of flaking stone. Beyond her the hill seemed completely sheer, and a dense hazel thicket covered the rock for a hundred yards. She looked at him holding on, with one hand out against the nearest boulder and his other hand pushing his glasses back onto his nose, and burst out laughing. 'Look at those old hags,' she said, pointing to the motionless birds on the rock. 'They're daring us to come down.'

In the hotel, after they had washed their feet, they went to the bar still feeling cold and stiff. She asked for cocoa and was told that there was none. Instead they drank hot whiskey. The alcohol was washed down by the sweet clove-scented water, lifting him into euphoria.

In the dining room they ate mutton, thick and a little overcooked, and covered in gravy, but it tasted strong and fresh. They drank a bottle of heavy Chateauneuf with a mildewed label. 'This is what bishops drink at Christmas, I'm sure of it,' she whispered. A solitary young Englishman at a nearby table ate bent over a plate of chops and bacon and sausages, pausing to drink from a pint of stout. When Schrödinger looked at him, he shook his head in wonderment.

He found himself set for her again on a warm current of drink and goodwill, the struggle on the hill a force against which to push. She was smiling at him, touching his hands and stroking his face, making him aware of its dry lines and creases, which the wind had burned and lifted into relief while her face bloomed. They talked idly about what had driven the builders to make such efforts to put up stone forts on the edge of nowhere, defending nothing, and what had made that barren upland so important. 'It was religion,' she said, 'war and religion: always enough money for both. I wonder where the sheep herders lived. Holes in the ground probably.'

'I think they were competing for the best view of the ocean,' he said. 'The more magnificent and meaningless, the more powerful they felt. Even if it was just for a few years: I am sure they ruined themselves quite fast.'

In the bedroom they lit a candle rather than turn on the harsh overhead bulb, and made love to the sound of male laughter from the bar below. They lay content and breathing deeply under the double blanket and stiff linen sheet while the candle tossed shadows on the wall. She touched his eyes delicately. 'I love seeing it naked – your face, I mean.'

'Blind, in fact.'

'Yes, I turn into a witch when you can't see me.'

'I sensed a change just then. A hideous grimace.'

'God punishing me for liking it, that was what it was.'

She was silent then, but he could tell that she was not falling asleep. Her eyes were open and her breath had become more rapid. She began to caress his shoulder, pulling at it as though to draw him closer. 'What's wrong?' he asked. When she did not answer, but sighed and leaned her head on his chest, he felt a sudden pressure on his heart. He sensed that the ground might be about to shift. What Quinn had told him flooded back, with a cold dread of what she might have to tell him. The tenderness he felt for her had returned, strengthened by their quarrel, and he could not bear the thought of the world outside this room leaning in, flicking on the light and studying their imperfect nakedness. He wanted nothing brought into this room that would make them more vulnerable to each other. We have what we need here, he wanted to tell her, in the warmth our bodies make.

'That man I was telling you about,' she said at last, 'the one who . . .'

'Yes,' he murmured, and felt relief, but also a pang of suspicion. Was this what she was about to confess, a gross submission to that dwarf? But he was also light-hearted, his fear of danger lifting. He had allowed Quinn to affect him too much. It was ridiculous to believe that she would risk so much in that room full of typing women.

'I haven't really told you it all. He scares me.'

'All what?' As he spoke he could feel his own arousal in the hollowness around the image that was forming of her alone with that runt. 'What is there to tell? Have you . . . did you?' The candle flickered quickly and went out, leaving them in the dark, in which the erotic heaviness of his jealousy felt safer.

'You can't be serious. God, not that. No, it's just that he uses the fact that he has knowledge about me, or thinks he does, to fix on me. It gives him an opening. He found ways of delaying handing over the package, especially the second time, and I was embarrassed. He claimed he had to ration them, but I didn't believe him. It was as if he wanted to have me available to him every so often, and once he wormed his way up to me on the street. Oh hello, I just happened to be passing kind of thing, right there in Merrion Row. I was afraid that he'd follow me home so I got him into a café. And I told you, he's one of those garrulous characters who can't stop stringing words together once they've started. The last time I saw him he was exulting over something, dropping hints like mad. I don't know how much to believe. I still can't see him as one of them, the republican crowd, they have this reputation for being such altar boys, very pure and upright. He's not like that at all.'

'Listen to me. You must not see this man again. He is a cheap crooked smuggler. A situation like ours, here in this country, it breeds fantasists. That is all he is, nothing more.'

'I'm sure you're right, but listen, there is something so horrible about his jabbering. I think he tells me more than he means to, and then I think there is something real behind it. He talks about a settling of accounts, how even the most faithful ones can be corrupted.' Her voice had taken on the man's northern accent, a hard level whine. 'We have to take a good hard look at our own sins, and accept what isn't easy so that we'll be hardened. We have to steel ourselves to do it and there'll be some who'll say we're pitiless, but there is a great chance coming, we have to take it once and for all.'

'Rubbish. The ravings of a crook who wants to seduce you.'

'Yes, he does, but that is what makes him talk, and makes me think that there is something to it. There's a sort of triumph in his voice. He's itching to say more, but then he gets uncomfortable and changes the subject. God, I can't believe I've allowed myself to get so beholden to him, but you feel sorry for somebody in a weird way, and then you start listening and not saying what you should have said at the beginning. I should have left this to you, but I felt you didn't want to know about the details, maybe that's unfair.'

She was shaking now, and he raised his hand to touch her cheek, which was hot and wet.

'The worst thing of all – the worst thing – they're not even any good. I think they must be defective, thrown out on a rubbish heap where he picks them up and sells them to eejits who don't know any better.'

'What are not any good?' he asked, though he knew, in a moment of despairing lucidity.

'I'm going to have a baby. His rubbers don't work.'

He seemed to himself to become completely still. He might have been waking from a deep sleep to find his body lagging paralysed for a few seconds behind his darting brain. She placed her spread fingers over his mouth. 'Say something. Please.' When he did not, she said quietly, 'Erwin.'

He lifted his right leg, as much to make sure that he still could move as to delay having to speak. The warmth of her thigh as his slid across it brought him out of his trance. He embraced her closely, folding her into an intimacy that his mind observed, suspended and wary.

'Of course,' he said, 'of course. Darling, for God's sake, you are sure? Yes, forgive me, of course you are. But you must not be upset. It's going to be all right, I promise you. I will be here. Please do not worry.' And he meant every word, scrabbling as he was on loose stones, reaching out a hand to her who was suddenly the one who had lost her footing. He thought of the rock up there, undermined by its own chemistry until a thin crust finally shatters and falls into the cave beneath it. 'We will be all right, really we will.'

'Do you have any idea what this means? I will have to stop working and I'll be disgraced. What will happen to the baby? I don't want it taken to an orphanage. But how can I look after it on my own?' This sudden loss of confidence in herself pierced him. It was obvious that she had meant to say none of this yet, and never so desperately. She pulled him closer and whispered, 'Why have you never wanted a child? I don't understand that. You are this child's father. It is such a mess. I wish I had never met you, and I love you.'

'And I you, and I don't regret for a moment meeting you. You are the most wonderful thing ever to have happened to me. I came so far to find you, and it was such an unexpected miracle.' He had thought of telling her the truth about Hilde's child this weekend, but the accretion of silence around it was too hardened to break through. Now this. She did not seem to have noticed his evasion of her question. There will be a moment for all that; everything will be made good. So he continued to hold her, drew the blankets higher around them, and soon they fell asleep.

The next day they walked east on the Kinvara road and left it after half a mile, climbing up onto the rock. They were talking more easily now that the shadow seemed to have lifted, about where she might go and how much longer she might work, and how she would live afterwards. He found himself assuming that he would be with her, although she never asked him to confirm it. As they climbed higher, towards a smoothly weathered grey hill, they concentrated on the work their legs were doing. The sheets of limestone had eroded here into overlapping fungal shapes, pitted and fluted. The roundness of the hill was an illusion, and they had to watch out for deep cracks between the sheets of rock.

From the top they looked down on a deeply cut inlet, an indentation in the larger mouth of Galway Bay, which had a quay and a few houses around it. He had remembered his binoculars today, and saw a man poling a raft from the entrance of the inlet towards the quayside. The raft seemed to sag and take on water, and was covered in what looked like wet leaves. As he watched he realised that the raft itself was made of long leafy ropes of weed. It floated on the incoming tide with unhurried thrusts of the long pole from the man standing in the stern, who did not seem perturbed that his raft was half awash.

They walked inland on the grey terraces, intending to work their way around the hill and back to the village. The rock became less fissured and they took longer strides and made good going. They were walking hand in hand when ahead of them they noticed some men standing in a half-circle looking downward. The dark blue of police uniforms seemed incongruous against the almost white slopes.

Some of the men held ropes and lamps. They were staring into a large gash in the rock, and as the couple walked up a tall sergeant noticed them. He lifted his hat to Sinéad and said good day, showing not the slightest change of expression as he did so, and went back to contemplating the hole in the ground. Sinéad asked a workman wearing an old suit what had brought the Guards to such a lonely place.

'A young lad's been found in Muckinish Harbour below. And there's been some clothes found up here.'

'You think he was washed out from here? Surely that's not possible,' Schrödinger said.

The workman looked at him. 'It's always been said you could throw a dead sheep in here and it would come out beyond in the sea.'

They saw the sergeant shake his head, a look of disapproval on his face. He said something to a junior guard, who took off his jacket and moved towards the hole.

She clung to Schrödinger as they walked towards a gap between the hills. He was conscious of the men's eyes on them as they crossed the bleak little valley. She was crying, pressing a handkerchief to her mouth. He tried to comfort her. 'That poor man. What a way to die,' was all she could say.

As they walked his mind ran on this landscape where the liquid state of matter was absent but its effects were everywhere, creating acids, dissolving, shaping, leaving only the hard stuff on the surface, where humans, he thought, must deal with it as best they can. Again he thought about the fierce permanence of life, not, whatever it was, some mystic unmechanical energy that cannot be explained, leave that to Heisenberg's rampant friends and to the priests. It is too tough for that; in the genes there must be a complex molecule, something that cannot be destroyed by the ordinary motion of heat that wears us down and will exhaust the world; an order at the root of our jittery dissipation. For a long moment it has been sheltered from that irreversible loss of heat and order; a kind of negative entropy. But it varies its structure. It must be, for evolution to work, a form that holds entropy off and is not mere repetition. An unyielding substance that nonetheless mutates. It is like a complex mineral, a crystal that is both beautifully regular yet can change. Here in this creased, folded landscape, each surface folding in more surfaces that only become visible when they are walked, everything bent on itself, distance is compressed into pleated stone. This space that seems so empty contains so much. Two adjacent hills, so easy apparently to walk from one to the other, but in between a gully that has almost vertical sides; and the energy needed to cross it has to be earned. Like the transition from one level to another, as an atomic structure changes. And the change can be a lift or a fall, as we know to our cost.

In the room that night she said, 'They were full of plans up there too, whoever built those walls. They must have been the envy of their little world. All that bareness. It's perfect without us, but it reminds me how small I am. It would be a cheerless place to die. Do you think that young fellow took his own life?'

'I suppose he did. But why would he strip naked to go into a cave?'

'Maybe he was mad and unhappy.'

'He probably was. He would have to be.'

'Well, he's at rest now. I didn't mean to mock you about the war. We knew a Protestant man at home who was in Flanders with the Irish Guards. He was very quiet about it. If you'd been in the British Army it wasn't something you talked about. Anyway he was a lovely old man. Nearly as old as you. He would come in and drink a glass of sherry with us at Christmas. He worked for one of those British insurance companies, Norwich Union or something. My parents were fond of him. I remember his moustache, I thought it was very English, very military. But he never said much about what he had seen, though I egged him on to talk. Only that on the worst Christmas he ever had he was up to his knees in mud all day and ate freezing cold beef out of a tin. So what was that about, with the bicycles in Galway?'

He answered the question she had not asked. 'Our worst problem was not mud. And I was far behind the lines with the artillery, or nearly always.'

'With your big gun.'

'A folly. A giant hammer.'

'The poor nails. I can't imagine it.'

'May you never see one.'

'Did you kill many men?'

'I don't know. It was hard to tell, we were so far back. That is what it is like, your sense of responsibility falls off inversely as the square of the distance, like the force of gravity. I kill you there, without moving from here. Think how it must be for a bomber pilot, four miles up in the air. Bodies you never see, never have to account for. Weightless murder. Your conscience ceases to be a burden.'

She was half asleep now. 'Tell me what you remember.' She slid onto her front like a warm animal before a fire, her mouth half-crushed by her weight against the yielding mattress, her voice distorted. But her plaintive need to hear him talk touched him, and he began to speak despite himself.

'They showed us the correct way to walk fast, to walk slow, to run. No huffing out or puffing in, no unnatural straining. We had to be mechanical but limber. "We want springs, not cogs," an officer said. "And we will make you spring." Driving a carriage you had to turn your head towards a superior officer and salute, holding the salute for a precise number of seconds. But if you were riding a bicycle you had only to turn your head smartly towards him, otherwise you'd become unsteady and they didn't like the look of tottering bicycles. It was like learning a language you knew you would have to forget if you wanted to stay sane. Schopenhauer says that necessary conversation is like marching compulsively side by side. Unconstrained speech is a free play of intellectual energy, like dancing, or indeed making love, I would say,' and he kissed her hair. 'Armies are the most boring conversations you can imagine.' She grunted softly.

'There was something so imperial about the heavy artillery. The Emperor's favourite casual dress was the simple unadorned tunic of the artillery officer, no braid or medals, or so we were told. He liked his big guns.'

He looked unseeingly towards the dark beyond the window, the sea on which ships were being tracked and destroyed. On the hills across the road the wind would be the only sound disturbing the silence above ground as the plants in the rock clefts consumed their modest portion of light; but under them the streams were rushing down to the sea, through caves with walls scalloped by the moving water. He closed his eyes. Bishop Berkeley once went into a cave where Viking raiders had found people hiding, long before Clontarf, and killed them in the darkness that hid hand from eye, men, women and children. *The bottom of this spring all overspread with dead men's bones* . . . That was what lay in the unobservable dark. We wade in the water, moving up and down, hoping to discover its depths and shallows; but who knows what our bare feet will touch in the rubbish and the mud?

He went on talking, sitting up in bed as the noise downstairs died away and there was nothing but the sound of the wind pushing gently against the window. 'In your great year of 1916 I was based at a village in the uplands north of Trieste. From a clearing outside the village there was a perfect view out over the gulf and Maximilian's white palace in its grove of trees. I used to sit on the warm gravel, beneath the Jerusalem pines, and look out at the water in the gulf playing with the light in the calm haze, and it was always so calm in the summer, a world away from the front, though you could walk to the line in a few hours. And the great reef above the city was hollowed and tunnelled with gun sites and trenches and caves. For us the Karst, for them the Carso. No difference. It was a disaster. They wanted to pull the leaves from the old Austrian artichoke and fork its rotten heart, and we were supposed to stop them. We should have given them their wretched city. Trieste is a dull port with good cafés; Belfast with better weather. It was the empty place in their heart, their yearning. Their lost dog.

'At the end of the summer the wind started blowing, a cold penetrating wind that knocked over tents and boxes, and made calculations for the drift of shells tedious.

'The shapes we give matter in space are such strange forms of the mind. Like the trajectory of shells: it is such an artificial thing, our idea of continuous motion, the curve created by air resistance that tends to stop the shell moving in every instant of its flight, the force of the explosion driving it on, gravity pulling it down. But we cultivated the perfect trajectory, as though it were just an elegant figure drawn in the air. We were good at euphemism, physics is very good at that: our language was full of plain geometrical terms. We talked about cones and arcs and spaces. Such as the area bounded by the surface of the ground and a sheaf of curved lines marking trajectories, an area in which the highest point is where a piece of shrapnel catches the head of a man and the lowest is where it strikes the ground. In between the two points is the dangerous space, beaten by the cone of fire. It's such a small space, and a man is hard to find inside it. It takes tons of shells to kill a lot of men. But not much energy to kill one.

'We needed to observe how the shells were striking. The unobserved strike was a possible strike, that was all; the barrage from ten kilometres away a fog of probabilities. Forward observation, sound ranging, flash counting. That's what made it unbearable: the need to see.

'The gun was gigantic. A train of lorries yoked together, with wheels as tall as men, inched the gun up the plateau. It was like moving a factory. The night we arrived the gun was hauled up to its position by lines of men stripped to their vests. In the moonlight I saw a hundred of them clinging to each rope, four dense crowds swaying like insects trapped on a line, hauling the huge thing with its barrel pointing down the slope. The wheels turned slowly on boards kept in place by men crawling after the gun and pushing the boards forward. We officers stood on a high rock looking down on them like overseers. It was terrible work: so heavy that every man looked both magnificent and strong, yet already broken and useless.

'By the light of torches they dug a hole for the base, and then the sections of the platform were bolted together and filled with concrete that the men turned and slapped and kneaded, but they kept running out of water and asking, "What sort of place is this, sir?" Then a line of rails was run across the platform and the barrel and breach and firing mechanism were rolled up and lowered onto the cradle. The shells alone weighed a third of a ton. So much *work* to prepare for killing. The gun had wheels for elevating it, like a bridge, and big recoil buffers filled with oil to absorb the shock. All this was a little childish and delightful, like having a giant toy engine, the barrel the cylinder, the shell the piston that kept on flying as far as its momentum would carry it. In the dark it resembled the Tower of Babel; but after the war I saw a picture of the Tatlin tower that the

Bolsheviks tried to build and it had the same shape, a machine for blowing people into the future.

'The gun, and there was a whole battery of guns like it, was supposed to terrify the Italians on the low ground. It was a breaker of walls and vaults. And men. To be safe from it they had to go very deep. When we blew out their caves they died of concussion, their eyes and lungs full of picric acid. That's what my physics came to in 1916. I'm sorry, this can't be what you wanted to hear, all this senselessness.'

But she said nothing, and he thought she might have gone to sleep. Then he heard her sigh 'Go on.'

'The thing could fire only about a hundred rounds before the inner tube of the barrel was worn out by the gases, and the temperatures eroded the rifling. It had a lifetime of only a few seconds, shorter than the half-life of certain particles. But it gouged and pounded the earth, the shell made a crater seven metres deep, and it shook the earth even when it failed to explode. The Emperor loved it and the generals had to like it too.

'The sound it made concussed the eardrums, so the men had to turn away from it and clap their hands over their ears with their mouths open as though they were screaming. Most of the time all we were doing was hammering the empty rock and the ditches our enemies had cut into it.

'In the first year I went up to Gorizia as often as I could. The gardens were lovely, the buildings untouched. Bombardment went on ceaselessly all around it, the Italians not wanting to ruin their own city. Their shells whooshed overhead while I sat with friends in a café near the Venetian castle, and our guns answered back, shells bursting on the Italian lines across the river. I was happy there. It suited me so well, being in the war but not of it. Of course in the end the Italians destroyed the town, they couldn't help themselves; there's something about a neutral place that the violent can't bear.'

She had rolled onto her side and was watching him through half-closed eyelids, holding his arm, but then he heard her breath come less often and more deeply, and could have been talking to himself for all he knew.

'One morning this temporary commanding officer we had been given, a major, ordered me to the front with him, the real front, not our billet miles away, to observe the fall of our shells. He was a fanatic, everything about him tense and severe, but apart from his eyes, which reminded me of uncooked eggs, he was completely unmemorable. I couldn't remember an hour after seeing him how to describe him, and now I can't remember his name. I'm not even sure he really existed as I remember him. We made our way through approach trenches up to the line until we stood to the south of a little mountain that we'd turned into a crazed wire- and cave-riddled eyesore. He told me to look out over the line. I asked how. He pointed to a ladder lying on the concrete floor of the trench. "Don't worry," he said, "we are out of range of musketry." A few minutes later four soldiers on either side of the ladder were holding it vertical, bracing their legs against the trench floor, each pair pushing as though they were holding the other at bay. I gripped the rails and began to climb, my binoculars bumping against the steps. My hands went cold with fear, and I felt a sick fall of vertigo through my limbs. I didn't dare look forward. I had to raise the glasses to my eyes, and I could not do it, I felt that I would fall and break my back on the hard edge of the trench. The major was staring up at me with a tight smile. I gripped the rail with my left hand and pressed the glasses to my eyes with the right. I shouted down that they should move it forward gently, and the sway brought suddenly into focus the wilderness of grey rock and wire and the human figures on the slope below me. Stretching away to the north in the intensified light of the glasses there was an abandonment of wire strung on metal rods or wooden stakes, as though a builder had cleared the ground and gone bankrupt before a brick was laid. I knew they were strands of wire as thick as a pencil, but from up there it looked limp and thin, string that a child could brush aside. I could see their parapets, the stone lip of their trench line, the piles of rock and sandbags. I saw immediately what the major must have known, that our shells were falling well short of the Italian lines, the rounds sending up a dust of pulverised stone. I cried out the estimated distances as best I could. I had been held up there for less than a minute, but my entire body crawled with fear. The air began to zip and crack around me. A bullet snapped by my right cheek. I slid down the ladder burning my hands on the wood, landed with a stumble and braced myself against the back of the trench. The C.O. steadied me with one arm, clapped me on the back and laughed, then walked away whistling a waltz.'

She made a small yearning sound, and he thought she was murmuring encouragement, but when he looked down her eyes were closed and her breathing slow and even. He drifted on in silence, memories floating by, fragments of the truth as vivid as dreams. You wanted to hear this and now I can't stop myself, this war that I couldn't give a meaning to even if I believed in it.

The gun was firing badly. We had been sent some smoky powder; fumes hung over our position, a ragged black flag for the Italian artillery to aim at.

They had an aircraft out looking for us, frail against a dark bank of clouds. Their guns found our range and shells began to fall nearby, and we had to find shelter. There were walls, like those loose lines of stone up above us here, but if a shell hit a wall it turned to sharp dust and needle splinters. Shells don't fall dead on stone. One of the gunners fell back with a long sliver of rock jutting from his head. We crouched behind the gun. Every few minutes a vicious cloud of fragments. We had four men wounded, and none of them by steel. We ran to a gap in the hill behind us and crawled down into a half-dark cave.

The dim light of electric lamps made our faces pale and hollow. It was dank and cold, and there was a thin film of water on the rock floor where the water seeped through from above. It smelled of sweaty cotton and wool, urine, excrement from the latrine niches cut into the rock. The feeling I had once when I looked into a vagrant's shelter in the woods outside Vienna, going into a bunker was like that – the fear of contamination by the wastes of those with nothing to lose.

That day they were targeting a hill to the north of our position, in the direction of Monfalcone, still covered in trees and scrub. When I crawled out of the hole I saw a fog of light-pricked smoke covering the hill, and the crashing, bursting sounds seemed to thicken the gases and dust. Flames ran along low declivities in the rock, trenches burned where ammunition had been hit. Runs of light dotted the hill. There was a roar of noise all along the heights. The woods were on fire, the trees burning as night fell, the white hornbeams burning like giant candles. The shape of the blaze became nearly circular, a horseshoe of massed flame and light and heat. In the morning it began to rain, and by then the hill was a dirty fireplace, with patches of glowing ash and clinker. Through the glasses men could be seen in the trenches, a long bayonet sticking up here or there. They must have been sitting inside the hill all night with their heads in their hands.

And yet I was almost relieved when the major ordered me forward to Monfalcone as an observer, though I knew the rolling bombardments meant a new attack.

I set off at night, walking with my sergeant, a printer in civilian life, wordy, well read, a social democrat, the most soothingly dull man I have ever met. Once he knew he had nothing to fear from me he would utter long discourses quoting Rousseau, Macaulay, Mill, Goethe, Dickens, Marx and Bauer. He was an expert on how national feeling was shaped by culture and technology, but he could never explain to me how these different arrangements had led us to this great rocky shit-heap. It may have been the man's droning certainty, his promise of a future of infinite reasonable tedium that kept him safe from the military police. It was like being tranquillised, it really was, he was a gentle, boring soul.

As we came towards the line giant searchlights illuminated the hills, sweeping across the cluttered surface of the rock, which was chalky white under the beams. Balloons hung in the sky, moving silently below the moon. Men with glasses leaned out of the hanging baskets looking for the signs, the flashes, the blast-swept earth in front of a howitzer, the fan-shaped print in the dust that gave away a Maxim. The balloons looked so innocent, floating on thermals that could have taken them over the Balkans, across the Greek islands, away from Europe altogether and out into the sky above Asia, away from the crowds fighting blindly over these stretches of arid rock.

It began to rain, not very heavily, but enough to wet us through, and the cold wind made the discomfort worse. In the darkness on either side of us we heard lost echoes of rifle shots. It was too far away from the line for sniping; perhaps the wind was playing us tricks. There were so many splits and holes in the ground we were afraid of twisting our ankles, and walked feeling our way.

My sergeant said, "These are bad lands, sir." The shortest sentence I ever heard him speak.

Under the next hill a line of thick squat mortars pointed straight up like black storage jars, firing shells over it, a dozen men in wet coats and forage caps standing around each gun, tending to it solemnly. We were close to the line now.

We went down into a communication trench. What soil there was in that place had turned to red mud and washed into the trenches; we had to crouch along smeared with dirt as we scrabbled through a sewer full of living bodies, rifles, clips, boxes, water-bottles, all fouled and soaking wet. The rain was much worse now, and my knees and hips were cold and aching in my wet trousers.

Around and ahead of us in the pale morning light the wire entanglements became deeper, and the Italian shelling was now exploding all around us, pulverising the rock. Showers of needle-like stone flew across the trench, a piece cutting my hand as I flinched and raised it just above the parapet. The cold was touching my bones, and I was miserable. And everywhere the smell of ordure, the unbearable stink. Two men relieved themselves side by side against the back wall and buttoned their trousers without wiping themselves.

When we reached the front-line trench we could not hear ourselves speak for the explosions and the loud stamping of a machine gun on a platform set into the trench wall. And the trench was such a massive thing, we took such pains; it was built out of solid rubble and cement, like a sunken fort. Built to last. I'm sure those trenches are still there, the last great achievement of the Habsburgs. Moments after we entered the line a flare went up, and then came down very slowly leaving a falling wake of burning powder. Ten, twenty more followed, glaring light over the low stands of wire and the litter between the lines. With the sudden quenching of the last flare a palpable stirring began in the trench around me, the men drawing carefully nearer to the parapet.

I shouted my orders to an exhausted, terrified young officer, who pointed behind me to a hole in the rock wall that an animal might squeeze down. It was covered from inside by a black canvas flap. When I pushed through, the long dirty face and wide eyes of a young man looked up at me from the dark. That fear again of stepping on the shit of hopeless men, of nameless stuff in the dark. My sergeant and I went down slipping and falling on the wide stone stairs in the drip of rain finding its way underground. The stairs wound in a steep spiral into the earth for about fifty metres, opening on a high cave where men were working at tables. The cement walls were reinforced with iron, and I could hear the sound of generators, of pumps circulating air, and grooved rails ran back from one dark gallery mouth in which there was a miners' car loaded with helmets and gas masks. A large metal cistern of water, its surface trembling as it registered the explosions up above, stood on the floor. I remember looking down at my reflection in the water which was stirring so gently and thinking that was what peacetime was like, a small disturbance of the surface that looked so harmless. At the back of the cave, under a trickle of water emerging from the wall, someone had placed a large boot that had turned white with calcium carbonate.

It felt like the literal bowels of the earth, dark and stinking; the place was suffocating, worse than the open trench we had left up above. Screams of unceasing pain came from one of the galleries. I reported to the commanding officer, a colonel, an old man or perhaps merely a tired one, and he told me that the Italians had concentrated hundreds of guns and mortars against this small stretch of line. "Hammer them," he said, "whatever you do, hammer them." I knew I had to go back up again and as I saluted I wanted to find some excuse, a miracle that would make climbing those slippery steps unnecessary. With a dry mouth and barely able to move for fear I somehow mounted the staircase, my sergeant following at my heels.

Back in the dreadful cacophony of the trench I looked through a fire slit. The sun was coming up behind us in a pall of fumes and water. The Italian line, a little way down the slope, was made of piles of stones and barbed wire. It halted on the edge of a destroyed wood, with stumps of trees among the mass of wire. The entire hill was otherwise burnt and swept of visible life, and it looked as though nothing would ever grow on it again. The rock had come to the surface like a pale-grey skull. There was nothing but the rock and water and wire, and heaps of rubbish that might have been dead bodies. A whitened yellow radiance was slowly drawn over this desolation. The rain stopped for half an hour and then came down again in a drenching curtain.

The trenches were so close together that it was difficult for our artillery to fire without hitting our own men. They were staring down the hill. I have never seen eyes so skinned, such attentive faces.

Beyond the Italian lines, and the railway embankment that ran past the foot of the hill, the city of Monfalcone was in ruins. The dirty face of the campanile clock lay on a pile of bricks. This is what we always seem to be left with: stopped clocks, charred paper, the jumble of houses, the evidence of crimes that will never mean anything and never be paid for.

Behind what was left of the town guns still fired. From the size of the flashes and their colour and the smoke they made, I was supposed to guess the calibre of the guns. The number of seconds from the flash to the report of the gun multiplied by 360 gave the distance travelled by the sound, and so we would have their range. But suddenly there was a thick concentration of shooting flame, fifty or a hundred guns together. Flashes lit and spent, lit and spent, again and again. All around the hill violent energies were unleashed, the cracking together of oxygen and carbon in fast reactions, heat and light and noise. We were under the guns in a world of blast waves, it was all shock, the most terrible battery, eardrums beaten and hurt. Most of the men retreated below ground. A heavy shell exploded close to our trench, slowing down the world as the blast plucked time and space into itself. It was such pure disorder. I remember a burst machine-gun barrel hissing steam like a kettle, a man's arm, fingers to elbow, appearing instantaneously beside me in the profound silence that all the noise created.

For hours the shells whistled and howled past each other above the town and the lines. I thought I could detect the enormous rush of our heavy shells among the rest, and far back among the Italian guns I could see the smoke of our shells exploding, but their fire did not grow any weaker. I retreated to the shelter of the cave when I could, but I had to go out to report to our battery on a telephone line run up for me from below.

The light improved as the sun rose higher, but the air was still so full of smoke and rain I could not be sure what I was seeing through the glasses beyond the Italian lines. Their barrage stopped, and ours soon after. Movement drew my eye to the wreckage of the town. A crowd of men on bicycles was swarming up a bare street cleared between ruined houses, an unmilitary wobble of black two-wheeled machines. They rolled on those delicate wheels in silence up towards the railway embankment, heading towards the gap of a bridge in dead ground that we could never hit. The bicycles climbed the hill, a holiday excursion of a thousand boys with their bottoms poised over their saddles, legs forked over the crossbars, their packs and spiked rifles pointing forward. They wore black-feathered hats that quivered in the freezing wind. As the gradient increased their bone-shakers paused at the top of each pedal stroke as though about to fall over, but they always kept going forward as their riders completed the stroke, their legs working hard against the wind and the weight they carried. The closer they came the more I could see of their faces through my binoculars. Some had the babyish ovals of Italian children, dark skin and dark eyes, and their hats were crowned with those extravagant plumes. They must have thought their bicycles the last word in style, rushing them to the front with such debonair speed. It was the craziest thing I have ever seen, a dream, but they were there. As far as I remember, I saw it in front of me, it was part of the general delusion of war, but how can I really have shared this picture with another human being? And then the guns on both sides started again, and the flat vicious shock waves seemed worse for the pause.

I telephoned our unit to say that there was too much counter-battery fire and that enemy troops were massing for an assault. I asked for my commander but a voice I could barely hear seemed to say that he was coming forward. The telephone went dead. Below the rear line of Italian trenches the wavering mass of cyclists stopped, vaulting elegantly from their bicycles as they neared the embankment, and then I could not see them. They must have stacked their mounts in neat rows on either side of the bridge before forming up.

They doubled under the bridge into the approach trench that led up the hill to their lines from the railway, their bodies flickering between the gaps in the sandbagged wicker fence that screened them. Sometimes I caught a good glimpse of them through a gap: one of the boys was swinging himself forward on crutches, in an easy slow toppling motion. He vanished behind the wicker panels again before I could focus on him properly. Our guns ranged back and shrapnel began to fall on the area behind the railway, but it was not well aimed and could not touch them.

By eleven, the fire was more intense than any I had ever seen. I was ordered back to the rear trench just behind the crest of the hill. I left word for my sergeant, who was still below in the cave, and as I went back along the approach trench I could see a vast wall of smoke stained with flame growing higher and higher, all the way north along the edge of the uplands and blotting out the hills to the east. It was a walk through ear-splitting shrieks and the violent pressure of waves moving at five times the speed of sound. I reached the top of our hill and threw myself into the rear dugout, crouching on the flat stone platform at the head of the steps. I was nearly as filthy now as the front-line soldiers, and my throat was parched. The Italian guns once more ceased firing. With frantic curses in Serbo-Croat from the NCOs, our men scrambled up past me carrying Maxim guns and ammunition belts and out into the trench. I tumbled out with them into the rain that was still falling steadily through the clouds of rock dust and choking yellow lyddite smoke, and the air cleared slightly in the quiet. Our guns had also stopped, but I had a ringing in my ears, and dust in my nose and throat. From down the hill mournful shouting rose and a horrible rottenness suffused the air: the mortar rounds must have thrown the older body parts about, and a sweet sharp stink of lethal minerals added to the reek. I drank some water from my canteen. A soldier beside me said, "I'd keep that, sir, we won't be getting any water for a while, we drink and eat once a day and it has to be at night. All this water and still thirsty. Dreadful ground, can't swallow blood or shit but soaks up water like a sponge." He spoke like a man making an observation on the weather. An officer came up and said that the colonel had been hit as he came into the trench, and had been taken down unconscious into the cave.

We could hear shouts in Italian now, whistles and pistol shots. A mass of men appeared out of the earth in a long line, hundreds of men wearing black-feathered hats like a chorus of woodlanders. Some of them walking ahead of the others wore breastplates of steel, helmets and bulky shoulder-plates, I swear to you they looked like dismounted knights in the wrong century. The lances they carried had long tubes on the tips. A few men materialised out of the ground ahead of the line: they must have crawled forward under cover of their own barrage. A tall man, his plumes nodding in the rain, stood up out of a slight hollow where a plover might lay her eggs. He walked a short distance and was flung aside by bullets, for shrapnel shells were now bursting above and in front of them. I had never seen it work on human beings before: the little metal balls finding their own trajectories but always together forming a rough cone with its apex where the shell burst in the air, and in that cone the small energies of the bullets met the living energies of men. So simple. An officer in our trench was beside himself screaming for aimed fire, aimed fire, and the Italians suddenly were running uphill over the broken ground in a charging, clumsy crowd. Some of them carried long ladders. Walking uphill today I felt what it was like, the brittle stones under my feet, a tilting, stumbling kind of walking, but they were carrying long heavy rifles, grenades, water, picks and shovels. The small stones were a trap for them. Sliding gravel. The little advantage of our small hill was enough. The huge menacing rush was thinned by the machine guns as swiftly as a cloud of insects goes ragged when it's blown by the wind. Many fell, just crumpled, bodies were thrown about on the ground by the bursts hitting them. The mass of men paused, sank into the rock a little and recomposed itself for another dash at the hedge of wire that was torn and askew but still hanging together six metres thick in front of our line. A few of the young men reached it and crawled through gaps, but these were nowhere very deep and their cries were audible beneath the cracking and juddering of the machines that were killing them. I saw two soldiers throw ladders on top of the wire and one of them began to crawl across, lifting his arm to throw a bomb into our trench; others were lying down and snipping strands of the wire with great pincers. Two of the armoured men threw out hooked rods with which they tried to pull back the wire, raking it in like hay. In our trench a man stood up as the steam poured out of the bulky jacket around the barrel of a machine gun and screamed in Serbo-Croat at the gun while unbuttoning his trousers. He stood with his penis in his hand, his face concentrated and terrified as he aimed and pissed down into the nozzle on the jacket. Then I saw a man swinging on crutches come a little forward of the line of advancing soldiers, his rifle strapped to his chest. His left leg was missing. He let the right crutch fall and took the rifle in his right hand and fired it one-handed, and the crutch must have caught in a joint in the rock because it stood upright as he came on. He fell, his other crutch thrown to the side. He tore at his uniform, his hand coming up empty in a throwing gesture, and then his body was kicked back again. His feathered black hat lay near his face as though he were kissing it. The pikemen in their coats of mail shoved their lances into the bushes of barbed wire, where their long tubes exploded. Crawling underneath, very small men pulled the tubes with them. The barbs must have torn their arms and backs, but the machine-gunners noticed them and depressed their muzzles. The men lay still, playing dead until the rounds came into the right plane, and then the bodies jumped as the bullets tunnelled through the soft obstacles. In amongst the wire there was no way out, it was all smoke, steel and laceration. Men died with their hands gripping the wire. But some of them were reaching the trench and tumbling over the parapet with bayonets extended, or tossing bombs.

Whistles blew. Men were crowding the second-line trench, pushing me out of their way. Some of our men were running back towards us over the open ground. The Italians had burst into the front line, and were coming over the trench shooting at the backs of our fleeing men. My sergeant was surely trapped in the cave beneath the trench. I heard the wounded screaming. Mortars burst around our trench, which was crowded with frightened men. Italian soldiers exposed in the gap between the lines were falling, their bodies piling loosely into a low wall. The Italians still able to run retreated to the front trench.

That major appeared beside me, smiling calmly. His was the only bland expression in all those shock-drawn faces. I had not thought of him for the past hour. He was holding the mouth- and earpiece of a telephone apparatus held by a cowering private, the line running back into the dugout.

Reinforcements were rushing up the eastern slope of the hill, and soldiers who had retreated from the front trench were being formed into units again, the officers tense and threatening, the sergeants implacable. Bayonets snapped onto rifles. An order was screamed and the trench emptied, men scrambling over the parapet and down the wreckage of the slope in the rain, picking their way around the carpet of bodies and the new holes opened in the limestone. Machine guns below found them, shrapnel whipped through the rain. The major watched them move onward, falling in clusters. I could see tears on his cheeks, but the smile never left his face.

Now there was fighting in the open between Italians coming up and our men going down, at least a thousand men on open ground in the freezing rain, shooting each other at point-blank range, fighting with bayonets and clubs, slaughtering with pick, knife, shovel, stone. The major was calmly giving orders; he seemed to have taken command. Some of our men began to run out of the smoke and rain now shrouding the front-line trench, their rifles gone. More and more of them. They were tripping and falling in a wild, slow run. The major was pale, his fury holding him stiff. He said the word "cowards" with astonishing emphasis. He was speaking into the phone, something like range five thousand, elevation six thousand five hundred, time fuse 144. Guns in action, Number One ranging. Within seconds an express train came screaming at us through the air, the thumping buffet of its passing instantly swallowed in the ground-shaking explosion just beyond the front trench. He began to grin, cheerful again, intent on the slope below him. I remember his pale, featureless face. He ordered all guns to elevate and fire three rounds of battery fire. The area around our front trench and in between our lines seemed to disintegrate, the giant explosions rocking us where we stood. I would have been knocked over if I had not been gripping the parapet, and I lost control of myself at that moment. My urine felt hot on my left leg, and cold and clammy seconds later. The shells in flight created an enormous rushing and howling, as though they were dragging a herd of frightened animals in their wake, an accelerated bellow of fear and disbelief. A steaming hole gaped where the front dugout must have been, a cavern with its roof torn off. He had given them no warning. These were our own big guns. He held the telephone away from him and whispered something I could not hear.

The front trench and the space between it and where we stood had been turned into a quarry. A few of our retreating soldiers staggered out of the smoke, their weapons gone, uniforms torn. They stared at us with dilated eyes, like surprised children.

Water-bearers could not get through for hours, and there was no food until after dark, as the soldier had warned. And I had lost all desire to eat. Men were calling to us for hours from the wreckage, in Italian, German, Czech, Slovene, in dialects that most of us could not understand, for water, for help, their voices monotonous and excruciating. The hill after the battle was like a burial mound blown inside out to reveal its dead. The thirst in the midst of all this water was dreadful; never enough water despite the constant rain and fog. Unless you caught rain in a helmet you must not drink it, blood and excrement were everywhere, no pool was safe. We could not look at each other. Squalor in the angles of the trenches. Bodies smelling to high heaven. A soaking desert. I smoked constantly to cut the stink. This is what we did with the ordinary energies of light and heat, tinkering with electrons.

The roads to the rear were jammed with vehicles and men: columns of lorries going down, columns coming up, the wounded packed into closed carts drawn by horses, blood dripping from the doors when they tilted uphill.

The rain stopped for a while and started again, a heavy, sheeting rain that lasted for two weeks. The trenches became torrents and sewers. The wind settled into its chilling winter sharpness. In November the snow began falling. There would be no new offensive until the spring.

But they had a hero: my sergeant, whose name was Braun, for it seemed he had distinguished himself in the defence of the forward trench. It was the acting commander's idea to choose him, the peacemonger and Jew, from among the mass of indistinguishable corpses; to judge what had happened there by what he wanted others to see. The smear of creative possibility that is the past for men like him. And the regiment that broke kept its honour and of course was never shelled by its own guns.'

He fell asleep a little later and woke up cold, still propped upright against the bedhead with his shirt draped around him. Rain thrown by the wind sprayed against the windows. He remembered speaking, but could not be sure how much he had said out loud, and he wondered whether the things he thought he had seen were not a product of the same disruptive work that could leave a crutch standing upright on a battlefield. The mind recomposing from its wreckage the possibility of a past. None of this happened to me, all of it did.

The next morning, the manageress said that the drowned man had not been from Ballyvaughan or the Burren. But an old man in the bar said he might have escaped from the industrial school in Salthill, across the bay. Sinéad muttered, 'No wonder he was sad.' Schrödinger could see the men discussing it quietly during the winter in the bar, when the last tourists had gone and the grey wall of rock would hem the village in on its narrow piece of land by the water.

Two guests had arrived from the capital the evening before, large men in blue raincoats and dark hats. At breakfast they and the other guests ate as though they had been confined in the hotel for months and were so bored they were incapable of speech. Only the two newcomers seemed to have any energy left, turning their big impassive faces on the guests without insolence or embarrassment. One of them looked at Schrödinger as though he thought he knew him, and said something to his companion, who glanced at Sinéad with cool appreciation and disdain. The contempt in a heavy male face: it is all the same face, damn you, Schrödinger thought as his eyes dropped to his plate.

He paid their bill while she waited in the yard. When he came out he could not see her and walked west under the bare weathered terraces that looked so smooth and harmless from the road. He thought of the young body underground, and how cold it must have been in the deep galleries, even in the summer, and the body would be dragged against the walls as the water fell towards the sea. As he turned back to the village he saw Sinéad coming towards him, a smile on her face, which looked beautiful and renewed. His breathing changed when he saw her and he felt the privilege he had been given, yet he was aware at the same moment of the sadness in his house on the other side of the country. He saw Hilde sitting with her hands in her lap in the small living room, waiting for her daughter to come downstairs, so that they could walk or take a bus into town. Anny might go too, entering into the spirit of it as she always did. The three of them happy without him, once they were out of the house. He felt that he degraded the time they spent together, the early mornings and late nights embittered by his carelessness and need. The life they had made – that he had forced on them, he accepted this, though it was sour and difficult to swallow – seemed damaged and unfinished. As he walked towards the young woman he was so sure he loved, he was consumed with pity for his former lover sitting undesired in the terraced house in that tree-shaded street, and for his uncared-for, unbearably needed wife, and for himself, bearing the cost of having it all ways. And his daughter. 'Uncle,' a euphemism for visitor or stranger. Even the way I hug her is not honest, he thought, I hold her carefully, knowing that a different word for what we are to each other would act like a flash of radiation on skin, perhaps changing its structure, an excited and dangerous state that none of us wants. And Sinéad was forming despite himself another kind of guilt, something else he had to deal with and to carry. He had hoped that she would free him from the demands of the ordinary entanglement they would always have become. Down in the body the mind sinks; the clear eye coats itself with grime. I thought I could rise above all this, but she can't give me the silence and clarity I need. I'm no freer than I ever was, bound in a confined space where my own energies shake me to pieces. And yet, after all, even despite the child she was bearing, it would be all right, and he was still in love. Arrangements could be made, not easily here, but a discreet house in a quiet suburb would allow them to get through. Clontarf would be ideal: a shame it was already taken. The thought made him smile as he neared her. She reached out for him, delighted that he was suddenly so happy again.

Yet later that day she could still feel the tension in him, after they had cycled back around the bay. The assurances he gave her were a relief, but she could sense that there was something nerveless about them. 'I've never felt so alone in my life,' she said to him quietly as the train picked up speed out of Galway. In their second-class compartment – there was no first-class carriage, and no one knew why – everything they said above a whisper could be heard by the other passengers, a man in a striped suit who looked like a lawyer and a woman in expensive tweeds, who with a flicker of her eyes established what she needed to know about them. 'I've acted as though I lived in Paris and I can't even go there to save my life. I'm here in Ireland and I am in terrible trouble. You are a good man, aren't you? Please be a good man, Erwin.'

In a low voice, without any emphasis that might attract their fellow travellers, he said, 'I will be good for you. I swear I will.' He meant it from the bottom of his heart, where he thought the turbulent currents could not reach, but he was unable to express the easy conviction that he knew she wanted to hear; he sounded even to himself a little shrill and appeasing. And the cold reality of what was happening to them slowly settled in the fug of coal- and tobacco-smoke that permeated the carriage. After an hour the train lost speed, and the exhalations of steam from the engine began to come slower, wheezing and separable from each other. The landscape passed by so unhurriedly that he could look at the fields of ripe wheat and see the small birds pecking at the stalks. The cattle masticated solemnly at the edge of meadows. He wondered if his daughter was being taken around the National Gallery again this morning, where Cuyp's paintings of cows would gaze at her with their mournful eyes.

By the time it reached Athlone the train was crawling. It stopped in the station, barely making steam. A guard slid the door of the compartment open and shouted something about fuel; Schrödinger had not penetrated his accent by the time he vanished. The lawyer muttered something about incompetence and paying the price for vanity. Sinéad smiled politely. The woman in tweeds said nothing. He went and stood in the corridor and smoked a pipe of his rough tobacco.

After two hours the whistle blew and the carriages were pulled slowly on across the flat plain, but their progress was so hesitant that the constant frustrated expectation of an increase in speed exhausted him. He imagined the stoker raking and raking, trying to get air up through the burning red mass in his firebox. Sinéad drowsed against the window. 'Burning duff,' she said quietly. Schrödinger looked up, startled, but she was staring out the window, and he saw the official in his suit and tie being fed into the blazing fire, a halo round his head.

In a stretch of flat, dark fields and bogland, empty as far as the eye could see, the train stopped again. A few crows drifted down from a line of trees and grazed in the rushes near their carriage. Above them was a broken layer of sheet-like grey cloud, so low it looked like fog. Schrödinger sat with his lit pipe in his teeth and couldn't bring himself to suck on it. Any movement seemed pointless. Sinéad slumped against the glass. The only sign of life was the birds scavenging the field. After what seemed like hours, doors slammed further up the train. A man in uniform appeared, wheeling a bicycle towards the line of trees. Schrödinger watched him reach it and swing up onto the saddle. He pedalled slowly eastwards, hunched over the handlebars.

It was dark when Schrödinger woke up, ash on his crotch, the pipe on the floor. Sinéad was still sleeping. In her corner, the woman in tweeds sat upright and alert. The lawyer was snoring in his. Schrödinger heard steam being released with a tentative explosive sound and the train began to move. He glimpsed two empty carts with horses standing in the shafts. Sinéad woke up and reached for his hand. His nerves were raw from his uncomfortable sleep, or he would have returned the pressure of her fingers, but instead he half-flinched and his hand drew back. She removed hers slowly and sat far back on the seat, looking at him steadily with wide unblinking eyes. The lights in the carriage came on, weak and yellow, but even in that light he felt reduced. After a silence that was already too long, he tore a page from the notebook in his inside pocket and scribbled in pencil, 'Forgive me. It has been a strange weekend. I was distracted. I thought we would be in that bog for ever.' She took the note and read it, then snatched the pencil out of his fingers. 'Don't make it any stranger,' she wrote. 'All I want is the part of you that can help me through this and be true. You know what I mean.' He nodded his head and took her stiff hand in his. Her body relaxed and she leaned forward. Her eyes were warmer, but she smiled without opening her mouth.

It was eleven by the time the train reached Dublin, after inching across Kildare at horse speed. They were numb with exhaustion and cramp. Their knees touched across the compartment, but what would a week ago have been an erotic grazing of skin was wasted on them now. The silent couple in the compartment made it impossible to break their own silence. As the carriage slid along the platform at Westland Row she yawned and turned her head to ease her neck without meeting his pleading eyes. The passengers got down, rumpled and shabby after twelve hours on the train. 'We'd have been quicker cycling,' he said as they walked back to the guard's van. They lifted their bicycles from the train and wheeled them down the ramp to the street. They stood facing each other under the high grey walls of the station. She laid a hand on his arm. 'I'll see you, then.'

'Let me ride with you – to see you home at least.'

'No, it's not necessary. I'm not likely to fall off in three hundred yards. I just want to sleep.'

'I understand, I think. I'll see you on Friday, in that case.' He leaned over awkwardly to kiss her and she raised her lips. Her kiss was dry and courteous. She put her left foot through the frame onto the pedal and pushed off, her right foot lifting and finding the turning pedal as it reached the vertical. He watched her as she worked to gain momentum and the figure she formed with the bicycle diminished along the dark street.

It was a fortnight later. He was caught on the street as he bent to unchain his bicycle from the railings around the garden in the square. The sun was setting and the shadow under the trees made the evening darker and colder. Yellow and brown leaves littered the road, the reason perhaps why Goltz made such little noise, and Schrödinger heard nothing until a voice spoke down into his ear. He jerked upright and stepped back, the chain dangling from his hand. Goltz did not remove his hat, which was drawn tight over his forehead; he stood smiling with his hands in the pockets of his long dark coat. He must have leaned over to speak so quietly, but he stood perfectly relaxed, as though the effort of stooping would demean him. He looked prosperous now: the coat was heavy and well cut, and his face no longer had the raw, weathered look that made him seem a little crazed. He looked like a man who had come into his own. His self-possession had become so enormous that it surrounded him, augmenting the menace of his body, which he held in check with restrained diffidence. 'Have tea with me,' he said. 'I have not been to the Shelbourne for so long.'

'I do not wish to have tea. And I must go home.' Schrödinger felt the weight of the chain in his hand, but the thought of lashing out with it worsened the bristling alertness that had taken hold of him. There was no one else on the street; the sentries on the government buildings across the road were too far away. I'm cornered, he thought, he knows the perfect moment.

'Oh, please, spare me the time. Do. We have so much to talk about. Come on, walk with me. Autumn is almost here now, and the trees on the Green are so beautiful as they change.'

Schrödinger stared at him, but he could feel the nervous tension in his limbs dissolving into a warm lassitude. The man's voice was charged with authority, he had the air of one who could command at will, and Schrödinger was drawn to him as though to a physical embrace that would make him safe, even as he wanted to wrap the chain around the saddle-post and utter some curt dismissal, or run and shout for help. He could not move. The man was too close to him and far too massive for any defiant gesture to work, and he had about him a delighted awareness of his ability to hurt. He said, with a playful smile, 'Do join me. We will drink tea out of china cups and watch the gentry. It's so quaint – like a zoo where dying species are on display. The Irish keep their former masters in a grand hotel. A museum for those who've lost.'

He turned and held out an arm, the gracious host showing the way to a visitor. Schrödinger's face was hot and he felt helpless, drifting on the tide that seemed to be moving in his blood. He moved onto the roadway, and the other man fell into step with him, ambling with a lazy swing, turning his feet outward in a parody of strolling. They had reached the corner across from the Natural History Museum before he realised that he was still carrying his limp chain. He brought his rucksack around and stuffed the chain into it, thinking helplessly of his bicycle. They walked at Goltz's unhurried pace up the wide street. When they were opposite the entrance to the government quarters Schrödinger had an impulse to call out to the guards on the gate, but he could not do it, and excused his silence by telling himself that this was the most watched-over place in a peaceful city, and no harm could come to him, as he moved in a helpless trance. They were walking in the full evening light, which gleamed in the windows of the soot-blackened houses on their side of the street, leaving the government offices in shadow. At the top of the street they turned to the right and walked in silence to the neighbouring square. Schrö-dinger hesitated once more at the door of the hotel, aware that there was nothing to stop him walking on and leaving his companion standing, but he noticed an old black car at the kerb, very high and long, a grand tourer from the years before the crash. An elderly woman sat at the wheel, bolt upright, her grey hair scraped back. She had a hard, handsome face, and stared at the street ahead of her as though to avoid a sight she found repugnant. Lounging against the rear wheel-casing was the little man, the smuggler grinning his ecstatic grin. It really was him, his head uncovered and his eyes darting after a young woman who was leaving the hotel. He was revelling in a private, insufferable glee. He is insane, Schrödinger thought, and look at the way he ogles that girl. They moved inside. Schrödinger was aware of his knapsack and open shirt as the doorman saluted Goltz in his expensive greatcoat.

Elderly men and women sat in the lounge to the right of the lobby, wearing coarse woollen suits in murky hedgerow colours. The thick pale curtains were swagged and tasselled, the brasswork gleamed. Waitresses stood at a sideboard piled with cream cakes and scones. The street outside looked raw and diminished through the tall, polished windows. The low wooden tables, the easy chairs and sofas, the linen and silver, were arranged to look perfect in the light the windows cast. The sofas were deep, and covered in a dark cloth patterned with flowers. Goltz – would he call himself that now? – found an empty sofa facing the entrance and spread himself across it, gesturing to the nearest armchair. 'Isn't this nice? Isn't this *civilised*?'

In this room, Schrödinger was aware of how embarrassed he was by the rolling cadence of the man's German, which he knew was not that different from his own. A couple eating neat triangular sandwiches, the man in a blazer and a tie patterned with diagonal stripes, the woman in tweeds, turned towards them and quickly away again, an ostentatious refusal of attention to the part of the room where the two intruders sat. The German called over a waitress and ordered two cream teas with cucumber sandwiches. He gazed around him with his smoky eyes. 'Look at them praying for time to turn back. You can almost see the thinning of their blood. Dreaming of England while they sit the war out here, in their decaying little city with their old automobiles and their empty churches. They sacrifice their sons to a lost cause. It's a rare sight, Professor, the last days of a race that has lost the will to live.'

Schrödinger felt that every eye in the room was on them, and was ashamed to be part of this weird tableau. He pressed back into the soft chair, minimising his presence; and he felt how flimsy his arms were. I cannot stop this happening, he thought, even though it sickens me.

'How was the west? Do you favour that kind of landscape? It's a little barren for me, I must admit. But still, you brought your own pleasing prospect with you, so you may not have noticed what a dreary place it is. You are quite astonishing, you know. I wonder you ever have time for solving the great problems of the universe. Cosmology seems hardly your style. I would have thought biology was more your thing.'

The sliding, jabbing sentences, the snide voice with its almost hypnotic cadence. It was obvious that he felt himself invulnerable, and the knowledge made Schrödinger sit still even though anger was choking him. When he found his voice it was low and emphatic.

'What is it that you want? If you have some fantasy of me being rich, of paying you off, forget it now. I defy you to do what you dare. Blackmail is a serious crime, and this is a lawful state, whatever you may think. You have no hold over me, none. My private life is no one's business and I have many friends here. I could have you imprisoned with a single phone call.' Even as he said it, he felt his own absurdity and weakness, the blustering gentleman high and dry, and knew that Goltz could keep him sitting there as long as he liked.

'What do you think I am, a fucking Jew?' Goltz asked in a louder,

258

harder voice and a sudden Prussian accent. The elderly military-looking man stared across the room in silent outrage. 'You think this is about money? I'm the richest man in Ireland. I've got the biggest prize of the lot, I've won something bigger than the Hospital Sweepstakes. Strange, by the way, how the men who run that lottery are friends of ours. Believers in destiny playing with loaded dice. They like certainty. And their cut.' Then he said, with the air of a friend digressing, knowing he would be indulged, 'The trouble with our hosts is that they are so sensitive, so innocent. And some of them are so indiscreet. Even being near someone who has seen what they shouldn't can taint you.'

'What are you talking about? I repeat, what do you want from me? I have nothing for you.'

The German ignored him. He paused and looked towards the waitresses, staring at one of them contemptuously. 'They are so slow, I wonder will they ever do anything well?'

He leaned forward and his voice dropped, soft and conspiratorial, almost confiding, and the Bavarian accent returned. 'As to what you have, I will be perfectly frank with you, who knows? Perhaps you've not been asked in the right way. And I have no idea really why I am talking to you. Perhaps somebody asked me to once, I can't remember. But it amuses me, and I'm at a loose end, that is the truth. I thought I could come here and start something useful. I had visions of a secret army marching across the boggy mountains of North Louth, operations around the lakes of Fermanagh. But it was not to be. I had better not start on that, I would bore you to death. Let's say we were badly advised. Landing in a field of farting cows on the night of a rainstorm was the least of my humiliations. God, the walking I've done. So now I'm just doing a little talking and collecting to pass the time. You see, for example, it has always amazed me what the scientific mind can do.' He gazed into Schrödinger's eyes and smiled, as though he were the most loveable person he had ever met. 'I have heard that there are bombs that create tornadoes, so that they twist and suck and tear up vehicles and men. And wind guns, imagine, that emit blasts of sound to deafen advancing troops. Parachute bombs that fall in clouds over bombers trailing long cords so that the planes will gently wind them in with

259

their propellers. Amazing things. What can be done, will be done – you know this as well as I do. And there is nothing that we can't do if we put our minds to it.' He sat back on his sofa. 'Of course they will be doing the same. They are a community of hate, the ones who started this, and at the very moment of their defeat, which is now, this very moment, they will use their twisted knowledge to unleash powers that won't spare their own children. It's up to all of us to prevent any further catastrophes.' His face took on a pious, regretful expression. 'They make destroyers of us who only wanted to live decently. And who knows what any of us can contribute. I speak in the most general terms, of course.'

'Spare me. Spare me. I've heard it all before. And if you knew anything about me you would know I have no interest in this awful stuff, and I have not done a practical experiment since 1914. This mad search for worse ways to kill each other is a cancer. Thank God I left.' But he was also thinking, is this what I've been waiting for? Please, not this.

'You left because you were fired. You tried to lick arse and you failed. You'll crawl again. Men like you always do, and soon, when this boozy sideshow is shut down. You would buckle like a sheet of tin.'

'You can bully me well enough, but you can't get blood from a stone.' And he remembered Hilde saying the same thing to him about Ireland, and felt even more helpless. 'I have nothing that you want.'

'You can think. That might be enough.'

'Not about the things that interest you. The mind knows where it cannot go, I have told you once already. Who are you? What the hell are you?'

Goltz turned his head lazily and looked around him. The room was emptying as the dinner hour approached, but the blazered old man and his wife still sat at their table near the window, gazing out at the darkening street and the trees and hedges of the park across from the hotel. A young girl wearing a white pinafore over a dark dress brought a tray on which there were plates of sandwich wedges and a tiered china cake-stand holding scones and jam and cream. Another waitress brought the tea. As soon as the plate touched the table Goltz snatched up sandwiches two at a time and bit and chewed them fast. He was impatient now. 'Insipid stuff. What you'd expect. Anyway, what were we talking about? Culture and all the rest of it. Restraint. What you won't do. We'll see. This country baffles me, it really does. I have friends here too, the ones who have not given up. Unfortunately they are not the most promising material, I saw that from the first. Quite hopeless, actually. They were rotten from the top. So-called leaders swilling pints of beer in pubs. I've had to teach them a thing or two about hardness.'

He stopped talking for a moment, and kneaded a small piece of sandwich with both hands. His voice fell into a dreamy register. 'If you're not prepared to treat the body as a thing that can reveal the truth, you'll never achieve anything. Think, for example, of a man tied to a chair. He is thirsty, disorientated, he is beaten every day when he least expects it. But nothing too severe. When he tries to sleep he is slapped awake. The light is always on. There is a bed inches from his chair, so that he has nothing to do but think of lying on it, easing the cramp in his limbs, closing his eyes. His back hurts. There is a basin of water, from which he can drink, but it's also used to duck his head. A few inches is enough to make him feel he's drowning. And he never knows when or if he will be shot. He lives in a state of heightened awareness. The end is always there, just out of reach, but as long as it doesn't come he hopes it isn't real. And one has to decide: live? Die? A tiny sphere of justice. Like you, I'm a microcosmologist. The little space where it all originates, where decisions are made.' He tore at the thin damp triangle of sandwich and stuffed both halves into his mouth and swallowed them.

His voice became brisk again. 'But the women are unbelievable. They're the ones who have sheltered me, driven me around, helped me survive. I eat well, my teeth are new, my suits well made. Hard, unbending widows and daughters who forgive nothing. The chief old lady runs a shop selling sober shirts and ties and uses me as she would use a gun. Thanks to her I glide through the city in that tall black Bentley. I feel like an undertaker's mute. Where she gets the petrol I dare not ask. And you'd be surprised who wants to be my friend. I'm like you, I have the gift of being invisible, but you are more careless. I've seen them all, generals and ministers and bureaucrats, a monsignor who knows His Grace, and of course the gentleman from the Sweeps. I dine in Rathmines and Rathgar. It's nice to be listened to with respect. You wouldn't believe the sweet nothings they whisper in my ear with their big confiding faces. But you, your games will have to stop. You can't juggle with knives for as long as you have and not expect the moment when you put your hand out an instant too soon and feel a blade slice into it. You'll stand on the stage nursing your bleeding hand and calling for help, but no one will come.' He took another bite of cucumber sandwich and reached for a scone, which he split with his thumb and spread with half an inch of cream and a glob of jam before biting into it.

Schrödinger grasped the arms of his chair and leaned forward, his face close to the man's chewing mouth. 'I don't know what you are talking about. And I don't want to know. You talk like a thug. You have watched too many gangster films. Why inflict this on me, this farrago of rumours and hints and schemes? You're something that's crawled out of the hell of men who can't control their need to hurt. You wander around in broad daylight and you expect me to believe you'd get away with this if you were what you imply you are? With your delusions of power, your omniscience? Is that what you are, some wretched Bavarian lunatic? You're nothing more than a cheap blackmailer.' He leaned back in his chair when he realised what he had said, bracing himself.

But all the German did was shrug, though his eyes were half closed and his mouth hung open. 'You're a coward and you're weak. What if your pathetic letter had *worked* in thirty-eight? What then, you pensionless hero? You think of yourself as a bearer of civilisation but you'd break down if you knew what needed to be done to keep you safe in bed. Let me tell you a story. It is set in Clontarf, yes, your bolt hole by the sea. The great Michael Collins, their magic cyclist, was having dinner one night during their little civil war at that small estate near the Guinness place. You know it? It's abandoned now, like all the rest. Well, there he was sitting big and vigorous in his strap-tightened uniform among his aristocratic admirers. Withering flowers twining around the hard man. It was the early summer of 1922. The day had been hot and the night was still breathless. Some married titled lady was there. The man who told me the story thinks that her presence was the measure of Collins's treachery. His castle whore, my informant called her. Candles in silver holders, cut flowers, crystal glass, an old burgundy dark against the white linen. The works. A diplomatic dinner to assure the old order that the new men would not run off with their spoons. And it was going well. But out in the garden a patrol was alerted: an assassin was somewhere in the darkness, waiting for the moment when the decorous movements of the guests in the well-lit dining hall would bring the traitor into line with his rifle.'

Their waitress approached them, but he raised his left hand without looking at her. His eyes staring into Schrödinger's dared him to look at the hand. The girl stopped, and then stepped back to her station by the entrance to the room.

'They found the man in the fork of a tall old yew tree, straddling a branch. His rifle was clean and well used. They dragged him down and beat him a little. A plain-clothes man went up the gravel path to the house and into the hall under the polished oak staircase, the long portraits of bearded gentry looking down on him. He entered the dining room where the guests were laughing in unison as often as they could. He saluted, took off his cap and apologised for the intrusion and stepped up to Collins's chair. He did not have to say more than a few words into his young commander's ear. He was one of his trusted men. What gesture was made in response? A flick of the hand? A nod of the head or a muttered two-word sentence? My amateur historian couldn't tell me, unfortunately. The man turned away from the table, left the house and returned to the garden. They tied the irregular's hands in front of him and clapped him on the shoulder, and set off down the drive, a group of young men out for a stroll on a summer night, the man in charge and four or five others in uniform. They crossed the road and went through the western gate of St Anne's. They could see in the moonlight the long lines of trees down the avenue, converging at the far end on the enormous white house, its windows shuttered, not showing a single crack of light. When they reached it, so ghostly in the moonlight, they turned to the left and along a sunken road that ran downhill by a stream. The darkness was deeper in there. The man with his hands tied could have seen if he looked up an elegant bridge curving over the stream, with a little temple at one end. He had – let us assume – never been in such a park before. They emerged from the road at the small lake. Just imagine the scene, though you know it well, but it was all new to him. A white classical pavilion set against a hill of cypress trees looking out over the still black water. But he was probably just a young country boy with his heart in his shoes and wouldn't have known an Ionic column from a lamp-post.'

Goltz still had his hand raised slightly and had not taken his eyes off Schrödinger. On the other side of the room the man in the blazer stared out of the window, hearing nothing, seeing nothing. The German's voice had become that of a man reciting a ballad, a story shaped by its fatal end.

'They walked on, and a soldier unlocked the gate to the coast road. They could see the lower slopes of Howth Head picked out in lights. Crossing the road, they reached a low wall and walked along it until they found steps going down. They helped the prisoner quite gently and soon they were on the mud surface of the channel. The tide was out. The ground was spongy, but not enough to stop them in their army boots walking out into the channel. They helped the prisoner across the shallow pools, lifting him under his arms. They came to the salt marsh raised above the floor of the lagoon. When they climbed up onto the grassy hummocks the sniper would have seen the meandering creeks, the mud pans, the tough grass, all pale grey and silver and black. One of the soldiers gave him a little push in the back and he stumbled forward. On the edge of a creek with undercut banks the soldiers stood behind him in silence. The man wearing ordinary clothes lifted a heavy revolver and shot the prisoner in the head. He fell forward into the mud, his face hidden in the film of water left behind by the tide.

'And a mile to the east the dinner party went on behind the tall uncurtained windows, the light from the room flooding the driveway. The cheese came in, the port went round. Nothing was said about the earlier intrusion. That is what civilisation is, *Professor*: the unhurried finishing of dinner.'

Goltz dropped his arm at last, retrieved his hat, stood up and walked across the lounge. Schrödinger sat with a plate of untouched sandwiches in front of him. Time passed. He rubbed his tired eyes.

Then he felt his right shoulder gripped tight and hard. For an excruciating second, fingers twisted into the muscle and he arched in agony, turning his head to see Goltz leaning over him. The man let go and wagged a finger at him, a smile still on his face, and walked out of the room. Schrödinger turned and saw him walk through the lobby. He looked down again, his shoulder now throbbing with pain, at the white triangles with the wet green wafers protruding between the slices of bread.

He heard an engine start up, and moments later the long black car passed the windows, its rear windows concealed by black curtains. The old woman held the wheel high, as though she were bearing something sacred. Her profile as she passed reminded him of an actress he had seen onstage thirty years before, raising a jar in her hands. *Potions from the womb of night.* He went on staring at his plate. The world finds itself in the mind; what tormented stuff it finds there now. The unleashed instinct of the bad overwhelms the rest. They need cruelty to forget themselves. The most stupid human will unbridled. What would old Schopenhauer, the healer of our useless energy, make of this bedlam? He never dreamed that the addicts of intensity would take over the world. He thought the good could sit it out, denying the flesh and banking the annuities. This thou art. The world is me, the single mind of which we're a part, but then I'm the raving maniac given a country to destroy, the killer in his tank. I'm part of this glib, restless thug who insults me to my face, bullies and threatens and hurts. It is no pleasure being part of him. Schopenhauer threw a charlady down the stairs, but he had to pay her for the rest of his life. No one pays for this, could ever pay for it.

He wondered if Goltz had even paid for their tea, and a well of hot anger uncapped inside him at the moment the waitress began to walk towards him holding what could only be a bill on a little metal plate. He watched her coming and had to suppress a scream of rage. This cheapness was unbearable. The young girl smiled at him. He lunged out of his chair and grabbed at the plate, but too quickly, so that his hand struck it and the plate spun to his right and smashed the cake stand on the table where the man in the blazer sat with his wife. The layered china plates burst, and fell in splinters on the carpet and against the window. The waitress's eyes widened, and she froze. She and her attacker stared at each other as tears began to flow down her cheeks. Across the room, the trim old man was standing up, furious and poised to fight, while his wife dragged at his arm.

In the first rush to embrace, nothing had changed. They walked arm in arm along the canal from Baggott Street. 'How are you feeling?' he asked, and as he did so he could tell that it was the solicitous care with which he asked the question that let her feel his distance from her. She answered vaguely. He had not been to her flat for a week; but the last time it was no less ecstatic than it had ever been to lose himself inside her, rushing towards her at the end to find what kept them separate gone. Waking from it in the same moment was also a taking on of heaviness, his body dragging him back and down. He knew that she felt this in him, but he could no longer pull apart the strands of his own regret and guilt, his fear of suffocation and his disenchantment. He wished to behave with kindness and dignity, and almost believed that this could satisfy her too. The memory of their early rapturous involvement in each other was becoming enough for him. The tense in which he thought of her was changing; he was beginning to store her, to treasure her like a memory. Hilde's pregnancy had been like this. Even before her body changed, the child slowly filling her made a separate world that he could not enter. The lightness he craved had been stifled by her calm concentration on her happiness, and he could feel it happening again. He was not repelled by her; it was not as gross as that, yet he was held off from her, and he felt a little untethered each time he took his leave of her.

At the lock by Harold's Cross the canal water was green and still. They sat on a hard slatted bench near the bridge. 'I'm in some sort of trouble,' she said quietly. 'I was called up by the superintendent of typists who brought me to an Assistant Secretary, this dry stick with no lips who smiled all the time. It was in an office I'd never have dared go near before, but he was very ill at ease himself. He asked me if I was aware of the code of confidentiality. I said I was. Then he asked me was I aware that *the severest penalties* would be imposed on any staff in breach of it. Oh yes, I was. Was I aware of any attempt to solicit staff to commit such breaches? I wasn't, but I wanted to say that the stuff we have to type should be used in a different kind of breach. Had I ever been approached by persons seeking information of a confidential nature? Was I aware of subversive talk? Other than my own, no, I could have said. But eventually the poor man seemed to get even more embarrassed and he finished by saying I wasn't to tell anyone about our interview. Miss McCabe said that she was sure Miss Ryan would inform the appropriate authorities – I think she meant herself – if she heard of anything *untoward* going on. Untoward, I ask you. She said that word as if she was eating a strawberry. And that was that. But I wonder if some poisonous so-and-so has told them about my article for Quinn. I'll lose the job anyway, but it would be nice to keep it for a while yet. I can pretend I'm eating too many potatoes, but by December I'll have to go.'

He wanted to ask her the question, but her denial in advance of what he suspected blocked him, and he was relieved that he did not have to hear her answer. The trance of impotence that the blackmailer – for that is what he was, he was sure, the money would be next – had induced in him began to lift. But not enough, and not for long: there was that strange entourage, the malevolent little creature and the hard clever-looking old woman. He resolved to speak to someone he could trust. Browne, perhaps. Have the man arrested – why not? I'm the leader's pet, the intellectual ornament of his backward state. They need me. Yet when he tried to think how he would describe his situation, his tongue felt tied. He could not explain what made him vulnerable, especially not to Browne, priest first, friend later. Even if they knew already he would never be the same in their eyes. And what would they do to her? State secrets that should remain invisible: jail, disgrace. If, that is, she had made the copy. Circumstances he couldn't control were rushing together, fast and violent. But how could the German know what she had done, know even that the document existed, whatever it was? The demand for money that he had dreaded he almost hoped for now. Banal greed would be a relief. And he could not disentangle the threat from the taunting, the overbearing pleasure the man took in his bullying. He can tell them nothing, it's what he sees in me that I can't bear to talk about to another human being, all the insult I've ever offered myself. It was best to say nothing.

The slatted back of the seat hurt his spine. 'I need you, you know that,' she was saying. 'I can't tell my family, if they would even speak to me. They would be mortified, not even begin to understand. I'd end up in a home. I'm completely alone, apart from you. All this, maybe the sack, disgrace, because we fell in love.' He held and comforted her, and his assurances were sincere. He would support her. He – in fact Anny, in whom he had confided and who accepted and gathered up the loose ends that he tore out like a tomcat on a rug – had found a room in a house in Greystones. In that Protestant village in Wicklow Sinéad's husband could well be abroad, serving with the British. There was a nursing home nearby. He enjoyed describing the place. He had gone there with Anny, so that he felt almost responsible for the arrangements. Yet as he talked about houses and trains, soothing and practical, her face became more closed.

'You sound like a kindly uncle. You might as well be talking about a child whose father you've never met. This is a real thing that is happening to us, and I feel – I think, sometimes, that you're turning me into a problem that can be managed and quietly put to one side.'

He denied it firmly and believably, yet there was an inert tranquillity in his tone that was worse than outright indifference. 'We must all stay calm,' he said. 'There is nothing to be upset about. You will be all right. This is just a problem we must deal with, that is all.'

'You may feel calm about it, but I don't. I'll be looked after like a poor cousin who's had hard luck. And I have to decide what to do with the child. I suppose I'll give it up for adoption. At least you're not sending me to the nuns.'

He picked on her small flash of irony. 'They would never survive the experience.'

She did not laugh, but stared at the back gardens of the dark Victorian houses on the other side of the canal. The hedges looked overgrown and dusty. Rough tar-painted planks made the walls higher. Her face was drained of colour and her eyes swollen, though she was too angry to cry. He knew that her pride would not allow her to ask him to do more. His admiration for her made him wonder again what it would have been like to live with her, and how much energy and passion it would take, but he could imagine the quarrels that would exhaust them. And if they did become an open secret he would have to step fully into the light. He could feel de Valera's remote, chilly silence. For a moment he thought of her in the same breath as his tormentor in the Shelbourne, pulling down the thin walls he had built around himself. He felt ashamed of the comparison, but the taint was there.

She was irritated by his silence. 'Why can't you understand what I am going through? I'm sorry, that sounds stupid and pathetic. I mean why can't you be here with me, now? I hate the feeling of being so incidental to you. But women are, aren't they? You keep them close to keep your distance. The way you love dilutes itself. Keep pouring water on the wine and by the end there's only a trace of it in each drop. You seem to think that will be enough. But these little splashes of you aren't enough. You offered the good stuff and that is what I want, not a ghostly taste of it.'

'It's not true,' he protested. He rose from the bench, which was torturing his back, and stood in front of her. She sat with her hands in the pockets of her coat, staring at the houses across the canal. He noticed a slight thickening of her cheeks and neck, and felt pity for her. 'I will always love you, you must know that.' He meant it with all the sincerity of the everlasting, beyond self and flesh and action. But he had an intimate, dreadful awareness of the futility of what he was saying, and of what he had become. *The impure self-willed man is born again and again.* The Hindu mystics were right. Standing watching her body change he had a moment of horror at the thought of endless, senseless rebirth, the stupidity from which he could not free himself stuttering on and on. This hellish return in the here and now, with her. Only once had he been able to rise above it, the moment years ago when the equation came. Now it mocked the endless failure that had followed it. He wished he could lift her up with him into an air of renunciation and calm, to show her that even if they never made love again they would remain indissolubly linked. 'How do you think that I could ever bear to lose you after what we have been to each other? I love you. Very deeply.' But it was the caesura that turned the last phrase into a qualification and she failed to hear it as he wished.

'I love my *cat*,' she snapped, staring up at him with her swollen eyes. He noticed that even in anger they were kindly, as if she seemed to doubt that the suspicion she had of him could be true.

'Please, please,' he moaned, pulling off his glasses and rubbing his eyes. A woman appeared at a rear window in a house opposite and he saw himself through her eyes: an ageing man pleading with a young woman on a canal towpath. 'If I seem hesitant it is because everything is so intractable. It is shrouded in fog. We can't acknowledge openly what we feel for each other. Normal life is nearly a crime. People hurt themselves for fear that God will hurt them. There are days when I don't understand you, not you personally, the Irish, with your cautious muffled speech. You look over your shoulder, expecting the worst, and of course you are quite right. I have become the same.'

She bent forward and gripped the front of the bench. 'That is half the trouble with you. You sail in here like a hero out of a bloody play and it charms you to dally with a native girl, but in the end we are all crude and strange and backward to you. We're a story to tell your brilliant friends, if you ever make it back home. You came for whatever safety and magic we could provide. You and your sacred formulas. Your precious mind. Did you really think you'd find what you needed here? You're afraid now that I'm going to do something really drastic. I can tell by the way that you treat me with kid gloves. Well, if it makes you sleep any easier, you can rest assured I won't play the vengeful hag, but only because I couldn't bear the stupidity of it.'

He denied it all, and the affection that hadn't quite lost its salt for them began to work again. After a while they found a way of joking about the false name she would use, and how he would have to visit her disguised as an eccentric professor from Cambridge, and the dangers of speaking with a German accent in Greystones. The evening grew colder as it darkened; the canal water looked thick and unhealthy in the failing light, and as they walked back towards town she fell silent again. At the corner of Hume Street she looked at him sullenly and turned away after a brief embrace. Her cheek felt taut and cool. Almost immediately she turned back, reached out and pulled him by his arm, hugging him to her. They stood for a moment with their heads on each other's shoulders before she took his hand and drew him down the street to the door of her building.

270

He was talking to Quinn in a restaurant near the Institute. Quinn looked shrunken, despite the renewed alertness in his eyes, which restored a look of sly delight to his face, though it seemed narrower and smaller. 'I'm feeling better,' he had said when Schrödinger walked in, as though to forestall any tactful expression of concern.

Schrödinger could not help saying, 'And you look better. I'm so glad. Still a little tired. Are you resting enough?'

Quinn made a deprecatory movement with his hand. 'I've been walking in Wicklow. On weekdays around Rathdrum you don't meet a soul – the occasional farmer, sometimes a company of soldiers running by in full kit, training for the big moment. If I'm lucky I'll see what I saw the other day, a raven and a peregrine away high up, dropping and diving on each other. It looked so graceful, the peregrine floating, barely using its wings, and suddenly darting down, and the raven circling with those slow wingbeats. It looked almost like a game, though with those two it was probably in deadly earnest. I hardly drink any more' – he gestured to his glass of dark-red wine, which seemed too heavy for him to lift – 'and I do sleep better, which is wonderful. I'm feeling that I've come back after a long time away. I have been absent, to myself above all. I can hardly remember what was eating me up back in the summer. Now I feel tranquil and indifferent. But the wound can be tightened painfully when I make an unguarded move – do you know the feeling you get after an operation?'

Schrödinger shook his head, thinking of the oculist's massive hands. He caught a waiter's eye and ordered a glass of burgundy.

'It happens when I talk to the wrong person, I get a sharp twinge and have a sudden feeling of panic. I was everyone's dustbin for too long not to suffer them telling me things I no longer want to know. So I have to listen politely. I can hardly turn around and tell them I'm not interested when I used to encourage them to feed me bits and pieces I could never use, admit that I was wasting my time. And since I've been away nothing's changed, except for the worse. The neutral mode's more unctuous. The ones in the know use it with hushed gravity as though there's someone listening all the time. Like the god who hears swearwords. Their impartiality grates on me, when I let it. Still, I've learned not to think about that sort of thing. More or less.' He took a small sip of the wine and lit a cigarette.

'Perhaps you're learning not to care about what you can't change.'

'I suppose I am. I never could find quite the right attitude for the artist. I should have been sitting quietly behind my curtains and not caring about anything except the beauty of my next sentence. If an army marches down the street, why look out the window as long as they leave me alone, with my mind intact?'

He has never mentioned his sentences before, Schrödinger thought. He felt at last that he could ask what would once have been an intrusive question. 'Your book – I know there is a book, forgive me, you probably don't want to talk about it – why have you never published it?'

Quinn looked at him through the little drift of his smoke. He shook his head, and for a moment Schrödinger thought he was going to brush the question aside. He drew on his cigarette and tapped off the ash at the tip. 'Well. If you rephrased that question in the third person plural you'd be more accurate. But you are right in the sense that I've given up trying. I have to assume that no editor will touch it, for all kinds of reasons, the war, but also' – he paused and shrugged, and stroked his glass with his fingers, and after a silence he gripped the glass and lifted it without raising it to his lips. 'It's the story of a little magazine. An editorial board that sets out to change the culture of a nation – the country is not named, it could be here or nowhere, but it's obviously a very small country – has become an end in itself, and the editors consume their lives in relentless argumentation and intrigue, falling out with each other and conspiring against one another and becoming reconciled after heartbreaking conflicts and the composition of long, useless polemics that only they themselves will ever read. They send each other enormous learned memos, letters as long as books. And barely anyone outside a tiny circle reads the magazine. They are big, genial men who never let up, never sleep, never forget a lapse and never look outside the little world they've made for themselves. They have uncanny energy. They argue over what to think about the latest treaty between the great powers, as though they were a power themselves. They believe that when they meet they represent something enormously important outside their meeting room, which is on the top floor of a house of ill-fame in a place like Soho or

Montmartre. Nothing significant ever happens to them. Nothing really worthwhile is ever produced. They never act; they only talk and write. They are more concerned with the purity of their language than if the language they speak is even alive. There is even a suggestion that only they can understand a word of what they are saying. But they have a strange cult of perfection, and criticise each others' writing mercilessly. The plot involves a young man, an awestruck acolyte, who is privileged to become a member of the board and drawn into their deliberations and in the end he's ruined. He writes an essay on the French Revolution. Ah, but in order really to understand that event, says one of his new masters, helpful and stimulating, you have to understand the whole of the Enlightenment. So the poor wretch spends a year boning up on Voltaire and Beccaria and Diderot, and adds a vast preamble, which becomes an even longer essay in its own right. And then he is told that without a penetrating analysis of the Wars of Religion he will never truly grasp what sparked that outburst of crusading humaneness. So he studies the Huguenots and Jansenists, Port Royale, the Saint Bartholomew's Massacre, and spends an entire year working on the Reformation and what led to it. When he's finally driven back to the Greeks he throws himself in the river with a manuscript of half a million words in a bag tied around his neck. It's a parable, of course, it's meant to be mad and comic, and a bit sinister. The Devils but also Schweik. But the truth is that I don't any longer think it's any good. Not good enough to fight for, at any rate. I can't bear to read it now, not a line of it.'

'It sounds at the very least unusual. A story of more than one kind of folly, all too familiar in a certain light. I think I might find that it cuts close to the bone. Is there really no one who would take it on?'

Quinn made another dismissive gesture with his cigarette and raised his glass, this time taking a long swallow. 'Did you notice, by the way, that report of the man who got away from the diehards who nearly killed him?' He changed the subject casually and politely, as though he could not expect his friend to know what to say to a summary of a book that did not exist.

'I try not to read the papers unless I have to. The news is atrocious and the print more tiring to my eyes. It is ghastly struggling to read small print that then depresses you.'

'There's nothing but bills of death to read, I grant you. So you didn't hear, then?'

'What did I not hear?'

'This fellow stumbled into a Garda Station in a terrible state, a revolver in his hand and chains and ropes around his legs and arms. He got away just before they were about to shoot him, because they thought he was an informer. He was one of the lads who declared war on Britain in 1939. They put bombs on bicycles, you may remember it at the time.'

'Yes, I do.'

'His friends had kept him awake for days, weeks by the sound of it. Beatings. He'd been pistol-whipped, they beat him with whatever came to hand, his throat was bruised. He was hardly able to speak. He had written a long, long confession to delay the inevitable. They would have shot him weeks ago, but he kept writing and writing, endless pages of self-accusing fantasy, implicating everyone he could think of, taking the blame for every single operation they'd ever botched. He must have lain awake night after night dreaming up new confessions. Well, the point is they moved him around a lot, but I almost passed out when I read that he'd been kept for part of the time in a house in Clontarf. Can you believe it? The one place no one would ever think of looking.'

Schrödinger sat very still and put his hands on his knees so that his impulse to tremble would not show. His face seemed to have frozen, and he was helpless to alter his staring expression. The waiter was approaching with a glass on a metal tray, and Schrödinger turned away from Quinn and tried to smile at the waiter to avoid having to respond. When the glass was placed in front of him he held it between his palms; it felt slightly warm. He looked into the impenetrable surface of the wine, which had a dense, heavy texture; the thought of bringing it to his lips nauseated him. He spoke haltingly, still staring into his glass, not trusting himself to look directly at Quinn. As he did so he could see his own bedroom, or Flaherty's, somewhere like that would be where they kept him, exactly the place in a similar house. Less chance of being heard, with a quiet back garden just beneath the window. A man in a chair, his head thrown back, blindfolded, blood on his vest, straining at the cords around his arms and legs. They could turn up the wireless. Kitchen things would do – towels, a basin of water. And somewhere in the house a man sitting in an easy chair, smiling to himself.

'I've never wanted to believe in this place, as you call it, this country more. I hate the endless despairing quibble about its reality, but I've had it now. I can't explain why. Reality seems to flicker. Reality *cannot* flicker, but here it does. If the quantum of energy were much larger than it is we'd see the world for what it is: a superimposed shimmer of wave paths, all there simultaneously, all the paths of light visible at once. We would see the shape of each eddying before our eyes, like a distorting heat haze, before one wave peaked and collapsed, becoming the only path actually taken, the only path real for that event. Of course we don't see any of that, because in our gross world quantum effects are so small. Not here, though, not in your country. We see the interference of waves about to break, a slow motion in which the possibilities are open and undecided. It's like being suspended in a fluid, sensitive to every flux. We know that there is a direction, that time will produce a clear answer as to where we were and what we were doing, but it never seems to happen. I cannot stand it any more, it is driving me out of my mind.'

Quinn stared at him, slowly nodding his head. 'I don't know what you're talking about, but in a way I'm not surprised. It's the times that are in it. Making all of us feel not quite ourselves. But you know, it's your country now too, whether you like it or not. And I'm sorry; I didn't mean to upset you. Shall we order some food?' When Schrödinger muttered agreement, the waiter who had been loitering nearby came towards them with a pen poised over a tiny notebook.

Part Four

Winter 1941

On the day of his consultation with Dargan he left the Institute intending to walk over to the next square south. As he reached the corner he looked at his watch, and saw that he was early. The wide street was flooded with cold air from the sea; he had to lean into the wind, and it chilled his hands. He wished he had remembered his gloves. The thought of returning to the office bored him, but shouldering the wind around the streets would be even worse. Instead he crossed the road to the Natural History Museum, which in two years it had never occurred to him to enter.

Once inside he understood why he had avoided the place. He was alone in the long downstairs room with an impassive attendant in a blue uniform, who sat by the door looking at his feet. Behind the giant elk, its antlers lifted high and wide, there were glass cases full of birds, their plumage fading, and small mammals showing their needle teeth. Badgers and foxes, patches showing in their ancient fur, stood on painted wooden rocks and artificial grass. He passed between rows of cabinets displaying butterflies and beetles; he pulled out a tray of pale, blown eggs. Hawks stood bright-eyed on short posts, their wings spread, ready to take off. Varnished cards told when the eagle or the snowy owl had been shot by Major this or Colonel that. In the days before the bird sanctuary, he thought; no wonder they needed it. His friend's gibe in Graz came back to him, from a time that he could barely imagine. At least the Irish don't mount the skeletons beside the corpses. Then the rows of cabinets blurred; the pain at the back of his eyes dazzled him, and he thought he could feel the heat of the overhead lights, though the room was cold. He left the building and walked back across the square, unlocking his bicycle and mounting it for the short ride to the eye man's rooms.

The light came from behind Schrödinger's head. Dargan moved closer, wearing his circular mirror on his forehead, leaning in and gazing into his patient's eyes through the hole at the mirror's centre. He never gets in his own light, Schrödinger thought. 'Wide now, that's good. Good, very good.' He is looking inside me; I wish he could change what he sees, make my eyes clean again. I do not want to be any longer what I am.

'I can't see any great progression. You do seem very tired, which doesn't help of course. Try to take it easy. The soreness and the strain could be caused by different things. Conjunctiva not as pink as I'd like. The cataract isn't ripe enough yet to operate. Don't smoke so much and be careful of the alcohol. Don't think about your eyes so much, and try not to read too closely for a while. A certain hyperaesthesia may be at work, so no excessive stimulation.'

'You think I'm hysterical. But really my eyes feel very strained and sensitive.'

'Good Lord no, man, I mean no such thing. But the way one lives affects one's eyes.'

'Yes,' said Schrödinger, 'I suppose you are right.' And he thought, this fellow always means more than he says.

He cycled back along the east side of Fitzwilliam Square, past the bare trees, his hands cold on the rubber grips of the handlebars. He had had enough of the Institute for the day, and rode straight on through Merrion Square. The hedges behind the railings looked stiff with frost and the wide street was nearly empty. He wanted to be home and warm, and braced himself for the full force of the wind blowing against him when he reached the river. Glancing up as he crossed from the last of the Georgian buildings to the poorer streets around the docks, he saw a rectangular plate on the corner house and he realised that he could no longer read the street names. No light seemed strong enough. He could see his eyes becoming grey and thick, like those of a cooked fish. I can no longer easily read what I write; if this gets worse I won't be able to read at all.

It's my body calling time, he thought. *Tonnaosta*: a good old age.

Getting on. A wave of old age. He had been looking up the meaning of *tonnachán* in his dictionary, a word that Browne had in a moment of anger uttered about O'Hogan, then pretended not to hear when Schrödinger asked him what it meant. An arse-crawler, as it turned out. The other word caught his eye. A wave of years that breaks over you, that drowns you before you are aware of it. An indeclinable Irish adjective.

Cycling across Butt Bridge with the sharp easterly wind pushing against him from the sea, he saw indistinct shapes in the river along the northern quays. He crossed in front of a horse-drawn van to the balustrade of the bridge. A ship was being warped silently down-river, no fanfare of siren blasts now. The river was in flood and a heavy swell moved through the turbid water. The ship was painted grey, made greyer by the fog that he now brought to the world. A big black balloon was tethered to the bridge and lolloped in the air a hundred feet above the deck. He could make out a gun near the stern and the red dab of a flag on the mast. There would not be a name on the stern, he knew, so he was missing nothing he might remember later when he heard news of another sinking. A windlass rattled loudly, and then a line lifted out of the water and stretched taut across the river from the south wall. The bow came slowly off the northern quayside until the ship was angled out into the river. It stayed poised like that, rocking in the swell, while two dockers unhooked the line from the south quay and tossed it down into the water. A boat was waiting there to lift it; he could see the boatmen turning their arms as they folded in the rope. They rowed back to the ship. The ship turned all the way downriver under its own steam and made choppy headway against the swell. It seemed to be receding into a soft mist that he knew was not really there. I see everything without precision, he thought. He thought again of the forceps picking inside his iris for the diseased lens. If thine eye offend thee, pluck it out. Pluck like a feather or a hair, and he shuddered at the idea of sharp metal inside his eye, which made him think for a moment he could live with this thin apprehension of the world. There was much that it was better not to see, but he felt the doubt recede once more in his longing not to feel that he was losing the shape of things that mattered. It will be like cleaning an old painting, he told himself; I'll feel the world is new.

He mounted again and cycled along the North Strand through the place where the bomb had fallen, the bare clay a startling emptiness among the low houses. A few women were standing on the open ground, looking around as if they had mislaid something. They reminded him of scavengers on a beach. The sea came in here once, he remembered. As he reached the bridge over the canal he felt the need to sit and rest in front of a fire countered by the dread of what he'd find at home; another night of isolation and silence would be unbearable. He turned, and cycled back over the bridge and along the canal to the library, whose windows shed light onto the stagnant green water. It was not yet five. A little way off the iron girders of Croke Park towered over the narrow streets.

The young woman behind the issue desk looked up at him, then down at her tray of index cards. He felt that he was intruding on the children who were engrossed in their books in a profound quiet. Their coats were draped over the backs of their chairs. The boys wore dark blazers, the girls the kind of dark-blue skirts and sweaters that Ruth wore to school. Older men sat reading at the back of the room. A man in a worn suit was taking furious notes from a volume of a large encyclopedia, his left arm protecting two more. He looked up accusingly for a moment, then began scribbling once more, his energy renewed. Schrödinger wondered if he was the man who wrote him letters about the arid bleakness of his godless foreign mind. This was where Flaherty had come almost every day, walking here along the sea and through Fairview. Anny said to Erwin, when the bonds that held their neighbours' lives together began to break asunder: 'That man's mother will leave a masterpiece behind her. He is suffering just from being what he is. In some ways you and he are alike, Erwin. But he at least knows that he is lonely. It would be worse if he thought he was normal.' The bitterness of her comparison astonished him; this wounding harshness from her was so unexpected that he couldn't speak for hours.

Schrödinger left the library after browsing the shelves; the well-handled books had a loose and yielding solidity that was pleasurable to touch. He mounted and rode back along the short stretch of canal.

Thoughts he tried to stop broke in. It was a time for overbearing men, gleeful and dangerous, their fluent menace leaning down into his body so that it felt awkward, diminished. This uncanny relentless energy, he thought, this buffoonish willingness to go on and on. Like the editors of Quinn's journal in the novel that he knew he would never be allowed to read. Goltz and that little thug, and even O'Hogan, fighting his rearguard struggle over and over again. And that policeman. They love their work. Flaherty did not, and nor do I, not any more. We wanted to be left alone, drifting uncommitted, but Anny was right, Limbo is too close to Hell for comfort.

Flaherty had been acting more and more erratically, drinking more publicly, and taking more days off work. 'He is sick,' his mother told the neighbours, again and again. 'He has awful migraines,' she said when Schrödinger asked after him one morning. And then her son resigned, left the Civil Service, the security, the pension. An unheard-of thing. It was said that he took to walking along the promenade in the middle of the morning when there was no one there but pensioners out for a stroll, and he would go across to the island, where he was seen once sitting on a dune staring out into the bay. He did not seem to mind that people noticed he was aimless; he remained tranquil and polite. At lunchtime he found his way to the pub on the seafront, where he sat and drank alone until the pub closed for the statutory hour, and afterwards walked to the library on the canal. His mother avoided the neighbours when she could, walking with her head down and crossing the road as if by instinct a hundred yards from anyone she knew. Schrödinger wondered what her son had studied all afternoon in the books on those shelves, among the children on their way from school. And he wondered where Flaherty went when he disappeared, and who had seen him last. Some said he'd gone to England, where disgrace could easily hide.

The policeman had come to see Schrödinger in his office on Friday afternoon two weeks before, when the square outside was nearly dark. Miss Nesbit let him in and excused herself, gathered her coat and left to meet her sister off the train from Cork. When she closed the street door, the Institute took on, Schrödinger immediately felt, the hollow stillness of an empty building. Sergeant Keegan spoke in a polite, formal, high-pitched tone: on the phone he had asked if he could 'call on' the Professor. He was a heavy-set man with grey hair and eyebrows that were overgrown and as black as his hair must once have been, the same colour as his jaded, unimpressible eyes. His mouth had a slack openness that a twitch could turn derisive, and Schrödinger realised that he had met him many times, in many forms, full of slow contempt and not a stranger to brutality. 'Routine enquiries,' the sergeant said; 'very much regret having to bother you. We must be vigilant in these strange times.' The preamble sounded tired from overuse. 'May I ask, Professor, if you have had any contact with a gentleman called Flaherty? John Flaherty? He resides at . . .'

'I know where he lives. He is my neighbour. I take it that that is the Flaherty you mean.' Schrödinger switched off his desk lamp with a quick flick of his finger; his eyes were smarting and he wanted softer light.

'Yes indeed. Formerly a clerical officer in the Department of Defence. May I ask whether you know him at all? Have you by chance spoken to him?'

'I have exchanged neighbourly greetings with him, no more than that. He is a shy man.'

'Ah, is that so?' The sergeant's strangely unctuous tone did not vary for a moment. Schrödinger thought he must be from the far south, but he could not be sure. It was as though he wished to let Schrödinger know that he was behaving with the utmost correctness, and also that he was on a leash, that as a matter of course he found his interlocutor implausible. Keegan's bulky torso hunched, as though he were about to sleep. He is so relaxed compared to me, Schrödinger thought, and the contrast unsettled him more. He leaned back in his chair and reached out to fiddle with a pen, then replaced it carefully on the desk, resolved to stay still as long as Keegan did.

'He did not talk about his work for the Department, ever?'

'We are hardly on intimate terms. Our conversations are limited to commonplaces as we pass each other in the street.'

'Indeed, indeed. Now if you will pardon me for enquiring, have you ever seen Mr Flaherty acting strangely? Did strangers of a certain

– of a dubious appearance, now, let me put it like that, ever call at the house, that you were aware of?'

Schrödinger moved again, crossing his right leg over his left, and felt the sciatic nerve pinch, but he could not bring himself to lower the leg again. Answer, he told himself, this has nothing to do with you, and yet he sensed that this man in front of him was a tugger on webs and that he must be treated carefully. He felt something unreliable in himself as he spoke. 'I suppose I would have to say that the man has been under a visible strain in recent months. He resigned his position recently, as you may know, and I never saw callers at the house, but yes, I have seen him in conversation with a man of strange appearance, once, in circumstances that struck me as odd at the time. May I ask *you* whether this interview is something to do with Mr Flaherty's disappearance? His mother is very upset, I need hardly say.'

He had never seen a more pitiable face than the old woman's when she rang the doorbell earlier in the week. She seemed to be struggling to hold off grief, and already sinking under its weight. 'He has not come home again,' she said, 'will you tell me if you see him or hear anything? He is a good boy, a good boy.' Anny invited her in but she would not come at first, and then allowed herself to be led into the front room. She sat upright and pale, drinking a cup of tea and refusing to cry. 'He went out to the library as usual this afternoon and he has not come back. God *forgive* me,' she said, 'I begged him to be careful. It is so unlike him. It's the cold that has me worried, these early frosts are bitter. If he has fallen down somewhere . . .' She stopped and pressed her closed fist to her mouth. Anny reached out to her, holding her free hand and her shoulder. Yes, she said, in answer to the question, she had gone to the Guards.

Keegan said, in a voice that lowered itself to a murmur the better to caress its stock of platitudes, 'I'm afraid it has, Professor, yes. We do have a certain interest in the case. Now if you don't mind, might you be able to describe the gentleman that Mr Flaherty was in conversation with on that occasion you mentioned?'

'Yes. He was a small man, almost unnaturally small. He had prominent teeth and receding hair. His eyes were large and prominent. Altogether an unpleasant appearance. One of those short men who, one can tell, wish to assert themselves against the world, if you know what I mean. Who is he, do you know?'

But Keegan had a face that could block a question with nothing but unspoken insolence, and said, 'Now that is most interesting. And by any chance did you ever see Mr Flaherty with items of a bulky nature? Parcels, I mean, that sort of thing.'

I have said enough, Schrödinger decided, I do not know where this will lead. 'No, I have not noticed anything like that.'

'Of course, of course,' Keegan said blandly, while under the grotesque tufts of hair that shadowed them his sullen eyes remained dark and hidden. 'Well, it is all a great shame, a terrible tragedy for the mother of course. But you have been a great help, Professor,' and then he murmured, 'Oh yes, that individual you described is someone we know well, not a savoury character at all. The other man must have had cause to regret ever knowing him, I would say.'

'I don't quite understand. You are speaking about Mr Flaherty as though you have some information about him. Do you know what has happened to him?'

'Oh I haven't a theory yet, no. But you'll have to forgive me there, Professor; I should have made myself clear. The body of Mr Flaherty has been recovered. The remains were found on the Bull Island. It is a most unfortunate case.'

Schrödinger felt the sergeant's low blow, and could not understand why the man would want to play with him. 'You are serious? But how did he die?'

'I'm afraid I'm not at liberty to say anything about that, since the case is under investigation. Do you ever visit the strand there?' When Schrödinger nodded, the sergeant asked, 'You were not by any chance having a walk there in the last few days?'

'No, not recently. But this is the most appalling news. The man's mother will be devastated.' He stood up from behind his desk and walked to the window, reaching into his jacket pocket for his pipe and tobacco, and lit up facing the glass, seeing himself draw flame into the bowl and smoke rising to the ceiling behind him. He could see the empty, twisted branches of the trees in the garden quite clearly, and the water dripping from the hedge inside the railings. I see better at dusk than at midday, he thought, my pupil enlarges and more light comes in.

'Yes, there is nothing like the devotion of a mother to her son,' said Keegan. 'She is a sorely afflicted lady. May she be given the grace to cope with her loss. But one other thing, if you don't mind. When did you see this other man in Mr Flaherty's company?'

'Earlier this year. In the spring, I cannot remember the exact time. It was in St Anne's, the Guinness demesne, near the house.'

'Is that right? Is that right? That's very interesting.' Keegan's voice was almost caressing. 'Near the house.'

Schrödinger would never be sure how it had begun, but there followed an hour in which Keegan skirted around some central unarticulated obsession, enticing his host into saying a little more, guarding himself a little less. It was as if the game released what was latent in the policeman and allowed him to show his capacity for studied menace. The man's immovable stance in the chair made Schrödinger more and more uneasy, and tempted him to say more than he intended. Keegan made the conversation circle, as though he were breaking a horse. 'You'll have to treat this in absolute confidence, Professor, but we suspect that the late Mr Flaherty was removing stores from the house there in St Anne's estate to certain individuals who have been conveying them out of the jurisdiction. Smuggling, if you will. Oh, everything has a price. Items in short supply there can be supplied from here, and vice versa. The curse of borders.'

'But how could he carry all that on his bicycle?'

'On his bicycle, now, is that right?' And he looked at Schrödinger out of hooded eyes, his lips forming the semblance of a smile. 'So do you think you might remember an occasion when you saw something of that nature?'

'Perhaps – now that I think of it – there might have been a package of some sort on his bicycle, from time to time.'

'That is *very* helpful indeed, Professor. I know how busy you must be. So many responsibilities. Things can slip our minds. Larger quantities they'd have been interested in, though, on the whole. It would take a horse and cart or a lorry. The man with the right forms, you see, can authorise anything. Daylight robbery. We inherited the

British love of bureaucracy. With the right notepaper you can get away with murder.' He grinned a little when he uttered the last sentence, but almost instantly afterwards his face relapsed into pious solemnity.

Through it all Keegan was courteous and deferential, but the longer it went on the uglier Schrödinger found him. He could imagine his violence, what it must be like to be alone in a different kind of room with this great snake squatting on his coils. But he dared to mention the small man again. 'He seemed so malignant. I was struck by that.'

'Malignant, is it? Oh I'd say that is accurate as a description. Give him a cause and he'll sully it. It will take more than a few blackguards like him to right the wrongs of our history, but they might be all it takes to ruin us. These boys are a little hasty. I fear there'll be more firing squads before we're through.' He pronounced this almost as a hope, with a lingering, bitter yearning.

By the end Schrödinger was having difficulty seeing the police-man. Deep within his eyes, tiredness was shifting from discomfort to a more insistent pain. He should not have smoked that pipe of bitter tobacco, and the main light in the room felt glaring. He wished he had not turned off his reading lamp, and thought of switching it on again and shutting off the overhead light; but the intimacy that would create – sitting illuminated by a single lamp while facing this man in the darkness – was unthinkable. The conversation meandered on. They talked about the city and the shortages, the dearth of women's bicycles, the miseries of the half-ounce tea ration and the inedibility of wheat-extract bread.

'So you do know who the little man is?' Schrödinger asked again.

'I think I might. If he is who I think he is, he is also smuggling, this again is in strictest confidence, Professor, items into this jurisdiction that are banned. Items in contravention of Catholic moral teaching. There is a certain kind of customer for that type of thing, human nature being what it is.' Keegan shook his head, to apologise for his lack of delicacy.

Schrödinger shifted on his seat in the harsh glare of the light. He wanted more than anything to rest his eyes, and to bring this interview to an end, but Keegan with his polite mockery seemed to block every way out.

'Why don't you just arrest him, in that case?'

'Sometimes you have to let a man run until you're sure you have him. But we will catch him. They always make mistakes. His particular trouble is that he talks too much. And Flaherty was a fool, God forgive me. There now, I should not have said that.' He looked down and said almost to himself, 'We'd have had them both.'

And then, before Schrödinger had time to wonder what he meant, Keegan asked about other neighbours, whether he had ever encountered strangers in the area; or indeed whether in the course of his work he had ever come into contact with men about whom he felt not quite right. Had he noticed, for example, any foreign gentlemen who seemed to behave in a questionable manner?

Schrödinger could feel the blood leaving his brain; for a moment he thought he was about to swoon. This is what it is like, he told himself, the steady light shining into the corner where you are cowering like a child. I should have reported it in the spring. The word 'duties' reverberated, and he remembered that he was a civil servant too, like all the rest of them. And then he wanted to indulge the impulse to protest at these irrelevant questions; to stand on his dignity, complain to the man's superiors, to his own protector, to show how arrogant he could be. But in a voice that sounded, he believed, almost neutral he said no, that he had not, and now if there were no more questions he would like to go home. I should have said this half an hour ago, he thought.

'Professor,' Keegan said, 'you will allow me to offer you a lift home. You have been extraordinarily patient, and I have kept you far too long. It is the least that I can do.' He stood up. Schrödinger felt very tired, and thought how long it had been since he had sat in a motor car. Traction without human effort seemed as luxurious as a bath in a hotel where there is always more hot water. But he had had enough of this, and dreaded twenty more minutes shut up in a car with this confiding bully.

'You are very kind,' he said, 'but I will need my bicycle in the morning.' And he refused the sergeant's offer to strap it to the roof of his car. When he left the building he saw the black car parked outside, Keegan already behind the wheel, his engine idling. As he rode away, Schrödinger could feel the man's eyes on his back.

At the railway bridge in Fairview he swung left onto the Howth Road instead of cycling along the seafront as he always did. The road was dark and sheltered, and there was almost no wind. He enjoyed the sensation of spinning along the tarmacadamed road. Large houses with long gardens hid behind bare trees. When he reached the junction with Castle Avenue he turned for home, and as he did so a dark car overtook him at speed, forcing him to swerve towards the footpath. After taking the corner the car slowed down, and he saw it turn into one of the streets of raw new houses planted amid the fields, where its engine noise died out.

Anny told him over breakfast that it had been a birdwatcher, out early looking for sight of a rare diver blown off its route to Africa, who had found the body in the tall marram grass. He lay face down at the foot of a sandhill. The blood had soaked into the fine sand. The man said to Anny – she knew him slightly from meetings at the shops – 'I thought he was resting. Blood on sand could be water. It never occurred to me that he was dead. God rest his soul.' He was too frightened to notice, he said, if there had been a knife. Only the police knew that. Schrödinger wondered if he could ever walk on the island again, and thought of the timid old man he had met in the spring.

Now, a week after the funeral, he could not bear Anny's silent reproachfulness. She avoided his eyes when she could, but without the coldness of real anger; it was as though she were ashamed for him. But he was numb. Shame was out there rubbing heavily against the walls, with him cowering inside, safe and insensible, knowing that he should take notice of it, open the door and scare it away, but he kept saying to himself, there is nothing that I can do. I cannot take any more. Since Anny's second visit to Greystones he could not coax back her old accepting self. Though she was as close to ignoring him as it was possible for her to be, she could not help talking about Flaherty's death. One evening she said, 'She can never recover. There is too much for her to bear. And the humiliation is terrible. To raise a child for this.' She picked up the book she had been reading when he came in, but without opening it. 'I think he avoided being alone as he would be when his mother finally left him.'

'I can't help thinking that she held him to her and pressed the life out of him.' But he knew that they were both only partly right. It struck him that Flaherty must have known that Keegan was after him. Perhaps the policeman had questioned him. He must have been afraid of him, of the little goblin who was his accomplice, terrified of life. And he had lost his small portion of it, for the sake of stolen shoes and spanners.

It was an 'uncertified death', a death that was not a proper death, neither murder nor suicide, but some point in between where motive or intention would never be determined because it had been decided not to look for them, and so the Church would bury him. An air of foreboding seemed to invade the congregation. The pale old woman sitting in the front pew flanked by her sisters and cousins looked as though nothing could reach her. Father McMahon said the Mass. The old priest was gravely solemn, and his eulogy was tactful, but he looked confused and troubled. When the Mass ended, the mother had to turn and walk down the central aisle of the nave, past benches filled by people she knew, who stood and turned inward and watched her with serious faces that betrayed nothing but heartfelt sympathy. To Schrödinger, watching from the back pew, all the spiteful discretion of which these people were capable seemed to wash away as they stood around her. He had come because he would now never understand why Flaherty – stupid, uninteresting, only half alive – could have disturbed him as he did. Perhaps, Schrödinger thought, he was the emptiness waiting outside the brightly lit circle of the artful and powerful, the silence of those who have stopped caring; but something about him was born of where he lived, intercepting the light and casting his local shadow. The mother was supported by black-clad women on either arm, and walked leaning on one of them, moving her feet hesitantly. Her black veil was thrown up over her hat, as though it would have suffocated her, and she took deep gulping breaths as she walked. She moved so slowly that the distance seemed unbearably long. She stared up at the organ loft and did not meet the eyes even of people who must have been her friends. As she reached the doors the mourners who had been sitting behind her formed a slow procession. Schrödinger waited until they all filed out before rising and following into the churchyard, where the mourners stood in groups and from which there was a clear view of the flat sands stretching to the mouth of the river.

At the interment on the southern slope of Howth Head the piercing liquidity of a robin calling from a fir tree cut through the priest's heartfelt recitation of the Latin office. The headland in its brown winter colours rose over the graveyard. The bay was visible down the hill, and he could see the point of the island, which looked from this angle like a flat blade of sand. They dug the grave deep, so far down that the heavy coffin became a small and irretrievable box when it was lowered by the diggers to the bottom of the clay shaft. They have left room for her, he realised. He walked down to Sutton and back along the coast. The lagoon was a wide channel of empty mud between the road and the island, which looked low and cold and barren: hills of grey sand and pale, rough grass. A flock of dunlins took off from the mudflats in a blur of thousands of wings, a wave forming and breaking and reforming, swerving in unison, too fast for the eye to follow as it flashed the birds' white bellies, then their darker backs. The swift cloud turned along the line of the old bridge, hovered over it for a beat and then blew on a sudden whim out into the bay, as though it had a single consciousness. Seafaring ghosts, thought Schrödinger, and remembered the old woman's wish to end in smoke.

Hilde and the child had gone to stay in Kildare, with a friend Hilde had made at a concert in the Gaiety, a woman who seemed to have taken amused and outraged pity on her. Hilde's last words to him were, 'We'll see you when you've swept away the mess.' For the girl it was an adventure; she kissed him goodbye and waved her small handkerchief wildly from the train as it steamed away.

Sinéad had been living in Greystones since the disaster in her office. She had fainted at work. 'I stood up and fell down. If I hadn't needed to pee I'd have stayed where I was.' Her supervisor Miss McCabe and one of the other women had lifted and half-carried her out of the typists' room to an empty office where they laid her on a couch and called for a nurse. The efficient sister who came took her temperature and her pulse and asked her briskly how long she had to go. The door was not shut properly; in the corridor Miss McCabe overheard. That afternoon a red-faced Principal Officer accepted Sinéad's resignation.

Despite herself, she liked the little bourgeois town facing the sea, with its hotels and prosperous houses neat and disdainful, turning its back on a country gone bad. Higher up there were houses with the best views and air, and she was lodging in a wide villa on a tree-lined street. At first she came up for days out in Dublin, but the more obvious her pregnancy became the less she wished to risk meeting some mortified friend in the streets around Stephen's Green and the government offices. He went down on the train. Her landlady, plump and brown-eyed, a widow from Monaghan, lived downstairs amid antimacassars and spotless carpets and prints of the English Lakes where she went hill-walking once a year. Sinéad liked to imitate her border twang. 'She's as sober as a judge and as straight as an arrow,' she said, 'but I like her.' And Mrs Johnson accepted that he was an old family friend, visiting this lonely girl.

They walked on the seafront, eating later in a café that stayed open in the winter. She was wearing a black woollen coat that he had not seen before. It sloped elegantly down and outward, giving her the profile of a well-fed priest, but she walked as athletically as ever. She looked warm and healthy and calm, and, he thought, more beautiful. 'Pregnancy suits you,' he said. In the café she took off her coat. Her belly was a neat hemisphere on a body that barely seemed to have changed.

'It's not as bad as it's cracked up to be,' she said. He reached for her hand, which she did not bring nearer, though she allowed him to hold it. 'I sleep well; I don't even eat as much as I thought I would. Mrs Johnson still pretends to believe my husband is in England. We have a nice little conspiracy being serious and discreet about what he's doing. She listens to the BBC and invites me down when the news is on, and we shake our heads at bad news, and it does cheer us up when the fascists get a bloody nose. She has a nephew in the RAF, so it's just as well I chose the Navy for my Bill. I've even made her sympathetic to the Reds. She has this doubtful way of saying "I suppose we're on the same side now." Sometimes I prefer the story to my real life.' She looked at him, holding his eyes, and spoke without reproach. 'It would be wonderful if there was a strapping young sailor coming home to me. Anyway, I've decided. I'm going to keep my baby.' Her voice was cool and neutral, as if she were telling him that she would have the steak rather than the lamb.

'If that is what you want, of course. I understand.'

'Good. I won't have it orphaned and adopted. I was mad ever to think of it. Those poor boys in orphanages with their pinched little faces. I don't know why I think it's a boy. Something about how high and small I'm carrying the baby, Mrs Johnson has convinced me of it. And I had nightmares for weeks about the lad who disappeared down that hole on the Burren. I wouldn't be surprised if he was an orphan or from the reformatory. I'll never do it.'

'You don't have to, and you don't have to convince me. I thought you wanted to be unburdened, but of course you must keep it if you wish. Being a mother on your own is, well, it is not easy, as you know. I meant what I said about providing enough for you and the child, as long as you need it. You must not worry about that.'

'All right. But I can't feel grateful to you, Erwin. It's conscience money, we both know that. Quite how I've gone from being your intoxicating lover to this, this settlement or whatever it is, I'll never know. A mistake that needs clearing up. Your wife is a lovely woman, you know. What a shame that you couldn't be satisfied with her. She's a kind of saint, really. If anyone had told me I'd end up liking her I'd have thought they were mad. The other woman and the wife. But we're all other women where you're concerned. Jesus Christ, what a mess.'

He shook his head and rubbed his hands over his face and up under his glasses. His eyes felt so useless: on the journey down he had given up reading because the print would not emerge from a blurred matrix of dark marks. Her anger broke on him, a thing to be weathered, that he deserved. This is what it comes to, he told himself, the amazing plenitude coming to this embittered nothingness, this impotent regret that I can't change.

'You think it costs me nothing. You can't despise me more than I despise myself. I don't believe in sin, but this feeling of having failed you, and myself, is very like it. It is hellish. Small drops of water fill a jar, and little by little I've grown destructive to myself, an idiot ruining what he's given. I'm trying at least to do the right thing for you now, though it may not seem much.'

'Such wisdom after the fact. The ruins piled up behind you, but unfortunately people are still living in them. Ah, Erwin, you get away with so much because some of your wisdom is solid and will last, or so I hear. Pure numbers, clear of all the messy parts of life. If you'd stuck to them, how happy you'd be.'

'If only it were that easy.' He thought, but could not say to her, how little she knew; which of us was ever truly happy, spinning out the threads from our symbols to the world? Even Einstein in America lives in the museum that Heisenberg wove around him, patronised like an old tortoise. And how happy can Heisenberg be, keeping his German physics pure in a sea of blood and rubble? But he lives in the eternal present, he will stay cheerful. He wasn't touching pitch. He may seem to have been up to his elbows in it, but if he was he cannot have known what he was dabbling in, though perhaps he did, and he was reaching down to open the plughole and let the foul stuff out. He'll always have clean hands.

They parted a little later with gestures that were strained and mannerly. He spent the time on the way back smoking and barely feeling the alternation of moonlight and pitch blackness when the train puffed through the tunnels, staring out over the dark, white-breaking waves where the line ran close to the sea. When the bay opened its arms wide he could see the lights of Howth in the distance to the north. The sting of conscience makes us human, he remembered, and wished it were something else.

The following week he borrowed a car from one of the Celtic professors, an old Mercedes Benz with a leaky roof, and used his petrol ration for three months so that he could take her out for the day. In clear, chilly weather he drove her as she asked to Parnell's house at Avondale, up in a green valley among the hills with a view down into a rocky gorge.

She told him stories of the great man's fall, not for having a married lover but for being found to have one. He wanted to mine iron and copper and gold in these hills, she said, so that the country could be ripped up and born again. He was the opposite of your friend, he wanted it all to change and for us to become ugly and strong.

She felt tired from walking in the grounds around the house. He drove to Rathdrum and they ate sandwiches in a pub overlooking two mountain streams that flowed into each other in a granite ravine. She drank a glass of Guinness. 'It's good for me. There's more iron in this than in those hills.'

She talked as the rushing noise of the water on the rocks came through the windows, her eyes on the bare trees on the hill across the stream. 'They knew what I'd done, or suspected it, but they wanted to cover it up and get rid of me quietly and I made it so easy for them. The sound of me hitting the floor that day must have been music to their ears. I knew you'd know what I did. I'm sure Quinn was as good as his word: he promised not to tell you it was me, but he should never even have mentioned it. I still don't know why I did it, really. I knew he couldn't use it. But it seemed important that someone should see it. If no one sees the way they talk in private who'll ever believe it? And Quinn has an obsession with the way they speak to each other when they think no one is listening. I'm sure it was a mistake I was given it to type. It should have been dictated to someone they could trust, Miss McCabe herself even, and of course they could trace it back to me, if it ever came out. How they knew Quinn had seen it I'll never know. They open letters, that's probably just the half of it. Anyway, I've been living on borrowed time. The memo was full of sneers at the futility of romantic gestures in the event of the worst happening. It said the important thing is to keep the water running, the trains – if there are any – and the fuel and supplies of food to the towns. It set out what would need to be done. It was all references to minutes, interdepartmental committees, "the view of the Department of Finance will of course be paramount", all that shite, if you'll pardon the expression. There was this assumption in it that the fellows who run the country would be left to get on with it by the "de facto power" as he called it, that responsible chaps would recognise each other and be able to work together. It was as though he were describing a change of minister. And then he says how it might be necessary to facilitate the identification of certain people of alien origin deemed hostile to the de facto power. There are some 4,000 of them and the Board of Works might wish "to take cognisance of certain eventualities, for example the need to allocate facilities of a temporary nature for housing that sort of person". That was the gist of it.'

Schrödinger muttered 'God save all here,' so clear was his memory of her stroking her cat that first morning in her bed.

'Exactly,' she said.

November grew more bitingly cold with every day that passed. He imagined that the time until the baby was born would go on as it had been arranged, difficult but civil, with regular visits and outings. But Anny had to visit her again; she felt responsible for finding her a hiding place so far away, and her neighbour's funeral aroused her need to help. On her return she looked shaken and it was obvious that she had been crying on the journey home. She broke down again in her bedroom where she had gone to change her shoes. He could hear her stifled coughing from downstairs. Later she sat at the kitchen table staring at her hands with inflamed eyes and spoke to him in monosyllables. He asked her what was wrong, and became angrily frightened when she shook her head. 'Please, has something happened? You worry me. Please tell me. Was she abusive to you? She can be very sharp.' She laughed, and shook her head, as though this was the most absurd thing she had ever heard. She said, 'I don't want to talk now. Let me be, please.'

In the morning, he found her sitting very still in the kitchen, as though she had not moved all night. She told him that Sinéad knew he was Ruth's father. She had let it slip without saying it, without in the least meaning to. She had talked about the child as she often did as a way of finding some common ground with another woman, sharing her own joy in the girl. 'I said something about her eyes being just like yours; it was the way I said it that made her realise. I must have smiled as I spoke. She went white. It was as though I had stabbed her. She couldn't speak, and just moved her head from side to side. I couldn't help myself then, and started crying. She mastered herself so quickly, that's the thing. She is so strong. We left the café and walked along the promenade. But I could tell that she was heartbroken. The sight of that poor girl holding herself together in that miserable place . . . God, what have we done? I don't know what to say. I suppose I should say that I'm sorry, but how did you hope to conceal it from her? She's too intelligent. She said, "I must have known. It's so obvious. I was blind because I wanted to be." She even managed to talk to me pleasantly as we walked along with the waves splashing up at us along the seafront. Indulging me. She can tell how fond I am of the child. But she is distraught. She feels betrayed and used.'

He looked at his wife, and for the first time it seemed as though she had found a way of seeing him for what he was. He raised his hands and covered his face, feeling numb. Anny did not reach out for him. She moved her chair back and opened the cupboard. He heard from behind his fingers the tinkle of china and the tap pouring water, then a match striking and flaring and the smell of weak gas. Anny sat down again.

'I was so happy when we were first together. It seems like a century ago. It was such a short time that we had together, just before and just after the war, but it was fine. Since then I've been holding on to something that's just a ghost of ordinary happiness. There have been other satisfactions, but nothing ordinary.' Anny spoke in a sad, congested monotone, but he could hear in her voice that she would not break down, that she was determined to confront him. 'Seeing that girl yesterday, I couldn't help thinking of what would have happened if I had been able to have a child; perhaps I would not have been so forgiving of you. I think about it a lot, I even dream about it, but it's always a dead baby in my dreams. It's horrible, this little foetus lying in a sort of cave with almost no light so that it looks black, shaped like a crooked finger but lying still and not moving. Awful. I should not have been so accommodating all these years. You have behaved so badly by not being honest with her. She can take rejection, but not this. It gave her some compensation to think that you and she would share this child, that you would have between you what no one else had.'

She took a deep breath and stood up. 'I am going to make tea,' she said. He lowered his hands and watched her pour boiling water into the teapot, put the lid on it and pull a thick tea-cosy over the pot.

When she turned back he was shaking his head and mumbling, 'Sorry, I am sorry,' as he left the room. He took his coat from the stand in the hall and wound a scarf around his neck with one hand as he opened the hall door with the other.

It took him three hours to reach Greystones. At Harcourt Street he flung his bicycle against a railing without locking it, and as he ran up the staircase he heard the announcement of the train's departure. The locomotive's gasping pace through the tunnels was intolerable. When it stopped at Killiney and did not move for an hour he regretted that he had not rung her to say he was coming, but he knew that she would not have come downstairs to the phone to speak to him.

He walked from the station in a cold, rain-flecked wind. After a long wait – he thought he could sense a quiet, urgent conversation within – Mrs Johnson opened the door. The hall and stairway behind her were dark, and he imagined a softly closing door beyond the carpeted stairs with its brass rods, but there was no sound. 'Oh. This is unexpected, Professor.' Her chubby, open face was tense; she stood in her flowered apron holding the door as though ready to slam it shut. He thought he could detect in her unease a feeling of distaste: she knew more about him now. 'I'm afraid Sinéad, Mrs O'Neill, is not here. She went out.' The woman's good manners struggled to cap the disapproval that welled from her. 'Don't stand there on the doorstep, we'll both perish.' In the chilly hallway they stood facing each other. He wondered if she would offer him tea. 'She is not well; she's really not at all well. I think she would prefer not to have visitors, to be honest.'

'But why is she out, in that case? I would very much like to see her, Mrs Johnson, it is imperative that I see her. There have been certain misunderstandings that I owe it to her and to myself to clear up, if I can.' The woman watched his eyes as he spoke, her scepticism giving her pain, wishing, he suspected, that she had never been drawn into this murky arrangement, her desire for a clean and honest outlook up here on the heights above the Irish Sea in danger from more guileful ways of facing the world.

'That's up to her, isn't it? Perhaps she has gone to the doctor. I can't tell you when she is coming back. And I have to run an errand now, so if you'll excuse me . . .' She moved her body imperceptibly towards the door so that he found himself turning with her, and the option of waiting was foreclosed.

'Will you tell her that I wish to speak with her? Most urgently.'

'I will do that, indeed. Good day, now.'

For the next two hours he walked around the village and along the strand, looking into pubs and the austere little café where they had eaten before, the bank and the small shops. He smoked as he walked, first cigarettes and then a pipe, the smoke filling his mouth dulling his anxiety a little. He walked along the road towards Bray in the hope that he would see her coming towards him, turning back after he had covered a mile and forcing himself to return to the house, where he hammered once again with the brass knocker, but more tactfully now, preparing himself once more to face Mrs Johnson's baffled rectitude. There was no answering sound of doors or feet. He knocked again more loudly, the reverberations of the sharp rapping falling dead inside the house. It was already dark. He stepped back and looked up at the first floor. The curtain in her window looked subtly different, but he could not be sure how, or bring himself to knock again. He walked to the station without thinking, moving instinctively, feeling consumed by sorrow of his own making. When the whistle sounded further down the line he walked halfway back along the platform, intending to find a bed for the night in a seafront hotel. But the engine steamed slowly alongside him, trailing a flat plume of grey smoke, and he could see her at the top of the stairs, silently looking down at the front door being beaten from outside; saw her walking back to her room, locking the door behind her and lying down on the bed. He turned towards the train and opened a door in the first carriage he found himself facing.

There were guards standing out in the road as he rode into the street, at least six of them, tall and broad-shouldered, their bicycles leaning against garden walls. An ambulance was parked by Flaherty's gate, and further up the street a car stood with its kerbside door open. He could see women standing awkwardly just inside their lighted front porches wearing troubled frowns, some of them rubbing their folded arms together. The parish priest was talking to Dr Feeney, the rival

300

to the doctor Mrs Flaherty hated, the two men holding themselves apart from the big guards and the ambulance men. Schrödinger dismounted and stepped towards his gate. A guard held out a restraining arm. 'I live here,' Schrödinger said, and the policeman touched his cap. Glass was scattered on the Flahertys' lawn from a jagged break in the front window on the upper floor. A large iron pan lay on the grass. No lights were on in the house. A shriek came from inside the front bedroom. 'You bastards. You hypocrites. You wouldn't lift a hand to help him.' Schrödinger noticed that the old archdeacon was pale, and that he looked near tears. He inclined his head to Schrödinger, who raised his hand in salute.

'You know the lady, sir?' the guard asked.

'She is my neighbour. What has happened?'

'She's locked the door and refuses to open it to anybody. Her sister rang us. The PP here tried to have a word with her and she threw a saucepan of boiling water out the window at him. He was lucky not to be hurt. Then she put the pan through the window. She's talking terrible rubbish. We can't leave her there; she'll injure herself or start a fire.'

After a few minutes two guards and the priest walked up to the door. One of the guards carried a long-handled mallet. Schrödinger saw him take a woodsman's stance and swing the hammer in a short arc. He could feel the energy of the blow dissipating through the frame into the brickwork, and thought again how easy it would be to knock these houses down. The glass in the door smashed loudly and tinkled onto the porch as the door burst open and the three men disappeared inside.

The hall light came on and spilled out onto the lawn, glittering on the broken glass. She was led out by the two tall guards, her arms held to her sides in their massive black-gloved hands. She was screaming in a voice that carried down the street that there were men on the roof, men listening through the tiles, and that she had a solicitor, she would sue, her roof was being ruined by them. The Corporation was a bunch of hooks, useless hooks. She screamed that her sisters were dirty no-goods. 'You're all *plámás*,' she yelled, and wrenched against the embrace of the two young policemen, who had her frail body packed tight between them. The priest stepped in front of her and uttered some quiet reprimand, but she looked into his face and laughed, a whooping contemptuous sound. 'Ah, you old jackass, what do you know about anything?' The old man's already high-coloured face flushed deep red and he stood aside. The guards brought her to the waiting ambulancemen, who pinioned her quickly and lowered her into a wheelchair. They secured her with straps across her chest and waist and legs, and lifted the chair into the back of the vehicle. As they did so she caught sight of Schrödinger and howled at him, spittle hanging from her lips. Some words formed in the anguished noise: 'You dirty hoor, you're a disgrace, a disgrace to the parish and the good name of the street!' and though her voice was yelping and distorted he was aware of all eyes turning on him. He felt as if he had been splashed with the contents of a chamber pot, and he stood there with the cold stuff dripping from him.

The ambulance drove off slowly, its engine dying away long after it turned the corner. Schrödinger could feel the neighbours' relief, and the lingering shame of having police in the street. A woman in a doorway across the road dropped her arms and shook her head. A man behind Schrödinger said to anyone who was listening: 'Thank God it's over, the poor creature, but how did it come to this?' Schrödinger did not know what to say, but nodded to him as he wheeled his bicycle up to the garage door and opened it. Anny was standing at the front window and he joined her at the gauzy net curtain. She looked at him briefly and said, 'Perhaps they were a happy family when the child was small.' She stood beside him for a few seconds. He was about to say something, but she turned and walked out of the room and he heard her mount the stairs slowly, more slowly than he had ever heard her move. At that moment he felt a rush of anger at her for her rewriting of the bargain they had struck with each other, the bargain which had always kept them whole.

Outside in the road, the guards walked their bikes in the direction the ambulance had taken. The doctor lifted his wide-brimmed hat to the priest and lowered himself into his car. The women had vanished from the doorways and the houses were silent behind their curtained windows. In the Flaherty house the hallway light was still on, shining on the bare concrete footpath. Soon only the old priest stood on the street, as though he were waiting for someone, taking small nervous steps on the pavement. In the silence the bare hedges seemed to tighten around the small gardens.

That night he had a dream about a dark three-masted ship, a training schooner of the old Habsburg Navy that he remembered seeing in the Gulf of Trieste one hot afternoon in the summer of 1915. The ship was moving with the complicated ease of its canvas-and-rope machinery through a still ocean under full sail. Then the sea turned black and angry white under a sudden cold wind. Rain sheeted down. Light was sucked out of the picture, the coast rocking in a dark fusion of sky and sea. The ship was running close to the high wall of the cliffs on the coast of Clare. The Burren is over there, he thought, this is not a good place for a ship. He was on the bridge, with torrents of water spilling across the inky tilted deck. The rudder lifted out of the foam, the wheel spun as though it were being driven by an engine out of control. In a moment he was no longer alone. A mass of people moving slowly and blindly, like winged ants, were inching up the acute angle of the sloping deck, and they were not subject to gravity as they crawled weightlessly towards him. Those in the front of the crowd were smiling, sneering, their hands stretched out, reaching for the spinning wheel. He could see that one pair of hands would become two steering fists, that the ship would turn to the coast, and that this would be catastrophic for him and for everyone he knew. But he could not move his legs. The headland in the offing looked low and easy, and instead of a sheer cliff it now had an angled stone slipway waiting to receive the ship with its cargo of voracious passengers. When they landed and ran up the wet black ramp he knew that the inhabitants of the country would be as helpless as ill-adapted, flightless birds.

He woke in terrible pain with his eyes streaming tears; he felt as if a handful of sand had been thrown into them and become lodged under the eyelids, which felt gritty against the surface of his eyes. He threw back the blankets and turned on the light, but he could barely see through the tears and pain. In the mirror both eyes looked red and swollen, and a pale discharge seemed to gather at the edges of the eyelids. He could not stand to look for long. He walked, whimpering with discomfort and fear, to the bathroom and splashed his face with cold water, but the relief was momentary and he could not bear to bring the roughness of a towel near his eyes to wipe the moisture off.

In bed again he lay in the dark, blinking as though he could remove with tears whatever was making his eyes so hot and irritated. It was like having tiny flies underneath the lids. He rested his arm on the bridge of his nose, trying to exclude the weak light that came through the slit in the curtains. Hours passed as he tossed and shifted, hoping for the relief of sleep, but it would not come.

At nine Anny called Dargan, who promised to see him as soon as he had a moment free. She helped Schrödinger into a horse-drawn cab that was the only transport she could find, and which had taken an hour to come. They were jogged into the city in a steady springy ride that he almost enjoyed, despite his nausea and pain. She kept the blinds drawn. By now the discharge was turning yellow. He was enraged at this disgusting betrayal by his body, and frightened that his eyes would be permanently damaged.

Dargan ran a warm wet cloth sprinkled with antiseptic over his patient's eyes, and lifted the lids with surprising delicacy to wipe away the discharge. 'Conjunctivitis,' he announced in his heartiest voice. 'And not a nice one, I'm afraid. But you'll live and your eyes will too. It came on fast, didn't it? I'll give you shades for the eyes, and no reading for a fortnight. And no smoking. A nurse will come with some balmy stuff later today.'

Once they were home again, he lay downstairs in the dark living room with the shade over his eyes, sitting well back from the fire that made his eyes stream. Every few hours Anny bathed them with warm water. He heard her washing her hands carefully afterwards. She was so gentle with him that he felt great affection and gratitude for her, and thought if only I could have been at one with her, what happiness we'd have had.

The pain slowly receded to a dull ache under the analgesics, and gradually flared again to a higher pitch of congested irritation. Once a day a nurse came to bathe his eyes with ointment and let the pus flow. She said that it was all fine; that it felt worse than it really was.

But he remembered men in the wet trenches on the karst suffering like this, and some had corneas so ulcerated that they went half blind.

Anny read aloud from the newspaper, but he was losing what interest he had ever had, and she too was repelled by the lists of battles and the relentless killing. They spoke less and less about events outside the house. But one late afternoon she went out for a walk and afterwards she came and woke him in his chair in the living room. She put down a tray on which there was a bowl of warm water with a clean cotton cloth folded over it, and the ribbed brown bottle of antiseptic solution that she used to clean his eyes. 'I've just seen a man being arrested,' she said. She was more animated and talkative than she had been for weeks. 'Well, just after he was taken. I saw him being driven away by the police. Just up the road from here in that new street. I heard a woman say that one plain-clothes man had said something to another about him being a German.'

'Where did you say?'

'That street of new houses on the way to St Anne's, you know the one I mean.'

'What did this German look like?'

'From what I saw he was a big fellow with a very high colour, and I couldn't really tell whether he was unhealthy or weather-beaten. He had rather large ears. But I just caught a glimpse as he sat in the car, through a window. He was smiling and laughing with the policemen. "Not a bother on him," as one woman said. Then he turned around and looked at me and for a second I thought he was smiling at me.'

Schrödinger kept his eyes shut, and felt his face stiffen. What she was saying had no meaning. He struggled to connect the scene that she described to something real. He had difficulty breathing, and wanted suddenly to go upstairs and lie in the bedroom with the shade pulled down over his eyes.

He managed to ask, 'Was he there long, does anyone know?' hoping that his voice would not waver.

Anny said, 'The woman I was speaking to recognised him all right. She thought he was a relative of the old woman in the house. Always gave her a cheery wave, she said, though she never said more than good day to him. But I don't think anybody knows.'

He woke next morning still trying to defend himself against the image of that man in the car. It was some ghastly coincidence, nothing more. Yet if it was him, he must have seen me come and go. The idea of him living so close, and yet his knowingness and swagger might have come from that. This can't be where it ends, he thought, in a suburban street where nothing ever happens, like a barely visible disturbance in the corner of a dark painting.

Anny had carried the heavy radio upstairs for him and set it on a small table by the bed. He would reach towards the illuminated dial in the darkness and turn the knob blindly from station to station, capital to capital, every voice militant or patronising, and the great washes of orchestral music they all played as a soundtrack to butchery. We have taken, soon will take, Rostov, Moscow, Tobruk, our tanks and planes and men are safe, their hour is numbered, our hour has come. When he could not sleep the voices of the bulletins fused into one icy voice emerging from the background hum. He entered a trance of boredom. Sometimes he clicked the set off and recited poetry to himself; he considered the structure, again, of whatever the substance was, maybe a protein molecule, that carried the genetic code and is so stable and so flexible. He resolved to read more about it when – if – his eyes improved. The questions nagged at him, drawing him down this cul-de-sac even though he heard a sneering voice, his own, asking himself – the way you live, explaining life?

On Vatican Radio one night he heard the Litany of the Saints and let himself be carried through the order of sanctity, the Mother of God, the angels, the patriarchs and prophets, innocents and martyrs, all the way down to the murdered virgins, Sancta Lucia, ora, Sancta Caecilia, ora, Sancta Catharina, ora. Ora pro nobis. Pray for us all you can, he thought. For freedom from the torments, ab imminentibus periculis, libera nos Domine, a flagello terraemotus, a peste, fame et bello, a spiritu fornicationis, a subitanea et improvisa morte, libera nos Domine. From the spirit of fornication, from sudden and unprepared-for death, free us O Lord. In Rostov, Moscow or Tobruk. And yet it comforted him as nothing else had for days, and he wished he could hear the periodic table read like that, from right to left, the great atomic masses first, then on through uranium and iridium and copper down to hydrogen, like a prayer for lightness, from the elements and their toils, free us, O Lord.

He tried to interest Browne in the idea when he came to visit. He was sitting too close to a hot wood fire. It was the only source of illumination in the curtained, stuffy room, a twilight that was meant to last another three days. The priest made an effort to be jovial, slapping the side of the stuffed armchair he had drawn to the other side of the grate.

'Why not? I'd like myself to recite the equations of quantum mechanics instead of the Sorrowful Mysteries. It would certainly be a penance, but they might lack the sonority the faithful have come to expect. You can't see them in the mind, apart from yours of course, but the contemplation of waves is an austere discipline, my friend. How are you? You look quite well, apart from your eyes, and they don't look as bad as I thought they would.'

Schrödinger had drawn the shade up onto his forehead in order to look at the priest in the light of the fire, his shadow enormous on the far wall. He could not tolerate his glasses yet, and Browne was a hazy bulk with a blurred, familiar face. 'Well, I'm very well. I thought my eyes were bad, and now I'm dying to have them back. Even reading a paper in a tiny point size would be delightful. When I finally have the cataracts out I'm afraid I will die of happiness.'

'You will put your new eyes to great use, I know that.'

They talked about the Institute, and the latest arguments about nothing among the staff, and O'Hogan's refusal to accept the Institute's real existence.

'Can it survive with people like him and those who think like him? I wonder what would happen if our patron were to meet with an accident.'

'I wouldn't worry. We're a branch of the Civil Service. Nothing is more sacred or untouchable. But I think myself it will survive because people, even those who are hostile, sense that it is important spiritually, blasphemous though that sounds, that we go on and give of our best. People feel that. And so in a way we have to be seen to be at our best. The Taoiseach sends his best wishes for your speedy recovery, by the way.'

Browne had spoken lightly, but with an emphasis on the word

'seen', and he had allowed a short silence to congeal around his statement before passing on the Taoiseach's greeting. It made the sentence hang awkwardly between them in the hot air around the fire. Schrödinger was aware of the heat scorching his shins, and wished that he could pull his chair back to a colder part of the room. His knees were almost touching Browne's.

'You know,' Browne said, 'there's a lot in the argument that science is the last secular refuge of truth, almost of saintliness, in this dreadful world we've made. There is something truly pure about physics, in the way that it traces the truth in symbols and follows the implications of their relationship even though it breaks the heart, as I think it sometimes does.'

Schrödinger closed his eyes and made a gesture with his head as the priest continued speaking.

'That is all physics wants: to discover what actually is, to see. Of course it is not enough; it does not have a true spiritual efficacy, as we would say; it ascends to God only so far, in the way a cloud does, rising as long as it is warmer than the surrounding air, cooling and reaching its dew point and then it cannot grow any more, its own mass compressing it. Its lightness has ceased to make it rise. This sounds like a sermon, I'm sorry. What I want to say is that with us the heat of desire rises and forms masses of such amazing material, cliffs and uplands of airy stuff, and eventually it meets the coldness of heaven and begins to break apart. We can't sustain that passion, that striving. It is how we fail. Our breath cannot reach God, it hangs there uselessly beautiful, unless we are aware of the contrary movement of his wisdom downward. Nevertheless yours is such a *high* calling, so hard to live up to. Perhaps, in a way, it makes impossible demands. But I would wish you to be calmer and even happier, if you'll allow me to say so. There is that in your science which is severe and chaste in its freedom from human needs. All of us can learn from that aspect of it. There now, I've confused myself, I hardly make sense. Anyway, you must come back to us soon, my friend, rested and renewed.'

Schrödinger knew that he was being rebuked, even warned. He was able to read the recent history of his need, its shifts and dreary failures, in Browne's ungainly manner and this oddly endearing admonition. He remembered what Quinn had said last winter about the Flaherty woman and how the Church would deal with her. She wanted to burn away the body, but I have almost succeeded. And he wanted to feel angry, to repudiate this less than subtle interference with his freedom, but he could not find the energy to assert himself when he thought of Sinéad angry and alone in that village twenty miles down the coast.

'I wouldn't presume to live up to myself,' he said, sharply enough to feel the need to laugh as he said it.

Browne joined in with relief, as though he had discharged an unpleasant duty. He made a pantomime of having lost something, patting the ground around his chair, 'Oh Lord, now where did I put that bag of mine?' as Anny backed into the room with a tray of glasses and a jug of water and a bottle of whiskey. She looked pale and her face was puffy, but she was making an effort to appear bright and wifely for the priest.

'Your satchel is in the hall, Father,' she said, and Browne settled into his chair again, making deprecating noises while she placed the drinks on a low table near them and poured two large measures and went to get the leather bag. 'You will stay for dinner, of course?' A smell of roasting meat had entered the room with her, and Schrödinger felt his appetite rouse. Yes, he thought, do stay, I need to hear you fill this silence for another few hours, displace all the air you want with your great unsullied body and impossible demands. 'No, no, I couldn't possibly, I would love to but I'm expected in Clonliffe at seven, you're very good but really no,' and as he protested he looked earnestly into Anny's eyes while opening the straps of his bag and drawing out a wide box neatly wrapped in brown paper and string, which he handed to Schrödinger. It felt heavy, as though there were something solid and durable inside it.

'A small token of regard, Erwin. I found it in a shop full of the most terrible paintings and the worst tat I've ever seen. But I couldn't resist it when I realised what it was. Now don't open it until I go, it's a whimsical thing.' He took a deep swallow of his whiskey to cover his unease. They began to speak of other things, and Anny said how quiet and cold it was on the coast in winter. Browne chuckled and said, 'Didn't you have high drama just up the road here last week?'

Anny said, 'Oh, you mean that man they arrested? I almost saw it happen.' She tried to smile.

'Did you really? Apparently the fellow has been loose, leading a charmed life for well over a year. A big bold cunning fellow, I hear, with a string of ladies and subversives looking after him.'

'How long had he lived there?' Schrödinger asked, aware that Anny would remember him asking the question before.

Browne said, 'I don't think anybody knows. You look quite drained, my dear man, of course this must be upsetting for you, forgive me, the proximity of a fellow like that, but there was never anything to fear. The net must have been closing in on him for a long time. It seems that the Gardai were tipped off about a particular house; they've been looking around here for a while. They found him sitting eating a great feed of bacon and eggs. Ah, but what could he do here, in any case? I wonder what he did with himself, all that time.'

Schrödinger said, 'Lived on his wits. Made the lives of those around him a misery. What men like that usually do. Did anyone tell you what he looked like?'

'He's supposed to be a large man, not young, but rather vigorous and outdoorsy, or so I'm told. Like the kind of man who rides to hounds. Does he sound like a neighbour? Have you been consorting with the enemy?'

'Not knowingly. But I might have said a cheery good day to him, for all I know, like all the other neighbours, or so Anny tells me.' But his voice sounded weary and irritated, out of tune with the priest's mood. A little later Browne found an excuse to leave, and said he would pray for his recovery.

After Anny had shown the priest out, she announced as she passed the door, 'Dinner will be ready in half an hour,' and walked straight back through the hall to the kitchen.

He sat and thought of the shoe salesman and the version of himself that he had performed in the Shelbourne, the man so familiar with Clontarf, the quiet village by the sea where mistakes are forgotten. And the poacher he saw on the beach last winter. The entrance to the road lined with new two-storey houses, full he assumed of teachers and clerks in government departments. The houses that looked so bleak and windswept that he had never had any desire to walk between them. All that toying arrogance, that confidence and swagger cooped up in that dreary street. If it was the same man. Who was laughing in the police car, a fantasist or a spy? He remembered what Goltz had said about collecting. On whose behalf? he wondered. Exhibits that think, with printed cards on their varnished mounts, wings stiff but lifted in a parody of flight. Planning for the time when there will be no neutral ground. And if it came to that, would I also recognise the futility of gestures and surrender once again, this time before I was asked? It is easy to despise a man for trying to save his own skin, he thought. They make cowards of us in advance. The moth learns to look blackened before the trees are darkened by smoke. The bureaucrat hedges his bets. And if it was true that Goltz could talk and walk and scheme and had no need to hide, whose bet was he? Schrödinger thought of that long, half-blind face, the hand turning the compasses to draw two bodies of unequal mass. He thought of a body tied to a chair in a bedroom like the one above his head, of soft metal buckling in a wrestler's hand.

In the shifting light of the fire he untied the parcel, reaching for his glasses on the mantelpiece. Inside the plain white box he saw what looked like a round, wooden tray made of polished hardwood. Beside it there was a small rectangular box with a white envelope taped to its lid. He noticed the regular arrangement of holes in the wooden disc, and the lines connecting them scored into the surface. They were nested pentagons, a diagram of a dodecahedron on a single plane, its twelve faces flattened, the lines representing the figure's edges and holes drilled at the corner points. He lifted the lid of the small box: it contained twenty white conical plugs, numbered, and a cord with a brass button at one end. He realised what the board was, and felt close to tears. It was Hamilton's puzzle, the toy that he had sold to a dealer, the game that was to have made his fortune and which failed before disappearing into a wilderness of junk. And the priest had found it. He ran a hand over the dark surface of the old wood. The central pentagon was labelled BCDFG; and he realised that there were no vowels on the figure, only the twenty consonants,

311

like an alphabet for elliptical secret words, or bowdlerised curses: G–d d–n. He had read that Hamilton used the names of cities and felt a mild disappointment that it wasn't true.

He took a handful of the pegs, which felt light and hard like ivory, and put them into the holes at the corners of the central pentagon. The point was to find a circuit on the edges of the figure, a trail such that every vertex was visited only once and no edge was travelled twice, and the final destination had to be the one you started from. No going back allowed, no crisscrossing of an already beaten track. He wound the cord around the five bone pegs and began to fill in the other holes, following the exact order of the consonants, laying the cord around each white corner piece, and found that he had completed the game without retreating along an edge, and had landed on each vertex once. The cord made an elegant twisting figure on the board. It was a problem in graph theory, a representation of the relations between things, and the graph on the twelve-sided figure had a Hamilton circuit because there were cycles in it of stopping points that included and exhausted them all and repeated none but the first and the last, the principle of least time for a traveller: the beautiful action he found in it, that Hamilton always found in the world, in everything except his own life. Once you move off the ideal forms you are lost, you find yourself going back, retracing your steps, spoiling the elegant shape of your journey and wasting time. Schrödinger held the board in his hands. He imagined the cities he would choose, and wondered if this twisted silk cord could trace the pattern of his own life; the cities he had lived in would almost fill the board, but he could see no way back to Vienna that would not mean walking in mud he had churned up in getting here. He unwound the cord and removed the pegs, and began to play the game again, this time inserting three pegs and tracing a different path.

He felt what a delightful thing it was, the better for being rare and having come to nothing. Browne's note read: *With prayers and hopes for your full recovery. May this help you to find your way back.* And the dodecahedron was the shape of the fifth element for the Greeks, the mysterious aether that is the ground of the stars, where none of us can live. His eyes were streaming now and he had to move away from the heat and smoke of the fire, and put the board aside. He went upstairs and lay in his room until Anny called him to eat.

At the end of the week Dargan came with the nurse. 'I hope you have been brainless and idle,' he boomed. Schrödinger tried to be jolly in return. 'I haven't read a line. I'm regressing to infanthood.' The hearty laughter died down while the oculist examined him. 'Let's see now. Nice, nice. Nothing to worry about there, still a bit congested, but the swelling is much less brawny. You'll soon feel better.'

At first his eyes were unbearably sore. He read passages of books in the largest type size he could find – a German translation of Chekhov, a volume of Yeats that Sinéad had given him, and even a few papers sent over by Miss Nesbit. The equations were readable, and their very concentration allowed him to think with his eyes shut for minutes at a time without the vacancy of boredom.

The day after he started reading, her letter arrived. The writing was clear and decisive, and almost easy to read. The letter was dated the day before.

Dear Erwin

I am writing this in a teashop on O'Connell Street. I don't even know why I'm doing it. You'll be relieved to know that Ireland is about to export me. It will ease the pressure on her conscience. And by the time you read this I will have been erased from her memory. I have an old schoolfriend who lives outside Liverpool. She's working for some branch of their air force and she says she can give me a room, and that there are other girls who will help and not faint away at the thought of a little Irish bastard. I will send you her address. I expect you to honour your promise about supporting us. Don't surprise me by being treacherous in that too. Of course I don't want to go away at all. I've taken only a few books, and I've asked Quinn to sell or keep whatever he wants. I think I may have quite a miserable life – a single woman with a baby, and who's going to want such damaged goods? They have no idea how damaged. But Ireland is what makes me really angry. I care more about the miserable streets of Dublin than the stones of Venice, though I wouldn't mind having a look just for the sake of comparison. But England is all there is for me, for now. It is the last place I want to be, but at least I can cut this knot you've tied so clumsily between us.

I may come back when you're gone; I assume you'll be on the first boat out when the war is over, if it ever is. Fleeing with relief, but full of stories about the customs of the barbarians. By then the standstill may be over and the country may crawl out of the stagnant pond it's crouching in. Whichever side wins, no doubt the cute men in Justice will be able to prove we were really rooting for them all along.

You believe in a mind that unites us all and never lets us die. We've all been here before. The world is just our dream of it. I am the world. Isn't that what the Hindus say? You are the world, all right. All this sympathetic vibrating, all this merging of minds beyond the transient flesh, transcending mere desire. It's your way of saying you mean the world to yourself. You're very like the men you claim to hate so much, the driven ones, though without their violent courage. And your Eternal Mind has a habit of letting women in so easily and forgetting about them. Each in her little compartment, hearing for a time what we wanted to hear. Maybe I'm already locked up in this ghastly contemplative brain, with all the other women stuck in here. Like a swarm. What a horrible thought.

I just saw Tony Ashman. He came in here as though he stopped here every day to buy a penny bun and a cup of tea. He must have seen me come in, though he made a great show of surprise and sat down and started booming out with that accent of his so the whole café was looking at him. He sneaked a couple of glances at this letter. When he heard I was leaving he made a great show of being upset and why had I not told him, and so on. He wrote out the names of people I should visit in London 'when I'm up', Skimper this and Tiggy that, great friends of his. He seemed to mean it kindly, but he is cold under all that playacting, full of his own rightness as you said once. He thinks we can't live with ourselves so we need him, them, after all. I don't know why I'm telling you this. As he left he said the strangest thing. 'You'll

314

find you breathe more easily not holding your nose.' I really wish he'd not had the last word, just as I'm about to leave.

That's it. I must go. You'll never hear from me again, not in this earthly life.

He left the letter on the table. He wondered about her friend, one of the girls who wanted to escape. Was she as passionate and smart? He had allowed himself to think of the moment when he would go into the room at the nursing home and see the baby. He remembered Ruth as an infant, her arms and legs flexing and kicking as she lay on her back, as though she were learning to swim; and the sudden grip of all her limbs, snatching and clinging, when she thought he might let her fall, which I will never do, he thought, which I have already done. She slept with her round, naked head turned to one side, her miniature fists held up in surrender by either cheek, a gesture of complete abandon. When she woke, her face turned calmly to the ceiling, her eyes staring at a point of light, vague shapes, the pressures of different forms coming near and receding.

At the moment when he realised that he would never see the child – might never know if it had lived or died – he felt his shame crash finally against the walls with a heavy shoulder, and felt them break and splinter. I should have gone back, he thought, that night in Greystones. I should have stayed there until she returned, and stood outside the door until she came downstairs. He swore at his unwillingness to face the awkward turns that the world demands, his fear of choosing a path, his need to lose his way. He thought of her sitting in an austere bedroom under a smoke-polluted sky, with her notes and her small shelf of books. He could not summon back the least desire for her, but Hilde had been right, nothing is ever wholly lost. It would be better if it were. And it gets worse, he thought; once we are entangled we can never free ourselves. The tug of hurt in space and time. What is physically ridiculous works for us, spooky action at a distance, and to our lasting harm.

That night he sat at the fire with his black eyeshade down. He had been trying to read and had paid the price, and was now denying himself light until he had eaten. The house was very quiet. He could smell cooking but he could not hear Anny in the kitchen. The silence was so unusual that he called out to her. He heard her move, a chair scraping back, and the drawer in the kitchen cupboard opening, then the clink of cutlery and the drawer closing again slowly with a slide of wooden tongues and grooves. It struck him that he had never heard the drawer closed so gently. He heard her slippers on the carpet as she entered the room, and her breathing. He could feel the warmth of her body beyond the heat of the fire. She was standing over him, just next to him. 'Anny?' he said. But she stood close, saying nothing. He raised the eyeshade and squinted up at her, her figure bleary in the weak light from the fire. She was standing by the side of his chair with a long knife in her hand. She held it tightly by the white handle. He could tell by the shape that it was the carving knife she used for cutting meat, which had been sharpened by the knife-grinder in the spring. He could recall without seeing the abrasions on the steel, which was, he thought, from Solingen. It seemed strange to think that they had brought a knife from Germany all the way here. Anny looked at him, standing no more than a foot away. She seemed unaware of him staring blindly up at her. After a few moments she said, 'Dinner will be a little while yet.' She turned and went out of the room and he heard the kitchen door close.

He threw some new logs onto the fire. In a few minutes it blazed up so hot that he wanted to pull his chair back, but in the sensual daze he felt his head become light and his eye muscles relax. He slipped the eyeshade down once more, and rested his head on the soft back of the chair.

Later the wind rose and shook the glass in the windows, showering them with rain.He thought that had woken him, but then he realised that the sound had been the closing of the front door. He slid the shade off his head, disoriented from sleep and very thirsty, and every sensation confused him. 'Anny,' he said aloud. 'Anny, are you there?' He stood up, feeling slow and helpless, anxious in the silence.

In the kitchen the lid of the oven was down; a tray of what looked like baked chops and sliced vegetables lay cooling on the stone surface of the sink. The room was full of the odour of meat and herbs, but the fat in the tray had turned opaque. 'Anny!' he called again, turning back into the hallway, 'Anny, are you all right?' Even though he knew that he had heard her leaving the house, the food going to waste made that so incredible that he went upstairs, telling himself that she too might have fallen asleep. Her bedroom door was open and the room was cold and dark, the bed neatly made and untouched. There is nowhere else for her to be, he thought, this is all the house we have, and the realisation woke him to a state of panic that he tried to control as he lifted an old coat off the stand in the hallway and worked his feet into a pair of wellington boots. The rain was beating on the windows more heavily now, and he picked up an umbrella as he opened the door and stepped out into the dark street. She could have gone to the right along the street, to a neighbour's house, perhaps she needed some domestic favour. He looked at the rows of houses in the rain, and it did not seem like a night for borrowing salt. He walked left out of the street and past the locked gates of the castle, and turned down to the sea, raising the umbrella and pressing it forward to defend himself from the wind driving the rain against him. A small body dressed in yellow oilskins and a sou'wester hat appeared suddenly to one side of his concave shield. He recognised the elderly man as the birdwatcher from the island, and realised before he spoke that he must be the man that Anny knew, the man who had found Flaherty, one listmaker found by another. His round face was contorted with distress.

'Good evening, sir, you don't know me. My name is Jones. I think . . .'

'Mr Jones, we have met. I think you know my wife, have you seen her?'

'I was just about to say, I was on my way to your house, she is down on the promenade by the baths without even a coat. She seems quite upset.'

Schrödinger ran, flinging thanks behind him. His umbrella turned inside out with a bursting sound, and he walked backwards for a moment trying to fold the ribs down, then gave up and ran on with the useless thing. The rain fell with relentless, soaking force. He had a crazy urge to run back and under cover of the wind and rain ask the man what he really saw. Did you see a knife? But now he could see the wall of the baths and the palm trees around it bending in the wind. Anny was not there. He crossed the road and saw the ladder leaning against the wall, next to a pile of tarpaulins and a covered

317

cart. He stood by the closed gate into the baths, his hair plastered to his head, his glasses streaming, trying to peer through the rain. The empty promenade curved away towards the city and in the other direction down to the bridge and the island. He could not choose. Then he wondered why workmen would leave a ladder standing upright, and tossed the umbrella onto the tarpaulin before shinning up the wooden steps. The flat roof of the changing rooms stuck out from the wall. In the teeming darkness he could see the surface of the pool lashed by the rain. He braced himself against the ladder. He thought he saw something move at the edge of the pool nearest the sea. What is happening to us? he thought, as the water ran down the collar of his shirt, and his coat hung heavy and sodden around him. And then he saw her, standing in her cardigan and skirt on the concrete surround of the pool and holding the rungs of the metal ladder that rose out of the water. He screamed her name, but the wind and rain whipped it away into their own turbulent medium. He crawled across the narrow roof and lowered himself to the ground, hanging by his arms as she must have done, but he could not believe that she was able. When he turned around she was no longer there. He cried out again, wiped his glasses with his sleeve and ran to where he thought she had been. The sea was high, massive and foaming with white spray against the outer wall. The wind coming off the bay was a heavy resistant thing, pushing him backwards. In the pool he saw the spattering creating ripples that interfered ceaselessly with each other. And with an awful moaning gasp Anny rose to the surface and flung an arm out, splashing and coughing and falling back again. He was sure he saw her pushing herself off the side. She has been on the bottom of this freezing sea pool, he thought, he could not bear to think how cold it was. He prepared to jump, then saw the lifebuoy on the board, hanging on its coiled rope, and lifted it off. The cork ring felt stiff and heavy, and he thrust it out from his chest with both arms, the buoy falling near her outstretched hand. She reached for it, a tentative and nervous gesture. She looked up and saw him kneeling at the poolside shouting her name. Her white face looked distraught; she is disappointed I am here, he thought, as he hauled on the rope and pulled her to the ladder and then up by both her arms. She was back-breakingly limp and heavy. He laid her on her side and rubbed her hands, and slumped down beside her on the cold wet concrete, panting for breath. She coughed and convulsed, then vomited. He sat up and wanted more than anything to be away from there, out of the flooding wet and cold, but wondered how they could ever climb out again. We will freeze to death in here, in this concrete pen. But when he had coaxed her up and half walked, half carried her to the gate, hoping and dreading that he would see some passer-by who could get them help, he turned and pulled the handle, and the gate opened without a sound.

She leaned heavily against his shoulder. The walk back to the house was a succession of halts and weaving movements, and sudden ungainly rests on garden walls. She was coughing noisily; he was afraid she would collapse. He was soaked through, his clothes adhering to his skin in a freezing poultice. When she rested once against a pillar she closed her eyes and sang tunelessly in English, the first coherent words she had uttered:

> *He sucks little bird's eggs*
> *To make his voice clear*
> *So he can sing cuckoo*
> *Three months of the year.*

They met no one on the street, but the pelting, freezing rain that hid them also humiliated and exposed them, a couple of vagrants sent out to lose themselves. Someone, he was sure, would lift a curtain, and the spectacle would be observed, and nothing would ever be said. When they reached the house he dragged her upstairs and pulled off her skirt and sodden woollen cardigan before rubbing her head roughly dry and wrapping her in a large towel. He left her sitting in the bedroom and ran a bath, glad that the fire would have heated the water in the tank, and walked quietly downstairs and called Dr O'Reilly, telling him that Anny had fallen into the sea while walking on the front, unable to think of a better lie, and returned to find her stretched out on the bed. He helped her up again and removed her slip. 'You must have a bath,' he said, 'please help me.' He realised how long it had been since he had seen his wife's body, and he found it intensely embarrassing, as though he were undressing his mother. He undid her brassiere and wrapped the towel around her from behind, holding it around her as he guided her to the bathroom. 'There, now, please get into the bath. Can you do that? Please, you must.' She stood swaying at the edge of the bath, looking stupidly at the clear water from which steam was rising. He snapped at her, his fear and compassion lost in an outburst of rage. 'You will catch your death! Get in, for God's sake, stop being an idiot. There isn't enough hot water for another bath. I cannot lift you in.' He left the room and shut the door, waiting with his hand on the knob. Then he heard sighing and the sounds of cloth falling onto the floor, and a splash, then a larger sloshing of water. He eased the door open and saw that she was lying back with her eyes closed. He could see her body under the water, her breasts refracted and shimmering under the bathroom light. 'Are you all right?' he asked. She did not look at him, but she nodded, her face dull and closed. He went downstairs with fresh clothes for himself and tried to revive the fire, but it was weak and smoky by now and the new logs would not catch. He stripped and towelled himself dry, shivering as the draughts in the room touched his body. Then a sudden panic at the silence from the bathroom. I should not have left her in the water. He ran upstairs. She looked at him when he opened the door. 'Come,' he said, 'you should be in bed.' Holding the big towel, he waited for her to rise from the water and wrapped her in the warm cotton. The doorbell rang, but he let O'Reilly wait while he led her into her bedroom and handed her a nightdress.

In the morning he started a fire, removing last night's heavy ash and twisting the newspapers into firelighters and cursing the bother of it. When it was burning he went up to her room with a cup of tea. As he jogged her shoulder she woke and turned over to look at him. She held his hand for a moment, and turned away again. Downstairs he looked at an *Irish Times* he had not used for the fire and found a box number for a general housekeeper in the ads for domestic help. He scribbled a note and put it in an envelope, wondering if he could leave her alone long enough to post it.

He was sitting by the fire with his eyes closed when she came down, bulky in her nightdress, a sweater and a bathrobe. She sat in the armchair across from him. Sleep had softened her face, but she was exhausted, and the look she gave him was blank and hopeless.

'How are you feeling?' he asked. He tried to let his question seem encouraging, but it came out bright and false. O'Reilly had said that she would survive. Complete rest, lots of hot drinks and soup. 'You'll be joining the hardy types at the Forty Foot on Christmas Day, Mrs Schrödinger, if you've a taste for icy swims.' He had given her a sedative, and left with his bonhomie and disbelief unruffled.

'I suppose I should say I am sorry. But I'm not, not yet at least. I am so tired.' She spoke dully but decisively, in a monotone that scared him.

'Perhaps we should see a doctor. A proper doctor, a sensitive psychiatrist. There must be a good person in the city. I will enquire. You are really not yourself. But first you must rest. I don't want to leave you alone. I can't describe to you how frightened you have made me. If only Hilde were here –'

'Yes, what then? Erwin, it would make no difference. I've endured them all, looked after Hilde and Hilde's child and would have looked after the Irish girl's too. I don't mind all that.'

'I know you would, I know how generous you are.'

She went on as if he had not spoken. 'They're all I have. Any lovers I might have wanted have long gone or were never able to tolerate your toleration of them. I've sat in that kitchen in this house under this endless sad light for two years. The bay feels so empty and dried out, or else the tide is full and it's this leaden water stretching off for ever. The spire of the church behind us is too high. It casts a shadow on the street, have you noticed that? I have no idea why these things upset me so much. I carry them around with me all day long. I met a neighbour the day before yesterday.'

'Who?' He asked because she paused and looked at her hands.

'You don't know her. She was all careful diplomacy as usual, always so polite. "A grand day, Mrs Schrödinger, maybe the rain will hold off." "Oh yes," I said and made a minute's talk in return. The usual stuff that housewives talk about. But nothing she said allowed me in. She is a nice person in her way, but I could never reach her. She knows I'm not interested in her retreats and sodalities and she probably suspects how we live, though she would never say anything unpleasant. A harmless greeting from a woman on the street. I came home and sat down and smoked. I must have smoked ten cigarettes. I was breathing tobacco and wearing it. I could see it on my fingers. I noticed that the kitchen walls were browning at the top like baking pastry because I smoke in there so much. And I could think of nothing but you. How you might as well be something I read about in a magazine. This war and the endless worry and all the running before that have used me up. I feel old and tired. I have not felt wanted for years. I have got by for so long on caring for you.'

He blinked and reached for her hand, which lay cold and inert in her lap under the momentary pressure of his fingers.

'You've drained the life out of me, Erwin. Look at us, Hilde, me, the child growing up with all this distance and subterfuge. I read the girl's letter, I'm sorry, I did, and she is right. We've followed you while you chase your wretched Golden Fleece. Anything goes that helps to get it for you. Look what you have done.' She sounded as though she could cry, but had decided not to, and she fell silent, looking into the fire, where the base of a small pile of logs was burning red under a black crust.

He thought of her harsh voice singing that ditty last night. And my voice is not clear, he thought, despite everything. He could see Sinéad, her stomach heavy, alone in a room where she had nothing to do but wait. 'Do you want to leave, to live on your own? You know I do not want that, but you know that you can, I would understand if you did. I need you very much, but I think I have treated you badly without meaning to; I thought that we had an understanding but I can see how difficult it is for you. You know I'm sincere when I say that you are more than a lover to me. You are very harsh now, cruel to yourself; I say nothing of what you are making of our life together. Surely our feeling for each other transcends all that nonsense about jealousy, it is so transient. Think of all the people who live together in lies and hypocrisy, who abandon each other at the first sign of honesty. Please try to think of how much else there is with us.'

She laughed weakly and made a bored gesture with her hand, flicking some invisible lint off her robe. 'Yes, we had an understanding, and I find I can't break the contract. I have made my bed, as they say, and I must lie in it. Maybe because of that I long to sleep, all the time. And no, I don't want to leave. Where would I go?' As she said this she almost smiled, and the ghost of her good humour was sadder than her pain.

He cut some bread later, and they ate sandwiches of brown bread and orange-coloured processed cheese that he found in the cupboard.

Browne recommended a man who he said could be trusted. He did so with his usual warmth, and pretended earnestly to be satisfied with the story of her exhaustion. 'Indeed, it is so hard moving to a new country, and at such a time. It's a miracle she has kept going for so long. But she will be in good hands.'

She saw the psychiatrist at his rooms, and did not like him. He wanted her in a bed under his care, but he had a waiting list. Meanwhile the weather was bitterly cold; the frosts at night left a thick fur of ice on the grass and the hedges. One night there was a fall of snow that quickly turned to slush. They rested together, she upstairs, he down; sometimes she joined him by the fire. She liked to draw the curtains back and sit in a chair looking out onto the garden towards the invisible sea.

For days after his soaking at the pool he had a heavy cold, and sat by the fire with his nose streaming and his eyes red and sore, but the infection in his eyes wore off, and he stopped fearing for his sight. He still read little more than the headlines in the newspaper. The housekeeper, a woman from the tiny houses around the bus station, came each morning to shop, tidy the house and work in the kitchen, and he looked forward to the meals she cooked. Her accent was like a kindly snarl, and he liked to hear her talk. He did not even try to work.

Time passed in a blur. He read one morning that the USA had entered the war. Now we don't have to decide, he thought. Someone else has seen our way clear for us. How simple it is. I don't have to make the choice he offered me, if he ever meant it, if he was ever real. He began to think that he might have found the strength to refuse, if they ever asked him to submit again. He tried to place the different versions of the man he had seen in some coherent order, but he was already becoming amorphous, moving backwards into the fog on the island.

He thought about the branching choices on a twelve-sided figure. If you start from certain points and try to end on a given vertex you may succeed, but sometimes it can't be done: there is simply no way through. We have been lucky, he thought. He drifted, stroking the edge of the Hamilton puzzle, the wood that felt so well worn despite the failure of the game to sell. Someone had played with this set often, and he wondered if Browne had really found it in a junk shop. He thought of the choice of consonants, twenty for the twenty corners. Hamilton chose well. The sounds made by stopping or diverting air from the lungs have more to do with the narrow twisted paths we really follow than the full and confident sound of the vowels. He wished he could finger the edges of a dodecahedron in three dimensions, and feel the way three pentagons meet at every vertex. Perhaps he could have one made. He wondered if he dared call Keegan to ask about the smuggler, and could not bear the thought of a conversation with him, even over the telephone. It was not his business, and never had been. The sergeant will find him; he is relentless, he is one of them. He could see them circling one another in the pit that was made for them. I don't want to see any more, he told himself, it changes nothing out there but it changes me for the worse. But he wondered who had used the knife on that poor man, and realised that he would never know.

A fragment of Alcmaeon came to him; he thought it was almost the only phrase of his that had survived: *A man perishes because he can't connect his beginning with his end.* The shell can't know its own arc. I can't finish my own sentence, and so I die.

Anny slowly grew stronger, and began to doubt whether she needed the psychiatrist after all. She dreaded the electric shocks that she knew he would give her; and she tried to lift herself a little higher each day out of the swell. She started to read again. He tried to encourage her. 'It will be better in the spring. This poor light and the endless rain and cold are bad for us,' he said.

She read a report in the paper that a vessel had come in with 7,000 tons of American wheat. 'How many loaves of bread does that give us?' he asked, and realised that he did not know how many loaves a pound of flour would make. Perhaps the bread would now improve. 'I'll think of it as American bread from now on,' he said. 'So how many loaves will it make, and how long will it feed us?'

'Three loaves to a pound,' she said, and they calculated, laughing like children. Forty-seven million loaves, they agreed, sixteen loaves for every person in the country, two a week, so around eight weeks' worth of bread. 'Wrong,' she said. 'Babies don't eat bread.'

One clear morning she suggested that they go for a walk. They wrapped themselves in coats and scarves and walked down to the bridge. The tide was out, and the flat grey sands seemed to stretch so far that Anny doubted the sea would ever come back. On the shore a flock of wading birds half a mile long picked soundlessly for the worms in their tiny burrows in the mud. They stayed watching from the bridge. Without saying anything to each other they knew that crossing to the island would still be too far.

Soon she was doing work around the house. 'I'll cook today, Mrs Nolan,' she said one Friday when the housekeeper came. That night she rolled pork around chopped apples and some prunes that she found in the cupboard and baked it in the oven. It tasted delicious, and she said, 'At least I haven't forgotten how to do this.' They sat for a long time over the food, passing bread and pepper and salt. It was as familiar and relaxed as peace could ever be. When they had eaten enough they sat over the greasy plates and talked about nothing, the weather, the lead weight of the bread. 'I would love to eat an *orange*,' she said.

'Soft white bread would be enough for me; I wonder if we'll ever see a proper loaf again.'

Later, as they sat in the warm living room, she looked at the mess around their chairs and said: 'We're getting old, Erwin; look at us with our books and our thick spectacles, our puzzles and old pens.'

'We are. But at least we're safe, I really believe we are now.' How often have I said this, he thought, and meant it? But now something has changed. 'I know I'll be with you at the end, wherever that will be.' He meant it sincerely, because he loved her, and wanted to bring her back, though it had never been and would never be enough. Can I be content with this, he asked himself, and if so will it be because I am weak and played out? Or will I rally for one last try, an old fool dazzling a woman young enough to be his daughter at some crowded party?

He looked at the grey rime of frost on the grass outside the window. He had longed for the ease of flowing forms and he had not found them, and now it was ice again, repetitive shapes and definite angles, this structure that is our reality. At least whatever it is in the cells that lets us live is not as stiff as ice; we can change. And we can't live there, he thought, in the fluid state where everything is the same in all dimensions: this cold complexity is what we are. Amplitude lessens as temperature falls. Yet even at absolute zero there is motion. We live so feverishly, but close enough to that cold limit not to be shaken into disorder. Or not at first. We hold together as long as we can, and it rolls up so quietly, touches first and recedes and only later breaks over our heads.

He thought, we've been lucky this time, and remembered the cat bricked up between the walls of the old house. Behind the wall nothing stirs as you approach it. You might break open the wall and find it stretched out, dead, a glove of short-haired fur and thin bones. But when the bricks fall in and the dust settles the cat lifts itself slowly, arches its back and yawns, its paws braced lightly on the floor.

Acknowledgements

The circumstances in which I have placed my main character – the starting point of the novel – are, however strange, nearly true. He did walk out on the Nazis in 1933, and did return to Graz, the centre of Austrian Nazism, in 1936. He did write a letter that he hoped would ingratiate him with the new regime after the Anschluss. He was brought to Dublin by a politician obsessed with mathematics and the Irish language. Schrödinger lived in the respectable suburb of Clontarf with his wife and mistress and her child, while carrying on affairs with younger women. And there was a German spy loose in Ireland for a year and a half, seemingly immune to capture by an otherwise efficient Irish security service, and protected by the IRA, among others.

I owe a great deal to the definitive biography of Erwin Schrödinger by Walter Moore, published by Cambridge University Press, 1989. It first inspired my interest in Schrödinger and I am indebted to Moore for my loose framework of fact about the man and his science, notably his account of Schrödinger's time in Graz and Oxford and his flight from Austria. He cannot be blamed, however, for my recreation of those episodes. I also relied on *The Historical Development of Quantum Theory*, Volume 5, Parts I and II, by Jagdish Mehra and Helmut Rechenberg (New York, 1987). I have on a very few occasions echoed and paraphrased Schrödinger's own words, notably from the books *What Is Life?* and *Space-Time Structure*.

I'm also indebted to the work of Carlo Cercignani and Engelbert Broda, the biographers of Ludwig Boltzmann, the memoir by Ludwig Flamm which describes Boltzmann's last weeks, and to

327

Arthur Eddington's *The Philosophy of Physical Science*. David Cassidy's life of Heisenberg, *Uncertainty*, and Paul Lawrence Rose's *Heisenberg and the Nazi Atomic Bomb Project* helped guide me through the fog of controversy. Thomas Hankin's *William Rowan Hamilton* is the source of all I know about that extraordinary figure, who rarely features in discussions of Irish culture. *Il Carso della Grande Guerra: le Trincee Raccontano*, by Antonio and Furio Scrimali, is an indispensable guide to the battlefields of the Lower Isonzo. I drew on the diaries of Giani Stuparich and Paolo Caccia Dominioni, soldiers on that front, and on the violently partisan contemporary reporting of Luigi Barzini and Bruno Astori. The late Nandor Balazs talked about his memories of Schrödinger. I have used these writers and scholars, and many more, as sources of inspiration and anecdote. None of them can be held responsible for the result.

The quotations from Franz Grillparzer are from the translations of *Medea* and *The Waves of the Sea and of Love* by Samuel Solomon, in *Plays on Classic Themes*, Random House, New York, 1969. The line from W.B. Yeats on page 16 is from 'To a Wealthy Man,' *The Poems*, edited by Richard Finneran, Macmillan, London 1983.

I would like above all to thank my editor Maggie McKernan for her sensitivity and tact. Georgina Capel and Anthony Cheetham know I can never repay them, while Graham Farmelo, Misha Glenny, Will Hobson, Helen Meany, Fintan O'Toole and Alan Samson gave me more than good advice. I wish also to thank Vinod Nargund and his colleagues at St Bartholomew's. Kelly Falconer at Weidenfeld & Nicolson was patient and helpful to the last. Carlo Feltrinelli, when I needed it, provided a refuge in which I was able to write. Merel Reinink has lived with this book, and worse, and the book is therefore dedicated to her and our two sons.